Fusi

Book Five of M...
By J.L.Mullins

Copyright © 2023 by J.L.Mullins
All rights reserved.

No part of this publication may be reproduced, distributed, or transmitted in any form or by any means, including photocopying, recording, or other electronic or mechanical methods, without the prior written permission of the author, except as permitted by U.S. copyright law.

The story, all names, characters, and incidents portrayed in this production are fictitious. No identification with actual persons (living or deceased), places, buildings, and products is intended or should be inferred.

Contents

Chapter: 1 – Underpinning Aura
Chapter: 2 – Humanity
Chapter: 3 – Questions and Requests
Chapter: 4 – A Lot to Take in
Chapter: 5 – Bloodstars
Chapter: 6 – Decadent
Chapter: 7 – Departing Makinaven
Chapter: 8 – A Hunter
Chapter: 9 – Archon Star Separation
Chapter: 10 – Abstract Guide
Chapter: 11 – Drop the Mistress
Chapter: 12 – Hallucinogens
Chapter: 13 – An Entirely Different Train of Thought
Chapter: 14 – Another Screech
Chapter: 15 – A Long, Long Day
Chapter: 16 – Particularly Pernicious
Chapter: 17 – Restraining Crush
Chapter: 18 – In the Ground
Chapter: 19 – You Earned It
Chapter: 20 – Back in Bandfast
Chapter: 21 – Aproa
Chapter: 22 – Five Percent
Chapter: 23 – The Right Call
Chapter: 24 – One More Thing to Practice
Chapter: 25 – Mage Hunters
Chapter: 26 – Challenges
Chapter: 27 – Alternate Interface
Chapter: 28 – Syphon
Chapter: 29 – By Design
Chapter: 30 – Finally Time
Chapter: 31 – Brutal
Chapter: 32 – It All Started with Some Chicken Soup
Chapter: 33 – Siphon Fascia
Chapter: 34 – The Normal Rate
Chapter: 35 – Black, Please

Chapter: 36 – Not Pregnant
Chapter: 37 – Vestiges
Chapter: 38 – Blessings Never Cease
Author's Note

Chapter: 1
Underpinning Aura

Tala couldn't wipe the smile from her face as she entered the Constructionist Guild's front entry room. The previous afternoon of plays had been amazing, the food fantastic, and the company enjoyable. She felt more relaxed and mentally level than she had in… She shook her head, still smiling. *It's been years.*

Even a frustrating breakfast with Mistress Odera hadn't spoiled Tala's mood despite the woman continuing to deflect anything resembling a personal question. *She wants to know all about me but doesn't want me to learn anything of substance about her.* She dismissed the mild irritant.

The breakfast food had been as good as always, and Tala actually felt pleasantly full for the moment. *I hope that lasts for a couple of hours at least.*

Terry had watched the plays with seeming dispassion, but he *had* watched. He'd obviously enjoyed the food.

At the moment, he was asleep, content, on Tala's shoulder.

Rane had enjoyed the afternoon as much as Tala from what she'd seen. He was meeting her at the training room later that morning.

After she'd finished breakfast, Tala had come to the Constructionist Guild to see if Jevin was available.

Now, a large part of her felt a bit bad coming to Jevin with her questions, especially just after Rane had so eloquently walked her through choosing a good use of her own time, and this wasn't fusing or recovering from fusing. Even so, these things were weighing on her mind, and it would only take a quick moment to drop through and move them forward.

She was scanned, and a *ding* resounded from the back.

At that moment, she remembered Grent. *Oh… rust… I really hope he isn't—*

Jevin came out, speaking quietly with the two Mages accompanying him. He smiled her way. "Mistress Tala." The two Mages bowed slightly to Tala and eyed Terry with a mix of curiosity and wariness but didn't speak.

Tala smiled at them but addressed the Archon directly. "Oh, Master Jevin, just who I was looking for." *Thank the stars.*

"It's good to see you, but we are just leaving."

"Oh?"

"Yes, these two are looking for advice on creating their Archon Stars."

Tala regarded the two more closely. "That's wonderful!" She smiled.

"Do you have any advice for the younger generation?"

Tala suppressed a smile. Both of the Mages were her senior by quite a few years. Still, Jevin was giving her an opportunity to help others.

Older Mages keep implying that that is important. And if she was being honest, she was realizing more and more how much she'd missed by skipping her time as an apprentice.

I wouldn't be here if I'd gone the normal route. That, arguably, might mean she'd have a better foundation. *No going back, now.*

She nodded once, passing off her extended pause like she'd been considering what to say. "What do you know about Archon Stars?"

The woman spoke first. "It is how we become Archons."

The man nodded. "Some mediums are harder to forge one within, and we should choose a medium that speaks to us. If none seems to, we should use diamond."

Tala thought, nodding. *Their masters didn't think they'd handle full information well...* They were both Guides. "It helped me to think of guiding the power, not forcefully, which isn't possible in most mediums." *Well, unless you have it inside your body... which they shouldn't do.* She hesitated.

They both gave her interested looks, and Jevin closed his eyes in a silent sigh.

Oops. "What I mean is, you won't be able to directly control the power within your medium. You need to guide it so that it *wants* to take the shape of the desired spellform."

Looks of seeming introspection swept across the Mages' faces, and Jevin smiled. "Thank you, Mistress Tala. That is solid advice." He gave her a meaningful look.

Tala smiled at the Mages. "Well, I'll let you two get to it. I do have a couple of quick, esoteric questions for Master Jevin." She turned to the Paragon. "Could I borrow you for a minute, or should I come back?"

Jevin considered her for a moment, then turned to the others. "Would you wait for me outside? I'll be just a moment."

They bowed to him, then to Tala, and departed.

"Now, 'most mediums'?" He gave her a wan smile.

"I apologize for that. I was thinking about working within your body versus without, but I didn't mean to… lead them down odd paths."

Millennial Mage, 5 - Fusing

He laughed, shaking his head. "You know, they'll spend days trying to understand the 'bit of wisdom the Archon hinted at.'"

Tala grimaced. "I am sorry."

He waved that off. "I know. It's an odd balance. I know you took an unconventional path, though I don't know all the details. Perhaps that is a tale you could tell, but some other time."

Tala found herself smiling. "I'd like that."

He gave a brief, genuine smile before professionalism fell back into place. "Now, I really do have to go. Your questions?"

"Alright, quick one first. Can you make me some inscribed darts linked to my anchor?"

Jevin considered for a moment. "To trap an opponent? Of course. That's a clever use of the anchor." He laughed slightly. "Well, I suppose it's very close to the original use of it, actually." He scratched his cheek, then nodded. "I'm sure you're aware that this use will cause the inscriptions to run out faster."

"I figured as much, yeah. Can you do it?"

"I'll put it together. Come back tomorrow?"

Her eyebrows rose. "That's soon." *Well, so much for just moving it along a bit... Do I really want to take time from my fusing for this?*

He shrugged. "It's just your bracers in a different form."

I can fuse as much as I'm able right before coming back, then use the walk down as a mental and magical break. After, I can fuse a bit, here, then walk back. She nodded. "Afternoon?"

"That's when I have time, so yeah."

"Will do."

"So, your longer question?" His smile didn't have any impatience despite his obvious time crunch.

"My Archon Stars can... combine."

Jevin nodded. "Master Grediv's treatise on liquid mediums implied such, and your ascension so soon after its dissemination made a connection fairly likely." He smiled. "Master Grediv's most recent pupil being with you? That made the association virtually assured."

She shrugged. "Well, yeah." Tala cleared her throat. "So, my understanding is that making an Archon Star stretches the soul, creating a tendril of sorts that can latch onto a magical item."

"True. That's one way to conceive of it."

"So, my question"—she swallowed—"is should I make as many small, weak Archon Stars as I can to stretch my soul, then combine them for my next bonding?"

"That..." Jevin frowned. "That is a fascinating question." He clucked his tongue, clearly distracted with his own thoughts. "Does a weak star stretch your soul in a meaningful way?"

"I... I don't know."

"We can test it if you like."

"You can?"

He chuckled. "Of course. When you come back tomorrow afternoon, we'll run a couple of tests. Do I remember correctly, you have a star already?"

"One, yes, and I could make another fairly quickly."

"That might be necessary, but we'll see."

"Will that take mental or magical energy to test?"

He gave her a searching look but then shook his head. "To analyze the star you already have, no. If we end up having you make another, then, of course, but that choice will ultimately be yours to make."

Tala shrugged. *Still probably a good use of time. Use the resources while I have them, and he seems quite happy to help those less powerful than himself.* "Well, I could come earlier if we're going to be doing testing."

He shook his head. "You are far from the only Mage I'm working with at the moment, Mistress. I have my day rather booked tomorrow. I do have time in the afternoon. I was going to suggest then if you hadn't. Let's say three hours past noon?"

After a moment's thought, she cocked her head. *Everyone seems pretty happy to help those weaker than them.* Instead of answering his question, she took the conversation for a hard left. "Why are you helping me?" She glanced over her shoulder. "Why are you helping them? It sounds like you are helping a lot of people. Surely, you have more useful things you could be doing with your time."

Jevin barked a laugh. "Hardly." After a moment's thought, he nodded. "There are two main types of Archon. The first is those who advance for their own gain. That's fine; that's wonderful, but it ultimately leads them to die or depart. Then, the others grow in power for some greater purpose. Most of us care for the fate of humanity." He laughed again. "Most successful people, in general, have that bent."

"Why?"

"Why? Because humanity is standing on the edge of a knife. People don't like those who rust the rest of us." He smiled sadly. "We need each other, so we need to help each other. True, I could be personally more powerful if I didn't help anyone else, but I can't be everywhere, and humanity as a whole would be worse off." He shrugged. "That's how I and most of my peers see it."

Tala found herself nodding. That was what she'd felt when talking to Grediv, Jevin, Master Himmel, and even Holly to some extent. They each had their own goals and eccentricities, but they all genuinely seemed to want humanity to succeed, as a whole, and they were willing to invest in new Mages to advance that goal. "I'll be here tomorrow, at three past noon."

"I'll look forward to it."

Together, Tala and Jevin walked from the building.

Jevin joined the others, and the three Mages got on a hovering platform before it lifted from the ground.

Tala examined it briefly. *Fascinating. There are inertial isolation scripts like on a dimensional storage item, but they isolate that which rests on the platform, rather than a separate space.*

"Oh!" Jevin's voice caused Tala to focus on him, thinking he had some parting remark for her.

Instead, Jevin's aura flexed back at the guild building's front and pulled the door closed behind her. He smiled and gave Tala a last nod before the wooden platform zipped up the spiral, leaving Tala and Terry to walk up alone.

Tala was locked in place, her mind an incoherent mess as she felt herself shaking uncontrollably, fear beyond any she'd ever felt overwhelming her for a brief instant.

She'd felt his aura clearly as it worked behind her. He hadn't had to reach past her; his aura had already been there.

More than that, though, his magical signature was deeply familiar. She'd felt it before, obviously, but she'd felt it more often than she'd truly realized.

The power surrounding Makinaven, that which was already under the control of another, unmistakably held Master Jevin's signature.

Fighting herself, she focused her magesight on the air before her, digging deeper, trying to find the power signature of the city itself.

She let out an unconscious whimper.

Master Jevin's aura underpinned all of Makinaven.

Millennial Mage, 5 - Fusing

*   *   *

Tala fell backwards, a headache not quite manifesting as she pulled her latest stitch tight, joining her soul, body, and spirit ever closer.

Her thoughts flickered back to the Constructionist Guild and Master Jevin.

It had taken her long minutes to overcome her shaking nerves after she realized just how extensive Master Jevin's power was. She'd slowly mastered herself, in large part because she simply couldn't conceive of the man's power and reach. *There's no way he actually holds authority over the entire city.*

He'd said he had god-like power within his aura. *No. There is no way his aura underpins this entire city.* She reassured herself with the repeated, obvious lie.

Strangely, it did help, even while she fully realized she was actively deceiving herself.

But that was in the past.

Focus on the present. She did *not* allow herself to focus on the fact that she was, *presently*, within that same aura. She did not allow her magesight to look deep enough to see it.

She groaned, stretching her arms wide and letting her legs straighten against the floor.

"I do not envy your method of fusing." Rane's voice was calm as it reached her from the far side of the training room.

She turned her head to glare at him. "Whereas you can just dump power constantly into your binding."

Rane shook his head a bit ruefully. "I am actually starting to feel a… pressure, if that makes sense. The bond is getting stronger, but it isn't doing what it's supposed to. I'm going to need to twist it, somehow, before I can fuse."

She grunted. "That's something, I suppose."

He laughed. "Oh, yes, your suffering is lessened because I suffer, too."

"That's how we humans work, Master Rane."

He grunted. "When we don't choose to be better? I agree."

Tala sighed, sitting up and pulling out her cold-water incorporator for a drink. "Way to make me feel like a rusting jerk."

He opened his mouth but seemed to think better of responding. Instead, he simply shifted from one deep stretch to another.

Tala cleared her throat, a thought coming unbidden to her mind. "Master Rane?"

"Hmm?"

"What form of government runs this city?"

He turned to look at her, not coming out of his deep butterfly stretch. "That seems an odd question for you."

She shrugged. "I just realized that I'd never really given it a thought."

He smiled. "Probably a good change, I suppose." He cracked his neck, bending fully back into the stretch. "There are two layers, really. There are popularly elected administrators for the day-to-day, and even year-to-year, running of Makinaven."

"And the other layer?"

"A guild holds carte blanche over major decisions."

Tala felt her eye twitch. "Which?"

"Hmm? Oh." He frowned, thinking. "I believe the Growers."

Tala felt herself relax.

His head shifted as he continued to consider. "No, that's Retindel... They have an almost identical system."

Millennial Mage, 5 - Fusing

She waited for a long moment as Rane shifted stretches yet again. Finally, she cleared her throat. "So…?"

"What?"

"Which guild rules here?"

"Well, not 'rules.' They—"

"Master Rane." She cut across him.

Something in her tone seemed to catch his attention because he sat up straight, looking her way. "Well, I'm not sure, but I *think* it is the Constructionists. I'd have to consult the Archive." He grinned, attempting to inject humor. "Or I suppose we could just ask the attendant."

Tala swallowed involuntarily. *Well, that makes sense if he owns the tree already…*

"Why do you ask?"

She didn't know how to respond. "I… I'm not sure what to say."

"What do you mean?" He was fully facing her, now, clearly a bit concerned by how she was acting.

"I think I realized something that might be a secret…"

He nodded, quirking his lips to the side in thought. "If you can share, I'm happy to hear, but don't break a promise or put anyone in danger to tell me."

Tala blinked at him. *That's… kind.* After a moment's thought, she nodded. "Did you notice anything odd about the power signature in the magic surrounding Makinaven?"

He shook his head. "Just that it was claimed, but that's standard for a city. If anyone could just grab onto a city's power, all sorts of chaos could come about…" He frowned again. "Your magesight is more sensitive than mine. What did you notice?"

"I think I recognize the signature of a Mage's aura threading through the power." She let that hang out there. *I can tell him more, depending on how he reacts.*

After a considerable pause, Rane shook his head. "Mistress Tala, you think you've seen a Mage's power, influencing the power around all of Makinaven?"

"No, Master Rane. I've recognized the signature of the aura which *is* the power around and throughout Makinaven."

He leaned forward. "Really? Who?"

A familiar voice came to her ear before she could respond. "Mistress Tala. We will speak of this tomorrow. I would appreciate your silence on the issue until then."

Silence rang through the room as Tala's entire body broke out in a cold sweat.

"Mistress Tala?" Rane was standing and walking toward her. "Mistress Tala, are you okay?" From his actions, he seemed to have not heard Master Jevin's request.

"Yeah. Yeah. I… I might be mistaken, so… can we talk about it tomorrow?"

Rane was kneeling beside her, concern clear in his expression. "Are you sure?"

"Yeah. I think that would be best. Ask me again, tomorrow night?"

That seemed to help him relax a little bit. "Alright. If you're sure."

"I am."

He smiled and stood, holding out a hand. "Want help up?"

"Yes. Let's spar. I need to clear my head."

Chapter: 2
Humanity

Tala let her mind expand, her focus broaden, and her body react on instinct. She forcibly pushed all thoughts of the tree's god-king from her mind. *Not helpful...*

Flow's hilt was at once perfectly smooth and easy to grip securely. It was cool, helping keep her hand from sweating while not sucking the heat from her hand. In short, it was perfect for her, contouring to her palm and fingers beyond the ability of any craftsman to replicate.

As she'd used the weapon more and more, Tala had noticed that as her grip shifted, gaining better form for sword work, the hilt had seamlessly shifted, maintaining perfect shape for how she was holding it, in that moment.

The grain of the wood beneath her feet was tight and smooth, polished to an almost mirror finish, yet, somehow, still allowing for firm purchase.

Her stance was relaxed, her muscles loose and ready to react at a moment's notice.

Rane lunged, driving Force toward her heart in a powerful thrust.

A flick of Flow knocked the point aside without conscious thought on Tala's part. She slid down the length of his blade, sending out ripples of power as the magic of the two swords conflicted.

She leapt forward with a quick step, maintaining the bind of their blades, the contact letting her know where his weapon was without having to see it directly.

Even as she closed and lashed out with a back-fist, leaving Flow in her off-hand, Rane spun around the strike, bringing his sword in an almost impossibly tight twist, cutting toward her back.

The next moments were a blur of attack and counter, rolling one upon another.

Force and Flow clashed in a staccato series of magical concussions that resonated in Tala's very bones.

It was a pleasant thrum that pulled a smile from her lips.

As the exchange continued, it became clear that Rane was more tentative than he had been in their previous fights. This allowed Tala to stand on an almost even footing with the big man.

Tala moved Flow through its three shapes with almost no effort, each blow seeming to reverberate through Force and into Rane's hands and arms.

Force was soul-bound to Rane, now, but Flow had a greater magical weight to it. Its bond to Tala was more deeply ingrained in the weapon than Force's was with Rane. Each merging Flow had gone through had bound it tighter with her. Those features both gave Flow's strikes extra oomph.

She didn't resort to any tricks, not for this first bout, instead relying on her skill, such as it was, along with her enhancements.

Rane wielded his massive blade with the dexterity of a calligrapher using their favorite brush and fine ink.

Even so, despite his skill and competence, Tala was becoming able to see more and more openings. Though, she was unable to take full advantage of any. However, she was able to alter her engagement in order to press him more closely around those openings.

As was usual for them, Rane's base skill slowly tipped the balance of the exchange, forcing her to extend herself ever more until, at long last, she couldn't recover quickly enough to stop his riposte.

She did have an instant to react, however, and she used it to great effect.

Force caught her ribs, lifting her free of the ground and tossing her into the nearest wall.

She groaned as she slid to the floor.

Rane grinned over at her. "You had me there for a minute."

She sighed. "You just had a moment of doubt in your abilities."

He cocked his head. "So, why not capitalize on that? You have a deep bag of tricks. You didn't use any."

She kicked back up to her feet. "Crushing your confidence wouldn't do any good in the long run. I need my sparring partner in top form if I am to improve."

He gave her a long, contemplative look. Finally, he nodded. "Alright, then." Rane frowned. "Wait... where's Flow?"

Tala grinned, pulling Flow from the floor at Rane's back. As Rane's inscriptions activated, throwing him into a forward flip to avoid the sword coming at his back, Tala stepped forward, reaching for his head.

As his head whipped toward her, she pulled her hand back so that she was moving away from him while he caught up with her palm.

Rane's scripts threw him forward regardless, slamming his forehead into her retreating palm.

The impact reversed the direction of his movement, even though she moved with him to soften the blow.

Once she had contact, she was able to twist around, taking him to the ground and pressing Flow, now in the shape of a knife, against his throat.

He groaned. "Ow."

"You okay?"

Millennial Mage, 5 - Fusing

"Yeah... Thank you for the soft landing."

She grinned down at him. "Happy to assist." She stepped back, offering him a hand up.

He took it, standing and stretching. "Again?"

She considered. Still feeling the tingles of existential dread, she nodded. "Again."

*   *   *

Tala had fully calmed and cleared her head after a few more bouts. After she thanked him for the training, Rane bid her goodnight and headed back to his inn.

Alone, she was able to dive back into her fusing with a renewed gusto.

She was going to be facing a god the next day, and she wanted as much strength as she could muster.

Yes, I need as many snowflakes as possible before I visit the forge. Who knows? I might just cool it off. She did not let her focus fracture.

When she absolutely had to take a break, her magesight aching from straining inward, she switched to practice with the iron spheres.

Since she couldn't easily turn off her magesight, only suppress it, Tala decided that forcefully turning it outward would help. Blessedly, it did seem to.

As she worked on her mental construct for marking her target, the paintbrush she imagined shrunk, as did the amount of magic she left on the target, allowing her to progress to the next balls up through the difficulties.

She marked and released the targets dozens of times per break.

As soon as she felt able, she would move back inside herself and crochet another step toward fusing. At most, she could do two stitches between periods of respite.

It was exhausting, deeply taxing work.

Ironically, the crocheting became a mental break as much as anything. *Maybe, this is why some people stitch as a hobby.*

Finally, hours after midnight, she found herself in need of a break from her internal magesight but mentally not up for painting targets with her power. She'd been struggling to form the image of a paintbrush delicate enough to pierce the mesh of this second-to-last ball for the past few breaks.

Why can't it just be marked? I have a near-perfect mental picture of the rusting target. She pictured the infuriating wooden ball in all its inglorious roundness.

The wooden ball within the iron-mesh ball took on a slight glow to her magesight.

Tala blinked, glancing down at her left hand where her middle finger and thumb were pressed together.

But... I didn't reach out to mark it...

It was true. There was no 'mark' of her magic on the small ball, the ball was simply targeted, no mark required.

I didn't grab it. I couldn't have. The mesh is too fine.

She picked up the iron ball with her right hand, the mesh so fine it could have served as bug-netting.

And now, it's just targeted.

She thought through the process. *I indicate my target by pointing, grabbing it with magic, or marking it with a mental paintbrush.*

Then what?

Then, I have to have an understanding of what I'm targeting. I connect that understanding to what I've indicated, and the target is locked on.

Why?

Why... what?

Why did she have to mark the target, grab it, or indicate it, to target it?

If I don't, how will the target lock?

Millennial Mage, 5 - Fusing

She cocked her head to the side. *No. I have an understanding of what I'm targeting. Why would I need anything else?*

The *click* of a mentality change rushed through her mind, shifting her understanding yet again.

Blessedly, her mental ruts were not nearly as set as they had been surrounding other recent revelations, so she was only left with a mildly splitting headache.

"Ow…" She glared around at the empty training room, Terry sleeping in his corner. "Fine… I'll sleep."

As she moved over to where she wanted to open Kit for the night, she hesitated.

A small smile tugged at her lips. *Might as well test.*

She pulled out the last ball, a complete, hollow sphere of iron. She swirled the ball, feeling the wood move around inside.

A wooden sphere, the same as all the others.

"Mine."

She *felt* her lock take hold, even though she couldn't see it, even with her magesight, and no evidence of the power leaked out.

She laughed, spinning in a circle. "I did it. I did it! *I did it!*" She laughed again.

Terry lifted his head for a moment, gave a half-hearted congratulatory trill, and lay back down.

Tala continued to laugh. A wide grin painted her face until a thought intruded into her mind like a shard of ice.

Her smile fell away, and her eyes widened, color draining from her face.

"Oh… oh, rust me to slag. My iron salve would be useless against someone who could do this."

*   *   *

Tala... did not sleep well that night. Not even during the last part of the night she actually tried to sleep through.

When Mistress Odera arrived for breakfast, Tala was wide awake and waiting.

The older woman commented several times that Tala was unusually quiet, but the observations never inspired a change, and they parted ways having barely said a few dozen sentences between them.

Tala spent the remainder of her time before her appointment with Master Jevin fusing as much as she could.

Three hours after noon arrived, Tala walked into the Constructionist's Guild entry, coming face to face with Grent.

"Mistress Tala!" He smiled, holding his arms wide.

Tala just stared at him for a long moment. He was one of the farthest things from her mind, at the moment, so she had no ready reaction to his sudden presence.

His smile faltered slightly.

She pulled herself together. She did *not* want another awkward interaction with this man. She took a deep breath, put on a polite smile, and bowed her head. "Master Grent, good day to you."

His smile faded, and he gave a slight, professional bow. "Good day. To what do we owe the pleasure?"

"I have an appointment with Master Jevin." *Right... the god-creature that's probably watching me right now.*

Master Jevin's voice filled the entry room—a comfortable volume for them both. "Yes. Welcome, Mistress Tala. Please head on back."

Her eye twitched, but she was most grateful to have an easy excuse to leave Grent behind. *Oh, thank the rusting slag.* "I have to go. Bye!" She waved to Grent as she moved past. Terry watched Grent as she passed but settled back down after he was out of sight.

Tala quick-walked down the hallways, refusing to let herself think on what she was walking into. *I'm already in the tree, and if he wished me harm, I couldn't escape before he enacted it upon me.*

Neither those thoughts nor 'not thinking about it' really helped.

Thankfully, she only needed occasional correction by Master Jevin's disembodied voice. *Directing me to the slaughter...*

A short minute later, she came into his office, and her mind forcibly returned to all the reasons she'd been nervous.

He controls the whole rusting tree. Despite the nerves, however, she found it incredibly difficult to really integrate that understanding. *Where I stand, he could snuff my life with a thought.* That should evoke terror. *Maybe, I've just gone numb?*

Master Jevin was sitting in one of his reading chairs, waiting for her. "How about you have a seat, Mistress? We've a lot to talk about."

Tala stopped. "Couldn't you just move me to the chair?" *Really? Poking the bear?*

A smile almost seemed to tug at his lips. "I could. So could Master Bob, but he'd have a harder time of it."

She grimaced. "That's... fair."

After a long pause, Master Jevin sighed. "So...?" He gestured to the chair opposite him.

Tala noticed that a small tea service had been set out, including a selection of scones. She begrudgingly moved forward and sat.

"Let us address the Leshkin in the room, shall we?"

Odd turn of phrase, but alright. She grunted her assent, snatching a scone to eat as she poured herself some tea.

Master Jevin gave a half-smile. "You have stumbled upon some rather... difficult information."

She grunted again.

"Do you have any idea how many people, within Makinaven, know even the small part that you've deduced?"

Swallowing, Tala shook her head. "Not many?"

"You are the only one."

She frowned. "I find that hard to believe."

He held up two fingers. "First, your magesight is incredibly powerful and detail-oriented. I doubt you have a true grasp on how rare a gift that is. There are *maybe* a small handful of Archons, living, who could perceive more than you." He grinned. "There are many who understand more from what they see than you do, but that's a separate issue." He dropped one of his fingers. "Second, now that you know, what do you want to do?"

"Get as far from here as possible." The response came out before she could consider how it might be received.

His smile never wavered. "Precisely." He dropped the second finger.

Oh. Yeah, that checks out. If basically anyone who figures it out leaves the city, there wouldn't be any here besides me.

He nodded, taking a sip from his own cup before continuing. "I see you understand."

She made a vague noise of assent.

"So. That part addressed, let's get to the meat of the issue."

"You are the god of this city."

He snorted. "Not inaccurate, but not what I'd pick as a descriptor."

"Oh?"

"I don't desire, seek, nor tolerate any sort of worship or veneration."

"But the power level?"

"Near so, yeah."

"What's that mean?"

"It means that I wouldn't want to test myself against the Forest Spirit—or any of the others—not even here."

That's probably quite wise.

"But effectively, yes. My authority, here, is without dispute."

"How? Why?"

His smile turned a bit sad. "Well, there used to be a trend, millennia back, to form your Archon Star out of a medium taken from a powerful thing of magic. I chose a simple wooden sphere."

No.

"Wood, taken from this very tree." His sad smile became lopsided. "It worked, beautifully. Little did I realize at the time that these great trees never really relinquish their hold on any part of their being. Even bits that fall, or are cut off, are effectively still a part of the whole."

"So, you soul-bound the tree."

"So, I soul-bound the tree before I was ever an Archon."

Tala sat back, slowly eating her scone and drinking her tea.

"I was irrevocably changed. The tree was immensely powerful, beyond the ability of any human to control or rule over, but it had no will of its own. So, the power *was* mine. The only possible result was that I was reshaped." The sadness came back in full force. "The tree had… knowledge isn't the right word, but it's close enough. The tree knew of beings that could bear up under its power."

"Leshkin." *And the turn of phrase makes sense…*

He shrugged. "Mezzannis, but close enough."

"So… you aren't even human?"

Master Jevin's eyes hardened, a deep rage seeming to rise within him. "What makes a man?"

Tala frowned, taking a delaying sip of her drink. *Wisdom dictates I do* not *answer that.*

When she didn't respond, he continued. "Is it his body? How much do you need to cut away before he is no longer 'he'?"

She had no response.

"Is it his mind? How many memories or neurochemicals, how much dura-matter needs to be altered before the person is fundamentally changed? Before a person's base nature is gone?"

Tala swallowed, setting her tea aside but unable to formulate an answer.

"No, Mistress. What makes a man, what makes a human, is the *soul*, and no accident of magic will take that from me." The room thrummed with power.

She felt a light dizziness that passed as she asserted her own will, locking herself away from his unconscious flexing of magic. Even so, her eyes flicked to his chest, her magesight immediately confirming what she knew would be there: his gate. *Human, at least at the level of his soul.*

"From that day, I have worked toward Reforging myself." He tsked. "Refining actually made the problem worse. Refining makes your body more purely what it is." His barely subdued rage at that was palpable.

I don't really understand that, but now doesn't seem the time to ask. "That must have been... difficult."

He snorted derisively. "Difficult? Extremely. Our inscriptions are based on being placed in human flesh." With a gesture, he indicated the most wooden-seeming portions of his face. "Even mild deviations can ruin everything."

Tala's eyes widened. "How, then?"

"I am bound to the tree. I did not age. I had time in abundance."

"But your inscriptions now…"

"Are human? Yes. That was the first aspect I reforged. Magically speaking, as a medium, my flesh is considered human." There was obvious pride in that.

"So, then, you're close?"

"Closer than I've ever been." After a short pause, he amended, "At least since my youth."

There was a deep weariness behind those words that Tala couldn't begin to fathom. She found herself frowning as she leaned back, letting the silence of his remembrance build and fill the space between them.

Chapter: 3
Questions and Requests

Tala slowly sipped her tea as she watched emotions play over Master Jevin's face. Eventually, she lightly cleared her throat. "If I may, how old are you?"

The sadness returned to the forefront as the dominant emotion evident in his features. "Old, Mistress. I was not lying when I said that humanity is all I have."

She glanced away, noticing the obvious deflection for what it was. *Alright, don't press, there.* "So, the tree."

"The tree." He nodded. "I am soul-bound to the entire city-tree."

"Can… you leave?"

He barked a laugh. "Oh, yes. It is… uncomfortable to be too far. That is one reason I remain on the front line against the Leshkin during the years in which humanity moves north, working against these ancient evils until my fellow man returns. I do go to the northern cities, but I return to the northern edge of the forest as quickly, and for as long, as I can."

She cocked her head in interest. "Not here?" She nibbled at her scone while he answered.

"Oh, no. This tree will be sealed up tight, and the spell-workings powered down. We have to do that so that the ambient magic can equalize once more." After a long moment, he shook his head. "So, do you have any questions?"

Millennial Mage, 5 - Fusing

"Way, way too many, but none really seem... important."

He shrugged. "Well, I'm here, if you ever wish to ask."

Tala considered for a long moment. She really did feel like he was genuine in his openness, and it caused her to realize something: she didn't really feel afraid any longer; she felt... heavy. Like she'd increased her own gravity to be near her limit. *But there is none of the energy I feel from such a challenge...*

It was a weight that seemed to settle into her spirit. *How many years has this man suffered, denied the one thing he cherishes above all: humanity?*

As she stared at her hands, a small plate moved into her vision. She looked up quickly, but Master Jevin was still in his seat. The plate, loaded with scones, sat in the air as solid as if resting on an invisible table before her.

"Scones help."

He's comforting... me? She glanced down at the scones and felt a smile break through her melancholy. She huffed a laugh and shook her head, but the solemnity of the conversation was broken. "Thank you."

He nodded, returning a slight smile.

"So... are the workers who've replaced parts of themselves bound to you?"

He shook his head. "Oh, no. The tree is still separate from me, though it is bound to my soul. They are simply gaining a weaker version of the bond I have." After a moment's pause, he amended. "Much, much weaker."

She sat back, considering.

Master Jevin tapped the armrest of his chair. "One last thing on this topic."

She refocused on him, waiting.

"I would ask that you not spread this information around. It could cause all sorts of issues."

She grimaced. *More secrets.*

"You can talk to Master Rane about it; I think avoiding that, now, would be a bigger problem than just telling him, and he's a clever boy. He'll understand the need to keep it to himself."

"But why would it be so bad for people to know?"

Master Jevin gave her a long look.

Tala shifted in her chair under his scrutiny.

"Can you really not think of *anything* that might go wrong?"

She opened her mouth, then closed it, thinking. After a moment, she found herself nodding. "Well, it might bring back that old trend of Mages seeking power and all that. Many would just see that it worked, not the costs."

Master Jevin nodded and waited.

"The mundanes would likely want to leave in vast numbers." She hesitated, then sighed. *He seems to want honesty.* "It *is* a bit creepy that you watch everything, all the time."

He raised a finger. "I actually don't. I have triggers in place to notify me of key things like your conversation with Master Rane on this topic, but for the most part, I see no more than anyone would."

"But people might not believe that."

"They might not."

"Shouldn't that be their choice? I mean, shouldn't they have the choice on whether or not to believe you and whether or not to stay?"

He cocked an eyebrow at her. "If you focus, could you construct what someone looks like under their clothing with your magesight?" He clearly already thought he knew the answer.

Can I? she considered. *Yeah, I suppose I could.* "I guess so, yeah."

Millennial Mage, 5 - Fusing

"So, do you tell everyone around you, 'By the way, I could see you naked if I wanted, I just choose not to. If that bugs you, you should probably not be around me.'"

"I obviously don't."

"Why not? Shouldn't that be their choice?"

Tala grimaced again. "I see your point." She groaned. "I still kind of hate it."

"Maturity requires doing things we don't like because it is right."

She gave him a deeply skeptical look. "Did you just state that being mature means telling unpleasant lies?"

He coughed, scratching his neck. "Let's not think too deeply on that one."

Tala snorted, shaking her head, but didn't comment further.

"But! We aren't here for me, not really. Let's discuss your questions and requests."

Tala nodded and smiled. "I'd appreciate that. Thank you." She poured herself another cup of tea as Master Jevin finished off his last scone.

"So, Mistress. You asked for throwing darts?"

"Ah, yes!"

He smiled. "Can I have the anchor?"

She unclipped it from her belt and tossed it to him.

He caught it with a nod. "You know, you could keep it in your dimensional storage. That might keep it safer."

"That... is a good idea."

"Though, now that you have these darts, that probably isn't as good an idea as it would have been before."

She gave him an unamused look that he ignored.

He pulled a small rack of throwing darts from a dimensional ripple in the air beside him. While holding the rack and the anchor, Master Jevin closed his eyes and exhaled.

Tala watched the man's aura grab inscriptions on each magical item.

He, somehow, pushed them together at a deeper-than-physical level.

He magically linked them, obviously. She sighed. She still wasn't used to instantly interpreting what her magesight showed her. *There was something to his friendly jab. I really need to get more used to integrating and interpreting what my magesight shows me.*

"There you go." The anchor and rack moved back to her, so she could take them from the air.

She clipped the anchor back to her belt and put the darts into Kit. Then, she reached in and pulled out one of the throwing weapons. "What's this metal?"

"Titanium."

She nodded, examining the gray metal. The exterior was heavily inscribed so that it could indicate a target. It actually looked a bit like a worm-riddled stick that had been stripped of bark and had the worm lines filled with precious metal. "I assume I can't target the world with this?"

Master Jevin laughed. "No, you can't target anything larger than your anchor space, so nothing larger than twenty feet across or so. And something that big will drain power like mad."

Tala frowned. "That is much less useful."

"Well, if you like the results, we could make a few layers of this, creating layers of entrapment."

She found herself nodding. "I think I like that, but I should test out the idea a bit, first."

"I thought as much, too."

"If this works, we could create an anchor for me, to help lock me in place, then another for the various layers of ensnared opponents."

Millennial Mage, 5 - Fusing

Master Jevin shrugged. "I mean, if we want, we could make your anchor variable distance. Let you mentally alter how close it keeps you, though things like that would be both more efficient and more easily controlled if you were to soul bond them."

"Could we then make the opponent snares variable? That way we wouldn't need to make it have multiple layers?"

He leaned back, nodding and taking a large bite of scone.

Where did that one come from?

Now that she thought about it, they'd eaten *way* more than had been on the tray when she arrived.

Huh, I suppose he has a stash of scones in his dimensional storage. Oddly, more than his kindly attitude, more than his ready answers to all her questions, the fact that he had a selection of snacks in his storage humanized him to her despite his insane levels of power. *Yes, Tala, he likes baked goods, so he must not be evil.* She kept outward expressions of her mirth to a small smile.

Master Jevin swallowed. "Yeah, that actually makes a lot of sense, again if you like the effect. The trick, I think, would be to have the distance set by the targeting item—either your bracers or the darts. Then, the bracers being on you would allow for active adjustment, without returning to the anchor. For the darts, you could set each before you threw it."

She leaned forward. "Oh! I like that." She was nodding. "After I test these." She lifted the dart in her hand.

"Yes, testing is a good idea." He grinned. "I look forward to seeing how they work for you." A small chuckle escaped his lips. "Most Mages want to keep opponents away, and any that are close enough to put a dart in are far, far too close."

"I can see that." Another sip of tea spaced out her next topic. "So... I was able to target the wooden ball within the final iron sphere."

"Hey! That's wonderful." He grinned her way, and she felt a wave of genuine warmth well up within her chest.

"Thank you. I am quite proud of it, actually."

"You should be. While it's a common series of exercises, not many have the capacity to enact upon the last ball." He gave a half-smile. "Do you want the next set?"

Tala's smile froze. "The next... set?"

"Of course! Did you think you were done?"

"Well... maybe?"

He laughed. "The next set are all fully enclosed in iron with varying targets inside. The first is the same wood but in a cube, instead of a sphere. Since you've never targeted a cube of the stuff, that's harder. The second is a different wood, formed into a ball. Third, another wood still, in another shape, which you won't be told, and so on."

She considered for a moment. "What's the final test?"

He smiled. "An unknown material, in an unknown shape, fully encased in iron, with no space around it."

"So, a solid sphere of iron with a bit of material at the core?"

Lines crinkled beside his eyes. "Bold of you to assume that the target would be in the center."

Tala groaned in anticipated frustration, but her mind was already sparking with the implications of such trials. "Yeah... that sounds like something worth working up to."

He held out his hand, and she returned the six spheres that she'd overcome. He then handed over the six new ones, each with a number, seven through twelve, stamped on the side and paired with a small notecard of information on the challenge.

"Thank you."

"I aim to assist."

She smiled. "So, I wanted to ask"—she gestured to the iron balls, even as he tucked them into a dimensional rift—"does this methodology make my iron salve useless?"

"Your passive defense?"

"Yeah."

"Not at all. To bypass it and target you, your opponent first has to have a spell-working that *can* directly target something, regardless of intervening space, which isn't actually that common. Then, even if they have the proper magic or inscription, they have to know how to use it in that way and be practiced in such a use. The last two are even more rare, proportionally, than the first. Even then, they'd have to overcome your will to affect you, and you always have the advantage in a fight for authority over your own body." He leaned back once more. "That contest of wills is actually one of the primary reasons such direct targeting is rare. It is much simpler to impart heat in the direction of a target than to target the specific thing you want to burn. You chose an... unusual path."

"So my teachers were fond of telling me."

He shrugged. "You have the magical weight to make it work when fighting at your level or below. You will struggle to work directly on those above you, but that is a fairly universal issue, regardless."

She nodded. "Thank you for the breakdown. So, the iron salve is far from useless but also nothing close to a universal defense."

"Well said."

She smiled contentedly at the praise.

"Now, your Archon Stars." He once again held out his hand.

She tossed him the iron vial containing her last star, still much weaker than Grediv had said was minimally required to become Bound. *Not that I need that, again.*

He caught it dexterously, removing the cap and looking inside. "Fascinating. For some reason, I assumed that the outside would have scabbed over once it was exposed to air for long enough, but it truly is a liquid medium."

"So it seems."

He smiled but didn't look up at her. "To confirm, you are alright with me performing tests on this?"

She almost responded with an off-handed "Sure," but something about his question gave her pause. "Is there danger?"

"Not particularly."

She gave him a flat look. "That means yes, but they're minimal."

"Accurate."

"So?"

He shrugged. "If I were to be malicious, I could overpower your will and forcibly bind you to something. This is too weak for a bond to a sapient creature, but I could think of a few things that would be detrimental to be bound to."

And the uncomfortable feeling's back.

"Oh, don't worry. I don't plan to do any of that." He laughed. "And if I did, you really couldn't stop me."

"Yeah... but you didn't have to mention..." She frowned, glanced at his eyes, and saw poorly hidden mirth. "Fine, it can be better to not tell someone all the ways you could harm them or invade their privacy. You've made your point."

He gave a slight bow. "The tests I will perform are perfectly safe."

Millennial Mage, 5 - Fusing

She waved an assenting hand, drinking more tea in stubborn silence.

He rose and went to one of his work benches, pulling out myriad tools.

As the star moved around, Tala continued to be able to tell exactly where it was.

Flashes and flickers of different magics radiated from the workbench, and Tala felt odd sensations coming from the Archon Star.

"What are you doing?"

"At the moment?" He glanced over his shoulder, a small smile evident, tugging at his lips.

Tala sighed. *He really likes destroying his own mystique.* "Yes, at the moment."

"Seeing if I can engender enough curiosity in you to draw you away from your tea." He gave her a full, mischievous grin.

She huffed a laugh and stood, resolutely refilling her teacup and bringing it with her.

He laughed, seeing her cup. "Good enough." He gestured to a hammered bronze sheet with silver-filled inscriptions worked across the surface.

"Why bronze? Why not wood?"

He smiled. "Well, the foremost expert on the human soul, in the last few hundred years at least, was a Bronze Archon, and she perfected the diagnostic inscriptions in that medium far beyond what I have time to develop in any other medium."

"Could you just use your aura?"

"Of course, but that would require *much* more power and still wouldn't be as precise in the information it could pull."

"Huh… good to know."

He gave her a sideways look. "Tallying up my weaknesses, eh?"

She decided to run with it, giving him a winning smile. "Anything you care to add to the list?"

"Caramel liqueur. It is most potent against me when contained in a smooth dark chocolate." He closed his eyes, clearly enjoying a memory. "And pair it with a full-bodied whiskey?" He shook his head. "*Mmm*, mmm."

Tala huffed a laugh. "Alright, alright. What have you learned?"

"This is, indeed, an Archon Star and can be used for a soul-bond to a non-sapient item."

She waited for a long count of ten. When nothing else was forthcoming, she turned back to regard him. "And?"

"I ran one test, Mistress Tala." He was grinning again.

"I thought you were busy today."

"When you get to be my age, you have to make your own fun."

"You sound like a librarian I ran into."

He snorted. "I don't doubt it; most Archon Librarians are of an age that they'd agree with me."

"Fair, I suppose."

Power moved through the bronze plate and the inscriptions engraved into it.

Tala watched power twisting around her Archon Star, now free of its vial and held, suspended, over the empowered item.

"Interesting."

"What is it?"

"I'm not sure. I need to run a companion test on you." He motioned with his hand, and a bronze plate moved from a nearby cabinet and settled onto the floor. "If you would?"

Tala shrugged and stepped onto the inscribed surface. As she did so, she felt Master Jevin empower the spellforms, and magic swept through her.

"Fascinating."

"Yes?"

"Your soul does have a tendril just free-floating, in addition to the connection to this star and your weapon."

"What does that mean?"

"Hmmm? No idea. I don't know of any specific use for a stretching of your soul."

"Does it weaken it? Strengthen it? Allow me to temporarily claim things?"

"No?" He shrugged. "These spellforms are registering your soul as quite strong, for a human, but I'd expect nothing else from an Archon moving toward Fused. Though, this would indicate that you have a bit more strength than that would imply. Soul exercises?"

"Every day."

"Seems to be helping."

"So, ignorant question, why is a strong soul good?"

He nodded. "Ahh, yes. There are too many words for the same thing. The strength of your soul is roughly equivalent to the strength of your will. They are intertwined and interconnected, to the point that they have never been proven to be different aspects of a person."

"But they've never been proven to be the same?"

He hesitated a moment. "Are your fingers and the bones of your hand the same? Are they distinct?"

"I think I understand. Which is the soul, and which is the will, in this analogy?"

"That's just it, we don't really know."

"That is massively unsatisfying."

He shrugged. "We don't know everything. Are you willing to create a star while being monitored?"

She thought about it for a moment. "Just a little one?"

"That should do, yeah."

Finally, she nodded. "I think the information we can get from it is worth the effort."

"Alright, then! Let's get to it."

Chapter: 4
A Lot to Take in

Tala felt somewhat nostalgic as she wove the Archon Star within her finger. She directed three void channels into its creation.

"That is fascinating." Master Jevin leaned forward. "It's already in a stable condition, with so little power. Truly, we Immaterial Guides have an unfair advantage here if we are willing to work within ourselves once again. Seems that working with a medium of your own body amplifies that advantage."

She just snorted. "Is that enough power?"

He shrugged. "I'm gathering all sorts of information from the creation process. It should be fine, though."

Tala pulled out a non-magical knife, retracted her defenses, and pricked her finger, pushing out the drop of blood containing her Archon Star. It dripped free even as her skin pulled closed once more.

The drop began to orbit around her clockwise, caught in the spellform radiating from below, which encompassed her.

Even as it orbited, completing one revolution every second or so, it moved up and down around her.

"Can you call this one to you?" He pointed to the drop hovering over the bronze plate on his workbench.

Tala shrugged and *pulled*. The drop zipped through the air toward her.

Millennial Mage, 5 - Fusing

She stopped pulling as it came within reach, and it entered into an opposing orbit around her, moving counterclockwise and vertically opposite of the other star.

Master Jevin leaned forward. "That... that is fascinating." He let out a laugh. "I feel like I'm saying that a lot."

"What? What did you notice?"

"Your blood is living, and you've soul-bound it to yourself, but the blood is too minuscule to fully contain the bond, allowing you to use the blood as a catalyst for the bond you wish to make." He shook his head. "Which doesn't even take into account the fact that it should *already* be bound to you as a part of your Bound body."

"What does that mean?"

"You've done the opposite of what I did. Where I accidentally bound myself to something far greater than myself, and that my bond had no right to actually affect, thus making me subservient to its power, you have bound yourself to something so minuscule, when compared to yourself, that it doesn't really count." He seemed to be considering. "Did you get your soul exercises from a book or from an instructor?"

"Well, trial and error, then confirmed by an instructor, finally found in a book."

He gave her an odd look but didn't comment on her long answer. "Which book?"

"Soul Work. Why?"

"Good, good. That is an excellent resource. If I'm seeing this correctly, you are going to want to make a *lot* of these stars. At least you will when you learn a couple more of the exercises in that book."

"Which?" She pulled out her copy, holding it out to him. The blood drops altered their orbit to avoid hitting her outstretched arm, even looping around it occasionally without any visible input from either of them.

Master Jevin took the copy and leafed through it. "The most recent, revised edition? And well-bound." He began to nod. "Master Grediv's work, then. He really did see something in you." His eyes flicked to Tala's for a moment, and he smiled. "Here." He passed the book back, two places held open for her.

"'Perpendicular Manipulation'?"

"Yes. When mastered, and if properly utilized, you can move your soul-bound items in orbits like those drops are moving in now. But you can do it on your own, without standing on a spellform." He laughed. "Even so, I'd say it would be impossibly complex, however."

She smiled. "I can reduce their effective gravity."

"Thus making it a much more feasible technique for you."

She frowned but nodded. *I can see use in that. Moving Flow from side to side would give me a lot more options in battle.* "Oh! Did I tell you that I figured out a new aspect of my gravity manipulation?"

He cocked an eyebrow. "Let's hear it."

She briefly delved into Join and Distinct.

"Fascinating. Your foundational understanding of gravity is... something." He smiled. "Thank you for sharing. That gives me much to consider." His eyes seemed to unfocus as he began to do just that.

Tala cleared her throat, drawing his attention back, tapping Soul Work. "And what's this second one? 'Aspect Mirroring'?"

He grinned. "You can cause any soul-bound item of yours to take on an aspect of you."

Tala cocked her head in confusion before returning her focus to the book and reading further through the description. As she did so, her eyes widened. "I can give my soul-bound items my same weight of magic and will so that they are as hard to affect as I am." She swallowed.

Millennial Mage, 5 - Fusing

"And I can cause my mass to mirror any of my soul-bound items and vice versa."

"Precisely. For most people, there is some powerful but limited utility in Aspect Mirroring, based on what they are bound to. For you, with your unique set of abilities?"

"I can have a cloud of blood around me, each drop taking hundreds of pounds of force to bypass and magically resilient to boot."

"Just so."

She dropped into a seated position as the implications crashed over her. *This would mitigate my issue with staying in place. It would be a* powerful *defense.* "There has to be a catch."

"A catch? No."

"So, why doesn't everyone do this?"

"Well, aside from it not being as useful to someone with a different type of Archon Star, and lacking your rare view and utilization of gravity, I imagine you will have four hurdles to overcome for it to truly be of use to you."

"Do tell?" She leaned forward, hanging on every word.

"First, mastering the movement of even a single soul-bound item into a consistent orbit around yourself is *difficult* in the extreme. Second, you will need to make it utterly instinctive for it to be anything but a known battlefield tool. Third, you will have to compound that difficulty *exponentially* to create a small cloud around yourself. Fourth and finally, you will need to find a way to split your Archon Stars into smaller stars."

She frowned. "I followed until the last, why?"

"In doing this, in using this defense, your stars *will* run into each other. By Master Grediv's postulation, that means they will combine. That will make the bond to you stronger, but that isn't useful for this utility. Correct?"

Tala nodded.

"Then, you will need a way to split them back apart, or you will have to be constantly making stars. There's the additional issue that the strength of the star will affect how it reacts, so you would have to be constantly altering your instinctual orbits for each drop as it changes in power level unless you can instinctively split them back down to the smallest size sustainable."

"Ahh... I think I understand the issue."

"I'm glad."

"So... why doesn't everyone want to do something like this?"

He took a deep breath. "First of all, I *might* be able to do something similar with Archon Stars in splinters of this tree if I could stabilize the spellform with as little power as you use, which given my aura control, I probably could. I could then also use my aura to effectively mimic the results you get from gravity alteration and soul work."

"So?"

"So, my aura and aura control already render it redundant. Anything that can get through my aura is going to be *much* too powerful to be stopped by the type of defense we are discussing."

"So... it will be useless when I advance far enough?"

"Not at all. Most don't devote themselves toward aura control and power as I have, and I would not recommend that path to you. You'd have to scrap your entire schema and start from scratch. You'd basically be in for a decade of uselessness until you could fully grasp the nuances of auras. Most Mages are in the same place as you and only develop their aura to a rudimentary level."

"Why?"

He shrugged. "The same reason most don't reinforce their body to the extent that you have." He grinned. "I certainly haven't. We each have things we focus on, and we cannot focus on everything, even with centuries or millennia to expand our understanding."

Tala was nodding again. "I guess that makes sense."

They fell into a companionable silence then, each consumed in their private thoughts.

*   *   *

After a few moments of thought, Tala decided to fuse a few stitches and began to work on that.

As she did so, she felt Master Jevin's attention return to her, but she didn't want her efforts to be wasted. *I'll engage with him again after at least one stitch.*

"Your soul is doing some crazy things. Are you fusing?"

She cracked one eye open to glare, only waiting until she saw him raise his hands in apologetic surrender before closing it once more.

Just one stitch. She exhaled slowly, fully immersed within.

Just over a minute later, she pulled the stitch tight and opened her eyes, stretching and taking more normal breaths. "Now, what did you want?"

"I don't know that I've ever seen soul readings on a person while they were fusing." He was scratching his chin. "I'll bet they've been taken, but I never really thought to look for them."

"Anything interesting?"

"Well, yes. I'd have thought that was obvious?"

She gave him an unamused look.

"First of all, as you would expect, your soul-bonds were vibrating in sync with the fusing."

"Wait... why would I expect that?"

"Because they are linked to your soul, and the bond is a part of it. Thus, anything that affects your soul affects your bonds."

"Oh. That does make sense."

"The best way I can verbalize these results, succinctly, is like this: The cord binding you to your knife just had another thread woven through it."

"That's…" She frowned. "I suppose that makes sense."

"Alright. Now, your soul, itself." He was nodding. "Your gate and your spirit, the two parts of your soul, both surged with power, intermixing before resettling back as they were, slightly more linked than before."

"Why is that unexpected?"

"Well, the way you described your fusing process, I would have assumed that you were slowly bringing the two into better fusion with your body, little by little."

"But it's more like three liquids in a jar. I shake it up, and they separate less each time."

"Interesting metaphor, but sure."

"Is that bad?"

"I don't believe so. It is likely just that your spirit and soul are being disrupted by your efforts to fuse, and it gives the described perception."

"So, when I'm done, the liquids will be fully mixed?"

"In the terms of your metaphor? Yes."

What would that look like? Well, she could see what it would look like in Master Jevin. "Wait… I can still see your gate. It isn't filling your whole body or anything."

"Ahh, yes. The joining is not at a physical level."

She nodded. "Right, but I'd still expect evidence throughout."

Master Jevin contemplated for a moment. "Think of the physical world and the next world as two cliff faces, bracketing an abyss."

"Alright."

Millennial Mage, 5 - Fusing

"So, your gate is a platform on the other side, which throws power across that chasm. Your spirit is a platform on the physical side that catches the power and allows you to work with it. With me so far?"

"I think so."

"So, what is your physical body in this analogy?"

After a moment's consideration, she smiled. "The portion of the physical world's cliff my spirit is anchored to."

"Precisely. So, then fusing is building a bridge between those platforms. Making them one. They are still distinct, like the legs of a tripod, but they are now unified into a whole, which is greater than the sum of its parts."

"Wouldn't that mean that I have a 'next world' self similarly linked in?"

He shrugged. "It isn't a perfect analogy. Such things never are, but some have theorized that, yes, we each have a spiritual body that is a mirror to our physical body, in which our gate is anchored."

"So, our spirit is anchored in our physical body, and our gate is anchored in our spiritual body?"

"That is the theory."

She grimaced. "That's a bit esoteric for me, right now."

"Fair enough." He grinned. "I've never really dug too deeply into it." After a moment's hesitation, he added, "Well, I did see if I could use the spiritual body as a template to recover my humanity, but I couldn't find a way. I don't know if that is because it doesn't exist, can't be used that way, or I simply never found the trick of it."

Some of the heaviness returned to the room at the mention of his nature.

Tala cleared her throat, searching for something to discuss. *We're talking about gates... Oh!* "You know, I've never asked."

His eyes came back to look her way. "Yes?"

"Humans without gates…"

Master Jevin tilted his head, waiting. When she didn't continue, he prompted, "What about them?"

She grimaced, again, but this time at her own lack of words. "They are what we were, but every means we have to verify humanity seems predicated on our gates." She held up her hands, trying to express her feeling of helplessness and lack of ability to articulate what she was asking.

He smiled, gesturing back to the chairs. "Come. Let's sit."

She nodded. As she stood, she pulled out two iron vials and *pulled* the two drops of blood into their separate containers. *Another thing to practice.* But that was for later.

She moved over to have a seat, and he sat opposite. "Humanity is a broken race."

Tala sat up straight, fully focusing on the Paragon.

"We were enslaved, this is widely known. What is not widely known, because it runs counter to the popular narrative of humanity's overcoming all odds, is that this was done to us." He gestured to his chest, to his gate.

"What do you mean?"

"It's theorized that in ancient days, a war, the likes of which we cannot conceive of, tore apart the planet, and so many beings died that the barrier between this world and the next weakened, letting magic in for the first time."

Tala found herself reaching for her tea once more as she listened intently.

"Beings and creatures of magic thrived. Whether they were here before or not, I've no idea, but as time passed, the division between worlds began to strengthen, repairing toward pre-calamity levels. That sent the magical races into a panic. Uncountable things were attempted, many of them using sapient creatures as a medium, and humans were a convenient, subservient test group." He took a deep breath, looking down at his hands.

"We were experimented upon."

"By the millions."

She nodded in understanding. "An arcane broke the human soul, giving rise to our gates."

"Yes. The trait was integrated into our genetic code as dominant and spread through the population."

"We are living holes to the next world." Her eyes widened. "Our cities. The rise in magic."

He nodded, giving a small smile.

"Us clustering together is like thousands of small perforations in a membrane, all close together. It stresses the boundary?"

"Yes, it weakens it."

"That's why we move. It isn't a backlash against our magic-absorbing scripts. It is a result of humans clustering together."

"The scripts are as much to reinforce the barrier between worlds as anything else. To shore up the membrane in the presence of so many perforations."

"And that's why they will never wipe out humanity."

"They need us to keep the barrier weak or magic will die." She rocked back, leaning fully against the back of her chair. She frowned. "So, is there only magic on this continent? Is the barrier fully repaired elsewhere?"

He shook his head. "It isn't well understood, but while certain locations can become incredibly permeable and then repair, the world as a whole seems to function near an average, held higher by our locations of abundant magic."

"But if everywhere is at the average, except the extreme highs, shouldn't the average be higher?"

He shrugged. "Yes, but as I said, it isn't well understood." He gave a mirthless chuckle. "It's not like we can easily travel the world to take readings across the planet. Every great while, an Archon with sufficient power will rise up and suffer from wanderlust. He or she will then travel far and wide, bringing us back news of the rest of Zeme. By this, we know that magic and things of magic exist across our entire star system."

"The... star system? There have been Archons in space?"

He gave her an odd look. "Of course. You, yourself, could reach the moon with relative ease and only a small amount of equipment if you so desired. I wouldn't recommend it, however. The beasts up there..." He shook his head.

She couldn't process that last comment at the moment, so she moved on. "What about the rest of it?"

"You mean outside our star system? Other stars? Other worlds? Other Realms?"

She nodded.

He shrugged. "To my knowledge, no human has exited this system and returned. It's possible that they just have failed to come back and are living happily on some far-distant world."

"That... that is a lot to take in."

"True."

Find an anchor; don't let your thoughts get sucked into the magnitude of implications he just put forward. "So, those without gates?"

"Ahh, yes. Humanity as we should be—before we were perverted and broken. They are true humanity. I've always seen them much as I see babies. They are defenseless in a merciless world. They are to be protected, pitied, and preserved to the best of our ability."

"That's a bit patronizing."

Millennial Mage, 5 - Fusing

He gave a half-smile. "I feel much the same about you. You may be a toddler to their infancy, but you are still woefully weak in a world that has no love for you."

"But it needs me." Somehow, she didn't really feel insulted by his words. *I am less than a child before what he could do.*

"But it needs us."

"Can they ever do magic?"

"Those without gates?"

She simply nodded.

"Of course, but they must approach it as the arcanes do. They must absorb the magic that surrounds us, cultivating it within themselves, hoarding it for use later."

"But our cities don't allow that."

"They do not." He looked to a clock on the wall. "But time has gotten away from us, and we both have much to do, I believe."

She stood. "Thank you, Master Jevin." Tala gave a deep bow. "You are so far beyond us, but you protect us, guide us, and—"

She was cut off as his hand caught her chin and forced her to stand upright. "I've already told you"—his eyes were hard but not unkind, and his hand was gentle but irresistible—"I do not want veneration or worship. I will take your thanks and nothing more." After a moment's pause, he pulled out a slate. "Well, that and three gold ounces for the darts."

Tala laughed, verifying the transaction was just that and confirming it. "Very well. Thank you."

"It is my pleasure."

Chapter: 5
Bloodstars

Tala strained, crocheting like her life depended on it.
I have so many things I need to do, but I can't let them distract me. I can do them on the side, but this is the first priority.

She didn't remain sitting, simply meditating as she worked. No, she moved through stretches and weapons forms; she brewed tea and looked out at the vistas presented through the training room's window. Winter had fully set in, and though the trees still held onto their leaves, they were covered with a white dusting throughout each day.

Fusing while distracted was slower for her, but it also forced her to make both the fighting movements and the fusing instinctive to a level she hadn't reached before.

I bet I can make it something that I do in the background. She nodded to herself. *Three days.* She'd give herself three days toward this goal. *Let's get to it.*

*   *   *

Those three days passed in a blur. She crocheted while eating, while bathing, and while sparring. She continued to fuse in her every waking moment.

After one day, her distracted crocheting was half as fast as her meditative work had been previously.

Millennial Mage, 5 - Fusing

After two, she was almost subconsciously continuing the fusing of her spirit, body, and gate.

By the afternoon of the third day, she had a slow fusing going in the background at all times, requiring virtually no thought and little effort.

Now, what else can I get done? She found herself grinning broadly throughout the rest of that day from the sheer joy of the accomplishment.

Perpendicular motion! She pulled out Soul Work and dug into the instructions.

Half an hour later, she was fairly irritated.

Perpendicular motion was not, actually, the ability to move a soul-bound item perpendicular to a straight pull. Instead, it required spreading out her aura and pulling Flow toward a specific part of that aura.

Even so, that actually made it easier to accomplish as it wasn't really a new skill, though it required a much greater control over her aura than she'd previously used.

As an interesting side effect, she discovered that she could hold Flow in place, within her aura, by exerting a constant pull to that location. It was *exhausting* but possible.

I can technically wield Flow without my hands.

While experimenting with that, changing Flow's shape and moving through various weapons' forms without her hands, Tala did other things.

The first was to *Reduce* the effect of gravity on her two blood Archon Stars.

She spent five minutes reducing each, getting the effective gravity as close to zero as she was capable. *Anything with mass is affected by gravity, so it can never actually be zero, though it is effectively so, now.*

As she did so, the drops began to rise. *Right! Find the point of neutral buoyancy, not just as low as I can go.*

That done, she began attempting to have the drops orbit herself.

It was... interesting.

If she moved her aura with each drop held in place by a perpetual pull, it mimicked what she was going for, but it was a heavy strain to do so.

In that way, she could move them to specific points around herself, however. *I can use this, too.*

Even with that cheat available, she did try to get the regular orbits to work, and as she worked on it more and more, she was able to have the blood do looping arcs around her one or two times before she had to catch or correct the motion with her aura. *That's something.*

With that in mind, she dove into Aspect Mirroring.

Here, while her efforts gave frustratingly little results, she didn't give up.

Two days of focused work, against a background of fusing and interspersed with sparring matches and meals, didn't give her the breakthrough she hoped for.

Finally, she swung by and had a conversation with Master Jevin, and her issue was immediately apparent.

Even though the book had told her how to accomplish it, she had misunderstood.

For those two days, she'd been trying to impose an aspect of herself onto her soul-bound items. That would never work.

To accomplish Aspect Mirroring, she had to *know* that they were a part of her, and she a part of them. Thus, they already had those aspects within, and she was just bringing it forward. Interestingly, it was very closely tied to how being an Immaterial Guide worked, so she should be better at it and learn it quicker than Archons of other quadrants, at least now that she'd actually understood it.

Millennial Mage, 5 - Fusing

Armed with that altered mindset and a renewed optimism, she only took another day to break through and gain limited aspect mirroring.

* * *

"Master Rane. I need your help trying something."

Rane looked up, tucked his book away, and stood. "What can I do for you?" He seemed a bit hesitant.

That made sense. Tala had been intensely focused for the last few days, barely speaking more than necessary. "I think I have this." She opened one of her iron vials and extended a tendril of her aura. With a *pull,* the Archon Star shot out, coming to rest within her aura, a foot in front of her chest. "Please draw Force. I want you to hit that drop of blood when I say to."

He nodded, drawing the sword.

Okay. She took a steadying breath. *That blood is my blood. That star is* my *star, a part of my soul. It is me, and I am it.* She closed her eyes and focused. *My magic supports it as it supports my body. My mass holds it in place.*

As the mental construct became fully manifest, she felt the drop become infinitesimally heavier, increasing the strain on her soul pull marginally.

She grinned, opening her eyes. "Now."

Rane attacked without delay, Force striking the drop of blood with quick precision.

Force imparted a hefty dose of kinetic energy through the contact, and the blood rocketed away, slamming into a far wall and imbedding into it.

"Oops…" Tala scratched the back of her head. "That is what would have happened if you hit me, so… success!"

Rane was staring curiously at the drop of blood as it zipped back to its place, pulled by Tala once more.

"Let me think…" *I want to block Force.* She began to nod. *Flow can block Force.* "Okay, one moment, then another hit."

He nodded in response, settling into a quick-striking position, Force held ready.

Flow is me, and I am Flow. First bound to me, before even my body. We are one. Flow is a weapon of defense and offense, and it can counter magical attacks. I can counter magical attacks. She blinked. *Wait… Wait!* "Rane, hit me." She locked the mental construct in place, straining.

He frowned but complied, striking for her side.

Force impacted with a concussion of power, and its magics dissipated.

Tala had to take a step to the side as the strength behind Rane's blow still moved her, but it was just that: Rane's bodily strength against her mass.

Rane's eyes widened.

Tala turned and retched, her head ringing, and her stomach trying to empty itself despite the scripts.

"Oh… rust me…" She looked within herself, then within Flow, and she understood.

Flow took the magic of the hit and distributed it throughout its own magical and physical structure. Mirroring that ability into her own body had caused every cell to try to pull itself apart at once. "Yeah… not doing that again."

Rane was kneeling beside her. "What do you need?"

"A minute."

He began rubbing her upper back as she knelt on one knee, laying across the other. "Does this help?"

Strangely, it did. She mustered a nod, and he gave a small, hesitant smile in return.

While focusing inward, she noticed that her background fusing had been disrupted, and she scrambled for a moment to catch the slowly unraveling strands of power and tie off the current stitch.

After much longer than a minute, she sat back, moving the wisps of hair from her face. "That… that was awful."

"If I can ask, what happened?"

"I tried to mirror Flow's defensive aspect within myself to allow me to take the hit."

Rane winced. "That sounds painful."

She nodded. "Yeah… I mean, it was better than being cut in half, so there's that."

He frowned, but Tala waved his comment away before he made it.

"I know *you* wouldn't have cut me in half, but that defense, as awful as it was, would stop that, too."

"What type of defense does Flow use to counter other magical attacks? I never asked."

"It felt like distributive dissemination."

He grimaced. "Anyone else would be in need of a healer, now."

"Good thing I focus on bodily resilience and healing."

"It does seem so." He gave her a sideways look. "You know, I'm still not sure if you are wise for choosing defensive magics that allow you to survive the odd things you try or foolish for trying those odd things."

Her tone took on that of an old sage. "'If you cannot help but leap from cliff tops, grow wings.'"

"So, you took that to heart. Wise, then?"

She shook her head. "Not wise enough to stop, but wise enough to know I needed something to prevent the worst repercussions."

He just grunted.

Tala pushed herself back to her feet. With a pull, she lifted her bloodstar from the floor where it had fallen and extended her aura to hold the drop in front of her chest once more. "Okay. Let's try this one more time."

Rane gave her a deeply skeptical look.

"You aren't going to hit me this time."

That seemed to mollify him, and he stood to face her once more, drawing forth Force in preparation.

Alright, so I don't want to mirror Flow's defense within me. She closed her eyes. *That blood is my blood. That star is* my *star, a part of my soul. It is me, and I am it. Flow is me, and I am Flow. First bound to me, before even my body. We are one. Flow is a weapon of defense and offense, and it can counter magical attacks. I am my bloodstar. My magic supports it as it supports my body. My mass holds it in place. Flow's defense is its defense.*

It was a complex mental construct, but she built it piece by piece. After nearly five minutes of focus, she had it in place.

Her eyes opened. "Now."

Rane struck, and Force hit the drop of blood, unleashing his sword's power.

The drop was pushed back by Rane's strength, but the magic of Force's blow was absorbed within the drop of blood.

The blood almost seemed to fizzle. So much kinetic energy was directed into and through it that the bloodstar struggled to contain it. After an instant, the lazy spinning swirl of blood inherent to her Archon Star was a tornado of force, causing the blood to spin faster than a top, only the coherence of the spellform within keeping it together.

Force, robbed of the magical portion of its attack, was deflected upward by the mass mirrored into the drop, even while the drop was pushed downward.

Tala's constant pull returned the drop to its proper location a moment later.

Rane stepped back, a grin evident on his face. "That is amazing! Aspect Mirroring, right?"

She nodded, breathing heavily and beginning to sweat despite the pleasantly cool room.

"I looked into that as it would allow me to implement Force's attacks with my own body, but I'm not a Guide, and so it will be a long road before…" He trailed off, looking at her with concern. "Mistress Tala?"

She wordlessly called the bloodstar back into its vial and capped it. She let the mental constructs fall apart and retracted her extended aura. With a groan, she sank to the floor.

"Are you alright?" He sat down in front of her.

"I think I will be." She rubbed her forehead with both hands. "I've proved the premise. Now, I just need to improve it."

"One more thing to practice?"

She let out a mirthless chuckle. "Yeah, one more thing to practice."

"Can I help?"

She leaned forward and patted his knee where it rested a bit away from her own. "You already have, Master Rane. Thank you for helping me test that."

He gave a nod of acknowledgment. "As always, I am happy to assist."

*   *   *

After another six days of dedicated training, their time in Makinaven was nearing its end. Tala had to start charging the cargo slots again, beginning the next morning.

They were in their training room, facing off for the umpteenth time, controlled violence a hair's breadth from being unleashed.

Tala stood, Flow in hand in the form of a glaive.

Rane stood opposite her, Force horizontal to the floor in a middle guard, point angled down to point at her heart.

She kept her breathing regular, speaking on the exhale. "Ready?"

His answer was just as unhurried. "Ready."

Tala lunged forward, two drops of blood streaking alongside her, carried in her aura, mirroring a mix of aspects from both herself and Flow.

Force struck Flow to the side, spoiling Tala's initial thrust, but she continued to close on her opponent, allowing the impact to carry her weapon in a tight arc, full circle to strike for Rane's other side with Flow in sword form.

Rane moved from his block to a back-cut, slicing toward Tala's unprotected chest.

One of her bloodstars dropped to counter his probing strike, dissipating the magic in Force's blow, and stealing the energy from Rane's swing.

Rane, for his part, rolled his head and neck out of the way of her horizontal slash, spinning to thrust Force's point toward her abdomen.

Tala instinctively flinched back from the hit; half-remembered pain forced the reaction.

Even so, she was able to move Flow in the way to partially parry the thrust, even as her other bloodstar dropped toward Rane's shoulder.

As the drop of blood mirrored her own mass, it was a credible threat to Rane and caused his defenses to activate and move him away from the incoming danger.

Rane twisted sideways, spoiling his own attack, though he didn't let that stop his assault.

They strove back and forth, Tala using everything at her disposal to counter Rane's offenses and strike at him throughout.

Millennial Mage, 5 - Fusing

She shifted Flow from one form to another with lightning-quick timing, always using the right tool to keep pressure on him.

She manipulated her bloodstars in tight arcs, countering Force and threatening Rane at every opportunity. She didn't successfully get them in place every time—or even half of the time, if she were being honest—but they were another weapon for use in staving off his relentless skill.

And she was succeeding.

Despite innumerable exchanges too quick to count, Rane wasn't gaining the upper hand despite his still obviously superior ability. He moved with elegant, powerful efficiency, but it wasn't enough to break through.

She just knew his defenses and limitations too well by this point.

She couldn't overcome him, but she could hold him off.

It was the most difficult thing she had ever done, combining virtually every combat technique she could safely use.

I'm not spraying acid at his face… no matter how much of an advantage it might give me. She honestly felt guilty for even considering it and pushed the idea from her thoughts. She also wasn't using her *Join* ability, but her mind was already split too many ways to make that a reasonable possibility, at least for the time being.

They strove back and forth, neither able to gain the advantage.

Unfortunately for Tala, her methods were *much* more tiring than Rane's.

Rane was in his element, using tried and true, well-practiced, well-honed tools and motions.

Tala, in contrast, was riding the razor's edge of her abilities and the tools at her disposal. Many of the things she was doing, she'd barely figured out, practiced, and refined in the last week. It was taking everything she had to keep going, and her ability to continue was rapidly nearing its end.

Rane must have sensed something because he suddenly disengaged and moved backwards, keeping Force up and ready. "A break?"

Tala knew that he didn't need the break, and he was just offering for her sake. She *almost* found that irritating, but as she tried to muster her anger, she found that she was too exhausted. Instead, she just grunted, sheathed knife-Flow, and flopped to the ground, panting.

He grinned her way. "That was fantastic. I don't think I've been so pushed since I tried to fight Terry."

Terry lifted his head from the corner of the room and squawked.

"Not right now, Terry, but I appreciate the offer."

Tala gave Rane an incredulous look. "Since when"—she pulled in a couple of quick breaths—"can you understand him?"

"I can't, but that was pretty obvious even so."

She grunted. "Fair."

Over the next minute or so, Tala got herself back under control. Her breathing leveled out, and her muscles calmed, unclenched, and relaxed. The headache was only slightly slower to fade. *Progress across the board.* She grinned broadly.

She glanced over toward Rane. "I'm feeling a need to celebrate."

"Oh?" He seemed hesitantly interested.

Over the last days, nearly two weeks actually, Tala had been so focused on her training that they'd done virtually nothing else. "I need to get the hide I left with a tanner,

Millennial Mage, 5 - Fusing

just outside the tree, but after that, I'd love dinner and maybe a play if one is available?" After a moment, she found herself nodding. "Before the play, though, you said that the views from your inn were spectacular."

"They really are."

"I did say I'd like to see them at some point, and our time here is almost done. We can watch the sunset from one of the observation platforms up there after dinner before the play. Plays usually start after sunset, especially in winter."

"That, Mistress Tala, sounds like an excellent plan."

Chapter: 6
Decadent

Tala was being a bit decadent, but she found that she didn't much care.

Her tea set was out and brewing a smooth chamomile.

A honey panna cotta was ready and waiting for her and her companion. They'd brought it with them from the restaurant. The sweet and creamy notes would be a perfect counterpoint to the tea.

Tala and Rane sat on a public observation deck that was connected to the inn Rane was staying in, but they'd claimed the outdoor space for themselves.

To be fair, no one else seemed much interested in this specific overlook. It might have to do with Terry sleeping just in front of the door, about as large as a truly terrifying dog, but Tala wasn't sure.

Could be almost anything really.

They were at a two-person table, one of three, and sat closer together than usual so they could both watch the sun as it continued to slip below the horizon.

They looked out to the southwest, toward the winter sunset, looking over the forest, over the plains beyond, and to mountains beyond even that. There was the hint of reflections or lights in the plains near the mountain, but they were only barely visible to Tala's enhanced sight with the direct glare of the sun before them.

"The world is so much larger than humanity's little corner." Tala didn't speak loudly, her voice barely above a whisper.

Rane responded in kind. "True words, Mistress."

They continued in silence for a long moment before Rane spoke again.

"One day, I'd love to see an arcane city. See our enemy and decide for myself how I feel about them."

She smiled, patting his shoulder. "You're surprisingly contemplative for a rage monster."

Rane gave her a side-eyed glare. "You know, I don't really like that about myself."

"But it is who you are."

He snorted. "We are what we choose to be."

She felt some of her contentment bleed away. "I never chose to be a Mage."

Rane glanced her way again. "I call rusting slag on that."

She frowned. "Excuse me?"

"You heard me. That's a lie."

Tala felt rage bubbling up within her chest. "My parents—"

He cut across her. "No. Mistress Tala, you are not a Mage because of your parents." He turned his full gaze on her.

She had been in process of summoning up words to lash out at him, but they died in her throat when she saw the intensity in his eyes.

"I've been trying to find a way of saying this to you for weeks, and now is as good a time as any." He took a deep breath, then continued in a rush, clearly desperate to get it out. "You're an idiot, but you can't see it. You're fantastic, but keep treating that like something that needs to be blamed on others."

"I'm a fantastic idiot?" A smile lifted one side of her mouth.

Rane nodded enthusiastically, seeming glad that she was understanding him. "Yes!" Then, his mind seemed to actually catch what she'd said. "No! No." He shook his head. "That came out all backwards. You're a fantastic *Mage*, and you're being an idiot."

She lifted one eyebrow. "Explain."

He swallowed, but he must have decided that he was committed now, so he plunged ahead. "Your parents dumped their debt on you, true and unfair, but *you* went to the Academy, and *you* chose your inscriptions. You chose to work at the classes, to learn, to excel, and to earn your certifications. The only reason you are a Mage is that you chose to be." He huffed, looking back out toward the spectacular view. "Your family gave you a shove, but you turned the unexpected stumble into a sprint at greatness."

Tala found herself glowering at the teapot.

"I told you that I've been trying to find a way of telling you this for weeks. I've had a long time to consider."

"That doesn't mean you're right."

He huffed a grunt of irritation, turning away. "I chose the restaurant this afternoon, yes?"

"Yes." She looked his way, curious where he was going with this despite herself.

He didn't look her way. "So, am I the reason we ate there?"

"Yes."

"The only reason?"

She considered. *No. Whenever he's suggested a place, if I'm uninterested, we go elsewhere.* "No."

"So, did you choose to eat there?"

She wrinkled her nose in irritation. "Yes."

"Even though I chose it for us?"

She grimaced. "Fine. I see your point."

Millennial Mage, 5 - Fusing

"This is important, Mistress." He glanced her way. "What your family did isn't unheard of, but it was distasteful, at least to me. I'm not trying to justify their choice, but you are not that choice. You are what you have done since that moment." He smiled. "There are always things we cannot control. We are what we do with those few things we can." His gaze returned to the landscape.

Tala hunkered in on herself, angry at how right he sounded. *That's pretty silly, Tala.*

She took calming breaths.

I'm not mad at him. I'm mad at them. She straightened.

The tea is well steeped, now. Tala took the moment to pour the tea for them both, setting Rane's cup in easy reach.

He glanced at her, tentatively. "Thank you."

She shrugged, taking a bite of the dessert. "Oh... oh rust, that's good."

Rane took a bite of his own panna cotta. "Wow! You're not lying." He sipped the tea. "This is a great addition. Thank you for suggesting and providing it."

She smiled, enjoying a sip from her own cup.

The sounds of the city of Makinaven were evident behind and below them, especially to her enhanced ears. Even so, the sounds of the forest at night were beginning to rise from before her, the forest already having lost the sunlight.

Bird song and calls, the hoots of owls, and the barks, yaps, and roars of various predators echoed in the far distant forest. None really overlapped, and none were too close to any other, but together, they added a pleasant background to the repast.

Tala let out a long breath. "You aren't wrong, you know."

Some tension seemed to bleed from Rane as he took another bite of the cooked cream. "You are an amazing Mage, more dedicated to improvement than almost any I've seen. That is not your parents' doing. You've made that choice."

She sighed, releasing frustration. "I've heard you, Rane. Can we drop it for now?"

He stiffened, then nodded, turning back to his dessert.

After a moment to collect her thoughts, she placed her hand on his arm. "You know, there's been something I've wanted to talk with you about, too."

He huffed a laugh. "It seems the time for such things." He glanced down at her hand, then to her face. "Is everything alright?"

She nodded.

"Then, might as well hear you out. What's on your mind?"

Tala smiled sadly. "How are you doing with the deaths of the guards on the trip here?"

His hand clenched in involuntary frustration, causing his forearm to tense and bunch, the strong, toned fibers obvious to her enhanced touch, even through his thin sleeve.

She patted his arm and withdrew her hand.

"I'm... not great. I know they made their choices, and I made mine. I know that in this line of work, even if I do my job perfectly, many people will die under my protection, and I have to come to terms with that. It is my job to make that number as small as I can. I won't let each death be a tragedy, dragging me down. I can't." He smiled her way.

"No. I don't think that's true."

He raised an eyebrow at her. "Oh? Do tell."

"Every death *must* be a tragedy, or we will become flippant."

He snorted, but he turned away, her words clearly hurting him.

She smacked his arm, forcing his attention back to her. "Let me finish." She waited a moment, giving him a fake glare until she was sure he wouldn't interrupt or ignore her. "It must be a tragedy, but it can't be *our* tragedy. We work to mitigate it, but that is all we can do, just like you said. We protect those we can and trust those in our care to make their own choices."

After it was clear she wasn't going to say anything else, Rane quirked a smile. "That sounds like parenting."

Tala laughed. "Probably a bit, I suppose."

"And, I'll point out, it sounds almost exactly like what I said."

"Subtle shifts can make a big difference in the long haul."

"Truer words, Ta— Mistress."

They both looked out once again, the last sliver of the sun dropping below the far-distant mountains. Dim lights had come on behind them, but they were subdued enough to not spoil the scenery.

At a great distance, probably two-thirds of the distance across the far plains to the mountains, the lights of a city became incredibly evident, now that the sun wasn't backlighting them. *So, they were lights, not just odd reflections of some water.*

"That's one of them." Rane had leaned forward. "That's an arcane city." He looked her way, clearly waiting for her reaction.

"So it is." She drank her tea and took another bite of panna cotta.

He glanced at her again, took another bite, and smiled. "Thank you." His eyes flicked back toward the city. "Aren't you more surprised? Curious?"

"Arcanes… they are just people, right?"

"What do you mean?"

"I mean, it's not like there's only a few dozen, who all enslaved ancient humans and are now plotting our downfall."

"True." He gave her an odd look.

"I'll bet that in that far city, two arcanes are looking this way, seeing our lights in this tree, and thinking 'There are the humans. They took that city from the Mezzannis before killing them all.'"

"That's not true!"

"I mean, sure? I don't actually know there are arcanes looking this way."

He shook his head. "No, I mean we didn't kill all the Mezzannis."

"Ahh, but we aren't told the whole truth, so why should they be?"

Rane didn't seem to have an answer for that. "So... you don't think that most of them hate us?"

"Oh, I've no idea. They might all be horrible creatures of torture and spite, but like you said, we don't actually know them."

"I said that?"

"Implied it, I suppose. You said you wanted to judge them for yourself."

"Ah, yeah." He smiled. "It probably won't actually happen, though."

"Oh?"

"Yeah, either I'm too weak—and I'd be in too much danger there—or if I wait long enough, I'll be too strong and they'll never let me approach one of their cities uncontested."

"That... that is a very good point." She patted his shoulder. "We'll figure something out."

"We?"

"Yeah! You don't think I'll let you go somewhere that unique without me, do you?"

He smiled, turning back to the view and their treats. "No. I suppose not."

All too soon, they were done, and Rane was leaning back. He let out a long sigh. "Well, we should probably get to the playhouse. I think the doors close in less than half an hour."

Tala nodded, standing and placing her items into Kit. "Alright. Terry?"

Terry flickered to her shoulder, sized for the perch, not breaking his seeming sleep.

She scratched his head affectionately, then smiled at Rane. "Let's go."

*   *   *

Tala was in heaven.

She lay within Kit, wrapped in a truly ludicrously sized bearskin.

The tanner had gone above and beyond, maintaining the fur, cleaning it, and conditioning it with a lavender-mint scented oil that would keep the entire thing smelling amazing and in great condition. He'd even included a tin of the stuff for touch-ups as needed.

These hides must be really valuable if one was worth this much work on the other. She didn't much care, though. *I'm never selling this.*

She'd woken up nearly a quarter-hour earlier, and it was probably her enhanced sense of touch talking, but she just couldn't bring herself to leave the luxury of the fur.

Another few minutes won't hurt anyone.

Even so, she did need to start her day. She began by restarting her fusing for the day, pushing the process to the back of her mind.

Finally, she reluctantly got out of bed, stretched, and dressed.

She looked back at the bearskin. "I'll be back. Don't go anywhere."

Okay, Tala, you're being a bit weird...

That was true.

She shrugged, placing her hand on one of Kit's walls and refilling the storage item with power. "Good morning, Kit."

Kit did not respond.

Tala moved through her normal morning routine, finishing with her bath and coming back up into the training room for the last time just as the sky was lightening toward dawn.

"To charge the cargo slots!"

Terry lifted his head, gazing her way.

She grinned and tossed a scattered handful of jerky pieces.

The avian's eyes widened, and a series of dimensional blips heralded him snatching each one from the air flawlessly. He ended his precise flickering on her shoulder, where he head-butted her cheek.

"Good morning to you, too, Terry." She looked around the training space one last time, noticing her bedroll in the corner where Terry had been sleeping. "Oh, right!" She gathered it up and pushed the whole thing into Kit, topping off the pouch's power once again. "Sorry for not folding and rolling it first, Kit."

The pouch did not respond.

"Alright, let's go!"

She checked out from the training facility, passing over the key and thanking the clerk at the front counter.

Terry carried her down the tree to the work yard, where her cargo slots were waiting.

Millennial Mage, 5 - Fusing

She charged them with relative ease, though she did have a bit of difficulty before she got used to the process again. *Nearly a month away from an activity really adds some cobwebs.*

Even so, she was just finishing up when Mistress Odera arrived so that they could go to breakfast together.

*   *   *

After another filling breakfast, Tala found her way to the marketplace in search of a gift.

Master Jevin had been incredibly kind to her, and she wanted to find a way of saying thank you. *Not that he's likely to be surprised. He could be watching me right now.* She shuddered. *No, Tala, he promised he didn't do that. Either trust him or don't. This waffling is a bit ridiculous.*

She was wandering through the various stalls when she saw one that caught her eye, attached to a large, brickwork building.

"Makinaven's Marvelous Munchy Makers?" *That seems promising.*

As she approached, she noticed that the stall tables were covered with display cases, each containing row upon row of chocolates.

There were other delicacies as well, but chocolate was definitely the most prevalent, underlying theme.

Perfect.

While scanning through those available, she found that there was a whole table of chocolates filled with liqueurs of various kinds.

One section of that table was dedicated to caramel liqueurs. *Exactly what I was hoping to find.*

But there were a *lot* of them. "Oh… this is going to be harder than I thought…"

A clearing throat sounded from behind her, followed by a soft-spoken voice. "Pardon me, but young master Reve would like to look at the chocolate liqueurs."

Tala turned, half-frowning.

Behind her, an Archon stood just in front of a deeply blushing young man.

The young man's voice was strong, but quiet, as he spoke to the woman, stepping up beside her. "Mistress Criada, please." He turned, bowing toward Tala. "My apologies. Please take your time."

The Archon opened her mouth, a stubborn look in her eye, but the young man cut her off, still focusing on Tala.

"I'm Reve." He held out his hand.

Tala regarded him for a long moment.

He was barely taller than she was with black hair, eyes dark enough to be basically black that were obscured behind magically-empowered glasses, and skin so pale that only a lack of sunlight could explain it. Lastly, Tala noticed a well-worn book tucked under his other arm.

Hesitantly, she took his hand. "I'm Tala. Nice to meet you," her magesight showed inscriptions but no keystone, "Reve."

He smiled. "Mistress Tala." He bowed again. "This is my instructor and"—he colored slightly once again—"chaperone, Mistress Criada."

Tala gestured to Terry on her shoulder. "This is Terry. He keeps me out of trouble, too." Terry trilled a soft affirmation without opening his eyes.

Criada huffed, interjecting herself into the conversation. "Be sure to keep that animal on a tight leash. Arcanous creatures have no place in human cities."

Tala regarded the tall woman with mild irritation before glancing back at Reve. "Maybe she should be in your charge, rather than the other way around?"

Millennial Mage, 5 - Fusing

She intended it as a mild joke to break some of the tension, but Reve winced.

Tala held up her hands. "I meant no disrespect."

Criada opened her mouth, clearly meaning to give Tala a piece of her mind, but Reve snapped his fingers. "Enough." There was a marked authority to his tone that brooked no argument.

Criada vanished.

Tala blinked at the spot the woman had been standing.

Criada was still there, but an expertly crafted illusion wrapped around her, keeping any sight or sound of the Archon trapped within and leaving no evidence of her presence.

It was expertly done to the point that even Tala's enhanced senses couldn't detect her, and only Tala's magesight let her see the illusion for what it was.

Terry, for his part, opened his eyes briefly and flickered around where the woman had been, seemingly examining the space before returning to Tala's shoulder.

"That... that's incredibly well-honed magic." She reexamined the young man. *A bent toward Immaterial Guide style magic, focused on waves of various kinds?* Sometimes her interpretation of other people's inscriptions was entirely unhelpful. He even had a portion of his keystone, now that she looked closer; it just wasn't complete. "Why aren't you a Mage?"

He scratched the back of his head. "She thinks I'm not ready yet."

Tala shrugged. "Well, if you trust your teacher, I'm not one to interfere." She glanced back to the waiting chocolates. "No reason we can't both look."

He bowed his head, once again, light glinting off his glasses. "Thank you, that is kind."

Tala glanced at the still-obscured Criada. She had to hide a smile as she saw the Archon's arms crossed and the woman seemingly squirming in indecision. *Or something…*

Reve followed her gaze and gave an apologetic smile. "Please forgive her. She is a bit overprotective at times."

Tala nodded, regarding the case of chocolates once more. "If I may ask, why is an Archon seemingly taking orders from an inscribed?"

He seemed to be conflicted, almost squirming before answering. "She was sworn to my parents before they died and vowed to protect me and raise me in their absence."

Tala turned to him. "I'm… I'm sorry to hear that." *That's heavy… Not something I'd tell a stranger, but I suppose I did ask… If someone asked me, would I lie?* She probably wouldn't. "I'm sorry. I didn't mean to pry."

He shrugged.

Change the topic. Congratulations, Tala, you just made things awkward with a complete stranger. "So, have you shopped here before?"

Criada seemed to have had enough because she waved her hand and the illusion dissipated. "Yes, we shop here often, and Master Reve, we need to get to the library for today's lessons."

He nodded. "Of course, Mistress. Let me just get one or two."

Criada crossed her arms again. "Very well."

Tala cleared her throat. "I'm actually looking to get a few for a… mentor?" She shook her head. "For someone as a thank you. Are there any of the caramel liqueurs that you'd recommend?"

Reve glanced her way, then nodded.

Over the next five minutes, they talked through those available, and Tala found him quite a pleasant conversationalist, at least around the topic of food.

Maybe he's just nervous or doesn't usually talk to strangers. He was nice enough once he came out of his shell a bit.

Eventually, Tala decided on a selection of ten chocolates, with Reve's guidance and some input from an attendant who had come over to help them both. She almost changed her mind when she learned the price. *Half an ounce, silver, per chocolate?* It was a bit ridiculously expensive, but it was what it was.

"Can you package it up? It's going to be a gift."

In the end, she parted with six silver for the gift-wrapped chocolates. She paid and placed the all-too-small box into Kit.

She gave a small bow toward Reve. "Thank you for the assistance. I would have taken much longer to decide without your help."

He smiled and bowed in return. "I was happy to assist, Mistress. Take care."

"You as well." She turned and walked away from the confectionery. *Now, I just need to find some full-bodied whiskey.*

Chapter: 7
Departing Makinaven

Tala found herself a bit nervous as she approached the third tier, Makinaven, Constructionist Guildhall for the last time, at least this trip. She'd found what she hoped was a good whiskey the day before, shortly after purchasing the chocolates, so she had both gifts ready to hand. *I hope they're well received.*

She did not want to interact with a bunch of people. So, before she reached for the door handle, she spoke under her breath. *This should trigger however he monitors the city.* "Master Jevin's aura is extended—"

"Mistress Tala?" Master Jevin's voice sounded in her ear. "What are you doing? What are you doing here? We don't have an appointment, do we?"

"No, I just wanted to stop by to say goodbye. I leave tomorrow."

"Oh, sure. Come on back."

The door opened in front of her, and she walked through with a small smile. "Thank you."

The standard scan and *ding* washed over her, but she ignored it. *That does remind me, I need to refresh my iron salve before we leave tomorrow.*

Master Jevin only had to direct her once when she'd hesitated, unsure of which hallway to take.

She walked into his workshop and glanced back. "It feels like you change the path to get back here every time I come. I'm usually very good at finding my way."

Millennial Mage, 5 - Fusing

"I have better uses of my time than ensuring I'm undisturbed by those who've visited in the past." He gave her a mirth-filled smile.

Something in his glance made her hesitate. After a moment, she started nodding. "By the stars, you do! You do rearrange the passages to get back here."

He shrugged, dropping the pretense. "Only when necessary. Some people have no boundaries." He lifted an eyebrow at her. "So, did you really just come by to say goodbye?"

She smiled in return, reaching into Kit. "That and to give you these." She produced a small cask and a wrapped box that looked minuscule beside the two-gallon mini-barrel. Tala set them on one of the central tables and stepped back. "Thank you for all your help and advice."

Master Jevin walked forward, an unreadable look on his face as he examined the gifts.

"You said you liked caramel liqueur chocolates and full-bodied whiskey." She gave an uncertain laugh. "It turns out that there are a *lot* of things that fall into those two categories, so I hope I chose well."

He glanced her way. "You... bought me chocolate and alcohol?"

She frowned. "Well, I didn't think of it in that way..."

"No. I..." He shook his head, waving off his own previous comment. "Thank you, Mistress. That was very kind."

She shrugged. "You said you liked these, so." She shrugged again.

Master Jevin seemed genuinely thrown.

"Are you alright?"

"I... Yes. I believe so." He picked up the small barrel. "This is an excellent vintage."

"Yeah, that's what the master distiller said." She smiled tentatively. "It's an eight-year-old, smoked-maple bourbon."

"That is a really excellent choice."

Good. It certainly cost enough... Ten silver was five days of food money for her, now that Mistress Odera and the Caravan Guild were covering one meal a day.

He unwrapped the box of chocolates, looking inside.

Tala tsked. "I'm curious."

"Hmm?" He looked up from the open box.

"Did you need to open it to see inside?"

"Oh, no. But it is nice to see with my eyes, rather than just my aura."

She found herself nodding. "Yeah, I can understand that."

Master Jevin capped the chocolates and regarded her once again. "This is really too much, Mistress Tala."

She waved that off. "It cost less than any number of things I've bought from you."

"It's not the cost, Mistress, it's the thought." He smiled, again. "Thank you, truly."

"Well, you're welcome." Tala looked around a bit awkwardly. *Okay... what now?*

"Would you like a glass?"

She thought about it for a moment, then felt a smile tugging at her lips. "You know what? Yes. Thank you. I'd like that very much."

Tala and Master Jevin spent the early afternoon sitting in his armchairs, sipping bourbon and talking of things of little note.

Finally, Master Jevin let out a long sigh. "I'm afraid I do have some work I simply must get done." He stood, offering her a hand up.

She took it and stood. "Thank you, again, for all you've done for me." She huffed a short laugh. "For all you've done for all of us." Tala shook her head. "It sounds ridiculous."

He shrugged. "Life is often a bit ridiculous. Thank you, for the gratitude." He smiled. "Now be on your way." His smile widened into a grin. "I hope to see you back here before too long."

"Count on it."

* * *

Tala stood at the top of Makinaven, on the platform on which she'd figured out she could fuse.

Terry stood beside her, just large enough for her to comfortably rest her right hand at the base of his neck, on his collar.

Rane was on her other side, arms crossed as he looked out at the surroundings. "This is magnificent!"

She looked his way, a self-satisfied smile unhidden on her lips. "Still think it was a waste of time to climb up here?"

"Absolutely not. I couldn't have been more wrong. We should have come here earlier and often."

Tala decided not to say anything further.

The gray light of pre-dawn was slowly coloring toward day. The day of their departure.

Tala found herself sad to be leaving. *I've spent more time here than in Bandfast…*

Still, Bandfast was a better base of operations for her current role, and she had a lot more work to be done before she could comfortably operate in these woods on a regular basis.

I have to go through them once more regardless. It had to be done, so she'd get it done.

She would try to avoid forest routes for a while.

Just until I get a bit stronger.

After another long moment, where they all enjoyed the world around them, Rane took in a deep breath and let it out in an audible sigh. "We should get going, if we're going to get all the way down in time."

Tala nodded. "Thank you for coming up here with me."

"Happy to, Mistress."

*   *   *

"Mistress Tala, do we really have time for this?"

Tala didn't answer Rane's inquiry as she quick-walked up to the tea stall in the tier-three market.

The grandfather bowed her way. "Mistress. Welcome back. I trust the drinks were up to your standard?"

"They were excellent, thank you. I'd like ten more pounds of each."

He blinked at her. "You haven't drunk all of it... have you?"

"Oh, no. Of course not, but I'm leaving the city, and I won't be back this way for a good long while."

He nodded in understanding and gestured. His son and grandson scurried around, quickly wrapping up her items. "Chamomile, mint, and espresso, correct?"

"Exactly right."

He was tallying in his head. "Individually wrapped bricks?"

"Yes, please."

"Then, ten silver, forty copper."

"How about an even ten silver for a bulk order and a returning customer?"

He grinned her way. "How about eleven silver for a quick turnaround?"

Millennial Mage, 5 - Fusing

She hesitated for a moment, then laughed. "Very well. I appreciate the speed." *He's right. I really should have offered more for the quick completion of the order.*

Rane was looking between them but didn't comment.

While his kin were working on Tala's purchases, the grandfather turned to Rane. "Master, can we get anything for you?"

Rane smiled and gave a slight bow of his head. "Thank you for the offer, but I am not in the market for such at the moment." He glanced to Tala. "She has shared some of your tea with me, and I can firmly say that if I ever am in need of such, I will come here, preferentially."

He bowed in return. "Thank you for the kind words."

Less than a minute later, they had the thirty parcels tightly bound and then bound together. Tala had confirmed the purchase on their slate, and she and Rane were departing.

As she was about to duck out, she paused, turned back to the grandfather, and bowed deeply. "Thank you for the products, the service, the speed, and the wisdom." She smiled and tossed a coin his way.

He caught it easily, glancing down, his eyes widening.

Tala departed before he looked back up, leaving him with the hefty five-ounce silver coin.

Rane gave her an incredulous look. "Any more stops?"

"Nope. I'm ready to go."

* * *

Tala finished charging the cargo slots for the day just as the driver swung up into place.

She waved to the guard, waiting on the ground below, looking up her way. "Ready!"

The Master Sergeant of the first guard shift nodded to her. "Thank you, Mistress." He raised his hand and dropped it to point to the west. "Let's move!"

His voice carried a note of command, and Tala thought she could detect subtle bits of magic woven through, making it easier to hear and interpret at a distance and over background noise.

I don't see any inscriptions. How used to command must he be for his natural magical pathways to have that effect? It was a humbling reminder of just how new she was to all this and just how competent those around her truly were.

Terry flickered to the front of the wagon, happily shifting from foot to foot, excited to exit the city once again.

Mistress Odera sat in the middle of the wagon, calmly regarding Tala.

The wagons pulled to a slow start, the guards moving into a protective formation immediately, even as the caravan navigated the streets of Makinaven's first tier.

They were leaving through the opposite gate from the one they'd come in through, so many weeks ago.

"Now, Mistress Tala. You'd requested I bring your breakfast to the caravan." She glanced down at the parcel sitting beside her. "I did *not* expect you to cut your arrival so close."

Tala smiled a bit sheepishly. "My apologies, Mistress Odera. I cut it closer than I intended."

The older woman grunted and handed over the cloth sack, which Tala opened gratefully. There was a nice spread of food, as usual much more than a single person should eat regularly. *I'll get used to this, eventually, and eventually, my stores will be full, and I can return to normal eating.* She looked up from the feast. "Thank you."

Millennial Mage, 5 - Fusing

Mistress Odera bowed her head, slightly. "The Guild is happy to provide."

Tala grinned back. "Oh, I am finished with my duties as a Dimensional Mage."

The Mage regarded her for a long moment, then nodded. "Thank you, Mistress. I think we will handle the outward trip similarly to the way here. From what you've conveyed in regard to your training, your capacities have expanded a great deal, but I pray we won't have to put them to the test."

Tala nodded in turn. "I'll continue my training as we travel if that is acceptable to you."

"I wouldn't have it any other way. I ask simply that you don't train to exhaustion."

"That sounds very reasonable." She was, at that very moment, fusing in the background, her magic moving through the now intimately familiar patterns of drawing her body, spirit, and gate closer into unity. *I wonder if this will be at all useful once I'm done fusing.*

Rane had touched base with Mistress Odera earlier, and he was to be the vanguard, staying just about a dozen yards in front of the oxen, at least for the first part of the journey.

The caravan was passing out through the gate, and Tala was about to pull out her bloodstars to begin working with them and her attempts at stable orbits, when the wagon's ladder creaked. Her eyes snapped to the front corner of their vehicle, in time to see a man pull himself into view.

He came up the ladder with quick, powerful motions, stopping to bow toward the two Mages, a half-eye kept on Terry while the terror bird regarded him in turn.

"Mistresses. I request a ride out of the city."

Mistress Odera seemed to be examining him. "Who might you be, and why do you request a ride?"

Tala did her own inspection. His gate made his humanity beyond question. His keystone labeled him a Mage, and his *realness* gave him a mid-to-high Archon feel, though his aura was tightly controlled. *As is proper.*

Her own aura was extending a perfect foot from her in every direction, mirroring her form as precisely as she could as a starting point for her chosen exercises.

The Archon was dressed simply, more like a forester or a hunter than a Mage, but his short sleeves left heavily inscribed forearms exposed, making his magic clear at a glance. In addition, he had a coiled line at his belt. It didn't look like cloth or leather. If she had to guess, Tala would have said it was some sort of empowered metal, and it seemed to be linked to him.

A soul-bound weapon of some kind? That supported him being an Archon at least.

He nodded to them both. "I am Zakrias."

"Master Zakrias, I am Odera, and this is Mistress Tala."

He bowed again to each. "Mistress Odera, Mistress Tala, a pleasure to make your acquaintance."

Polite for someone who just jacked a ride. Tala quirked a smile. "So, Master Zakrias, to what do we owe the pleasure?"

"I'm heading to the west to hunt and harvest, and I will be on my own two feet for the foreseeable future, so I thought letting a wagon work for me for a couple of hours would be a boon."

Mistress Odera nodded at that. "I can understand that. Please, join us."

Tala tilted her head in interest as Zakrias sat. He chose a spot near them, not too close, and well away from Terry. She pointed to the avian. "He's Terry."

"Familiar?"

"No, friend."

Zakrias gave her an interested glance but didn't inquire further.

"So, are you with the Harvester's Guild?" Tala did her best to not lean forward. *I've not met a harvester before.*

"I am, yes."

Very nice! Better to get his thoughts than whatever guild official would be working the reception if I inquired there. "What's that like?"

"Well, it's dangerous but enjoyable work." He stretched up, then leaned back on his hands, planted behind himself. "I have to know myself and my abilities to the utmost, and I still dance with death every single time I go out."

He was clearly a bit self-satisfied, but he likely had a right to be. To Tala's eyes, he had the look of one whose appearance was influenced by magic, meaning he looked far too young for how well he carried himself. "So, you meet fascinating new life forms and then kill them?"

Zakrias smiled a bit quizzically. "That about sums it up, yeah. Though, I try to know my opponents before I kill any. There is a delicate balance to be had, and over-harvesting can rust up a whole region." His expression darkened. "Some idiot wiped out a good portion of the apex predators to the south of the city, and it's been chaos in that region for weeks."

Tala swallowed involuntarily.

Don't look away; don't let him know it might have been you.

She cleared her throat. *Don't panic; it could have been someone else.* "What happened?"

He shrugged, irritation clear on his features. "They somehow lured in so many creatures that I found what amounted to a small pond of blood."

Well, that's an exaggeration. Or… not me? "That's… gruesome."

"Tell me about it. I found it because a bunch of Leshkin were swarming the area, and I had a bounty on their arms."

She swallowed. *Did they come for me or the blood?* She had her iron salve back in place, but she still was *not* looking forward to going back into the forests for an extended period. Then, she processed what he'd been saying. "Wait... arms? Do you mean weapons or arms?" She waved one arm to demonstrate her meaning.

"Oh! Weaponry, sorry for the confusion." He grinned. "Anyway, whoever had caused the bloodbath had royally ticked the Leshkin off, too. I came upon them as they were beginning to sweep the surrounding woods." He shook his head. "As I said, all sorts of things can be thrown out of whack when you don't know what you're doing."

Tala glanced to Terry and found him regarding her with what could only be a mischievous glint in his eye. Tala glared back, then tossed a bit of jerky over the side of the wagon.

The avian flickered after it, then to Tala's shoulder.

The Archon frowned at her. "That's an odd thing to train your friend. If I throw a treat away, come to me?"

Mistress Odera chuckled. "Oh, he went for the treat. Coming to her was his own decision."

Zakrias cocked his head for a moment, then his eyes widened. "Oh, you're an old one, aren't you?"

Terry trilled, then resolutely tucked his head down to return to seeming sleep.

Tala cleared her throat, desperate to change the subject away from what was most likely the aftermath of her escapade. *You don't know that.* But she did. "So, what's that on your belt? A weapon, right?"

He glanced down. "Ah, yeah! This is a beauty." He pulled the coil from his belt.

Millennial Mage, 5 - Fusing

"It's not a whip… right?"

"No, but that's in the right direction. At its basic level, it's just a cord, but the center is a tightly braided strand of muscle fibers. It lets me use it almost like an appendage."

She blinked at him. "What for?"

"Well, I'm an Immaterial Guide. I focus, generally, on kinetic energy, and my inscriptions excel at manipulating, and increasing, it in anything I can touch."

Tala found herself nodding. "And that counts." She indicated the empowered cord.

"And this counts." He grinned. "Nearly unbreakable and can be healed back together with relative ease if it ever truly is overcome."

A bit like me, I suppose. This was going to be an interesting couple of hours.

Chapter: 8
A Hunter

Tala looked around at the surrounding lands on this, the western side of Makinaven. She'd not been out this gate, so it was all new. Even so, it was pretty much the same as out the other gates: farmland, orchards, and more odious industries, such as tanning.

As the caravan continued away from Makinaven, crossing through those fertile lands, Zakrias turned the conversation to her. "So… what can you do?"

Tala hesitated for a moment, then shrugged. *He was fairly open. There's probably no harm in responding in kind.* "I'm mostly aimed at being magically reinforced and self-healing."

His eyes twinkled with barely contained mirth. "So, you just take beatings?"

She gave him a half-glare. "Hardly. Offensively, I manipulate gravity."

He seemed a bit disappointed, his expression clearly falling. "Oh, an area of effect, support fighter then."

"Hardly." Tala grinned at the Archon.

He perked up at that. "Oh?"

"I work on individual targets, manipulating their gravity as it relates to specific other things."

He frowned. "That's not how…" He shook his head and laughed. "Never mind. Who am I to say how your magic should work?" After a moment's consideration, he regarded her critically. "How are you at opposed casting?"

"I honestly haven't practiced it really at all." She scrunched her face in irritation at the admission. "I've been meaning to practice but just haven't had the time."

He grinned. "I'll bet you a silver that I can cool your left hand to an uncomfortable degree faster than you can force me to drop mine." He extended his left hand at his shoulder height.

Cool? Ahh, he's able to manipulate kinetic energy on a level to affect the heat energy of something. That would require *incredibly* fine control.

I wonder if Rane's defenses would counter incoming fire by moving out of the way or by cooling the area before it was affected to counter the incoming heat? Probably worth asking. She hesitated. *No, he's a Creator. He can't cool an area that way… right?*

Her eyes flicked back to Zakrias' face. *Right, talking to someone else.* She quickly flicked her thoughts over what he'd said. "How will we determine 'uncomfortable?'"

He shrugged. "When you say so. If you can keep enduring it, it isn't uncomfortable enough to count."

"That's not exactly fair."

He shrugged again. "If you don't want to wager—"

She shook her head, cutting him off. "No, not fair to you."

He hesitated, then barked a laugh. "I like you! Let's make it a gold."

"No, no. A silver is fine. This should be interesting." Tala touched her left middle finger to her thumb unobtrusively, focusing on the man's hand, getting ready to target it.

"Mistress Odera, would you give us a 'go' signal?"

The older woman shrugged, clearly focused on things other than the conversation between the two Archons. "Go."

Zakrias twitched his right hand, and his soul-bound cord flicked out, connecting with the back of her left hand.

Tala locked the mental image of his hand in place and *targeted* it. The hand began to glow in her sight. *Got you.*

Increase. There was incredibly heavy resistance to her enactment, but she gritted her teeth and bore down.

If her normal workings on inanimate objects were like blowing against a feather to move it across a table, this was like blowing on a lead ball. Not wholly ineffective but frustrating to an incredible degree.

Zakrias, for his part, was frowning, even as Tala felt a building pressure and heat on the back of her hand.

Iron salve for the win! She grinned.

"That is a fascinating defense. It's like my power is struggling to catch hold to even *start* contesting you."

"Give up?"

A smile grew across his features. "Hardly."

The resulting contest of wills was incredibly boring from the outside. For all intents and purposes, they were each simply staring at the other's hand.

Even so, the internal struggle was intense. *Why is this so hard? Shouldn't it either succeed or fail?*

No, that wasn't right. She had to use her magical weight to impose her will, her working, onto a resisting target. *I'm not doing that, though.*

Effectively, she was tossing out the spell-working at her target and simply adding more oomph behind that toss in the hopes of making it take effect.

Yeah, that's not right. I don't want to enact and leave the working to its own devices; I want to make sure it takes hold.

Millennial Mage, 5 - Fusing

But how?

Zakrias' face broke into a broad grin. "There!" The iron salve was still interfering with his working, but he'd worn through enough to begin affecting her, and suddenly, his will crashed into hers. He grunted, his smile slipping.

Tala felt the strain of his will, his magic, his power, fighting for dominance over her hand. She instinctively responded. *Mine.*

A ripple of... something slammed into his working, pushing it back to his bound cord.

Oh! I see. It's a fight for authority over the target. Master Jevin had explained that to her in a way, but she hadn't really understood and integrated it. Now, it was obvious.

Gravity is mine to manipulate as I wish. That hand is my target. It is mine.

The feeling before was like throwing her glaive. She had great strength but could only impart so much of it as the spellform moved away from her. Now, it was as if she was properly braced and charging forward, glaive in a firm grip.

Her power, her will, her magic claimed his hand's gravity as her own. Her spell-working clicked into place, taking hold and beginning to increase the effective weight of the appendage, if slower than she'd have liked. Zakrias' own magical weight was still resisting her, even if it couldn't throw off her working entirely.

Tala's focus on his hand, however, had loosened her own defenses, and his working was beginning to affect her as well.

A minute passed in silent struggle, each able to affect the other but just barely.

Her gravity increase was working despite his resistance, but the hand wouldn't drop. *How is he still keeping that up? It should feel like having an armored guard hanging from the tips of his fingers.*

He didn't even appear to be flexing to keep the hand up. *Wait. His muscles aren't contracted at all. How is his hand staying up?*

On her defensive side, her hand was becoming *cold.* She knew she'd already have frostbite without her enhanced recovery, but she refused to give in.

After another long minute, in which ice began to form across her hand from moisture pulled from the air, she was beginning to have trouble focusing through the pain. *Not all enhanced senses are a boon...* She should talk to Holly about reducing her pain receptivity.

Even so, her magesight had locked onto *something* around his hand. The truth finally clicked into place. "You're stealing the kinetic energy from your hand."

It looks like he's sequestering that energy for later use? That was fascinating, if true. It was also the type of information that he'd probably never share.

Worth asking though.

He grinned triumphantly in reply. "I am." His voice came out a bit strained. "But I must say you are taking a lot of power to resist."

"It seems more like you're taking the power, storing it for later?"

His eyes widened in surprise, but that was the only reaction he showed. "A Mage must keep some secrets."

Tala gave a pained snort. "Fine, fine." After a moment, she frowned, gritting her teeth against the cold. "We really shouldn't be depleting your inscriptions before a hunt."

He shook his head. "This isn't pleasant, but it's my most efficient ability. You are forcing me to use a lot more than I'd expected, but I can still do this for *days.*"

After a moment's hesitation. "Wait... I won't have to do this for days... right?"

She forced out a short laugh. "Forever, unless I undo it." She involuntarily jerked, her body rebelling against the ice crystals now forming within her flesh.

"Oh..." He swallowed, considering for a brief moment. "What do you say we call it a tie?"

Rust that! I don't want to lose. Then, she thought about it.

You're being foolish, Tala. There is literally nothing of consequence on the line. Take the tie.

Tala nodded quickly before she could change her mind again. "Yes."

She immediately reversed her casting. *Reduce.* The resistance to her working vanished, as Zakrias was no longer opposing her, and she easily claimed full authority over the gravity of his hand. Thus, she was able to quickly move his hand back to experiencing normal gravity.

She likewise allowed him authority over her hand, to reduce the strain on his magics, and Zakrias, for his part, immediately flooded her hand with controlled heat, making way for her to easily repair her damaged flesh.

That was kind of him. "Thank you for that. It wasn't necessary."

He shrugged and smiled. "No need to strain your healing when this takes so little from me."

Tala's working finished restoring his hand to normal gravity, and a bit of an awkward lull fell over them.

Mistress Odera didn't care, she was busy doing... something.

Tala's magesight told her that the Mage was keeping careful tabs on the caravan and their surroundings despite her closed eyes. *Yeah, that tracks.*

If the silence persisted, it was going to be a long remainder of Zakrias' trip.

What to ask, what to ask… oh! "Hey, I've been wondering."

Zakrias turned his gaze back to her. "Hmm?"

"There are an unusually high number of fire-aligned creatures in this area."

"Yeah, that's true. Not a question, though." He grinned.

"How has the forest not burned down?"

"Well, that's actually an interesting bit of trivia."

"Oh?"

"You see, the local Archons some… six? Eight? Something like that. Six or eight cycles ago noticed the increase in fire creatures. Specifically, a large number of them were breathing fire, and in the forest, as you guessed, that's bad."

She chuckled, and he smiled in turn.

"Thus, they went on a hunt for the fount, which was granting these powers, to put a stop to it, but as they searched, they realized something." He paused for effect.

Tala decided to play along. "What did they realize?"

His smile widened. "They realized that there had never been a forest fire of any great magnitude. Not in living memory. Not even since the number of fire creatures had increased."

After another pause, she asked, "So, why not?"

"Well, they had no idea. So, they investigated. As it turns out, there is an arcanous creature, a kind of bear, that goes through the forest, devouring any open flame."

"Just one?"

"Well, supposedly they are only seen individually, so there's never been a confirmation of more than one."

"What does it look like? I'd hate to kill it on accident."

Zakrias laughed. "It's a massively powerful creature, Mistress. It takes power from every spark and seems incredibly efficient in its means of storing magic. As to how it looks?" He shrugged. "All that anyone's ever seen is smoke in the form of a bear. Whether it is smoke coming off some body underneath or it truly is made of smoke, I've not found proof either way."

She looked at him skeptically. "A bear, made of smoke, that eats fire."

He shrugged. "I've seen one myself."

"What, do they wear silly hats and pants, too?"

"No... why?" He looked incredibly confused.

"Well, if you're making up stories, you should go all the way."

He shook his head. "If you don't want to believe me, you don't have to."

Tala glanced toward Mistress Odera.

The older woman smiled, even as her eyes remained closed. "He's not telling you lies, Mistress. The beast, or beasts, have been spotted throughout the southern woods, and there has never been a recorded forest fire in this region." She seemed to hesitate. "Well, no, small blazes seem to crop up, they are an integral part of the lifecycle of any forest, but there are never any large enough to threaten the trees."

"So, fires in the forest, but no forest fires."

"That seems to be the case." The older woman still hadn't opened her eyes, and she kept them closed as she fell back into silence.

Tala turned back to Zakrias. "My apologies for disbelieving you, Master."

"It is understandable, Mistress. I was skeptical, too, until I encountered one."

"Huh, the more you know, I suppose."

Zakrias nodded, then finished the saying, "The stranger the world reveals itself to be."

Tala found herself nodding. She'd definitely found that to be true. "What is something that you wish you'd known before you became a Harvester?"

He tilted his head in consideration. "Are you thinking of becoming a hunter?"

She shrugged. "It's good money, and I've enjoyed harvesting when I could in the past."

Zakrias grunted. "Not the worst reason, I suppose."

"So?"

"Hmmm…" He seemed to consider the question. "Well, the first thing is that being a devastating attacker is a liability more than an asset." He chuckled. "Sure, it will keep you alive, and you should definitely keep some overwhelming, quick-kill workings in your secret storage, in case things rust through, but in general?" He looked back to her. "You need clean kills, in the sense that you want your target to die clean: no mess, and no destruction of anything you might want to harvest."

That made sense. "Yeah, but that's pretty obvious, right?"

"Your gravity attacks. Do you have much harvestable material when you kill with that?"

"Well," she thought for a moment, "in general, no. No, I don't."

"Exactly. I'm sure it's a great working: clever, effective, quick, and efficient. But with it, you'd be a poor Harvester. Without it, you're missing key tools from your powerset."

Tala frowned. "What do you use?"

"Me?" He grinned. "I use everything. I impart kinetic energy into little objects to pierce their vitals. I give motion to the air, creating sounds surrounding my prey that distracts and gives me the advantage. When I can work it, I can begin processing them before they die. If you give two portions of flesh kinetic energy in opposing directions, and you are precise enough, they shear apart more cleanly than under the finest blade."

She blinked at him, seeing him in a new light.

Zakrias was a hunter: brutal, efficient, and meticulous. He was old, and that meant he'd survived on his own in the Wilds for years—probably decades. He had a calm confidence that spoke of a perfect understanding of his own capabilities. He would likely never enter a situation when he wasn't sure of victory, and he would always have a plan of retreat if anything diverted from his plan.

He was a hunter.

A predatory smile briefly stole across his lips. "Ahh, there it is. You understand. Being a hunter, a part of the Harvesters, there are only two paths."

She waited, already sure she knew the gist of what he was going to say.

"You either die quickly, or you learn to think like a predator. That doesn't mean you fight every fight or defeat every foe. It *does* mean that you know you can defeat every foe you fight, else you don't fight it."

Tala considered, her eyes flicking to Terry, still sitting on her shoulder. *Like Terry.*

She had a brief curiosity if Terry or Zakrias would win in a fight but quickly dismissed the idea. *Not a productive line of thought.*

Zakrias leaned back once more. "But that's why there are so few of us, and why we still make such good money." He grinned, the predatory tint to the expression had faded. "What does it take to be a caravan protector?"

Tala opened her mouth to answer, then hesitated. After a moment's thought, she sighed. "Mistress Odera would be a better person to answer that question."

Mistress Odera's eyes snapped open, and the older woman regarded Tala critically. After a long moment, she huffed, smiled, and nodded to her junior.

Tala rolled her eyes. *I'm still an Archon, old woman.* Even so, she smiled.

Mistress Odera thought for a moment before nodding. "The most important part of being a Mage Protector is that you are defending something, as stands to reason. More specifically, you are defending something fragile, that is very nearby. A Mage defending a fortress or city can allow attacks through, they can move to other defensive positions, and they have the in-place defenses supporting them."

Zakrias nodded, listening to her words.

"A Mage Protector of a caravan does not have a defensive structure to utilize, they cannot retreat to a better position, and those around them cannot take the attacks if they fail. Such a Mage must be able to engage the enemy and hold them back, defeating their assault, rather than simply enduring it."

He hummed in contemplative thought. "I've heard similar descriptions, before, but never quite in that way." He nodded. "I understood that it is much more difficult than manning the defensive towers around a plain's city, but I'd not considered why."

Tala interjected. "There's also that around cities, waning cities excepted, there is much less magic, so the beasts that attack are weaker. Out in the Wilds, as you know well, they are stronger."

He pointed at her with a smile. "That's the explanation I've heard before, and the one that I'd have expected."

"No less true," she hedged.

"Oh, of course not. It is arguably the largest reason the Wilds are so dangerous."

Zakrias turned back to Mistress Odera, and the conversation wandered on, touching quite a few topics before it wound down.

Millennial Mage, 5 - Fusing

By that point, they had left the bowl around Makinaven behind, and Zakrias was seeming ready to depart.

"Thank you, Mistresses, for your hospitality, the conversation, and the ride." He stood, bowing to each of them. "Take care, stay safe, and may we meet again in a time of peace."

Mistress Odera bowed back to him. "May that be sooner than we could dare hope."

With a parting smile in their direction and no visible flexing of his muscles, Zakrias launched from the wagon, sailing away through the trees.

Tala cocked an eyebrow. "I thought he said he'd be walking."

Mistress Odera snorted. "He's showing off. I'd bet every ounce of gold to my name that he'll be walking as soon as he's sure he's outside our range of detection."

Tala grunted. "Probably true." Even so, though, she was incredibly intrigued. *He can fly.* That was something that she would be dearly interested in figuring out for herself.

Chapter: 9
Archon Star Separation

Tala spent the remainder of the day working on her bloodstar orbits. She had a breakthrough when she realized that, like she'd learned with Flow, she could have the bloodstars pull themselves toward her, instead of the other way around.

It was still a drain on her soul, meaning that she couldn't do other soul exercises to the extent that she normally could, but it didn't take any active thought, and the strain was small enough that she thought she could probably do it nearly constantly.

Now, enforcing a mirroring of her magical resistance and mass onto the bloodstars was still a great strain, so she focused on that aspect. There was the additional issue that when she was mirroring her mass, the difficulty of maintaining the orbit increased exponentially, but that was to be expected.

By the time they stopped to camp for the night, the two drops of blood were spinning around her in tight, oscillating circles, almost exactly as they had under the influence of Master Jevin's spellform.

The forest seemed to be more favorably disposed to them on this outward journey as they didn't have to navigate around nearly as many blockages of any kind, and they had yet to see a single Leshkin.

However, there had been a few arcanous encounters that the guards had dispersed with ease.

Millennial Mage, 5 - Fusing

Nothing had required Rane's intervention, let alone hers or Mistress Odera's.

Almost as if summoned by that thought, Tala felt the approach of something large and obviously magical.

She turned, looking through the surrounding forest.

A large, jaguar-like creature that was armored with chitin, rather than having fur, was charging their way. Its motions were more like a bull than the great cat it closely resembled. It clearly weighed an immense amount.

In truth, large didn't begin to accurately describe the size. It was easily as massive as two of the caravan's oxen, combined.

Rane had noticed as well, and he, flanked by two guards, ran to intercept the incoming threat.

Tala considered adding a gravity manipulation to the creature to assist, but she decided that was unnecessary. *Rane's got this.*

A screeching, hissing roar of challenge echoed off the trees as the cat's head dropped lower, its pace increasing as it sprinted all out across the last hundred yards.

In the very last stretch, it leapt, seeming to be attempting to drop on Rane like a rockslide.

Force split the creature from its snout to its back right hip in a single blow.

Tala had barely tracked Rane's movements as he stepped with the strike, spinning under the attack to stand beside the beast as it splashed to the ground, blood, guts, and viscera falling through the new divide in its body.

His strike, diverting to the right, had ensured that the body didn't impact either of the guards who had come forward to back him up.

Tala pulled out Ingrit's list and found what she'd remembered; the chitin was prized for certain types of armor. The guards said something to Rane, and he laughed, clapping the closest on one shoulder. He gestured, and Tala was able to interpret what was being said. Rane had given the carcass to the two guards.

She sighed, watching the guards drag the corpse back to be properly stored, even as the drivers were unhooking the oxen. *Those are on Ingrit's list. So, they'll be valuable.* Still, she knew that Rane had done the right and generous thing. Those guards could have left him to it, but they'd put themselves in danger, to be ready if he needed them.

Tala dismissed her mild disappointment. It wasn't like she had a right to the harvest. *Zakrias is right, my main magical attacks aren't exactly conducive to harvesting.* And Mistress Odera was right to keep her back from the fray.

I want to fight... But she was unarguably the most critical individual in the caravan. Without her, their dimensional storage would cease to function, and the caravan would be lost.

I'm just glad I get to fight at all. She was colossally torn. On one side, being a Dimensional Mage for the caravan was the cushiest job she could hope for. If she wanted, she could sit in her room all day, training. She'd make good money and have her needs seen to, but that would be so boring.

Not to mention that she'd have to sit on the side and let others defend her. *And without combat, I'd stagnate.*

Being a Mage Protector as well mitigated much of that. The second position earned her higher pay and let her engage threats. *I just still have to be wise in what engagements I participate in.*

In truth, she *should* be following wisdom's path, regardless of what position she held, but she *wanted* to dive in and fight every battle.

Millennial Mage, 5 - Fusing

As a Harvester, that would put me on the path to an early grave. She wasn't a Harvester and might never be, but the sentiment was still true enough.

Tala nodded. *This is good for me. I should be learning discretion, and this forces that.*

One thing at a time, Tala. Well, she was fusing in the background through her every waking moment, so that was a given. *Two things at a time, Tala.* She cracked a smile at the thought.

The bloodstars held the potential for so much utility that she needed to put them first since fusing was a given. *Get the orbits stable and second nature while mirroring my magical resistance and mass.* That was the first step.

It was still exhausting to mirror those aspects, but even with her work through the day, added to what she'd been doing the last few days, had caused great improvement.

She was getting some interesting looks on occasion from the guards, but not every one of them noticed. The bloodstars were still just single drops of blood, after all. If they weren't moving, it would be very possible that they would be all but invisible.

While she was strengthening her soul toward the task of constant aspect mirroring, she needed to figure out how to split one of her Archon Stars. *If it's even possible.*

But that was a task for tomorrow. Now? Now was time for dinner.

*　　*　　*

As it turned out, Amnin was head chef for the return trip as well, and she really came through. Over the next three days, Tala ate like a city lord's entire family, and she had no expectation that that would reduce as the trip continued.

Apparently, all the support staff had been asked to delay their departure for this oh-so-important cargo load. They'd wanted no chance of having the caravan short-staffed, so all the workers, guards, and drivers were the same as those who had come with them from Bandfast. The only exceptions were new additions to fill the slots of those who had died on the trip out.

Not for the first time, Tala considered only eating while on assignment. That way she'd never have to pay for her own food. She could, in theory, survive on her reserves while between journeys, but that would mean that she would be starting each voyage with her reserves depleted.

Too dangerous. Even with endingberry power flowing through her and iron salve on her skin, it was her finally nearly entirely full reserves that really gave her a sense of security.

That, and she'd have to be hungry for days at a time. *Not a good choice in any respect.*

They weren't heading straight north, and not just because the forest made straight-line travel functionally impossible. No, apparently some Archon had an area of research set up to the northwest of Makinaven, and a part of their journey to Bandfast was a supply drop to the reclusive woman.

As they traveled, Tala had spent her time working on her ability to hold aspect mirroring, as well as attempting to figure out how to split a combined Archon Star.

The results of her labor were two magically and mass mirrored bloodstars moving in quick orbits up and down around her as she stared at a third Archon Star.

This third one was a combination of two others, which had each been as weak as she could get the spellform to stabilize.

It wouldn't separate.

Millennial Mage, 5 - Fusing

Her manipulation of magic couldn't guide the two apart.

It wouldn't obey a will-infused command to separate.

Massive gravitational pull in opposing directions on each half hadn't split it.

It wouldn't be pulled apart by her aura, wrapping around two parts of the spellform and pulling.

Flow couldn't cut it in half.

It simply wouldn't split.

Today, as lunch was laid before her on a massive tray, Tala decided to dive into the spellform to see what was actually causing the binding. *If I can't find any distinction between the drops within the star, then I might have to approach this entirely differently.*

"Thank you." She smiled at the assistant cook who had brought the food to her on top of the moving wagon, even as he climbed out of sight.

"You are most welcome, Mistress!" he called back up the ladder.

She began to absentmindedly eat the roasted sausages, salad, and bowl of sliced fruit.

She directed her magesight to dive into the Archon Star within the blood hovering before her, locked in place by her aura.

Just as she'd expected, the spellform was a self-contained, infinitely looping knot that resembled a monkey's fist knot, if the loops interwove and braided together at irregular intervals.

The power was evenly distributed, flowing around and around while going nowhere.

Exactly as it should. She grimaced but continued to probe.

After a little longer, she still hadn't discovered anything of consequence. *I have nothing to compare it to.*

She pulled back her magesight and called one of her bloodstars to her, immediately diving in with her sight.

This one, she'd made stronger at the time of its creation before leaving it to self-sustain.

A powerful cord of power, looping in the exact same pattern. Tala blinked, then leaned closer. *One cord.*

She pulled over the newest, combined star.

Sure enough, her memory was correct. *Two cords.*

The knot was built as if someone had made it with two cords at once, weaving them through the pattern identically, side by side.

"One for each star, combined now." That had to mean something. "It's not one cord; it's two." She wished she'd tested this with Master Jevin around or at least his soul-scanning, empowered plates.

With incredible delicacy, she tried to grab onto one of the two strands with her aura.

She didn't have the nimbleness with her aura to accomplish the feat.

Alright then. She pulled out Soul Work and flipped through, searching for one of the exercises that she'd read over but put aside for the time being.

There you are. Aura Scripting. She'd initially been incredibly excited because she'd thought it was a way to create spellforms using her aura as either the medium or spell-lines.

It wasn't. *That has to be explained elsewhere…*

It was a series of exercises meant to build up her aura control to the point that she could form scripted words with her aura. Others with magesight would be able to read it, if their magesight was active, so it had *some* base utility, but in general, it was just a series of dexterity drills.

Perfect.

It was time to expand her exercise routine.

Millennial Mage, 5 - Fusing

* * *

"Mistress Tala?" Mistress Odera placed her hand on Tala's shoulder.

Rust. Rust. Rust*!*

"Are you alright?"

Tala let out a disgruntled sigh, opening her eyes to glare at the surrounding forest, slowly rolling by. *Two days. I've wasted two days.* "No. I'm ticked."

The corner of Mistress Odera's mouth lifted. "I gathered."

Tala frowned. "What? How?" She was being very emotionally contained and hadn't done anything in anger, keeping her features calm and placid.

"Mistress, your aura is violently flashing 'rust' over and over again."

Tala blinked at the woman, then felt herself coloring. "Oh…" Once she'd managed to form letters, then words with her aura, she'd taken to forming her aura into as many words as she could, striving for fine control over it. Rather than coming up with random words, she'd begun simply writing out her thoughts. "Wait… If you can read that…"

"Yes, Mistress. You might want to find another way to practice."

Tala's color deepened. "You could have told me days ago." Her voice was quiet.

Mistress Odera seemed a little taken aback. "You really didn't know?" She patted her shoulder. "I thought you were being intentional about it. I've gathered such great insight into how you think, and I'd thought that was your intention, even if you were being circumspect about it. Why else would you always refer to me as 'Mistress

Odera' in your thoughts, while almost every other Mage you think of lacks the moniker?"

Tala frowned. "What now?"

"You think of me as Mistress Odera, while Master Rane or Master Grediv are just 'Rane' and 'Grediv' in your thinking."

She blinked at that. "I... huh... I guess I hadn't noticed that." Tala frowned. "I wonder why."

"I'm no mental Mage, dear. There are precious few human ones, but if you find one, ask them." She cleared her throat. "But this is all beside the point. What's wrong?"

"I've been refining my aura control for dexterity in an attempt to"—she glanced to her combined star—"do something I'm not sure is possible."

"Mistress Tala." Mistress Odera gave her a level look. "Your aura is writing out 'Archon Star separation.' Being vague won't work if you continue… that." She waved her hand, indicating the words that were continuing to flicker. "And I am not being nosey. I'm monitoring the entire caravan with my magesight. Your aura writing is like a beacon right beside my head. I couldn't ignore it without retracting my magesight entirely."

Tala grimaced, purposely pulling her aura back to her skin. As she'd done more and more aura and soul exercises, they'd become second nature with increasing ease.

"So, dear child, what happened?"

Tala decided not to deflect again despite the clearly offered option to do so, with that last inquiry. *Child indeed.* "My aura can't grab onto the distinct threads within my Archon Star."

"Oh? Why do you think that is?"

Because it wants to rusting stay useless slag, Tala growled internally.

Millennial Mage, 5 - Fusing

"Is the cursing really necessary, dear?"

Tala blinked at her, then noticed that her aura had started to extend and write out her thoughts again. She clamped down once more, holding it firmly contained. "Sorry about that…"

"My question?"

She sighed. "The power isn't really a thread, it's a current. It's like trying to grab a river. Even if you have a big enough tool, the best you'll do is grab some water, not pick up the river and redirect its flow. It also doesn't grab the current downriver and drag the water back and to the new path."

"But, in this case, the river is flowing in a circuit, right?"

"That's correct."

"So, why not divert the river directly? The current will loop back around and follow the new path. Right?"

Tala opened her mouth to answer but stopped. *Why not?* "One moment."

How should I approach this? She returned her focused magesight to the Archon Star.

She picked out the pattern in the flowing magical spellform, the two rivers of power, streaming side by side.

I can't just grab the flow—that is useless. I can't even grab the magic and redirect it. It's too stable for magical manipulation to be useful. I might be able to strong-arm it, but that would be an effectively useless solution for me.

Blocking a river would create a lake or just cause the water to flow around the blockage. *I need a new path for it.*

She hesitated.

No, it should flow into the form of an Archon Star on its own, once separated. What I need is a redirection.

It wasn't exactly like a river. The power was flowing according to its own nature, rather than in physically restricting banks. So if she shunted the power away, it should reform as she desired.

Alright, then. Let's do this.

With her newly trained dexterity, she stabbed her aura into one of the two streams, angling it against the current to create a sloped shunt. More than that, she *pulled* on her bond with that one stream, while holding the other in place with a similar pull.

Power shot up the aura ramp, prevented from flowing as it wanted to but acting by its nature, nonetheless.

Even as it was distorted away from its natural path, the magic was still bent and aspected to form the pattern for an Archon Star, thus, it almost immediately began flowing through the loops and twirls of the Archon Star spellform once more.

In less than a second, the entirety of that stream had been shunted off to the side, reconnected, and was now floating, self-contained beside the star that it had just been interwoven with.

Tala's aura flexed, pulled in opposite directions on the two drops of blood. They moved apart with ease, leaving them hovering, distinct and perfect before her.

Mistress Odera and Tala stared at them together.

"That worked."

"So it would seem."

Tala looked to her superior. "You didn't know it would work?"

"I'm not an Archon, dear."

Tala grunted.

Mistress Odera cleared her throat. "As someone who isn't an Archon, this might be an ignorant question."

Tala turned to regard the woman curiously. "Yes?"

"Shouldn't they be identical?"

"Of course. They are—" Tala looked back to the two drops of blood and instantly saw what Mistress Odera was talking about, now that she was looking for it.

The second star was a perfect inversion of the first, from which it had been pulled.

"Oh. That seems… bad." She looked to the older Mage. "What happens when you invert a spellform?"

"Depends on the form? For some, it doesn't matter. For others, it reverses the effect generated."

They regarded the two hovering bloodstars.

After a long minute, Tala swallowed and cleared her own throat.

"The question is, then, what's the opposite of a soul-bond."

Chapter: 10
Abstract Guide

Tala, Rane, and Mistress Odera sat around a table, in the fading, late afternoon light of the forest campsite.

Dinner was done, and the guards were bringing out the light constructs as the Mages continued to study Tala's inverted Archon Star.

Rane scratched the side of his head. "Every test I've run seems to indicate that it's identical in use."

Mistress Odera nodded. "I have to concur with Master Rane."

Tala found herself nodding. "Well, the only thing I can still reasonably test is recombining the two stars." She looked to the two other Mages. *No way am I trying to form a bond using an inverted star.*

They each took a moment to consider before nodding.

"So, what's the worst that could happen?" She looked to each in turn.

Rane shrugged. "They could negate each other, and your soul could be harmed in the backlash."

Tala's eyes widened, and Rane hurried to continue.

"But that shouldn't be much, given how weak they are."

Tala grimaced. "Soul damage is soul damage…" She looked to Mistress Odera.

"Master Rane is correct. That is likely the worst-case result." She hesitated. "But some, even weak, spellform interactions can be catastrophic. I once knew a dissolution

Millennial Mage, 5 - Fusing

Mage who could create devastating effects with the smallest amount of magic I've ever seen." She shook her head. "He claimed that his theories would have allowed him to wipe out an arcane city, if he found the right materials to work with, but he died before ever bringing that horror to reality."

"That's... certainly terrifying."

She patted Tala's arm. "I highly doubt that your blood is that theorized material."

That was small comfort, but Tala still chuckled, attempting to break the tension.

Mistress Odera pointed to the iron vial in Tala's hand. "Do the combination in there, so in the worst case, it shouldn't blow up the camp."

Tala blinked at the older woman. "Would the iron vial really help?"

The Mage gave a small smile. "The depths and wonders of magic should not be restricted." She shrugged. "But we should be fine, yes. There is a whole range of things that *could* wipe out this camp but would be redirected by iron. The number of things that wouldn't be so deflected is vanishingly small." After another moment's thought, she added, "I'll put a shield around it as well, just in case."

Tala nodded her head reluctantly. *That's not actually that comforting.* Still, it was better and wiser to test this here than in a city. She briefly thought about walking a ways into the woods, but anything that would be negated by such a short distance that she could walk it wouldn't have ever been a threat to begin with. *Not with Mistress Odera's shields on hand.*

Tala moved both minuscule stars into the vial and held it above her head as they came into contact.

Mistress Odera created a miniscule shield around the vial, hugging tight to Tala's wrist, sealing off the space inside.

After a long moment, it was clear that nothing was going to happen.

"Huh." Tala lowered the vial and looked inside, Mistress Odera's shield vanishing. The two drops of blood sat side by side, unmerged. "Well, that was anticlimactic."

"What?" Rane leaned closer, trying to take a look.

"They're just resting side by side."

"So, they're acting as Archon Stars are supposed to." Rane held out his hand.

Tala grinned. "I suppose." She handed over the vial, letting the other two Mages examine the contents.

Finally, Mistress Odera sighed. "Well, this tells us nothing except that they are no longer *as* compatible as your stars normally are." She snorted. "But that really doesn't say much." After another moment's thought. "The researcher we're resupplying might be a good Archon to ask. Until then?" She stood. "I need to get some sleep. Master Rane, you have first shift?"

Rane nodded. "Sure thing."

The older Mage bid them goodnight and returned to the cargo slot for the night.

Terry lifted his head from the far side of the table where he'd been resting.

"You planning on hunting tonight?" The avian had been going out most nights, taking advantage of the caravan's fixed location to range farther than he did during the day.

He trilled, standing and stretching.

"Well, be safe, alright?"

Terry flickered over and lightly headbutted her cheek.

"Thank you."

Rane looked between them and smiled. "What about you, Mistress Tala? Up for a bout before sleep?"

She grinned. "That, Master Rane, sounds wonderful."

*   *   *

Tala swept Flow upward, toward the inside of Rane's right knee, even as one of her bloodstars dropped toward his right shoulder.

Force, which had been about to slap into the side of her neck, was jerked away as Rane's inscriptions moved him backwards, out of range of both strikes. Or, it would have, if Tala didn't push Flow into the form of a glaive at the last moment.

Flow impacted Rane's leg, throwing it outward and eliciting a pained grunt from the big man.

Even so, Rane didn't slow, using his muscles to spin with the hit and reduce the damage he took. As he did so, his right leg, which had just taken the hit, shot out behind him, counterbalancing his torso as he leaned forward, thrusting at her.

Force's tip cracked into her sternum, throwing her backwards, the bone groaning in protest and only her endingberry power keeping it intact. There was a nice little dip in the reserves, too.

Tala gasped at the impact as she landed, rolling with the momentum to come back to her feet.

Rane had followed close after her, Force already descending for another devastating blow.

But Tala had seen him coming and anticipated his tactic.

A bloodstar imposed itself in the striking line for the big sword, and Tala mirrored Flow's defensive abilities into the star. *I really need to have this in place as standard.*

Force stopped cold on the slightly flattened-out drop. Rane grunted again, in surprise this time.

Tala grinned. *It worked!* She'd ensured that her aura was beyond the blocking drop, and pulled *hard* on the soul-bond even as Force was intercepted. The pull had prevented the drop from being knocked aside or forced down. She laughed, launching back onto the offensive.

They strove back and forth for another minute or so before they called the engagement a draw.

Rane's leg was beginning to give him difficulty, and Tala's head was aching from mirroring Flow's defenses into her bloodstars. *I really should be doing this alongside my mass and magical weight.* She'd considered it before, but until now, those two aspects had been enough to exhaust her. *Time to add in defensive mirroring.*

Rane slumped down on one of the benches still out from dinner, and awaiting breakfast, and drank deeply from his canteen. "You are getting much better."

Tala sat facing him on another bench and shrugged. "I've got more weapons than you do. I effectively have four hands, and still can hardly take advantage of any holes in your defenses."

Rane chuckled. "That's a part of it, sure, but you are genuinely getting much better. Your form is better every day. You are well-braced to take hits and move smoothly between attack and defense. If I had your skill after three months of practice with just one weapon, I'd be proud. You're working with three distinct forms, plus hand-to-hand combat, and the use of your bloodstars. You've only been learning this for, what? Two months?"

"So, barely better than you'd expect."

He shook his head. "You aren't a prodigy, no, but your mental and physical enhancements *are* making this easier for you to both pick up and implement. A year from now? You're going to be a terror."

Tala gave a small smile. "Careful. Terry's the only terror we have for comparison."

Rane laughed loudly, then. "True enough. But even so, you might just be a match for him in a year or so."

She fell into contemplation at that. *Is it true?* Maybe. Only time would tell.

He frowned, then. "Your manipulation of your stars."

"What about it?"

"How are you doing it through the iron on your skin?"

Tala cocked her head. "What do you mean?"

"The iron blocks magic, right?"

"Yeah."

"So…?"

Tala shrugged. "An aura is, by itself, not really magical. It can be expanded via magic—Mistress Elnea's lessons and Master Jevin prove that—but the aura, itself? It's basically just an area of rule and authority for one's soul, and a soul cannot be stopped by iron."

Rane was nodding by the end of her explanation. "I hadn't thought of it that way." He smiled. "That does line up with what Soul Work says."

Tala grinned. "Well, I have been reading that book quite often." Unfortunately, no other book had unlocked along with Soul Work, but she had continued to read those that came to her, ready to read. *I need to at least know where to go for information if I need it.* She grunted, then. "Go, catch Mistress Odera before she's asleep and get that leg seen to. You're on watch, and I want my protector in top form."

He nodded his thanks as he stood. Even so, he had to comment, "The day I have to protect you from harm is a day we will all fear what's coming."

He took a few slightly hobbling steps away before pausing.

"That came out a lot darker than I intended."

Tala nodded. "Yeah, that was a bit grim."
They both grinned.
"Hurry up. I want to get some sleep, too."
"As you say, Mistress. I'll be back shortly."

*   *   *

Tala slept fitfully that night.

Nightmares woke her up a half-dozen times.

On the plus side, they were varied. She had the usual ones associated with her crushing debt, and her family's abandonment of her, but there were others that left her weeping until she was able to wake up enough to get past them.

The first was that her eldest brother, just three years younger than she, herself, was now in the exact situation she had been in.

After she left home, they'd acquired more debt and eventually sent Caln off to the academy, saddled with the new debt.

There, he tried to find her, but she ignored all messages from him or her family, and their paths never crossed.

That was a silly fear for more reasons than she could count.

Primarily, it would have taken long enough to build up such debt, that it would have had to be one of her younger siblings, if not the youngest. Also, if Caln had been sent to the academy, then there was really no way that their paths would *never* have crossed. *Unless he didn't want to see me and actively avoided me...*

That was possible but still unlikely. She shook that concern off.

Another horror consisted of her returning to confront her family and them simply not remembering her.

Millennial Mage, 5 - Fusing

Nothing she said or did could convince them that she was once a part of the family. They were polite but utterly baffled as to who she was and why she was bothering them.

That had taken a lot longer to calm down from.

A third new nightmare was much simpler. It was just that Master Jevin had been evil, and she was still in Makinaven. He was manipulating her senses, making her think that she was free, but in reality, she was his prisoner and would be forever.

She shuddered. It didn't help that the least realistic part of those dreams was that Master Jevin had made a mistake which allowed her to realize the predicament that she was in.

Nearly a week without nightmares, and suddenly, they're back, and they brought reinforcements.

Cups of chamomile helped, but in the end, she abandoned sleep well before dawn.

Even after her morning routine, the sky was still dark, the gray light of pre-dawn barely beginning to color the sky.

Even so, the cooks were in the chuckwagon, working away.

She just had to charge the cargo slots to be done with her required activities for the morning. *Still probably a bit too early, though.*

Mistress Odera was on second shift for the night, and Tala waved to her, deciding to head toward the smell of cooking food first.

Amnin greeted Tala warmly as she approached. "Good morning, Mistress."

"Good morning, Amnin."

The chef's eyes flicked to Mistress Odera, sitting on top of the cargo wagon, but quickly returned to Tala.

As Tala considered it, she hadn't been around the woman without others around this whole trip.

"Would you be willing to come inside for a moment?"

Tala smiled. "I'd love to." She kept her breathing steady. *I'm being invited into a cook's wagon!* She walked around to the back of the vehicle, where Amnin opened the door and ushered her inside.

As Tala stepped in, she suddenly remembered that she needed to charge the cargo slots, and that she was hungry, not really that interested in whatever was in here. *I have so much I need to do.* "Hey, could I get something to eat? I've got a lot to do this morning."

Amnin grinned, holding out an inscribed wooden coin. "Here." The wood was nearly the same color as the copper inscribed within it, making the magic nature of the coin hard to discern.

Tala glanced at it, then sighed, shaking her head. "I really have a lot to do—"

Amnin cut across her. "Hold this for me, and I'll grab your food."

Tala sighed. "Fine." She took the coin.

Amnin looked at her expectantly.

"So, are you going to get my food?"

Amnin frowned, then closed her eyes, putting a hand to her forehead. "My apologies, Mistress. I need you to power it."

"I don't know what it does. I have no mental construct." Tala grimaced. "I just want food, Amnin. I can get myself something if you're not willing."

Amnin held up her hands. "I know it will be inefficient, but please? I'll get you an extra chocolate puff-pasty."

Tala considered. *Those are really good.* Finally, she sighed and connected a void-channel to the coin. Power pulsed outward from the inscription, and Tala blinked.

What was that? She looked down at the coin. *What is this?*

"Better?"

Tala frowned. "What's going on, Amnin?"

"Welcome to the Guild, Mistress." She was grinning. "I was asked to officially induct you to some of our more obvious secrets."

"More obvious?"

"Well, those that would be, without interference."

Tala looked around, seeing... something in the air with her magesight. "You will tell me what is going on. Now." She didn't raise her voice, but Amnin visibly paled.

"Right. Right." Amnin swallowed. "Abstract Guide spellforms."

"That's Conceptual magic."

"It is."

Tala had Flow in her hand, in the form of a sword before she could think, the blade pointed at Amnin's chest. "Explain."

Amnin raised her hands. "Please, put that away. You are in no danger."

"How are you affecting me?" *Is the magic so pervasive, so powerful, that it's getting through my iron salve?*

"We're not—at least not as it was described to me and not as was guessed."

"Well?"

The cook looked down at the sword. "Can you put that away? Please?"

Tala thought back to Brand, how he'd tried to knife her at nearly their first meeting. *Is this how that will end?* She frowned. "One moment." She took the wooden token with her and stepped back out, sheathing Flow. "Mistress Odera."

The Mage glanced her way unnecessarily. "Yes?" She didn't shout, but the word carried to Tala with ease.

"Can you and I chat in a quarter-hour or so?"

"Certainly."

Tala nodded and stepped back inside, sure that the older woman had seen her enter the chuckwagon. *I'd have said she was seeing me in the chuckwagon, but these scripts probably make her uninterested in what is happening within.*

"Was that really necessary?"

"If anything happens to me, she will come looking."

Amnin sighed. "She really won't."

Tala frowned. "Explain."

"I can't without making you jumpy again." She held up her hands as Tala placed her hand back on Flow's hilt. "Can I just explain from the beginning, please?"

"Be quick about it."

"The interior of the wagon is inscribed to make it uninteresting, not worth examining, and easy to forget. It's a kitchen. Everyone's seen a kitchen before. Amplifying that isn't hard. It also tones down the interest added by it being a mobile kitchen. The working isn't sufficient on its own to make those genuinely interested forget about us, like the Wainwrights." She gave a small smile. "They make overtures in every inter-guild meeting for access to our wagons. The other guilds don't understand the Wainwrights' obsession."

Tala felt herself smile, but it was without mirth. "Because they see nothing interesting about your wagons at all."

"Precisely." Amnin cleared her throat. "I say that we aren't affecting you because you never let it drop. Brand conveyed that you never lost interest or stopped talking with him about what we do."

Tala's eyes widened. "But other Mages…"

Amnin nodded. "By Brand's report, just as expected, the other Mages in your previous caravan slowly lost interest in the oddity of eating arcanous meat and never investigated further. If you were to bring it up to them, it wouldn't be new information, simply something that they'd never gotten around to investigating."

"But I didn't lose interest."

"No, you didn't."

My iron salve. "So, the scripts passively make everything about your guild seem uninteresting."

"Not the whole guild, just parts of our facilities and our wagons."

Tala waved off the correction. "And actively, you push on Mage's minds so that even if they do notice something, they won't ever get around to investigating."

Amnin nodded.

Tala sighed, falling into contemplative silence. *This doesn't make sense. How is this possible?* She didn't know, but she would find out.

Chapter: 11
Drop the Mistress

Tala looked around the inside of the chuckwagon, taking in the disks of wood, subtly affixed at regular intervals around the part of the chuckwagon's interior that she could see. Each radiated power that just barely registered to her incredibly sensitive magesight. *I suppose that magics meant to help in evading detection would have to be harder to detect, by its very nature.*

She shook her head. *I'm getting lost in the weeds.*

What was the core issue, here? She nodded. "How do you even know Conceptual inscriptions? You aren't a Mage. You're not even—" She'd been about to say that Amnin wasn't inscribed, but as Tala focused on the woman, she noticed a double ring of inscriptions in each of the cook's armpits. *That would be painful to receive.* "You are inscribed."

The cook shrugged. "Just two simple scripts. One to protect me from the inscriptions I work around, and another to make us magically uninteresting."

Tala glared. "Do you have any idea how valuable that second spellform would be to humanity?"

"It only affects things it entirely contains."

"So, couldn't we use it around every city?"

"It is, already. Where do you think we got it?"

Tala blinked at that. "What?"

"Have you ever investigated how the cities' magical systems function?"

"Of course not, I'm not a Builder."

"But isn't it interesting, how they've created such extensive, interlinked networks?"

"Of course, but I can only look into so many things."

Amnin shrugged again. "As you know, I'm not a Mage. I can only tell you what I was taught—which wasn't much. The scripts we use are used in almost every guild, in their most secretive facilities." She chuckled. "By what I was taught, the Mages gave us these scripts when we were recognized as an official human guild."

"Then, wouldn't they be on the lookout for them?"

"I've no idea. I've not interacted with any Mage besides you. Discounting a few exchanged words as required for anyone in my position, that is."

"So, where does your education in magic come from?"

"The Culinary Guild, of course."

Tala groaned. "So, we're training Conceptual Mages, but not actually making them Mages, keeping them segregated, and not taking advantage of them."

Amnin scoffed. "Hardly. I don't want to be a Mage, Mistress. I'm a cook. Just because I know what these specific inscriptions do and can switch out pre-inscribed disks if they wear out, it does not mean I'm qualified to be a Mage."

Tala sat down beside the entrance, placing her head in her hands, the wooden token pressing against her forehead. "I'm going to need a bit to process this."

"Take all the time you need. That coin's for you, after all." She chuckled again. "It's not like we have a lot of those laying around. Keep it powered, and you'll be welcome in here whenever you wish. If you lose it, or it runs out, I can't replace it. Maybe the Guildhall in Bandfast can."

Tala groaned again. "Thank you. I just need a minute." She hesitated, a few scents standing out to her as she drew in a deep breath. "And bacon and coffee."

Amnin patted her shoulder. "Bacon, coffee, and a little space, coming right up."

* * *

Tala sat on the cargo wagon roof facing Mistress Odera.

The older Mage had her eyes closed, seemingly ignoring Tala as she ate.

Conceptual magic. She shuddered again. *There are Conceptual Mages, scattered through humanity.* No, that wasn't right. Just because they could activate conceptual inscriptions didn't make them conceptual mages.

After all, I could get that time inscription, which would let me always know exactly what time it was, but that wouldn't make me a Time Mage. That actually made Tala feel a lot better.

So, just some basic conceptual inscriptions. That's not really news. I knew that there are some human Conceptual Mages out there, somewhere, just not very many. It makes sense that items wouldn't be unheard of.

And that didn't take artifacts into account. *Would we even recognize a conceptual artifact?*

The average person probably wouldn't, but Archons surely would... right?

She thought back to the inside of the chuckwagon. She'd *known* there was magic involved, known exactly where to look, and it had been hard for her to see.

Nope, it's very possible that conceptual artifacts are just being missed. Blessedly, artifacts didn't really survive outside of waning cities unless a Mage was sustaining them, so there shouldn't be unknown conceptual artifacts in any city but Alefast.

Probably worth looking into.

"Well, it's good to see that you've stopped writing out your thoughts, but even so, you are clearly in turmoil."

Tala's gaze snapped back to Mistress Odera, whose eyes were still closed.

"You're shifting, scratching, sighing, and grunting. Unless you picked up *another* new project, something is bothering you."

Tala sighed, then noticed she'd sighed and grunted in irritation. Then, of course, she noticed that and scratched her cheek in frustration.

Mistress Odera grinned broadly. "Proving my point, dear."

Tala shook her head. "Fine. What do you know of conceptual inscriptions?"

"Abstract or Concrete?"

She thought back to her conversation with Amnin. "Abstract."

"Very little."

Tala glared. "Concrete?"

"The same."

"Why did you ask me to specify?"

"Because I was curious."

Tala scoffed but decided not to quibble. "So?"

"So there are a handful of items that can be made with conceptual inscriptions. Some Abstract, some Concrete, and they are a mix of Guide and Creator."

Tala nodded, leaning a bit forward, even as she ate more of Amnin's offering of placation.

"Some are banned and actively watched for. The Constructionists *can* make an item that draws consumer attention, giving merchants or shop owners an advantage, but that is… frowned upon. Another that is banned is one that makes the veracity of your words seem greater, regardless of the evidence." She shook her head. "Not a great thing for anyone to have."

"Are any legal?"

"Oh, of course! Some are positively silly, reducing how awkward someone appears or making someone or something seem less interesting."

"Couldn't the second one allow you to get in places you shouldn't or do things that you shouldn't?"

"The ones I know of can't force away genuine interest. They just tip the scales. They can't make someone ignore a thief they are looking right at, for example. That said, of course it can be abused. So could items of invisibility or capture. In the end, they are tools, and we try to be in the 'trust but verify' vein for things."

Tala grunted. *That all lines up with what little Amnin could explain.*

"Why this interest?" Then, Mistress Odera started nodding. "Our mysterious arcane visitor."

Tala opened her mouth to say 'no,' but in truth? That was one reason the chuckwagon's inscriptions had been so shocking to her. "That's a part of it, yeah."

Mistress Odera nodded. "I received a message that we have a Paragon monitoring the region closely as we head back for Bandfast. Additionally, the Archon we'll meet up with later today is a powerhouse in her own right, though she's a bit eccentric." She grinned. "Some think that she loves fungus more than people, or some such nonsense, but the truth is more nuanced. She likes her research and doesn't really care for formality." The older woman shrugged.

"What else can you tell me about her?"

"Well, from what I know, she followed an older school of thought and made her Archon Star in a sphere formed from a giant mushroom stalk."

"A Mushroom Archon?"

"There have been stranger mediums, Blood Archon."

Tala snorted a laugh. "That's fair, I suppose." She hesitated. "Why did you bring her up?"

"Well, her section of this forest is much more... set, at least for now. We'll have almost a straight shot out of the forest once we get to her. That doesn't mean we'll be out of harm's way, but it should be a predictable route as far as days of travel required."

Tala nodded. "That will be a welcome thing to get back to."

"Regular schedules are a blessing, indeed. There is also the fact that she hasn't abandoned her research in the last thousand years."

She hesitated. "Wait. So, when the forest cities wane...?"

"She and her assistants stay."

"How does she survive the Leshkin?"

Mistress Odera shrugged. "You'll have to ask her yourself, but from what I know, she's one of only about a half-dozen Archons who ignore the migration of humanity."

"Thus, we should be safe near her."

"Well, I doubt she'd intervene if an ox steps on you, but we should be relatively protected from arcanes, powerful magical creatures, and the like."

Tala nodded. "Thank you."

"I am happy to be of assistance."

Tala examined the woman for a long time then, as morning continued on, passengers got their breakfast, and the caravan prepared to depart. *There is a lot to her that I don't understand at all.*

Finally, Tala began charging the cargo slots but addressed the older Mage as she worked. "You are quite familiar with Archon Stars."

Mistress Odera stiffened but otherwise didn't react.

Tala let the silence stretch on as she completed her work, charging each slot with ease.

Finally, the Mage opened her eyes and regarded Tala. "That wasn't a question."

"But you still understood what I was asking." Tala brushed off her hands. "I'm done with my Dimensional Mage duties."

Mistress Odera nodded in acknowledgment. "I have not attempted to bond a star."

"That much is obvious. You'd be a fount or an Archon." Tala sighed. "But that answers my question. You've made one."

The woman scoffed. "One? No."

Tala raised an eyebrow. "Oh?"

"Mistress Tala, I've made hundreds. Among living Mages, Archon or otherwise, I am likely the one with the greatest understanding of that particular spellform, regardless of medium."

"Is that why you had so many tests, ready to hand, to examine my inverted star?"

"Yes." The Mage frowned. "I will admit that that did vex me. I'd never considered inverting the spellform."

"So, how do you have hundreds? How have you not swallowed one?"

Mistress Odera pulled out a viciously sharp snarl of glass, holding it out toward Tala. Even holding it caused a few small lacerations and punctures on her fingers and palm, spots of blood beginning to form almost immediately. "I'm vicious."

Tala's eyes went wide. That burr of glass contained an Archon Star.

"Nothing requires the medium to be a sphere, and the compulsion is never strong enough to convince me to pop something like this between my lips. I have these little devils made of various materials so I can satisfy the itch to make the star, then I wait for an Archon to notice, ask for it, and I let them destroy the thing."

Tala found herself nodding. "Master Jevin."

"He was very kind."

"So, that works? Why wouldn't every Mage do that, when they reached this point?"

"Other Mages prefer death to bleeding all over the place. Or they hold out hope that they just might be able to become Bound, so they work their hardest toward making the attempt. I hold no such delusions."

Tala sat back. *That makes sense.* "So, how long will this solution last?"

"At least for today."

With that solemn answer, the two fell back into contemplative silence.

* * *

It was just after noon when the forest began to darken.

While there were clouds in the sky, barely visible through the canopy high above, it wasn't the simple darkness of a cloud stealing across the sun, and it was very much tied to this portion of the forest itself.

Where most of the trees that Tala had seen in this place grew only a single, high-level canopy, this section seemed to have sprouted many, overlapping layers, giving the forest floor below the feel of twilight, even around high noon.

Everyone was on edge as they moved into the darker section of the woods, even though they'd been expecting it. After all, mushrooms preferred dim light.

As they progressed deeper in, the air became heavy with moisture, small ponds, streams, and creeks crisscrossing the space in what was obviously a meticulously designed water system.

After an hour of travel, they found the first mushroom.

Standing about half the height of a man, the mushroom was short and squat, with a top that spread wide and sickly yellow striations throughout.

They all knew better than to get close. They'd been briefed on the types to expect, and how to avoid the dangers.

That one releases spores that dissolve anything they touch. The only saving grace is that they are heavy enough that they fall almost straight down and only do so if the fungus is disturbed.

It actually reminded Tala of ending trees, except that the fungi's dissolution was chemical and organic in nature, rather than magical.

I'd probably be fine. No reason to test it, though. There would be nothing to gain, except knowledge of her own capabilities.

Stop that, Tala. It would be colossally foolish to test your inscriptions and endingberry power against a plant. Maybe if there was something tangible to gain, but only then. *Maybe.*

More mushrooms of varying kinds and ever-increasing sizes began to dot the landscape around them, among the trees, as they pressed on.

Here, there was what could almost be described as a road through the vegetation.

Hard-packed dirt in two obvious lines marked a clear and easy path for the wagons. There was even the occasional, simple bridge over some of the larger waterways.

Tala frowned as she examined the path. "I know this is supposed to be a safer area, but isn't taking the same route each time dangerous?"

Millennial Mage, 5 - Fusing

"It might be if anything could be waiting in ambush. This area isn't really large enough to inconvenience the largest magical predators. In area, it's smaller than most cities."

Even with that reassurance, Tala felt deep discomfort at following such a path through any portion of the Wilds.

The forest didn't get any darker as they progressed, and as Tala examined the canopy above, she could see evidence of pruning in the upper reaches. Clearly, someone had taken a good deal of time to have a narrow range of brightness in this section of the forest.

Over the next hour, Tala began to notice great swaths of lichen-like growths, covering sections of the forest floor, seemingly decomposing the detritus on the ground. Eventually, it was a unified layer, covering everything other than the two dirt tracks that the caravan continued resolutely down.

Finally, when the light was beginning to fade, they came into a much larger clearing, centered around a massive stump that was covered with mushrooms the size of houses.

As their back rider came into the clearing, a voice filled the space.

As Tala looked around, she saw that the mushrooms, themselves, were vibrating to create the sound. The result was a deep rumble, with quite a bit of sub-vocal resonance, which vibrated in their chests, even as they heard the spoken words.

"What are you doing in my woods?"

Mistress Odera didn't even open her eyes. "We are delivering the goods you requested before continuing on to Bandfast."

A small woman appeared beside Tala, her voice soft and smooth. "Oh, why didn't you say so?"

Mistress Odera opened her eyes then and bowed to the woman. "Mistress Noelle, I presume?"

Noelle waved her off. "Just Noelle."

Mistress Odera hesitated. "But, Mistress—"

Noelle cut across the older woman. "Drop the Mistress, or I will end you." She gave a tight smile.

Tala almost laughed, but she couldn't see even a hint of mirth on the woman's face despite the smile.

Mistress Odera regarded the Archon for a long moment, then nodded. "I am Odera, and this is Mistress Tala. Master Rane is the other Mage Protector for this caravan."

Noelle grinned widely. "Tala, Odera, Rane!" She shouted the last, and Rane turned to regard the top of the wagon. "Pleased to meet you." Her voice carried to Rane, once again out in front of the lead wagon, and he gave a marginally confused partial bow in her direction.

Tala cocked her head. "So, Noelle…" She stopped there. It felt weird to address an Archon without their moniker. *I'm really settling in to Mage social norms.*

"Yes, Tala?" Noelle's lips were pulled up into a small smile. She seemed to enjoy the lack of formality.

"I assume that you are the primary Archon of these fungus-filled woods?"

"But of course." She gestured to herself. "Can't you tell?"

Tala looked at the woman more closely, then. Noelle was short—shorter even than Tala herself. She had bob-cut, dark blonde hair that seemed perfectly clean and styled despite the mugginess in the air. Even though her aura was held in tight, Noelle seemed to be letting just a bit out, for Tala's inspection.

Tala frowned. "Fused? How are you only Fused?" The inscriptions that she could see pointed to the woman being a Material Guide, focused on something close to plant life. *Fungi, most likely.* It was a guess, though likely a correct one.

Noelle leaned in close. "The questions you should be asking are: *How* do I only look Fused, and why do I want you to make that assumption." She smiled mischievously. "Now, how are you magically inert, even while clearly affected by innumerable active inscriptions?" After a moment, Noelle winked. "Well, except your eyes. How did you manage that color? Not a Ruby Archon, are you? They are oh so boring." She sighed, shaking her head as she turned to Mistress Odera and held out her hand. "Give it over."

Mistress Odera seemed to relax as she tossed her barbed, glass, Archon Star to the smaller woman. "Thank you."

Noelle's hand twitched, and a puff of glowing powder surrounded the glass, even as it flew through the air. The powder seemed to draw the power out from the spellform within the glass before dissolving the glass itself. "Happy to assist, Forbidden."

Mistress Odera bowed her head.

Noelle laughed, suddenly standing in front of the older Mage, grabbing Mistress Odera's chin, and lifting her head. "None of that. Come, you all are tired, and I want my stuff." She hesitated, then glanced to Tala. "And you have *so* many questions to answer." She walked over to link arms with Tala. "Let's go."

She moved with Tala, and Tala didn't resist, even as the little woman walked them off the edge of the wagon's roof.

One mushroom after another sprang up under their feet as they progressed, each lower than the last until they stood on the ground.

Noelle looked back toward the wagons. "You! Giant!"

Rane was, obviously, already staring at the two women, and he seemed utterly baffled by what was happening.

"Rane!"

He startled, then walked their way.

"Good boy. We've a lot to discuss, including why your souls seem to be halfway in sync with each other. I've been trying to synchronize mushroom souls for *years*."

Tala gave her a puzzled look. "Mushroom... souls?" She decided to ignore the other bit.

Noelle shrugged. "Souls, spirits, magical underpinnings that allow for the defying of natural law. Take your pick."

Tala opened her mouth to try to form a response, but Noelle snatched up Rane's arm with her free hand and took off at a brisk walk toward the fungus-covered stump.

"Come, come. They'll unload what needs unloading."

As if at the words, Tala saw a dozen other Mages exiting the house-sized mushrooms before them. *Oh, they actually are houses...* It was going to be a *very* odd evening.

Chapter: 12
Hallucinogens

Tala kept up with the diminutive woman leading her and Rane each by an arm.

Rane, for his part, was quite confused as to what was going on. "Mistress Noelle—"

The Archon spun on Rane, briefly releasing Tala's arm as she thrust her finger into his face, cutting him off. "You get one warning, Rane. I am Noelle. Use your universal moniker on others, but I'll have none of it."

Rane pulled back, looking cross-eyed at the finger still aimed his way.

Tala briefly reflected that the gesture was a lot more threatening from a Mage than a mundane, and it was uncomfortable, even from one of those.

He nodded. "Yes, Noelle."

Noelle smiled up at him. "Good boy." After patting his shoulder a couple of times, she turned back, easily catching Tala's arm and moving inexorably forward once more.

To his credit, Rane recovered quickly. "Noelle."

"Hmm?"

"Where are we going?"

"Oh, to my workshop. I need to examine the two of you."

At that moment, Terry flickered into being on Tala's shoulder.

Millennial Mage, 5 - Fusing

Noelle stopped dead, looking at the avian, then to Tala. "Oh, you two are very interesting. You should—" She cut herself off, shaking her head. "No. That would be foolish." She met Tala's gaze. "Get stronger, bond the bird, then come back." She pointed back and forth between Tala and Terry. "I will be fascinated to see how that settles out."

Then, the latest distraction dealt with, Noelle snatched up Tala and Rane's arms once again, leading them onward.

Tala cleared her throat then. "So, we're going to your workshop to test us for... soul-syncing."

"That's one name for it."

Tala sighed. "What would you call it?"

"Soul-syncing." Noelle's tone was perfectly level.

Tala huffed a short laugh. "Fine."

Strangely, she was finding herself relaxing, just a bit. She realized that a part of it seemed to be related to the change in her surroundings. Even in Makinaven, trees and wood had dominated her environment. *Apparently, mushrooms are better.* Well, they were different at least.

Tala returned her focus to the matter at hand. "Naming aside, what is it?"

They were to the base of the stump, and Tala was able to see wide stairs carved into the dead tree, up which Noelle led them both as she answered. "People and things that are around each other for enough time start to fall into sync. A rock resting on the forest floor will leave an impression. It will change the mini-biome of the area, affecting what can live there and how well it will prosper. Given enough time, the rock will become almost indistinguishable from the surrounding forest floor."

Rane was frowning. "So, that sounds like a passive process."

"In that sense, it is." Noelle let out an exaggerated sigh. "Things that are truly in sync can act as a single magical unit."

Tala cocked her head to the side in thought, even as she took a quick step forward to thread around a variation in the width of the stairs. "Like a soul-bond."

"Like that, but without the combination of the spiritual being required."

Tala nodded. "Hence 'soul-syncing.'"

"Precisely." Noelle smiled. "Soul-syncing is more like a rock. Is a rock a rock? Or is it a collection of molecules, fused together? Why should that one rock be a unit, magically speaking, but be separate units the moment they break apart? Why does a molecular bond impart magical oneness?"

Tala had honestly not ever considered that portion of magic theory. "I mean, I can target a part of something. So, I could target a portion of the rock, without it needing to be broken apart."

"Ahh, but are you targeting a part of the rock, or are you targeting a smaller rock, that happens to be fused with others, as part of the larger?"

She didn't really have an answer to that. *That's an interesting question, probably worth considering at some point.* Tala had no idea what the implications were of either answer, but she was sure that it would be fascinating to investigate.

Noelle turned them inward, facing the side of the stump at a seemingly random place in their ascent. By that point, they were so used to following her lead that neither of them registered that she was leading them into a solid wall until they had stepped straight through it.

Tala craned around, staring back the way they'd come at the perfectly normal-looking, open doorway. "Why can't I see any magic?"

"Because the effect isn't magical."

Tala turned back around to frown at Noelle in confusion. "What?"

"It's an incredibly precisely controlled, regulated, and focused hallucinogenic effect."

"That's not how hallucinogens work."

"Oh? You're an expert?"

Tala opened her mouth to argue, then closed it. Finally, she sighed. "Magically manipulated, but not magical in nature."

"Precisely."

"What could you do with that kind of fine control?"

Noelle tittered slightly. "Well, I'm actually a two-thousand-pound leopard, but I've convinced the local Mages that I'm one of them and use that to lure my prey back to my lair."

Both Rane and Tala stopped dead, trying and failing to pull free.

Even so, Noelle stopped as well with an overdramatic sigh. "Relax. I'm joking."

Tala felt an almost irresistible urge to laugh but managed to contain it.

Rane began chuckling, but his eyes showed that it wasn't genuine.

Noelle looked back and forth, between them. "Oh, my apologies."

His laughter stopped, and the air was suddenly a lot clearer.

Tala blinked, looking around. The effect was similar to being in a smoky kitchen and stepping outside for the first time in hours. *I didn't even notice the stuff in the air.*

"Of late, my spores tend to shape themselves in attempts to meet my subconscious desires. It's dead useful much of the time, but there's a reason I don't work in a city." She winked and started forwards again, or at least, she tried.

Tala found that she easily resisted the small woman's pull, now.

Noelle grunted. "Ahh, right."

Tala found herself bristling with irritation. "You've been manipulating us since we were at the wagon, haven't you?"

The older Archon sighed. "Technically every interaction is a form of manipulation, but yes." She thought about it for a moment. "Actually, most of it was keeping you socially off balance." She grinned at the two. "Come on. We're almost there."

Tala and Rane shared a long look. Terry let out an indifferent, quiet chirp, continuing his fake sleep. Finally, Rane shrugged. Tala gave a half-grin back his way and shook her head in resignation.

Noelle had walked about ten feet down the corridor before stopping and turning to regard them. "So?"

They followed after her, and she led them another dozen yards or so before they came out into a large chamber, open to the air above them.

This is in the center of the stump. Odd to have the entrance hidden, then open the space itself to the outside for anyone to drop in. The woman likely had other security precautions, regardless.

As Tala looked around, she noticed that the layout was very similar to Master Jevin's workshop. There were even a couple of dasgannach in glass jars. "You're studying those, too?"

Noelle looked to where Tala was pointing. "Oh, yes. They are utterly fascinating. Every researcher worth their metal has at least one to experiment with." She smiled widely. "Besides, those are arguably fungi."

Millennial Mage, 5 - Fusing

Rane frowned. "I'm not an expert on fungi, or whatever that is, but it's moving. Aren't fungi, by definition, non-motile?"

Noelle grimaced. "You sound like Darmin."

Tala looked to the woman. "Darmin?"

"My research assistant."

Rane looked at the moving mud, then back to the woman. He seemed to decide on ignoring her deflection. "So… how are they fungi?"

"…I want them to be."

Tala huffed a laugh. Then, she realized what the woman's reason was more likely to be. "You want to control them."

Noelle regarded her for a moment. "Well, obviously."

Tala shrugged. "Why not just soul-bond one?"

"They are sentient enough that their assent, as well as mine, is required for the bond."

Rane started nodding. "But not sentient enough to choose to bond."

"Precisely. I've tried making an Archon Star of their chosen food, but even if I put the star in, by itself, they refuse to eat it. No matter how long they are kept from other sustenance." Noelle sighed. "It doesn't help that they seem to not need to eat."

"They don't need to eat?"

"Not really. I've never had one starve under my care, and I've left one without food for centuries. Never did take that star…" She sighed. "It didn't shrink or become less motile, either, so it wasn't actually 'starving' or anything."

Tala was frowning. "Wait, Master Jevin said that they don't have any will to speak of."

"That's true. If will was water, they'd be a desert."

"Then how are they sentient?"

"Oh, Tala. What makes you think sentience requires a will?"

She blinked in confusion. "What? Isn't that the definition of a will? Of sentience?"

Noelle shrugged. "Sentience just means that they are capable of making a choice between utterly equal options."

"What?"

But Rane was nodding. "The starving donkey."

Noelle pointed to him. "Precisely."

"Starving donkey?" Tala was lost.

Noelle looked to Rane. "You or me."

He shrugged. "It's your workshop."

She smiled. "Fair enough. The postulate is that if you place a donkey between two utterly equal sources of food, water, shelter, et cetera, then there should be nothing to allow it to choose one over the other."

"Alright."

"So, if there is no 'reason' for it to choose one over the other, will it starve?"

"Of course not. It will just pick one."

"How?"

Tala opened her mouth, then closed it. After a long moment, she shook her head. "I don't know."

"Sentience! Sentience, my dear, is the ability to make a choice that seems to have no reason behind it. The starving donkey is just a hypothetical extreme to illustrate the point."

Tala grunted. "I suppose." After a moment, she shrugged. "So, that's not will?"

"Oh, no. Will is the ability to make a decision *against* reason. It is a step beyond mere sentience. Many humans are perfectly sentient but never do anything that is too hard or that is opposed. They lack will." She shrugged. "Or their will is weak, however you wish to state it."

"I think I get it. So, bonding a dasgannach?"

"I'll figure something out eventually, but that's not why we're here."

Tala cleared her throat. "Right, soul-syncing. Why, again? I don't think you've said."

"Ahh, yes. It's simple. I want to inscribe and empower every fungus in this region as one."

"Why would that be useful?"

"Well, then I could make a small script on, say, that mushroom"—she pointed to a rather plain-looking specimen growing from one of the tables—"and it would affect them all."

Oh! Wow… that… That would be rusting useful. Tala started thinking through the various implications. *It'd be like aspect mirroring, without needing the conscious effort.* It was how her elk leathers functioned. They were, magically speaking, one item. *Shared pool of power.*

"I can see you've realized at least some of the advantages."

Tala nodded, but Rane was frowning. "You said that Mistress Tala and I are moving toward soul synchronization?"

"I said you were half-synchronized."

"Is there a difference?"

Noelle laughed, walking over to a cabinet and pulling out a set of tools. She then lifted two that had identical handles but wildly different tops. "These are half-identical, right?"

Rane nodded.

"So, are they moving toward being identical?"

"Oh, I see."

Noelle nodded sagely. "Good. You see, I assume that you two spend a lot of time near each other, yes?"

They glanced at one another and shrugged. Tala responded. "Yeah. We're friends, sparring partners, and we're both Mage Protectors for this caravan."

"Right, so your bodies and souls have fallen into sync. You aren't becoming one, but you *are* becoming intuitively aligned. Your heart rates are not identical, but they are sub-rhythms of each other. You breathe either on beat with one another or directly opposed. You fall into step. Tala, you lengthen your stride, and Rane, you shorten yours."

Tala tsked. "What does that mean?" After a moment's hesitation, she frowned. "Wait. How could you even know this, even if it were true?"

Noelle looked at them. After around five seconds, she nodded. "Confirmed. If you're looking for it, it's hard to miss." She hesitated. "Well, if you have the perceptual acuity to notice. As to what it means? Well, what you two have is the physical side of things. I've found it most often in guards or long-term friends. Some marriages, and many research associates."

"Darmin?"

She waved that off. "No, his bio-rhythms became subservient to mine almost immediately. One morphing to match the other isn't true synchronization."

Rane pointed at himself and Tala. "So how do you know that's not what happened here?"

"Because of the second part. But the physical side first. Mushrooms can't do that, their rhythms are set by nature, and their environment. I can force such alignment, but that causes the same issue as one suborning the other."

Tala groaned. "Can you get to the point? I feel like you're spouting nonsense, trying to sound profound."

Noelle laughed again. "You're funny"—the mirth left the small woman's face—"I like you."

Millennial Mage, 5 - Fusing

Tala felt the color drain from her face, but she had no idea why. *What is wrong with me?* She swallowed involuntarily.

Rane shifted. "So…?"

Mistress Noelle sighed, glancing between Tala and Rane. "Fine. I don't know what it means, alright? All I know is that certain things can have a sort of resonance between their spirits, which is partially reflected in the physical. I've seen it in predators and prey; I've seen it in people who've hated each other for years; I've seen it in people who just met; and I've seen it absent in couples after more than a century of marriage."

He cocked his head in confusion. "So you don't know what it means, or what it affects, but you can detect it?"

Mistress Noelle waved that away. "Oh, I know what it *can* do, and what I'm trying to do."

There was a long pause.

Tala took a seat, waiting. *Think small thoughts. Don't notice me, here.*

Rane, for some reason, didn't sense the frustration coming from the Archon. "Well?"

Mistress Noelle grunted and flopped down on another stool. She glanced to Tala and saw that she, also, was sitting. Noelle smiled happily at her, then turned back to Rane. "You're distinct. Each of your magical pulses, cadences, and rhythms is compatible with the other's but are not the same. Your heart rates aren't identical, but they are harmonious." She shrugged. "I'd bet that you are far more effective, magically, against each other than you would be against anyone else."

"Still haven't answered my question."

"Haven't I? I want to unify life forms magically, without them having to be linked physically or spiritually. That magical link often *manifests* spiritually or physically, but it doesn't require it."

"And Mistress Tala and I are…?"

"Physically in sync, which implies a soul-synchronization and hints at the possibility of magical unification."

Tala sat up straighter at that. "Hang on. What are you planning on doing to us?"

"Hmm? Oh, nothing. Just take a bunch of measurements."

Tala's eyes narrowed as she regarded the woman. She didn't want to antagonize her, but she was definitely not going to be forced into unity of any kind with another person, not even Rane. *Nope. I am me.*

Mistress Noelle seemed to sense her hesitation. "I swear to you that I will only take readings."

"If only oaths were binding."

The woman sighed, pulling out a slate, manipulating it for a moment, then pressing her thumb to indicate a confirmation. She passed the empowered item over.

Rane walked over to read over Tala's shoulder.

"This is a contract stating that you will only take readings."

Mistress Noelle nodded. "And if I do more, you, or your heirs, will be entitled to a ridiculous sum of money, mainly your weight in gold, for any infraction."

Tala cleared her throat. "I'm very heavy."

"It really doesn't matter, Tala. I'm not going to do anything but take measurements."

Tala shrugged, feeling at least a little bit better and looking to Rane.

He shrugged, too. "She could probably just compel us if she has as much skill with targeted hallucinogens as I suspect. At the very least, she could render us unconscious, do as she wished, and be done with it. Her asking for our agreement shows something of her character."

Mistress Noelle straightened a bit. "It does, doesn't it."

Tala rolled her eyes. "Very well."

The Archon stood, clapping her hands in glee. "Wonderful! Let's get started, then. I have just a bit of set-up that I need to do to perform the tests." She waved a hand, and one of the cabinets opened, showing a selection of random snack foods and bottles of various liquids. "Help yourself."

Tala and Rane did just that as they watched the elder Archon work.

Mistress Noelle retrieved a large array of bronze plates, each inscribed with spellforms that reminded Tala of those Master Jevin had.

She moved around an open space to one side of the workshop, placing them in two mirrored patterns. Once that was done, the Archon pulled out bronze wire and carefully ran it in an intricate pattern between the various plates, wrapping around small, raised pins.

All in all, it took her nearly half an hour to get all set up.

"There we go. Tala?"

"Yes, Noelle?"

Mistress Noelle smiled at her. "You stand there, please." She indicated the center of one of the two formations. "Rane?"

He started walking toward the other.

"Good boy. Right in the center, mind you."

When they were both in position, Mistress Noelle clasped her hands. "Are we ready?"

The two nodded.

"Alright! Let's begin."

Chapter: 13
An Entirely Different Train of Thought

Tala hoped to the rusting stars that Mistress Noelle was going to get good use out of this data. *Anything for this to be worth it...*

The Archon had asked them to sit still, stretch, chat randomly, argue about a topic of her choice, and a few other odd things. In the end, she seemed satisfied with her data.

"And that does it. Thank you!"

Tala and Rane both slumped a bit, stepping away from the spellforms and moving to stools near where they'd been standing.

It was dark outside, easily seen through the opening in the ceiling above. Despite that, there was still plenty of light to see by.

As it turned out, the walls were covered in a bioluminescent fungus that produced enough light to allow even a mundane to read with ease.

Oddly, the luminescence was almost lilac in coloration, which gave the workshop a bit of an otherworldly feel, but Tala didn't find it objectionable.

"Now"—Mistress Noelle sat down at the table with them—"what can I do for you two? You'll be departing in the morning, and your caravan is safe for the night. So, you'll already get a good night's sleep."

"Dinner?"

Mistress Noelle smiled. "Your chuckwagon will have some food for you when we're done here."

Tala almost stood up right then, heading toward the exit, but Rane caught her gaze, raising an eyebrow questioningly. *Right!* "So, I have a question about Archon Stars."

"Oh?" Noelle perked up. "What do you want to know? They aren't my expertise, per se, but I'll answer if I can."

"What does the inverse of an Archon Star do?"

"The... inverse."

"Yes."

"You want to know what happens when a custom spellform, unique to the caster and medium, is inverted perfectly?"

"Yes?"

"How, under the heavens, would I be able to answer such a specific, theoretical question?" She had a playful glint to her eye.

If Tala had to guess, she'd have said the other woman was hunting for a compliment. Instead of playing into her desires, Tala decided to subvert them. "Not theoretical."

"What?"

Tala held out the iron vial with her inverted star held within. "It's not theoretical."

Noelle took the iron vial and removed the cap. "Tala, that's an Archon Star." She looked in again. "I'll want to ask you about the medium later, but let's stay on track."

Tala held up a finger. "That's the thing. *This* is how I make Archon Stars." She opened a different iron vial and *pulled*, causing one of the stars she'd been using for orbital practice to come out, hovering before Noelle.

Noelle shrugged. "They're both Archon Stars, but for different people."

Tala opened her mouth to object, but Noelle cut her off.

"I know you made both. Well, you flipped this one, right?"

"That's right."

"It also resonates with your soul. I imagine you can manipulate it as you can your originals?"

"Yes."

"Good, right. So, first thing. This isn't inverted, it's inside out."

Tala frowned. "What?"

"Inverted, the spellform goes left when it should go right, etc. This is inside out. It's like you grabbed the spell-knot and twisted until it rolled around and came to rest with what used to be inside, out."

"But… it looks almost identical to being inverted."

"Ahh, but it isn't."

"How do you know?"

Noelle gave her a bit of an irritated look. "Fine. I know because an inverted Archon Star must be made intentionally that way, not manipulated after the fact." She shook her head. "One, willingly made, willingly taken, binds your gate to your body. Closing your gate and returning you to the natural state of humanity."

Tala's eyes widened, and she opened her mouth to ask the obvious question, but Noelle cut her off, again.

"Yes, your Forbidden friend knows. I've never heard of a Mage taking that path. It is willingly giving up on human magic. That's no life." She shook her head. "Not to mention that humans without a gate only have a lifespan of a half a dozen decades. A few more, if they take good care of themselves. The luckiest might reach a hundred and twenty years of age, even with magical healing and maintenance."

That's a lot shorter than I would have guessed. She frowned. *Poor Adrill and Brandon!* Tala shook her head in frustration. "Is there anything that can be done for them?"

"Stop them from creating or ingesting an inverted Archon Star."

Tala hitched at that. *Wait...* "How do we not have half our Archons accidentally creating the inverse form?"

"As I said, it has to be intentionally formed. The first Archon Star that they make is their regular star, regardless of how they make it. That's one of the *many* reasons why there isn't a set spellform that works for every Mage or Archon, even in a given medium."

Tala grunted but didn't know of anything that would counter the woman's point. *It lines up with what I know, too.* "What if they were born without a gate?"

Mistress Noelle gave her an odd look. "So, that's an entirely different train of thought. Do you not want your answers?" She lifted the iron vial slightly.

Tala shook her head. "Right, right. So, how does an inverted Archon Star do that?"

Mistress Noelle gave a half-smile. "That is also not what we were discussing, but the answer is quick enough. As an Archon Star binds the physical body to the gate, an inverted Archon Star binds the gate to the body." She hesitated. "Well, no. That's wrong but close enough for what we're discussing. In essence, it pulls the gate back from the next world and binds your spirit to your gate, returning them to a single whole."

"I don't really understand." She frowned. "And isn't that just what it would do if I swallowed it? What if I tried to use an inverted star to bond with something else?"

Mistress Noelle shrugged. "It's not exactly clear, especially since it's simply not done, so there aren't many subjects to study." The Archon gave Tala a hard look. "Do not experiment with such things. My *guess* would be that it would rip your gate, your soul, from your body and implant you into what you were trying to bond. That would kill your physical body. Best case, you would be a fount inside of whatever you placed that star within, your mind gone, and your spirit in bliss, either in this world or the next."

Tala tried to process that. "And the worst?"

"I won't pretend to know the worst, but *a* worse outcome would be that your cognizant spirit would be trapped inside the intended bound thing, with your gate closed, and an eternity ahead of you, hoping that your prison will one day be destroyed by the inevitable expansion of our local star."

Tala swallowed and cleared her throat. "Well… yeah. I won't try that."

Mistress Noelle snorted. "Good."

"So… what about my inside-out star?"

"Oh, yes. This would create a bond to your soul, just like a regular one, but this would bind to your subconscious mind, primarily, with your conscious mind having to work to get any sort of control or ability to use the item or link."

Tala blinked at the woman a few times. "What?"

Mistress Noelle sighed. "Right now, anything that you've bound to you is consciously connected to you. You could act on it subconsciously with enough training, but it isn't natural. This would make that the natural point of connection. If you ever wanted to consciously decide how you were going to utilize that link, you'd have to train toward that end."

Tala frowned. "Your spores?"

Mistress Noelle waved that off. "Oh, no. That's something else entirely but good memory."

You only said it a couple of hours ago…

"Now, this is an odd case because you'd already bound the blood to yourself with a standard star form, so this inside-out form is simply being housed inside an over-bound vessel."

Rane interjected then, "Wait. Wouldn't a subconscious bond be so much more useful?"

Mistress Noelle gave Rane a long, long look.

He didn't react.

Finally, she shook her head. "Are you in perfect control of your subconscious?"

"Well, of course not."

She nodded, giving him a moment.

"Oh… Well, I mean… That…" He frowned. "So, it's subject to the whole of your subconscious. But for a normal bond, properly trained, it does what you want subconsciously."

"Precisely."

"You could have just said that." He hunched a bit, glowering her way.

She shrugged. "You got there, eventually." After a moment's pause, during which she seemed to be verifying that Rane had no further questions, Noelle turned to Tala. "Now. Tala."

Tala gave her a wary look. "Yes?"

"Blood? What on Zeme possessed you to use blood as a medium?"

Tala sighed. She briefly walked Noelle through her process, how she'd discovered the spellform, and how it just seemed right.

There was a long silence. "Wow… you're lucky I wasn't on your elevation examination council."

Tala frowned. "Why?"

"Because I'd have killed you on the spot."

Flow was in Tala's hand before she had time to fully process that.

Mistress Noelle was holding up her hands. "Hold, hold, Tala. I'm not going to harm you."

Rane had Force in hand, but Tala hadn't seen him draw the weapon. Neither of them set their blades aside, but they allowed the woman to continue.

"That story is suspect as *rust*. If Xeel hadn't already warned me about your potential stalker, I'd assume you were a puppet for some arcane." She hesitated. "Well, being Bound makes that unlikely, and since you're moving toward Fused, it's basically impossible. That said, as a Mage? I'd have to assume that your star would trigger your transformation into an abomination that would take out at least a few Archons before we could put you down." She shrugged.

"That's... kind of horrible."

Mistress Noelle sighed. "I'd have been wrong, but in some cases, it's better to lose one potential Archon than multiple that are already of that stage of advancement. Humanity needs all its Archons and more." She shrugged again. "It's harsh, but there it is."

Tala and Rane both grimaced.

"But I wasn't there, you advanced just fine, and you are clearly an asset to humanity, not a lurking danger." Mistress Noelle smiled at Tala, and Tala felt the implied threat in her bones.

She swallowed involuntarily again and nodded.

"Good. Now, anything else I can do for the two of you?"

As much as they both wanted food, they didn't want to miss this opportunity. As such, they talked through some of their abilities and how they were utilizing them. Mistress Noelle, while obviously powerful, wasn't a front-line fighter like either of them, so she only had general pointers and critiques to offer.

She was able to expand on quite a few of the exercises contained within Soul Work, and once Tala had fully described it, Mistress Noelle was in agreement with

Millennial Mage, 5 - Fusing

Master Jevin about her constellation of protection, should she ever be able to reach that level.

Mistress Noelle did, however, have one laughably obvious suggestion, which left Tala a bit dumbstruck as to why she hadn't thought of it earlier: place the bloodstars within a non-magical item.

A non-magical item couldn't be bound, so the Archon Star wouldn't be used, and having the drops fully, tightly enclosed would mean that her manipulation of the bloodstar would move the item it was embedded within.

Tala eagerly pulled out two tungsten balls, the gravity of which she'd reduced until they were neutrally buoyant or at least close enough.

After all, with the mass I'm mirroring into them, the added weight will be pretty negligible.

"Tungsten?"

Tala nodded to the other woman's question.

"Perfect. Let me see…" Mistress Noelle said while digging through her workshop cabinets. After a few minutes of searching, she exclaimed in triumph and pulled out a strangely shaped, black and orange mushroom.

There were inscriptions set into the fungi's surface and looked as if they might be interwoven within it as well.

Tala was utterly unfamiliar with the medium, so she didn't have a good guess at what it would do.

"This is a tungsten manipulation inscription."

Rane frowned. "That's oddly specific."

Mistress Noelle shrugged. "I try to have basic manipulation items aimed at common materials. With Makinaven so close, tungsten is more common than you might think."

That did make a certain amount of sense.

With a small pulse of power through the copper inscriptions, Mistress Noelle tapped the first of the tungsten balls. The texture changed, seeming almost like putty, and it began to shift.

Working together, Mistress Noelle lengthened the ball into a rod an inch across and a foot long. Together, she and Tala placed two of Tala's bloodstars central to the rod's circumference, at the dividing points that would demarcate the tungsten stick into thirds.

Mistress Noelle then tapped the rod, again, and it looked as it had before in texture.

"What did you do?"

"Made it more malleable and more able to have its bonds and structures rearranged."

"How?"

The woman gave Tala a puzzled look. "Do you really want a lesson in material magic, now?"

"Ahh, right. No. Thank you."

Mistress Noelle shrugged and smiled, turning back to face the other ball.

They then embedded the remaining, non-inside-out bloodstar in a second, neutrally buoyant sphere, leaving that ball in the round shape.

Neither the stick nor the ball was an ideal application of Mistress Noelle's suggestion, but they were ready to hand, easy to implement, and they would allow for the sort of testing that Tala would need to understand the capabilities and limitations of embedding her bloodstars in non-magic items and take the idea further.

These current items would, if nothing else, give her larger surfaces to block with.

Even if Force won't be stopped quite so easily.

Still, if it worked as she hoped, she could utilize something similar in a thousand different ways.

She imagined a shield with three stars embedded in a triangular shape. In theory, she could control it perfectly, and have a shield protecting her blind spots, autonomously.

Well, at least without my hands being required.

Besides, if the idea didn't work, she could always retrieve the drops later.

Her eyes widened. *No! Not a shield, just a triangle of metal that I can then affix to an empowered shield.* A thousand new ideas flickered through her mind, and a grin spread across her face.

"Noelle."

"Yes, Tala?"

"You are amazing. Thank you."

"Of course. I am happy to assist."

* * *

The whole caravan slept soundly that night, safely beside the mushroom town.

Amnin had come through for Rane and Tala the night before, and they hadn't gone to sleep hungry.

The morning was no different, and Tala enjoyed a hearty feast after her morning stretches, exercises, and magical drills.

Mistress Noelle didn't see them off, but her assistant thanked them on her behalf, both for the supplies they'd delivered and for their time in letting her gather data for her research.

All in all, it was a fairly uneventful morning.

As they trundled away, Tala turned to Mistress Odera. "Was the delay just so that we could bring those supplies here?"

Mistress Odera frowned her way. "What?"

"We delayed our departure for nearly a month. Was it just so that we could resupply this place?"

"Oh! Stars, no. This was just a side stop on our way back to Bandfast. The shipment will be passed on from there."

"Any idea what it is?"

The older woman shrugged. "Not particularly."

"Aren't you curious?"

"No. If someone tried to tell me, I wouldn't stop them, but I'm not particularly interested in what sort of bulk goods needed transportation out of the forest."

"That's... fair." She grinned. "Do you have anything specific for me today?"

Mistress Odera cracked an eye, looking at Tala. "What do you plan on doing if I say 'no?'"

Tala pulled out the tungsten ball and rod. "I need to practice manipulating these."

The Mage frowned. "Show me."

Tala shrugged. "Sure."

She extended her aura out a foot from her physical form, then pulled one of the bloodstars in the rod up to a point above her head.

It acted exactly like Tala had expected. The rod had no stability at all, acting like a pendulum and top in one. The bloodstar had no axis stability, and if it had, it was a drop of liquid in a small spherical cavity, within the metal.

Tala then focused on the other bloodstar and pulled. She jerked the rod into a fixed, horizontal position. The motion caused it to start spinning even faster.

Even so, it was where she'd wanted it to be. With practiced effort, she began to move it around herself.

It felt awkward to be seated, so Tala stood and moved through a staff form.

From the outside, Tala would have guessed it looked ridiculous.

Millennial Mage, 5 - Fusing

First of all, she kept her hands tight in front of her chest, while she used her aura and soul pull to manipulate the item.

Second, it was *very* small as a staff.

It was the right diameter but a fifth the length it should be.

Mistress Odera watched with her physical eyes, as well as her extended magesight. In the end, she nodded. "I don't think you'll want to use that as a primary weapon, but if you train to have that sweep your blind spots and the openings created in your own defense when you wield Flow, it could be incredibly effective." She shrugged then, closing her eyes. "But what do I know? I'm not a melee fighter. Keep an eye out and intervene if you feel you could lessen an injury or save a life. Otherwise, you're free to practice as you like."

"Thank you, Mistress."

Tala then set about training.

Apparently, the mushroom-filled section of forest ran more north than south, so they were barely leaving the domain of fungi by the end of the day. By that time, she had the tungsten ball, a bloodstar at its heart, orbiting her just as the naked star had.

The tungsten rod had been much more difficult. She found that with precise tugs on one of the bloodstars, while the other was well controlled, she could spin the rod in defensive twirls that *should* knock away most weapons and lighter attacks. It wouldn't do much against Force, but that was to be expected.

This was a proof of concept, more than anything.

I should ask Rane to spar with me, with a practice weapon. That would let her test out this defense.

Rane should be available after dinner.

The ball, she hadn't found much use for, but she knew that was a temporary thing.

If nothing else, she could pull it to an outer portion of her aura with a flickering powerful pull, then release the action before the ball reached the point of origin. That caused the tungsten to shoot out away from her. It wasn't fast, not really, especially when compared to how fast she could throw the ball, but it didn't take her arm.

Toward that end, she could hold the ball in place with her aura and soul pull and crank its gravitational attraction toward a target up before releasing it.

It was unideal because as its pull increased, so did the strain on her soul, but it did work. *I'll have to try some variations.*

Though, there were likely other issues she wasn't considering.

All in all, as they set up camp for the night, Tala felt that it had been a very productive day.

Chapter: 14
Another Screech

Tala spat out a weird collection of dirt, leaves, and other detritus as she vaulted back to her feet. "You lied to me!"

Rane grinned as he kept his relatively short training sword up and on guard between them. "How so?"

"You're better with a bastard sword than with a greatsword. Why the rust is your main weapon a greatsword?"

"Better reach? Even this has better reach, though." He shrugged. "Skill doesn't come into play as much when fighting beasts, and the greater range is useful. But this?" He nodded her way. "Fighting one on one, skill factors far more."

Tala pulled a stick from her hair, then hesitated, thinking back to his words. "Wait… what is your best weapon?"

He shrugged again. "The one I learned first was a simple club, so I am most experienced with that, at least time-wise. As to my best weapon, skill-wise?"

"Yes." Tala tried not to grit her teeth.

"I think longsword would fit that role." He shrugged. "Swords bigger than that"—he tapped the bastard sword—"like this one and Force, just take a bit of modification to the movements and tactics. Give me a shield and I'm even better." He grinned.

Millennial Mage, 5 - Fusing

Tala took a deep breath and let it out slowly. She was used to losing, but she'd been getting better, improving her form and technique. "So, you're still not using your best weapon."

She'd thought she was catching up to Rane.

She'd been mistaken.

Rane had taken her apart in less than three exchanges in each bout that they'd had that night. More humiliating, however, was that without Force's magics, a single hit wouldn't take her down. Rane had to weave around her defenses, scoring multiple blows before he could gain an opening through which he could trip her up and knock her to the ground.

"You *are* getting better." His tone was sincere enough that she really didn't have much choice but to believe he was being honest.

Tala sighed. "That's kind of you to say, but it feels like a lie."

He shrugged. "Whether or not you believe me, it's true. You even used that rod to block a couple of my attacks." His eyes flicked to the tungsten rod, now orbiting Tala in slow, regular circles. "It is disconcerting to have that thing whipping around you."

Tala had to grin at that. She'd been able to fend him back quite a few times with the unconventional weapon. Without it, the bouts would likely have ended even more quickly. Though, in truth, her use of that extra tool made his victories all the more impressive.

"I have a suggestion, if I may?"

She nodded.

"I think you should practice two-fold. First, we should work with some of the guardsmen who are interested to fine-tune the movement of your defensive bloodstars through the weapon forms you're practicing. Then, that placement can become second nature to you."

Tala found herself nodding. "We'll have to modify them again when I change to more useful items."

Rane shrugged. "It'll be good exercise, either way."

"What's the second aspect?"

"I think you should defend against me with just the rod. No attacking, just watching for my attacks and blocking them."

She thought for a long moment, then nodded. "Yeah, I think that makes sense. It will pair well into the first aspect."

"That was my thinking." He smiled. "Shall we?"

Tala grinned back. "That sounds great. Thank you."

* * *

It was the middle of the night, and Tala was keeping herself awake to be alert on watch for the second half of the night.

She'd used a few different things to accomplish that increasingly difficult task.

The first, and most obvious, was a copious amount of coffee. Irritatingly, now whenever she drank coffee, she saw that horrified healer's face. *I'll cut back soon… when I don't need to stay awake.*

On top of the coffee, she exercised her soul and her magic, alternating and interspersing that with physical exertion to keep herself from falling asleep just because she wasn't moving enough.

Of course, she kept her fusing progressing in the background. She couldn't easily tell how much she had left to fuse, but it was less than when she'd started. *Obviously.*

At the moment, she had expanded her aura in front of herself, covering an almost ten-foot sphere above the wagon top. Within that sphere, she moved through her soul exercises and used them to manipulate Flow and her tungsten rod in a mock duel.

Flow was in the form of a knife, with the training sheath secured in place.

As the two items clashed, Tala was imagining little figures wielding the small weapons in a death battle. Flow was about to defeat Rod once and for all when something tickled her magesight.

Immediately, Flow was in her hand, and her rod was floating behind her, ready to defend. She stood, spinning to face the source of the horribly familiar feeling.

The empowered lights spaced around the caravan's camp cast a large bubble of light, and at the edge of that light, beside a large trunk, stood a small form made of vegetation.

Oh… rust.

"Leshkin!" Tala hissed out the word with enough force that the guardsmen stationed on watch atop the chuckwagon could easily hear her, without it being a shout that would carry into the woods.

One of the guards looked to her as Tala pointed, using that to orient toward the threat.

An instant later, the *twang* of a crossbow announced their response.

Only one? She nodded. *Right, the lesser only take one.*

As the bolt struck home, the tiny creature threw back its head and let out a skin-scraping shriek.

The inscription on the quarrel activated, and the Leshkin puffed into a disconnected cloud of leaves, which tumbled aimlessly before settling to the ground.

Silence fell over the clearing as the creature's scream seemed to echo in Tala's ears long after the origin of the horrible sound was gone.

Don't sigh in relief. In the stories, that's always when the answering cry comes.

One of the guards, Carl, if Tala was seeing and remembering correctly, let out a long breath, and Tala barely was able to hear his words. "That was a close one."

As if in answer, another screech sounded, off in the forest, then a second a bit farther away, then a third farther still.

Tala glared across the distance to the chuckwagon as one of the other guards glared at the offending man. "Rust you, Carl. You just had to say something."

Well, at least I remembered his name correctly.

Carl hunched his shoulders and grimaced. "Sorry. I was just happy the danger seemed to be past."

"Never assume the danger is past, Carl… that kills people."

"Oh, oh, wow, I, uh, I didn't know that…" He then turned and glared. "Is what I would say if I was a superstitious moron! They were out there before I said anything."

The other two guards just shook their heads in mock solemnity. "Take responsibility for your actions, Carl."

Tala barked a laugh, grateful for the breaking of tension. It let her refocus and consider the situation. They likely had incoming enemies. *Prep the caravan for danger.* "Carl!"

The guard spun her way. "Yes, Mistress!"

"Go wake the other Mages and a second unit of the guard."

"Yes, Mistress!" he called back.

Tala checked the time by looking up at a clear patch of sky overhead, toward the east. After a long moment, she grunted and shook her head. *I can't tell anything from that, not at the moment in the least.* "Wake the drivers and cooks, too. We might need to depart quickly."

Millennial Mage, 5 - Fusing

Another set of screeches sounded to the south and east. They were still a ways off, but if Tala had to bet, she'd say they were closer than before.

She swallowed. "And be quick, please. There's a good chance that we might be fighting until we get clear of the forest."

Carl waved in affirmation as he sprinted across their campsite and bolted through the door into the cargo slot in which the caravan personnel were sleeping.

Tala topped off all her items, clipped her sheath to her belt, and called out to her friend. "Terry!"

Terry flickered into being beside her, even as she moved to recharge the cargo slots. *Who knows what the morning will bring.*

"Leshkin may be incoming. Do you want to wait in the cargo slot?"

Terry regarded her for a long moment, then shook himself.

That came as quite the surprise to her, and she frowned. "Really? Are you going to fight?"

He shook himself again, then flickered to her shoulder and head-bumped her cheek.

She had to grin at him as she scratched the back of his head. "You just want to watch out for me, eh?"

He trilled happily.

"Thank you, Terry. I'm glad to have you around."

*   *   *

Tala was in her element.

Flow moved flawlessly through the undisciplined bunches of lesser Leshkin, always in the form most useful at each given moment. Behind her, the caravan retreated at its best pace, making for the edge of the forest to the north.

Her tungsten instruments foiled enemy lunges with inelegant, choppy motions, but they were effective. Only the metal's inherent acid resistance kept the two blunt objects useful as they moved around her while she butchered her opponents.

She even used her inside-out star, spoiling her opponent's steps whenever possible, though it was much less useful in that regard.

She was not practiced in manipulating four bloodstars at a time, so she was bouncing between them as quickly as she could, even while she forced the endingberry power within herself to remain active and at the surface, lessening the injuries she took from claws, teeth, blunt strikes, and acid all. What damage she did take was rapidly healed by her regenerative inscriptions.

Her elk leathers were holding up acceptably, though she was having to top them off a couple of times a minute.

At the moment, the recharging was little more than an occasional, added distraction for her already straining mind.

Difficult as it was, she was loving it.

At her back, a half-unit of guards stood with large shields braced and interlocked against the acid splashes her attacks fostered, sending bolt after bolt in a regular cadence into strategically chosen Leshkin, keeping the pressure off of her as best they could.

They were a stalwart sector of calm that allowed Tala to more efficiently focus on the opponents coming at her from every other direction.

Strangely, the monsters didn't seem interested in getting past Tala, apparently content to throw themselves against her in irregular waves.

A dozen yards to her right and just ahead, Rane fought, supported by the other half of the unit of guards.

The Leshkin would engage with him but only when he attacked them first. Otherwise, they seemed only intent on getting past him to better surround her.

So, they are most likely after me. Were they sweeping the forest this whole time? Did we just get lucky until tonight?

The sky was lightening toward dawn, so she corrected. *Lucky 'til last night.*

The caravan had packed up, geared up, and begun its retreat behind their defensive line.

There had been brief talk of pulling everyone in close and having Mistress Odera put up a shield against the Leshkin, but it was agreed that that would not end well.

They had more than a day's travel left before they exited the forest, and there were *far* more Leshkin this time than the two Juggernauts they'd resisted before.

The strain would pop their defenses far before they were in the clear.

So far, most were lessers, but a few warriors and knights were beginning to appear among the weaker foes.

Tala and the rest of the caravan were, effectively, executing a fighting retreat, one step at a time.

A second unit of guards waited a hundred feet back or so, mounted and with spare mounts for all those currently engaged in the active defense. They were also armed with crossbows and shields, though they would have a hard time utilizing the hooks on their belt to re-cock the weapons while on horseback.

The mounted guards also had the standard spears as well, which they would use if they had to act as a relieving force, but that wasn't their current role.

One of Rane's guards took an acid splash to the face and fell back, screaming.

Three mounted guards swept forward, one dismounting to take the injured man's place, while the other two helped that burned man up on the recently vacated horse and rode with him back to the caravan for immediate healing.

Redundancy and keeping the injured out of the fight. It was a good task for them and kept Tala and Rane from worrying about the mundanes with them. Mistress Odera could have the man back, ready to fight once more, in a matter of minutes.

As she continued to fight, she again noted that there wasn't an endless, never-ending tide of Leshkin.

They came in groups and packs with seemingly randomly varied spacing, which gave Tala and Rane time to move backwards to keep pace with the retreating wagons.

And while this was absolutely fantastic practice for virtually every one of her techniques, she had a feeling that it was going to be a *very* long day.

* * *

Tala was exhausted.
Cut, duck, kick a Leshkin back.
Acid rolled across her skin, cutting caustic lines in her elk leathers, even as it repaired itself. Tala maintained two void-channels to the garments, praying that it would be enough to keep them from being overwhelmed.

The caravan was still retreating behind their backs as monsters swarmed up from the south in an unending tide.

She needed a break, or she was going to make a mistake and be overwhelmed. Thankfully, they'd set up a short command phrase for her to indicate such a need. "Stepping back!"

She'd heard Rane use it several times already, and it worked just as well for her as it had for him.

Millennial Mage, 5 - Fusing

The guards behind her surged forward, moving around her to plant their shields between her and the next batch of Leshkin, short swords drawn to replace their crossbows as they hacked the Leshkin back.

Some of the mounted guards came forward to use their spears to reinforce those on the ground.

Tala took deep breaths, using the moment to guzzle the rest of the endingberry juice from her flask, followed by water from her incorporator and jerky straight from Kit.

Terry was perched on the back of the chuckwagon, eyes watching her intently across the distance. He'd not interfered at all throughout the long morning, but there hadn't been a need.

Now that noon had come and gone, even Tala's high endurance was reaching its end.

Rane had cycled out a few times already, though he was back in the fight at the moment.

The guard units were switching out every half-hour or so. That let them rest for the majority of the time. Though, that rest included a stint as the mounted backup and another as the crossbowmen on the wagon roofs.

It's alright for me to take a breather. I've earned it, I think.

Tala had been out of the fight for less than a minute, when the Leshkin swept around the guards, ignoring them almost completely to rush at her. The horses of the mounted guards shied back despite their combat training.

After all, anything got a bit skittish when a tree came for it.

Tala grunted around the jerky. *Well, that settles it.*

There was no longer any doubt that they were targeting her. *Even after more than a month, they remember me...*

There had been countless paths to go around her and those fighting with her, but the Leshkin had largely ignored the potential.

Now that she wasn't on the front line, they were bypassing those who were, making it laughably obvious that only their obsession with her was keeping the creatures from catching the caravan.

Tala cursed, swallowing and pulling Flow back into her hands in the form of a glaive to cut across the necks of those rushing her with animalistic intensity.

The jerky lodged in her throat.

Chaos reigned.

Even as Tala gagged on the improperly chewed jerky, her attack killed four Leshkin but also sent a spray of acid at the backs of the guards who had relieved her.

Their armor protected them to some extent, but the damage was still done.

Tala had to briefly bend over, hacking to clear her throat.

The creatures still facing the guardsmen's shields were able to batter through the suddenly agonized defenders, and Tala's desperately-needed break became a desperate situation of an entirely different kind.

No. Now able to breathe again, she didn't let herself freeze as the men and women who'd been fighting beside her were taken to the ground.

Tala lunged forward, accepting slashing cuts to draw closer, slaying as many as she could, while she tried to cover the mere feet between her and the falling guards.

A Leshkin that she couldn't counter without slowing down latched its wicked fangs into her left shoulder. Its claws sunk into her side and leg as it whipped its head back and forth like a dog with a bone.

Tala screamed in rage and pain as she stretched over and drove Flow down, through the top of its head. As she struck, Flow changed from a knife to a sword, allowing for a strike that she couldn't have easily accomplished with any other weapon.

Millennial Mage, 5 - Fusing

With a twist and forwards sweep, Tala ripped the Leshkin open sufficiently to end this vessel's life.

The thorns of its being still clung to her, making her inscriptions struggle to push out the invading material and close the wounds.

But her mind was on the five figures just before her.

She swept low with her tungsten rod, aiming to knock the Leshkin from atop the bodies on the ground.

She mainly succeeded, though it put a great strain on her soul to do so.

She was scraping the bottom of her reserves.

Putting most of her weight on her uninjured leg, Tala took up a firm stance before the guards on the ground, her every trick coming to bear. Thankfully, both her legs would soon be effectively undamaged.

As a group of Leshkin knights came into view, rushing her, she dropped all three with *Crush*. It took two rings each. They were blessedly much weaker than the juggernauts that they could meld into.

The warriors were too numerous for her to use that limited casting on them, but she still tried messing with their effective gravity.

She found that reducing their gravity really didn't do much as they could use the vegetation in their feet to grip the ground and move with very little difference. It didn't even take them that much time to adjust.

Making them heavier, however, caused stumbling and eventual destruction, but that took nearly thirty seconds to achieve. So, she targeted those the farthest away, trying to bring them down before they could reinforce those she was actively engaging with Flow and tungsten.

Blessedly, the steady *thwack* of quarrels into the swarm of Leshkin let her know that she hadn't been abandoned. *Not that they could let me go that easily.*

Mistress Odera's voice came to her, then. "Retreat, Mistress Tala. We must risk a shielded retreat. I am preparing now. Master Rane and his guards are already moving this way."

Tala glanced down and back at the guards still on the ground. They weren't moving much, but she could see evidence of life, still, despite the blood and acid liberally speckled around them. *You know, some of that is definitely mine...* "No, not without them."

She felt herself settle in, firm in her resolve. *I will not leave them behind.*

Chapter: 15
A Long, Long Day

Tala was completely surrounded, barely fending off the Leshkin that swarmed around her.

However, swarmed wasn't exactly accurate. They were like a pack of dogs, circling and lunging at her whenever they thought they perceived an opening. The empty eyes of the lessers, fixed on her with a cold detachment, added a creepiness to the situation, underlying the terror and desperation that Tala already felt. She'd been able to keep her focus off their eyes for most of the battle, but now, surrounded and almost entirely on her own, she couldn't, not any longer.

Even saying that she was fending them off was not accurate. She wasn't fending them off, not in the individual sense like keeping back a lion with a whip. She was slaughtering them by the dozen, creating an ever-rising low barrier of plant matter around her self-assigned charges while she danced around the group, killing the vicious plant people that just kept coming.

After a heavy, near silence that had extended for what felt like an eternity, Mistress Odera's voice finally replied. "Advance into their attack, so that we can get the wounded with less interference. Be ready to retreat when I say."

Hah, I knew she could hear me. The thought was fleeting across her exhausted mind. "Agreed."

Millennial Mage, 5 - Fusing

The quarrels buzzing overhead increased in quantity for a short space of time, opening a hole for Tala to move deeper into the Leshkin tide.

With another curse, this time for luck, Tala lunged into that opening and away from the humans on the ground.

From what little she could see, the Leshkin pursued her, ignoring the guards as they passed over them.

Alright, now to survive.

One of the warriors must have seen her glance and intuited something of her priorities, because it disengaged, moving back toward the downed guards.

Growling, Tala threw one of the prison darts at its retreating form, and after hearing a satisfying *thunk*, she dove away, deeper into the Leshkin ranks.

The Leshkin warrior screeched in confusion as it moved backwards, even as it continued to try to run forward.

Tala laughed, her exhaustion continuing to cloud her mind.

Flow was moving in constant, looping circles by that point. She no longer had a wall of safety, in the form of guards. That had allowed her to focus her efforts and maintain a modicum of control over her surroundings. It had been a great strategy, which she'd used for the whole of the day so far. It was no longer an option.

Now, she was a solitary island of humanity in the middle of a frenzy of inhuman monsters.

Breathe. Strike, block, dodge. *Focus.*

As she fought, she became one with Flow to an extent that she'd never achieved before.

As a glaive, Flow decapitated three lessers with its blade, then struck a knight that she hadn't seen approaching before that moment, driving it back with the butt of the staff.

As a sword, the weapon lashed out to either side, taking eyes and driving life from these temporary forms as Tala advanced on the knight that was still stumbling backwards.

Right hand raised in a familiar gesture, Flow striking out, gripped in her left hand, Tala forced *Crush* to latch onto four other knights, driving them to the ground, then squashing them to sappy paste.

As a knife, Flow drilled into the still-stumbling Leshkin knight almost as fast as a sewing machine's needle, stitching a path of holes from its groin to its all-too-human, rage-filled face, completely ignoring the wooden armor along the way.

That knight burst apart.

Good to know, sufficient punctures can end them, too.

A circular sweep of her glaive gave Tala a bit more space, enough to see a juggernaut coming in the distance.

Flow moved to her left hand as her right hand came up, her arm extended, her palm out. Her first two fingers were pointing toward the sky, the second two bent down. All four fingers and thumb were tucked close together. The target was acquired. *Crush.*

The juggernaut was being dispatched, but it had cost her a moment's concentration, leaving her defenses imperfect.

Even as her rod swept aside a pair of Leshkin swords, and her sphere knocked a lesser back with a hit to its sternum, a spear drove through Tala's low back.

Flow swept around, severing the offending weapon, even as Tala dropped to a knee, a cry of pain ringing through the forest and easily heard over the rustle of foliage and periodic Leshkin screeches.

Terry flickered into being behind her, gripping the spear with his beak and ripping it free to drop to the forest floor before he vanished once more.

Millennial Mage, 5 - Fusing

Tala gasped, spinning to decapitate the monsters who had swung for Terry and been unbalanced by his quick disappearance.

Her flesh was already pulling back together, but the echoes of pain were building. The endingberry power merely mitigated injury in this fight with the Leshkin, when it would have negated it against any other foe. The power was anything but ideal under these circumstances, but it was enough to keep her limbs attached and her life her own, at least for the moment.

"Mistress Tala, retreat. We've got them." The Mage's voice was clear in her ears, and it caused relief to wash through her. *One task left.*

Tala didn't argue, turning on her heels and advancing back the way that she had come.

The caravan was quite a ways away by that point, but Tala could make it. *I have to make it.*

She cut a path free of the closest press of Leshkin and began sprinting. There were no signs of the fallen guards, so she was reasonably certain that they had, in fact, been retrieved.

Remembering her last fights with the Leshkin, she took her anchor into her left hand and Flow in sword shape into her right, even as she kept moving.

True to form, a juggernaut tried to take her from the side, this time erupting as if from the ground to her right.

Tala *pulled* with all her soul's might and managed to get her tungsten rod and ball between herself and the two-fisted punch barely in time, mirroring her mass onto the three bloodstars within.

They were driven back past her, stealing much of the viciousness from the attack.

Even so, when the fists hit her, one in the shoulder, one in the hip, the impact made her bones creak.

The blow had the entire force of the juggernaut behind it, its massive body uncoiling to continually add power behind its fists.

She dropped her anchor, even as she was launched up and back.

She stalled out in the air ten feet from the anchor as it bounced to the forest floor.

Looking down, she saw the Leshkin warrior that she'd darted earlier, stumbling around, clearly disoriented.

In that moment of clarity and understanding, she almost laughed. *I've been dragging that fellow around all over the place.*

As her momentum began to run out, she enacted *Crush* on the juggernaut still so close to her.

Two rings had burned away to empower that effect when she came back to the ground, landing beside the warrior.

Flow took its head, and Tala caught the falling dart from among the newly created detritus.

The juggernaut, for its part, was kneeling over her, struggling to adjust to the increased gravity as another ring burned away from her right hand, slamming the creature into the ground.

As before, the giant wasn't disabled completely by three rings worth of power, and this one used its remaining mobility to burst into two knights, breaking her lock and freeing it of her spell-working.

Tala cursed. *Great. They're learning.*

Still, she was able to dive between the two new knights, snatching up her anchor and continuing her sprint toward the caravan.

With every unit of guards active, and Tala, herself, now finally in clear view, a veritable cloud of bolts whistled around and past her, sinking into the Leshkin behind her as she ran the final stretch to slap into the back of the chuckwagon.

"She's here!" a guard on the wagon top called unnecessarily.

A fully enclosing version of Mistress Odera's signature shield blossomed into being around the caravan, sealing the humans away from their attackers, at least for the moment.

It was a long moment before Tala caught her breath sufficiently to push herself up off the chuckwagon's rear step, where she'd collapsed after her desperate sprint.

I made it. She grinned openly. *I did it!*

She'd had help, of course, but no one had had to come rescue her. She'd made good, wise use of her powers, and she'd protected others besides.

The guards. She immediately called up to a guard on the top of the chuckwagon.

She informed Tala that the injured were being tended to in the cargo slot where the caravan personnel were quartered.

After thanking the woman, Tala walked quickly to the cargo wagon and pulled herself up onto the step before opening the door and striding inside.

She found her destination with ease, after a brief search, and Tala talked in a quiet voice with the servant who'd been put in charge of overseeing the injured guards.

While Tala had still been fighting the Leshkin, Mistress Odera had been able to see to the worst injuries and stabilize those who had made it to her. Among them were the guards that Tala had stood over, defending with her body as much as her blade and spell-workings.

Unfortunately, the guards' injuries had been too severe for a quick heal. It had been to the point that even with Mistress Odera's healing, they would be on bed rest until the caravan reached Bandfast. Still, they would all survive.

All five are alive and will be whole. Tala smiled triumphantly at that.

The servant assured her that she would see to it that the needs of the injured were met and that they were kept as comfortable as possible for the remainder of the voyage.

With that reassurance, Tala thanked the servant and left her to her work.

I need to see what's happening with the defense.

As Tala opened the door and stepped back outside, the strangely reverberatory sound echoed between the wagons and penetrated the space around her.

It was immediately stressful, announcing each Leshkin attack. That was compounded by the fact that such attacks happened at least every second or so. *I need to see what's going on.*

Rane was coming down the ladder as she came out of the cargo slot, in her way if she was to get to the cargo wagon's roof.

There was concern in his voice as he met her gaze. "You look whole. Are you okay?"

Tala nodded, her triumphant smile now a small, tired thing. "I am, thank you. What about you?"

Rane grimaced. "I was useless out there. They never wanted to truly engage me. I felt like I was chopping at a river, trying to change its course."

Tala snorted a laugh. "You did help, I promise you that. And even with your help, I was dancing the edge, there, for a bit. I don't want to imagine what it would have been like without you."

That thought reminded her of her spent castings. She glanced down at her right hand and grimaced. *Twenty-one. I used twenty-one rings to enact Crush.* She only had nine iterations left.

Millennial Mage, 5 - Fusing

I'm going to be so glad to change over to the passive gravity manipulation, across the board. She still needed to address the great strain placed on that inscription set by fast enactment, but there was potential there, to say the least.

Rane clapped her on the shoulder. "You did fantastically. I imagine you're hungry?"

She nodded. "Famished."

With a sly grin, he nodded. "I'll get the cooks to start bringing you food. You tell them when you've had enough, alright?"

She smiled gratefully at that. "That sounds wonderful."

"You'll be up top?" He indicated the direction he'd just come from.

"That's the plan."

He nodded and left, another smile obvious across his features.

As Rane dropped off the side of the wagon, down onto the little ground beside the vehicle, inside the bubble, Tala swung out and climbed up the ladder.

In the center of the roof, Mistress Odera sat cross-legged, sweating despite the cool winter air. Her eyes were closed but not clenched shut. Her breathing was regular and deep, but even still, her effort was obvious.

The oblong bubble surrounding the caravan moved with them through the forest at a steady clip, a testament to the woman's power and experience.

The drivers were spurring the oxen on as quickly as the beasts could safely move. *We might make it, yet.*

Tala turned her gaze outward and felt herself pale.

They were surrounded by juggernauts, moving along with them through the woods.

As the wagons advanced, the juggernauts in front of them were nudged backwards at a slow walk for their massive frames. Even so, they attacked relentlessly with myriad weapons.

A great club user stood beside a Leshkin wielding a sword and shield. Another struck with a greatsword that put Force to shame, if only in its sheer size. A warhammer added its strikes beside a war-pick as well as a long spear. And on and on the variety went; short spear and shield, axe with reverse spike, maul, and others that were too obscured to make out clearly.

If Tala was counting correctly, and that was in doubt due to the constant ripples across the shield's surface, there were at least ten of the giants, maybe as many as fourteen.

Tala cracked her knuckles. "Time to do this right." She was still mildly embarrassed that she hadn't dealt with the last two juggernauts on the last leg of their voyage to Makinaven. *I'll correct that, now.*

Her thumb and middle finger came together, and she immediately targeted the two most forward of their advance, ramping up their gravity as quickly as she could without using the *Crush* mental constructs. She didn't want to burn out her inscriptions from the strain.

Unfortunately, the last one she'd dealt, the one that had split into two knights to foil her spell-working, wasn't an outlier, and they were showing their cleverness.

As soon as their gravity was altered sufficiently to be noticed, the two juggernauts cracked apart into knights, breaking her lock and spoiling the working before they faded from view.

Cursing them, she, nonetheless, immediately targeted two more juggernauts, ramping up their gravity as well. Before that reached inconvenient levels for the creatures, two more juggernauts returned to the front of the shield, renewing the attack. These wielded polearms of differing kinds.

Millennial Mage, 5 - Fusing

She couldn't tell if the new arrivals were completely new juggernauts, taking the place of the departed, or a new combination of the same knights. *No, they couldn't be a recombination, that is much too quick for that.*

It was disheartening to see her enemies replaced so quickly, but still, she persisted, attempting to relieve some of the strain on the shield for Mistress Odera.

Over the next half-hour, Tala tried all sorts of things to get around their new understanding of her magics, but nothing worked.

Each juggernaut that she forced to split was replaced shortly thereafter, and the weaponry they used continued to alter, covering the gamut from dual daggers to one with a war scythe. If anything, they seemed to be testing if any given weapon affected the shield more easily.

Blessedly, that didn't seem to be the case, and the shield held.

Even so, there was just no end to them.

Do they have that many? Or were they recombining, somehow? *We are surrounded by great trees...* It was most likely a combination of having juggernauts in reserve and the knights going to recombine and then returning.

In the end, she was sure that the majority of the juggernauts attacking the shield were, in fact, just recombinations of those she'd previously forced to disassociate.

To her horror, as she became better at identifying the individual Leshkin, she became increasingly certain that at least some of those that now harassed them were ones that she'd slain that morning.

Is a spawning ground that close? Are some of their heartseeds that close? It was a disheartening thought. *Even if I do kill them, they'll just return in short order.*

She had a brief desire to strike out and hunt down whatever hiding place contained the heartseeds so near to hand, but that would be colossally foolish, so she squashed that desire for the time being.

Finally, she had to admit defeat. At this point, she was just wasting inscriptions. So, with a growl of irritation, she stopped trying.

As she'd been trying to contribute, even while being carted along, the cooks had been bringing her a feast's worth of food, even by Tala's standards. That meant that it would have normally counted as a feast for a small family. The deliveries of sustenance continued, even now that she'd stopped working with her gravity manipulation.

She had done a *lot* of self-healing throughout the morning, even despite her defenses, and that had put an incredible strain on her body, inscriptions, and reserves. Thus, even as she continued to devour the food, she could feel a vortex of her power breaking the food down in her gut and shunting the nutrients and energy outwards to refill her reserves and help return her to top form.

Between bites, she topped off each of her bound items, even refilling Terry's collar despite it not really needing it. Still, the act allowed her to have the terror bird near, and that gave her some additional comfort.

After that was done, she recharged the cargo slots, just in case. *Who knows what the rest of the day will bring?*

Beyond that, she made a note to refill them as often as reasonable, probably every half-hour to hour.

It is going to be a long, long day.

Chapter: 16
Particularly Pernicious

Tala was surprisingly well-rested, despite the stressful circumstances.

The long day had turned into a long night, but everyone aside from Mistress Odera and the drivers had gotten more than a full night's sleep, at the Mage's insistence. Even the drivers had been switched out to get the rest that they needed, even if less than would have been ideal.

As morning passed and drew ever closer to noon, Tala knew that Mistress Odera couldn't hold on much longer. They still weren't out of the forest despite their best efforts, and even if they did make it before the Mage had to drop her shield, it would be a near thing.

They really couldn't risk that disaster. Normally, Tala would have left the dealing of the issue to others, but Tala wasn't willing to risk that either.

What would Mistress Odera do if our positions were reversed? Tala looked around at their caravan, the guards, their crossbows, and the surrounding Leshkin, barely obscured by the rippling, blue-tinted shield. After a moment's thought, a grin spread over her face, the seed of an idea manifesting. *That just might work.*

The nugget of inspiration firmly in mind, she went to talk with Rane and the Guard Captain. Thankfully, her idea was simple enough that they readily agreed, helping to fill in the details and preparing for the fight to come.

Millennial Mage, 5 - Fusing

It wasn't a truly new idea. In fact, if Mistress Odera's shield had been easier to drop and re-raise, they likely would have been doing something similar all along. *Well, that and if they could be sure the Leshkin wouldn't just return in short order.*

By the time the sun was directly overhead, and Mistress Odera was swaying, all preparations were in place for the bursting of the bubble.

The older woman's voice came to Tala's ear. "I can only hold on for another minute or so, Mistress Tala, prepare."

Tala nodded. "Already done." She looked to the crossbowmen crowding the wagon top. "Soon, now."

They fell into position, the front-rank kneeling and the second rank moving up to stand right behind them.

Each guard had a pre-cocked and loaded crossbow ready to hand, in addition to the one in their hands, and they each had a primary and secondary target preselected and assigned.

They each also had anti-Leshkin spears and broad shields arranged on the wagon top within easy reach.

The chuckwagon had a similar complement of ready guards. Rane stood at the back edge of that wagon top, ready to take out his assigned targets and then engage any surviving enemies as needed.

He also had his massive harvest bag slung over one shoulder. If the opportunity presented itself, he was going to grab as much as he could from the Leshkin juggernauts.

The drum-like reverberations of impacts to their shield continued unabated, their enemy either unaware, or uncaring, that the situation was about to change.

As Tala did one more sweep of their surroundings, focusing to see through the active shield the best that she was able, she caught a glimpse of something glimmering ahead of them. She looked closer, her eyes starting to ache from the strain. *Sunlit grass?*

"We're almost to the edge of the forest!" She glanced to Tion. "Plan B." Plan A had assumed they'd need to continue at a steady pace for an unknown length of time.

The driver nodded her way in acknowledgment. Under Plan B, he would force the oxen to their top speed—something they couldn't maintain for very long.

They'd have to rest a short way into the plains, but they would be free of the forest. *Finally, blessedly free.*

There was also a danger that the mass of their magic going faster than recommended would draw down a creature of magic on them, but they'd agreed that the small chance of that was an acceptable risk.

Mistress Odera started to cough. "I'm sorry. That's all I have." Her eyes snapped open, but they were blank, the woman already unconscious.

As the Mage tumbled backwards, a ready and waiting servant caught her and lowered her gently down on a pad behind her.

The magical, bubble-like shield burst, and Tala yelled, "Fire!"

The simultaneous *click*, *twang* of so many crossbows was almost deafeningly loud. The almost instantaneous responding wet *thunk* of the bolts striking home in Leshkin foliage brought an irresistible smile to Tala's face.

Leshkin weapons swept through the open air, and the giants found themselves unbalanced as their intended attacks on the shield protecting their prey was suddenly met with no resistance.

Rane lunged off the back of the chuckwagon, even as the vehicles picked up speed.

Since each juggernaut took eight bolts to be overwhelmed by the inscriptions, the first volley only dropped five of the mammoth creatures. Each guard let their fired crossbow fall to catch on its strap as they raised their second weapon.

"Aim!" After a single, quick breath, during which Tala ensured all the guards were ready, she bellowed, "Fire!"

A second, slightly less unified wave of bolts took down five more juggernauts.

Rane, still airborne from his powerful leap, swept Force in a precise arc, beheading two juggernauts, something he could never have done from the ground.

Twelve down. Her gaze searched the dimly lit terrain around them, searching for the remaining opponents.

The guards reloaded and fired as quickly as they were able, falling into the second phase of Tala's plan, even as Rane verified that no Leshkin that he needed to deal with were close and pulled on his big-game harvest bag, scooping up the first two piles of Leshkin remnants, securing the juggernauts' armor and weapons, along with the guard's bolts within the piles of vegetation that used to be their attackers. They'd get rid of the plant matter when they had more time.

Tala had finished her quick sweep of the battlefield. They were surrounded by a small army, mostly knights, but a few more juggernauts were beginning their charge forwards. In the distance, she *thought* she saw more movement, but it was far enough away, and there were sufficient enemies close at hand, that she filed the sight away as non-critical.

Tala lifted her right hand, two fingers to the sky, and locked onto the closest two juggernauts. The two that were about to slam their weapons into the back of the chuckwagon.

The two that Rane had trusted to her care. A smile tugged at her lips.

These two were hers, now. *Crush.*

The automatic compounding was too slow, so she triggered the ability manually, again. *Crush.*

She couldn't let them break apart and ruin her casting. *Crush.*

She *would* ensure her magics took their toll. *Crush.*

The four near-instantaneous castings on two targets tore away eight of her remaining nine rings and obliterated the two Leshkin she'd targeted, sending their spirits off to respawn as effectively as the enchanted bolts would have.

The timing was such that Rane was able to scoop up the remains of those two next before he continued around the caravan to gather what he could.

The guards were sending a steady spray of quarrels outward into the surrounding knights. They were working in blocks to select targets and bring them down with systematic efficiency. So, even with a requirement of four bolts per Leshkin of that form, the plant bodied-creatures fell in droves.

Tala verified that their path was relatively clear ahead, and the guards with good line of sight in that direction were ensuring that the few Leshkin in the path of the wagons' headlong rush were primary targets.

Rane had finished his harvesting frenzy and was engaging any Leshkin group that seemed in danger of drawing too close.

She let out a long breath, allowing her tension to ease, if just slightly. *This is working. We're doing it!*

Overhead, one of the massive, far-reaching branches creaked and swayed, causing the light filtering down to flicker and move oddly.

Tala looked up in time to see a tide of humanoid vegetation dropping toward their heads like a massive stalactite of death.

Millennial Mage, 5 - Fusing

"Above!" *Rust you, Tala, you had to ruin it, thinking we were in the clear.*

The back line of guards immediately bent down to grab spear and shield, rushing to raise them against the new avenue of assault.

On pure instinct, Tala lifted her right hand, locking onto one of the foremost Leshkin, an ax-wielding knight that was almost directly overhead. *Restrain.*

Her final golden ring burned away, and her working stole the Leshkin's kinetic energy, jerking it to a halt, midair. That energy was then repurposed to calculate and apply the exact level of gravity necessary to maintain that beast's current position as a stable orbit.

The knight was still for only an instant before those behind it began to slam into and bounce off it. Since the magics were still at work, continuing to drain away its kinetic energy to feed the working, fighting to set the Leshkin into a fixed position, it wasn't forced downward just yet, despite the cascade of bodies ramming into it.

The actual effect was to cause something comically similar to inserting a spoon into a stream of water as each knight tumbled into those next to it.

The net effect was to prevent any from landing directly on the cargo wagon's roof.

The chuckwagon was not so lucky.

If only I'd still had another casting. Another idea came to her, then, and she began delving through her seemingly useless *Crush* and *Restrain* scriptings. *Maybe...*

Thankfully, that roof had a larger complement of guards, given that they'd not had to leave room for Mistress Odera or the servant meant to care for her. The Leshkin landing there were met with an interlocking platform of shields, bristling with inscribed spears.

Even so, the impact bowed the defenses, and one of the crossbowmen was pushed off the side of the roof by the pressure of the inner guards having to bend down under the impacts.

Another guard, Carl, shouted in alarm, lunging outward to snag the flailing woman and throw her back.

Unfortunately, that meant that he was now falling in her stead.

Tala watched in horror as Carl slammed into the ground, all the breath seemingly driven from him.

The woman he'd saved spun, reloading her crossbow and rallying her block to target the Leshkin bearing down on Carl, even as they crouched under the shields held aloft by their brethren.

The crossbowmen on the cargo wagon facing the other vehicle focused on the enemies that had survived atop the bristling defense. There was a worrying number, even so. For the moment, they were held up on well-braced shields, but that couldn't last—as Carl's situation clearly demonstrated.

The wagons were continuing at their rapid pace, almost as fast as Tala would have jogged, and Carl would soon be left behind.

Tala had a moment to consider before she cursed and jumped free of her wagon, giving a screech that was as close to a Leshkin's cry as a human could produce.

Every enemy head snapped to orient toward her.

Initially, this allowed the guards to continue reaping their vegetative harvest, but as Tala landed in a roll, the true result quickly became clear.

Answering screams assaulted the humans, disorienting most of the guards and even breaking some eardrums.

Every Leshkin turned fully toward her and *moved.*

Some simply ran, others launched themselves in her direction, and they all maintained a lock on her, the best that they could. They still struck at the guards near them.

Millennial Mage, 5 - Fusing

Tala staggered; the inscriptions surrounding her ears protected her from direct damage, but the sound was still startling enough that it fouled her footing for a step. In the end, she came out just a bit better than the average guard.

She couldn't see what had become of Carl, but she had other things that were far more pressing for her at the moment.

She dove to the side, avoiding a pouncing cluster of knights, and as she came to her feet, she saw the sheer magnitude of what she was facing.

Well... rust.

There were at least a hundred knights and three juggernauts that she could see easily, all incoming.

I can't outrun that; I certainly can't fight through it. She had an instant of panic, then a calm washed over her, and she knew what she needed to do.

After only a moment's hesitation, Tala turned, unclipping her anchor, and threw the empowered device with all of her considerable might.

She'd aimed carefully between trees to the northeast, away from the heading of the caravan but still closer to the edge of the forest.

I hope. It wasn't like the forest ended on a perfect latitude line.

In a nauseating blur, she streaked through the trees. More than anything, it felt like falling in a twisting, nauseating tumble. She slammed into the ground, coming to a stop at least a hundred yards from the caravan.

I gained downward velocity through the whole of the Anchor's arc? That did make a sort of sense, she supposed.

Unfortunately, her desperate thinking wasn't enough to distract her body from what had just transpired. Tala violently tried to vomit but was prevented by her inscriptions.

It felt akin to someone preventing her from inhaling toxic fumes by punching her in the throat; it was *probably* better than the alternative, but the difference might well just be academic.

Leshkin cries of rage sounded behind her, and she screeched back, around her dry heaving, afraid that they would reorient on the caravan with her suddenly farther away.

She turned to glance over her shoulder, her entire body shuddering at the repressed expulsions, and discovered her fears were unfounded.

The enemy was in hot pursuit.

Of all things, it almost looked like the juggernauts were picking up knights.

No. Her eyes widened as the first massive Leshkin cocked back to throw its payload.

Terry flickered into being beside her, sized for riding. He trilled, nudging her with his head, trying to help her stand.

Tala felt herself laughing manically as she quickly snapped up her anchor from the ground, where it had fallen, and clipped it to Terry's collar. She hopped on his back as the first knight crashed into the ground beside her, pulverized into near dissolution.

Unfortunately, they had enough latent power to pull back together and lunge toward Terry and Tala.

The avian ducked under the first attack and shot off into the woods, Tala tucking down against his neck.

"Go north! Terry, where are you going?" She started patting his neck, trying to get his attention as if he wasn't well aware of her and where she was.

Terry squawked back at her, and she looked behind just in time to see a series of seven knights crash across what would have been their clearest path to the north.

Millennial Mage, 5 - Fusing

I didn't see those incoming. They likely would have slammed right into us, if we'd gone north. She briefly considered using her gravity alteration inscriptions on their pursuers but knew that they wouldn't be useful. *Best case, I'd increase the number of enemies trailing us, even if it did mean they were weaker as individuals.*

There had apparently been flanking forces of Leshkin lessers moving through the forest parallel to the caravans, and they were now screening off easy escape.

Oh, that's the distant movement I saw… Yay me? She growled.

Well, at least the caravan will get free. They're probably close enough to Bandfast that they might make it with an hour or two to unload if they're quick about it and don't stop to rest. She found herself unsurprisingly at peace with the idea of dying to let the caravan survive.

She didn't *want* to die, but she didn't find that she was really mad about it either. *Huh, I suppose that's progress? I* actually *don't* want to die.

Terry, for his part, was showing how he'd survived for so long.

He darted around trees, even using his massively powerful legs to run up trees a good way before vaulting off to clear groups of incoming Leshkin.

Tala had Flow in hand, lashing out at any enemies who drew within striking distance of any of its forms. Though she didn't have training in mounted combat, Tala was able to move Flow through the more maneuverable shapes, allowing her to reposition her weapon with ease to strike in almost any direction.

Her tungsten rod and sphere were likewise moving around her to foil enemy advances, but she wasn't nearly as effective with them as they were still new tools in her arsenal.

She made a mental note to add mounted combat to the list of things to work on if she survived.

You know, I can definitely imagine burning all these rusting tree people. Maybe I should try to get some fire inscriptions... She then immediately threw the idea aside. Fire was too hard to control properly. It was sloppy and weirdly weaker than she'd have assumed or wished.

She still remembered an odd demonstration where a Mage at the academy had turned a powerful flame on a block of ice.

Tala, young and naïve, had expected the ice to flash boil in a glorious explosion. Young Tala had wanted to burn things, allowing the fantasies of such to drive her toward understanding her keystone. After all, only after the keystone was complete could she get other magics.

But her hopes were crushed that day. Sure, the ice lost in the end, but it took *hours* to melt down that person-sized block of ice.

That particular lesson had been focusing on something about heat capacity, but what young Tala had taken from the instruction was that fire was lame.

It would have been like watching a bunch of guards struggle to overcome a mundane rabbit: disgustingly disappointing.

Terry lunged to the right, pulling Tala's focus back to the present.

Flow, in the shape of a glaive, cut down a particularly pernicious lesser Leshkin, and they were suddenly in the clear—at least with regard to enemies.

They were, however, once again deep into the forest.

The Leshkin were still close on their heels, but Terry could outrun them in a race.

They were in the clear.

Tala grinned in relief.

Millennial Mage, 5 - Fusing

Just then, a whip, skillfully wielded by a juggernaut, cracked out, wrapping around her waist and jerking her from Terry's back.

She had one thought as her grip was broken and she lost her seat atop her avian friend.

You just couldn't have rusting waited to celebrate, could you…

Chapter: 17
Restraining Crush

Tala continued cursing herself as she was whipped backwards.

She did, however, pause her inner tirade for an instant chuckle. *Ha, 'whipped backwards.' Because I'm being pulled by a whip.*

She jerked to a stop and back to the matter at hand, immediately moving forward after Terry, her anchor preventing her from getting any farther from her partner's collar and the dimensional anchor affixed there.

The strain was too great on the juggernaut's weapon, and the woven length of vines frayed and shattered behind her, just leaving the length wrapped around her waist.

Tala, once again, slammed into the ground face-first, her mind overcome with nausea.

Terry trilled, and Tala's enhanced hearing heard him slide to a halt and juke back her way.

Because of that, her dimensional sliding came to a quick end.

That was… unideal.

Even so, she still had enemies bearing down upon her from behind. She needed to keep moving.

With a great effort of will, she pushed herself back up to stand on her own two feet, or at least, she tried.

The portion of the vine whip that had wrapped around her was now anchored deeply into the ground, seemingly growing roots, even as it spread across her. Even with her enhanced strength, she was stuck fast.

Trapped as she was, Tala still wasn't helpless against the Leshkin who were almost upon her.

Her sphere slammed into a lesser's chest, knocking it back as her rod tripped up a warrior only a handful of feet from her.

With Flow in the form of a knife, Tala sliced across herself with almost frenzied abandon, feeling her endingberry power drain to defend from each cut, followed by the distinct magical signature of the elk leathers expending power to pull back together.

The vines, also, continued to grow, even as the cuts tried to pull back together. Thankfully, the heat of Flow's blade, even in knife form, had somewhat cauterized the vegetation, making it much more difficult for the plant to regenerate.

Get... Cut, slash, flail. *FREE!*

She was finally able to jerk herself out of the suffocating vines, and she stumbled upright.

Terry almost tackled her from behind, knocking her onto his back once again.

She barely caught his collar and righted herself as the avian veered to the side and away from the jagged wave of oncoming enemies.

Blessedly, Terry was able to steer back northward, circumnavigating the screaming mini horde.

Now on the lookout for it, Tala was able to intercept, or otherwise thwart, myriad thrown and long-range attacks.

Terry outright dodged any thrown Leshkin while barely slowing.

In a couple of instances, Tala felt dimensional energies build within her friend, but they always faded without him flickering away to leave her to her fate.

His instincts are telling him to abandon me, but he's not leaving.

She suppressed the wetness in her eyes. Now was hardly the time for sentiment, and blurry vision could well get them both killed. Still, she could do nothing about the grin tugging at her face.

Despite everything, she was still keeping a tight rein on her aura, only letting it extend in specific places to allow for the manipulation of her bloodstars.

Something deep within her made her feel that it was utterly imperative to keep her aura restrained and under her control. Wisdom prevailed as she continued to listen to that deep something. *If help is coming from Rane or the caravan, they'll have to find another way to find me than tracking my aura.*

They were making a *lot* of noise, between them and their pursuers, as Tala and Terry continued their skirmishing retreat, circling north as much as possible. *They can probably hear this ruckus from miles off...*

She *really* hoped that nothing else would follow that sound and find them, adding to the complexity of the situation.

Finally, when the inside edge of the tree line was in sight and the gloriously brilliant, snow-covered grasslands were before them, their progress hit a snag of monstrous proportions.

Two juggernauts slammed into the ground directly in their way, blocking the narrow path between two trees just a hundred yards in front of them.

Not seeming fazed in the slightest by their ballistic impacts, the two vaulted to their feet, weapons at the ready. Each held a tower shield that was actually on the small side for them, while still being just taller than Tala, while she rode on Terry.

Millennial Mage, 5 - Fusing

The one to Tala's right wielded a greathammer one-handed that was large enough that it would easily have required Rane to use two hands. The other pointed at her with a flanged mace of dark, dense wood—clearly, a gesture of violent intent.

Her first thought? *I want those weapons for Flow.* It was an odd, disjointed thought as she'd not focused on that when surrounded by juggernaut weapons. It was probably because she was nearing the end of her mental endurance, and her thoughts were becoming less directed.

Her second thought? *I really want to survive this...* The significance of that thought didn't register in the slightest as she immediately began mentally scrambling for a way out.

Terry could change direction and take them away, once again. After that, they could try to circle around once more, but she had no idea if it would work or if they were being shunted toward more Leshkin or some other threat to the east.

The avian couldn't fight a juggernaut safely, and Tala certainly couldn't bypass them on her own. *He's not dying for me, not if I can help it.*

She could throw her anchor once again, but given the level of intelligence the Leshkin were demonstrating this time around, they might just snatch the empowered item from the air, and she'd be well and truly trapped.

She had a brief mental tableau of a juggernaut holding her anchor in one hand, while the other slammed its massive weapon into her again and again in an endless cycle until her magic ran out, and she was pulverized for the last time. *I wonder how many that would actually be? Twice? Three full-body heals?* It probably wouldn't be more than that. *I suppose it depends on the exact nature of the damage.*

But she was getting distracted in a moment where she couldn't afford distraction. She did have one idea. It was out there, but it meshed with her understanding of her own magics too well not to try.

Well, let's do this, then.

"Straight on, Terry. I need to try something. I think it will help get us out."

Terry trilled, deep and rumbling, almost a war cry.

Tala's grin returned as she extended her right hand, first two fingers pointing up, second two curled downward. All fingers, and her thumb, were tucked in tight as she oriented her palm toward the juggernauts.

She locked onto both. That had been expected to work. Even without rings to burn, the targeting inscriptions should still function. Still, she felt a thrill at the first success, no matter how expected.

Now, the hard part.

She had modified her inscriptions on the fly before. Holly had helped her enact *Crush* upon herself while suppressing the recursive portion of that inscription, and it had worked exactly as she'd hoped. *Totally useless in the end, but it had worked.*

That had been suppressing and diverting power away from a portion of her inscriptions. What she was doing now was quite a bit more convoluted and would require her jumping power through her flesh. She wouldn't need to mold that power into true spell-lines, thankfully. She wasn't adding functionality, she was just hot-wiring two bits of spell logic together in a sequence they hadn't been inscribed to fire. *Should work though; they are compatible, and my mental model is rock-solid.*

Indicating the first targeted enemy, she ordered *Restraining,* followed immediately by a command toward the second: *Crush.*

Millennial Mage, 5 - Fusing

Her power rushed through the spellforms, but there were no rings to work with.

Tala grabbed the *Restrain* functionality and guided it, stealing all kinetic energy from the Leshkin on her left and channeling that energy into the *Crush* spellform trying to enact upon the second juggernaut.

She screamed in agony as the inscriptions embedded in her right breast were burned away in their entirety to fuel a twisted hybrid of their original purpose, forced as they were to work in a way out of sync with their design.

But it worked.

The hammer-wielding foe froze in place, clearly struggling, and at every thwarted twitch from the colossal beast, the mace-wielding enemy was driven toward the ground.

The kinetic energy wasn't doing the crushing. No, that would never have worked. That stolen energy was powering the multiplication of the gravitational constant on the second.

It only worked because of the immense power of the hammer-wielder, jacking up the gravity on the second Leshkin so fast that it couldn't divide into knights to escape.

Incidentally, it was also burning out the flesh of Tala's chest as she acted as a catalyst. The gold of the inscription was long since gone, but the spellform was stable and would continue until it couldn't any longer.

I may have made a terrible mistake. She couldn't scream; she couldn't even draw breath. Only four barely scraped together void-channels kept her body from being sucked dry of power.

As the mace-wielder was crushed into oblivion, there was no longer anywhere for the kinetic energy to go, allowing the spellform to dissolve into nothing, freeing the first beast from kinetic thievery and Tala from her self-created agony.

Tala slumped forward, left hand pressed to the right side of her chest as she gasped in a breath for the first time in what felt like hours.

Rusting rust! It had worked, but there was a reason that using uninscribed spells was inadvisable.

Terry continued his sprint toward the one remaining juggernaut, a host of smaller Leshkin still close behind Tala and her avian transportation.

This is it. She looked up, seeing the foe that she'd been unable to contain. *I have no tricks left.*

In retrospect, she could have waited until they were closer, and that might have allowed them to bypass the ambush before the hammer-wielder could move again, but as it was an untested spell-working, she hadn't been willing to commit them to the extent that that would have required.

"I'm sorry, Terry, but—"

Tala's eyes widened as she watched Force take the giant's head from its shoulders. Rane rode past the still-upright body, precariously standing on his horse's saddle to get the height needed for such a blow.

Over the body of the first juggernaut, a hail of bolts shot, dropping part of the wave behind Tala and Terry.

Rane had arrived with two full units of guards and none too soon.

His voice was crisp and filled with an air of command. "Come on!" He dropped down into a more stable seat, hooking his feet back into the stirrups and grabbing the reins to wheel around and charge back toward the plains. As he drew close to the Leshkin again, he freed one foot from its stirrup, leaning out of his saddle and opening his harvest bag to scoop up one of the shields and the mace.

Millennial Mage, 5 - Fusing

Tala laughed with barely contained glee. *We're going to live? We're going to live!*

The guards continued their steady rain of bolts, softening up and slowing the Leshkin in pursuit.

Tala, for her part, threw anchor darts at the remaining shield and massive hammer. It only took her eight attempts with her left hand to sink a dart into each as she and Terry drew closer and swept past. Her right arm was not working as she desired, due to the pain in her chest.

I'm glad the ones I missed will be dragged along just the same.

And then, she was out, the full light of day unobstructed before her despite the canopy extending overhead.

The guards were in full retreat atop their own mounts, twisting in their saddles to fire backward as they rode.

Terry overtook the horses and passed them by, head tucked low, utterly focused on the line of daylight ahead.

They burst into full, beautifully blinding light, and Tala felt tears fill her eyes.

Free. I'm blessedly free of that cursed forest.

* * *

Tala took long, slow breaths as she lay on her back, looking up at the cloud-speckled sky.

She had collapsed, arms thrown wide, on the cool white snow, close to a quarter-mile to the north of the forest. She flexed her hands open and closed, picking up snow and casting it aside, uncaring of the melting snow that slowly seeped into her leathers. *They'll be fine.*

She sent a pulse of power their way to top them off, just in case.

Terry was asleep, curled up on her stomach. A mound of snow was piled atop the right side of her chest, but it didn't really relieve the burning sensation still coming from the burned-out flesh in her right breast.

The guards had headed back to the caravan, which was resting close to two miles to the west.

Rane was waiting with her as she stared at the beautifully tree-branch-free sky. *It's been too long.*

The Leshkin had turned back a few hundred yards past the tree line. They had escaped from their erstwhile pursuers.

The Leshkin withdrawal hadn't been a hard stop. Instead, one by one, they'd slowed down and eventually turned around to return to the forest until the few that were still following were taken out by the guards' precise shooting.

But that was past now.

Tala was free of that ghastly forest. *I'm not going back. Not for a long, long time.*

She'd be sad to miss out on seeing Jevin. *But he'll come out in… sixty? Yeah, sixty years or so. I can see him then.*

It would definitely be better for everyone if she stayed out of that forest. *At least until I can deal with Leshkin much more efficiently.*

"Are you okay?" Rane's voice was soft but reached her easily from where he sat, cross-legged, a few feet away.

Tala grunted. "I think I will be. How's the caravan?"

"All the Leshkin followed you. We sustained a few injuries as they departed but not too many."

"Carl?"

"He was mostly unharmed, but he was just trying to sit up as one of the last knights ran past. Its foot clipped the side of his head just wrong and…"

Tala's eyes widened. "Carl's dead?"

Rane's own eyes widened in turn. "Oh! No, it just caught on his scalp and… damaged it."

Millennial Mage, 5 - Fusing

She frowned then. "Will he be okay?"

"He should be. A couple of the other guards were able to grab him, and get him in the chuckwagon. They got the flap back in place and applied cold pressure. It should be alright until Mistress Odera wakes up. She should be able to sort him with ease."

Having your face ripped off. Tala shuddered. It put her own pain in perspective.

…Still didn't make it hurt less, though.

She tentatively poked at her chest, wincing at the pain.

She'd burned through her endingberry power without even realizing it, and though her inscriptions were actively working to break down the destroyed flesh and replace it with new, healthy tissue, burn wounds were notoriously hard to heal no matter the means, magical or mundane.

Rane cleared his throat and asked again. "Are you sure you're going to be alright? I've never seen you take this long to recover from something."

She grimaced. "Seems that fire wins again." *Stupid element.* It hadn't even been fire, not really.

"Fire?"

"Fine, fire's proxy, heat."

"Does it have something to do with what you did to the two juggernauts? I don't think I've seen you use that working before."

She sighed and gave him a brief explanation.

"Huh. Well, I'm not surprised that it worked."

She cocked her head. "Really? Not going to chastise me for doing something 'incredibly foolish' or the like?"

"Hmm? No. Guides patching together spellforms is a time-honored tradition in the heat of battle. The more experienced Mages can pull it off with little in the way of side effects, but your consequences are in the vein of what a first attempt should produce."

She grunted. *Well, I'm finally average at something.* She huffed a laugh.

"What's so funny?"

"Of all the things for me to be average at." She shook her head.

He grinned back. "Well, you're alive." His smile took on more of a mischievous glint. "And I have quite a few harvests for us to work with." He patted the large canvas sack on the ground beside him. "I think there are a couple greatswords in here that I can meld with Force for a bit of added magical weight. If we split the loot, I'm happy to give you the other part of my share"—he seemed to stumble over what he was going to say before catching himself and continuing—"for a reasonable price."

She nodded. *That's right you won't just give it to me.* "That sounds reasonable. I think I might have a use for the armor, too." She hesitated, then laughed. "I can probably use most of it, unfortunately. I'd love to sell it, to get a better payout."

"Don't be too sad, the protection payout should be close to what it was for each of us last time. Fewer injuries, no deaths, but overall fewer beasts beaten back."

She shook her head. "Hard to believe that that was fewer."

"More concentrated. That makes it seem worse." After a moment, he shrugged. "I suppose the next two days could bring anything, though."

Tala sighed and pushed herself upright.

Terry flickered to her shoulder without otherwise seeming to move.

She scratched his head and whispered to him, "Thank you, my friend. You really saved me today."

He trilled softly and nuzzled her in return, without opening his eyes.

Louder, she addressed Rane. "We should get back to the caravan."

Rane stood, offering her a hand. "That's probably a good idea."

Tala let him assist her in standing. She was exhausted. "Lead the way, Master Rane."

Chapter: 18
In the Ground

Tala and Rane walked back toward the caravan, Rane leading his horse, Terry riding on Tala's shoulder.

She had slipped on her shoes because even though her feet didn't generally sink into the cold, wet mixture of snow and toppled grass, it was a little bit more comfortable to have the footwear on, and she saw no need to choose discomfort with no upside.

Tala had given Terry a large amount of jerky as she'd lain on the ground and continued to flick it out for him at regular intervals. *I need to restock my stash of this stuff. Terry has definitely earned all I can get for him.*

She and Rane were mainly silent as they trekked across the frozen ground. Game trails crossed their path every so often, but they didn't see any sign of life close by. Their goal was obvious, given the caravan's chosen resting spot, atop a rise that was easily visible despite the distance.

There were some mundane birds flying about in the distance, and Tala thought she caught glimpses of deer or elk on occasion, on far hills, but she couldn't tell if they were arcanous or not. *Probably doesn't matter.*

There really weren't that many purely mundane creatures in the wilderness, now that she thought about it. Most found their way through a fount one way or another, picking up innate magics or dying as a result.

She did see some things glinting with colored light here and there, peeking through the snow. But it was hard

Millennial Mage, 5 - Fusing

to get a good look with the white snow around. There wasn't any power coming from them, so she decided that it wasn't really of consequence. *Probably just odd, shiny rocks.*

That thought only lasted until they came to the top of a rise and saw a crystal wolf, statuesque in death, curled up on the ground.

No magics remained for them to determine if it had been a bearer of crystal powers or the victim of them.

Not much difference in the end. Though the lack of a visible wound implied that it had died from crystallization, rather than being killed while such an entity.

Rane groaned. "This might be bad."

Tala found herself nodding. "I thought Master Xeel said he was going to clean up the crystal fount. Wasn't that over a month ago?"

"This isn't evidence that he hasn't. For all we know, this is from that cleanup." He shrugged. "Though, Master Xeel also said he cleaned up Terry's fount." Rane gestured at the avian to emphasize his point.

Terry let out an angry hiss but didn't otherwise react.

"So?" Tala glanced to Rane. "What do we do?"

"Get back to the caravan and report it. I'll handle that report. As to the caravan, they should be safe enough, with clear sightlines and the light of day, but we shouldn't leave them down two protectors for much longer."

Tala sighed, sweeping the area with her normal vision and magesight together, just to be sure. There were a surprising number of lumps under the snow. *More than elsewhere.* She walked over to one and moved the snow aside.

A crystalized bunny huddled among the dead grass. "Another, here." The next mound looked like a cut stone block, weathered with countless years. "Part of a ruin?"

"The fallen arcane cities." He had a mischievous glint in his eyes.

Tala nodded, sagely. "Right. This area used to have a few."

Rane snorted. "I was mainly teasing. There were more magical research stations than cities. A few fortresses, for the various groups to posture against each other with. There were other, less mundane things, but there shouldn't be any evidence on the surface, at least not from them." He shrugged. "But those could be anywhere, even under other ruins."

Tala uncovered more mounds, finding a mix of crystalized animals and plants, along with other remnants of past civilization. Some of the smaller ones were locked into very lifelike poses, and Tala tucked those into Kit. *They're pretty, even if in a morbid sort of way.*

Rane interrupted her perusal of the various mounds atop the hill. "We should get to the wagons."

She sighed and nodded, straightening as she placed a particularly lovely specimen away. It was a falcon in flight, wings tucked in close for a killing dive. *I wonder how it managed to survive the fall from the sky.*

Crystal's lattice structure could survive a lot if it took the stress correctly. *That's probably it.*

"Alright."

They continued on their way, faster this time, following the rise and fall of the land, making a straight line for the caravan. Rane kept a tighter rein on the horse as they walked, ensuring they took a path that the animal could traverse, which wasn't that hard as the terrain here was almost universally gently contoured.

As they neared the base of a dell, weaving through some spare, bare trees, movement behind a bush caused them to freeze. The bush itself was mostly just snow-covered sticks this time of year, but they were prolific and did obscure their vision somewhat.

A crystalline doe hobbled past the plant, brushing the bush and causing the entire thing to crystalize and shatter. The resulting pieces were small enough to virtually disappear among the fallen snow.

Rane placed his hand on Force, letting the horse's reins fall. The animal took that as a cue to stay where it was, and it began rooting through the snow to get to the grass underneath, seeming unconcerned by the arcanous creature so near at hand.

Tala placed her hand on Rane's arm. "Don't, Rane. You are *very* susceptible to that thing's magic."

He stopped, turning toward her and waiting for her to continue.

The doe's front leg was broken, barely hanging on by glittering tendons. That was likely the only reason they'd gotten this close. It was regarding them with absolute stillness, as if utterly uncertain of what to do about their presence before it. Its gaze wasn't hostile, but it didn't seem afraid either.

It was the look of a prey animal that had recently found itself to be a predator. Old instincts were warring with new-found knowledge and power.

Tala could see magic swirling around the creature. "It's healing. We can't leave it."

He moved once again to draw his weapon, but Tala stopped him again.

"I've got this." She brought her left middle finger to her thumb, targeting the deer. *Increase.*

She began ramping up the deer's effective gravity as quickly as she was able without using the *Crush* mental model.

The animal shifted slightly, then simply continued to stare at them. It was seemingly unable to decide if it should run, even as its hooves began to sink deeper into the turf under the influence of its increased effective weight.

The two humans stared at the magic-infused animal as the seconds ticked by.

After half a minute, Tala began to frown. "That's more than enough to crush a juggernaut to oblivion."

Rane shrugged. "Crystal can be incredibly strong?"

The deer continued to sink, driving its three good legs into the ground until its belly pressed down through the snow.

The magic continuing to swirl around it was enough proof that it wasn't dead, but it wasn't moving, not really.

Why isn't it struggling?

After a minute, the belly of the creature began to sink into the ground as well.

Tala threw up her hands in frustration. "This is madness! It should be experiencing more than three-hundred times normal gravity, now. Something is obviously happening, but it's still intact."

Rane had his head tilted as if considering. "Do you think it's not moving because it sensed the attack and shifted into its most stable, resilient configuration?"

"That would explain—" The faint sound of cracking cut her off. "Finally."

He was frowning. "Mistress Tala, that's not coming from—"

A loud *crack* reverberated through the ground under their feet. Immediately thereafter, the beast vanished, dropping from sight.

The tinkle of shattering crystal, along with a wave of magic, signified the end of the dangerous animal.

By the origin of the pulse of power, Tala knew how far it had fallen. "Master Rane, what could be sixty feet underground, here?" She hesitated. "Well, whatever the deer shattered on is that deep."

"An abandoned well?"

Tala gave him a deeply skeptical look. "That the doe *just happened* to be standing over when I targeted it?"

He gave a half-smile. "That does seem to beggar reality."

"Just a bit." She smiled in return.

After a short moment of consideration directed at the new hole in the ground, he glanced back toward Tala. "Do you think it's safe to go look?"

Tala frowned at the dark opening, then sighed. "Terry, can you go look?"

The terror bird lifted his head and gave her an incredulous look.

"Not to tell us what you see, obviously. I just want you to test and see if it's stable. If it isn't, you can flicker away."

He tilted his head in thought, then vanished from her shoulder, appearing beside the hole, the size and weight of a small horse. Rane's horse lifted its head and eyed Terry suspiciously but didn't bolt. Rane took that hesitation as an opportunity to grab the hanging reins.

After a long moment, Terry stomped with one taloned foot, pausing to see if there was any effect.

When nothing happened, he jumped up and down a few times.

When that did nothing, he flickered back to Tala's shoulder and curled up.

"Seems safe." She nodded toward Rane.

Together, they walked to the hole and carefully looked down. "I can't see anything."

Tala's enhanced vision was better than Rane's natural eyesight. "I can. It looks like a storeroom of some kind. The deer crystalized some boxes, which broke open. They were filled with... something. I can't quite see." She hesitated. "Should I go down?"

Rane looked at her like she was insane.

"Fine, fine." She held up her hands. "It was just a question."

"Do you detect any magic down there?"

She looked again to confirm what she already knew. "Not at all. Even the deer's power is dispersing as I'd expect, no barriers or dampening fields that I can detect."

Rane smiled. "Good. Then, it shouldn't be urgent. I'll get it reported. Then, the Archon Council in Bandfast will likely send someone to take a look. If it's a low enough priority, they'll create a mission that any Mage or Archon can take."

"You mean, they might pay us to come back?"

"Could be."

She grinned. "That sounds like an excellent plan."

Rane seemed oddly contemplative as he regarded her. "What?"

"I'd think that such places would be..." He seemed to be struggling to find the right words. "Unpleasant?" He shrugged. "Unpleasant for you."

Tala cocked her head, frowning. "Why in Zeme would that be?"

"Well, for most people, being crushed to death is unpleasant but probably fairly quick in the event of a ruin's collapse. For you, you'd survive for..." He seemed at a loss for words again. "I don't even know how long you could survive under tons of rock. I'd have thought that would be off-putting."

She regarded him with something akin to horror. "Well, it is *now*." *That would be an awful way to go. Nothing I could really do, no way out, my scripts keeping me alive in my suffering.* She hesitated. "I could simply divert power away from my scripts and let the end come?"

He considered for a moment. "I suppose, if you did it in the right way, that would work. Otherwise, you'd just fall unconscious, and your scripts would reactivate." He tsked. "Your gate doesn't close when you're unconscious, right? I remember you saying something like that."

She crinkled her nose. "Yeah... that's true."

Rane cleared his throat, seeming to realize that he'd brought up a bad subject. "Even so, I'd be happy to come back to explore if you're up for it."

She gave him a long look, then shook her head. "Maybe. It might be interesting, at least. Let's go back. We've delayed long enough."

They began walking again.

After another quarter-mile or so, she glanced his way. "What would we have been likely to find down there?"

He shrugged. "The most mundane thing would be a forgotten cache of food and supplies from an earlier cycle's defense of these plains."

"Right." She nodded. "The Leshkin wars."

"Wars is a bit dramatic. Humanity mainly sets up defensive positions and kills Leshkin by the thousand as they recycle their souls back to the forest."

Tala had a thought. "Is that why there is so little undergrowth?"

"What?"

"In the forest, is that why?"

Rane paused. "Maybe? If they grab onto any plant life, other than their great trees, and twist it to grow them a body, instead, that would thin things out a bit."

She grunted. Even if that were a factor, there were likely other factors at play. "But back to the ruin. At the least, it's a forgotten human supply cache. At most?"

He shrugged. "There are some vestiges of a few of the ancient enemies of mankind. In other cases, some have yet to be rediscovered in the prisons they were locked in by early Mages."

"Which do you mean?" She was listening more intently, now.

"Well, several liches were buried by early humans who didn't know any other way of dealing with them."

"Entomb them in the ground?"

"Them and their whole fortress. They couldn't risk a phylactery being among the spoils."

"So, what? They sank whole towers?"

He nodded. "Towns, too. Cities, in some cases."

She snapped her fingers. "I always thought that the tales saying that the heroes put an evil Mage 'in the ground' were saying they killed them."

Rane laughed. "Probably, more often than not, that's exactly what was meant, but from what Master Grediv has told me, early human Mages buried a lot more of their problems than they knew how to eliminate. Modern Archons try to hunt down those that they can and end the threats for good, but it isn't always easy. Ancient Mages didn't want anyone freeing the beasts, so they didn't keep records of the burial sites and did their best to hide any and all evidence. In many cases, they supposedly altered the stories so that those couldn't be used to suss out the hidden prisons."

"That's one way to do it, I suppose."

Rane shrugged. "Geologic activity frees some every so often or battles unknowingly fought atop them. So, it's worth hunting them down as we can."

Tala nodded. *That makes some sense.* "What others do you think fall into that camp?"

For the remainder of their walk, Rane told her short accounts of the myriad worst enemies of humanity. He

Millennial Mage, 5 - Fusing

spoke of beasts composed all of smoke; of sythenians, humanoids capable of killing with a look; of horrors made of shadows and darkness; of the endless Black Legion; of immissusi—men who changed into beasts under certain influences, magical or mundane; of creatures who lived by drinking vital things from humanity; and many others.

The vital drinkers reminded her a bit too much of dasgannach. Even so, when she mentioned the seeming connection to Rane, he didn't think the motile mud and metal was the source of myths of bloodsuckers or any of the others, but he did admit that he could be wrong. It wasn't something that he'd studied extensively.

Tala loved the old stories. After all, she'd modeled her very magic after such stories, depicting humanity's first heroes. Therefore, it was hardly a surprise that the rehashing of those tales, even if only in passing, was a wonderful way to spend a walk through the countryside.

*   *   *

Tala and Rane arrived back at the caravan without further incident.

Rane handed over his horse to one of the attendants, and they went to meet up with the drivers and sergeants. Terry seemed content to stay with them.

Dron, the head of the caravan's guards, gave a shallow bow to them as they joined the ongoing discussion. "Good to have you two back." He then met Tala's gaze. "Mistress Tala. Thank you for leading the Leshkin away. I don't think we'd have had an easy time breaking free if the attack had continued at that intensity."

Tala gave a tired smile. "It was the least I could do. I'm..." She swallowed. "I'm fairly certain they were after me, specifically."

Dron nodded, not showing any surprise in the least. "That is what we'd assumed as well. Do you know why?"

After a moment of shock, she shook her head. *Glad I didn't try to deny or obscure it...* "I have some guesses, but they are just that."

He gave her a searching look before nodding again. "I believe you. Sometimes beasties take a fancy to something and act against their pre-discovered nature. I've heard of a few Mages who've seemed to cause similar, if less extreme, reactions from the forest terrors." A smile tugged at his lips. "I hope you don't begrudge me when I say that I will be recommending against allowing you to take forest contracts for the time being."

She gave a nervous laugh. "Yeah. That makes sense. I'd been giving it some thought, and I wasn't planning on taking any anyway."

All the guards seemed to relax a bit at that. The two drivers simply smiled in commiseration.

She cleared her throat. *In for a copper...* "I do apologize, however. While I didn't intend to put the caravan in danger, it seems that I did, nonetheless."

Dron smiled once again. "Apology accepted, Mistress. Your diversion saved lives, and it seems that no one is likely to die as a result of the Leshkin. We came out ahead, by my count."

"Ahead?" Tala frowned. "I don't understand."

"Well, the forest was *much* quieter on this outward journey than it really should have been. The likely reason, looking back, is that the Leshkin were sweeping the woods, looking for you, killing or driving off anything that could have posed much danger."

"But we still had to drive off beasts daily."

Dron waved that off. "Nothing like the number or power we were prepared for. It is unusual for every guard to survive on a leg of a forest journey." He gave a sad smile. "The hazards of the job."

"Well, that does make me feel a bit better."

"Good." His joviality faded a bit. "Now, I assume you know not to take that as a reason to venture back in. We got lucky in that we didn't encounter any Leshkin until we did. Likely the mushroom-infested region helped with that, but even so."

"Oh, I understand. No forest travel for me until something changes."

Dron nodded. "Good to hear. Now, we were in the middle of discussing the plan going forward."

They talked through some logistics and possible paths. Tion ended up having the most to say, there, as the head driver.

In the end, they decided to let the oxen rest another hour or so, then push on once more, making camp as usual for the night. If they did that, they should arrive at Bandfast before nightfall the next day.

Tala smiled unconsciously at that realization. *Home. We're finally going to be home.*

Chapter: 19
You Earned It

Tala had had a rough couple of days, and that didn't even account for her still-healing chest. The burns caused by shorting out her *Crush* and *Restrain* inscriptions were taking a lot longer to heal than most injuries she'd taken, though they were mostly recovered by this point.

Taking everything into account, as the wagons began moving once again, Tala realized that she was mentally and emotionally exhausted.

As foreign as it seemed to her, she felt like she should not be training right then. So, going against the habits she'd tried to build over the last couple of months, Tala gave herself a bit of a break that afternoon. She simply relaxed on the cargo wagon's roof, watching the rolling plains slide by.

She hadn't realized how much she'd missed the open air, but it seemed that her time in Makinaven had given her a new appreciation for wide-open spaces.

Their caravan must have given off more dangerous vibes than usual because they weren't attacked even once as afternoon slid toward evening.

Tala did see some arcanous beasts watching them at a couple of points, but none tried their luck.

Thankfully. She shook her head at the idea of having to defend the caravan. *We're all exhausted.*

It was nearing evening when Mistress Odera finally joined Tala on the roof, moving slowly and deliberately.

When she saw the older woman, Tala rushed to her aid. "Mistress Odera!" She offered her a hand up, and the other Mage took it.

"Thank you, Mistress Tala."

They moved back to the center of the roof, where Tala left the cushioned central seat for Mistress Odera.

"Thank you, again." As she settled down, Mistress Odera sighed in relieved weariness. "Now, I'd love to hear your version of this morning's events. What happened after I passed out?" After a moment's hesitation, she shook her head. "No, go back a bit before that. I only caught snatches as I was too near my limit at that time to truly pay attention, but I believe you organized some strategies for when the shield came down. Is that correct?"

Tala nodded, then launched into an abbreviated version of events, not pausing until she'd explained Rane and the guards coming to her rescue in the end, and their safe departure from the forest and final escape from the Leshkin as a group.

Mistress Odera nodded, finally commenting then. "It sounds like it went better than we had any right to hope. It also seems blindingly obvious that they were after you, for some reason. I'd suspected on our inward journey, but there can always be oddities and anomalies."

Tala nodded. "That's what we concluded as well."

"We?" Mistress Odera gave her a searching look.

Tala shrugged, glancing away. "Master Rane, myself, the guards, and drivers."

The older woman gave a small smile. "Ahh, good. So, there's nothing tucked away. No building rumors we might need to deal with. That makes things simpler." She regarded Tala for a long moment before nodding. "It is almost always better to be forthright about such things."

Her eyes narrowed. "Did you know that they would target you before we entered the forest?"

Tala jerked her focus back to Mistress Odera. "What? No! Of course not."

The Mage clucked her tongue, humming contemplatively around the motion. "What about before we departed to head back to Bandfast?"

Tala hesitated, then. "No? I had fears and wild speculations, but I didn't know for sure."

Mistress Odera grunted. "Your fears, we discussed. I still don't agree with your anthropomorphizing of the greater Leshkin, and so if that is truly all that you had to go on, I am satisfied that the danger was not fully expectable."

"Well, and my defensive magics being based on endingberry power."

She sighed and shook her head. "That isn't news, either." She held up her hand before Tala could add anything else. "Nor is your iron-based protection. We *should* update the Archive with the possibility of those links, however. Things could have gone much worse. Many caravans would not have held up so well under such an onslaught, and we are nearing the Leshkin surge for this cycle. Only a century and a half or so before the height of that threat."

Tala frowned. "What do you mean?"

"Surely, the Leshkin wars aren't unknown to you."

"No, of course I know of those, at least in part. I meant, what do you mean by 'many caravans wouldn't have held up?'"

"We are somewhat, but not entirely, uniquely able to survive as we did. I have one of the greatest defensive powers for caravan protection duty of any Mage currently working."

Millennial Mage, 5 - Fusing

Tala was about to scoff and roll her eyes at the arrogance but then considered for a moment. *She can fully isolate and protect a caravan as it moves, for hours, all while it is under heavy assault.* In the end, Tala had to concede that Mistress Odera might actually be right about her abilities relative to other Mage Protectors. "Go on."

The side of the woman's mouth pulled up, and she clearly had intuited Tala's thinking, but she didn't comment. "Second, we have an incredibly high number of guards for our relative size. Thus, we had more defenders per area of the caravan. That is due to you. Your high-capacity cargo slots and their proportionally increased cargo necessitated more guards, and their space efficiency concentrated that defense onto only two wagons."

Tala smiled at the compliment, oblique though it was.

"Master Rane is very destructive of single targets, and he is incredibly efficient in his use of power and inscriptions in that destruction." Mistress Odera shrugged. "True, that is no different from any Mage using an artifact as a primary means of attack, but that is still a factor in our favor."

"So, we were uniquely suited to survive."

"We were distinctively designed to survive."

Tala frowned. "Explain."

Mistress Odera shrugged. "Things like this are always a possibility. So, the Caravan Guild tries to ensure that forest ventures are well-suited."

"Ahh, so you meant that many non-forest route caravans wouldn't have held up well."

"That is accurate. Yes."

Tala shrugged. "That's fair. Though, I suppose, this is close to what we'll have for other routes, right?"

"We'll often have fewer guards, but otherwise, yes." After a moment's thought, she shrugged. "We probably have about the optimum ratio of guards to wagons, at this point. In truth, we might have more guards for some of the plains routes, if we have sufficient passengers, but then, we'd need passenger wagons anyway, which would drastically lower the ratio we're discussing." She seemed to consider further. "So, as I said, we were in a very good position for the danger that we encountered."

The conversation continued as Tala asked some pointed questions about being a lead Mage Protector. Her short stint trying to operate with Mistress Odera incapacitated had shown her that she had a lot to learn.

Mistress Odera seemed to be ready and even to have been waiting for Tala to show such interest. Thus, they spent the remainder of the afternoon's travels, that night's dinner conversation, and their time until first watch continuing Tala's tutelage in the finer points of leading a caravan's magical protection.

Mistress Odera also gave Tala a list of reference materials to look into, when she had time, and Tala added them to her growing to-read itemization. *The Archive tablet is looking more and more appealing.*

Even though that tablet would be an amazing resource, she doubted that she'd ever want to fully give up on physical books.

All in all, she had quite a lot to process as she lay down for the first half of the night.

She did her best to compartmentalize, as she'd have plenty of time to think while on second watch, and she didn't want to keep herself awake through what little time she did have to sleep.

* * *

Tala's irrational irritation at being awoken by Rane lightly knocking on her door was reduced by the large jug of coffee he proffered to her when she opened it.

Millennial Mage, 5 - Fusing

He gave a tired smile. "I know you're supposed to be cutting back on this stuff, but yesterday was… rough." He glanced behind himself, at his own door. "I'm going to sleep. Nothing to report on watch."

Tala grunted her thanks as she took the coffee, but then she found herself on the roof, sometime later, before she had formed truly coherent thoughts.

Well, I got up here, and I seem to be scanning the surroundings. She swallowed the coffee already in her mouth. *And we're all alive.* She shrugged.

It was a cold night, not that it bothered her. As such, she used the temperature as an excuse to pull out her massive bear pelt, wiggling it back and forth, just a little, to get it out of Kit's relatively small opening.

The pelt was glorious.

She stood with the fur of her adversary draped over her shoulders to cascade down around her feet. The scents that had been worked into the cleaned hide were phenomenal over and above the feel of the thing.

Terry was curled up on part of the bear pelt that was splayed on the wagon top.

As Tala turned to continue her surveillance of the dark terrain, the pelt moved with her, carrying Terry in slow circuits as well.

That made her smile, even as she took another swig of coffee.

Now. Running a caravan's magical defenses. There really was so much to consider. The Mage Protectors *technically* outranked the guards, but they weren't in charge of them directly.

A senior Mage Protector had to balance diplomacy with decisive action at need.

Not sure that will ever be my role… or if I even want it.

The more Tala dug into various aspects of Magehood, the more she was seeing what Master Jevin had warned her of: humanity needed its Mages more than the Mages really needed humanity, at least on a personal level. It would be all too easy for her to untether from human society and do what was best for her and her alone.

Doing so wouldn't cause the collapse of humanity—she just wasn't that unique or important—but if too many Mages did so? *We'd all be rusting dead.* Or effectively so. *Who wants to be the last survivor of a dead race?*

She grimaced. *So I need to be pursuing my own interests while keeping the larger needs of humanity in mind.*

She let out a long sigh. *No wonder they don't bring this up at the academy. I'd have laughed them off and ignored the lesson, then.*

But now? She still was tempted to treat the idea as silly, but she felt like she was beginning to turn on the issue. Now that she'd fought beside mundanes, wandered through more cities, and realized that her disenchantment with her family was not a reasonable condemnation on humanity as a whole.

Could things be better? Absolutely. But how could they ever change, ever improve, if those who disagreed and had power simply left?

I want to be a part of humanity, and I want us to thrive.

She chuckled and shook her head. *I thought I was thinking about caravan defense.* But everything in a Mage's life was interwoven. *Probably in any human's life, actually.*

A person's foundations and the foundational framework of society were inextricably interlinked. *Humans can't live without humanity, and humanity is nothing without the humans that make it up.* It was a ridiculously obvious assertion, but it still felt important to her.

Millennial Mage, 5 - Fusing

She smiled contentedly, opening Kit and *pulling* her bloodstars out.

She spent the rest of her watch in meditative, but still observant, silence, moving her rod, ball, and naked bloodstar in interweaving orbits under a star-lit, winter sky.

* * *

It was mid-morning the next day before anything of note really shook up their voyage across the plains.

A small family of thunder cattle had been spotted in a somewhat hidden depression, just a quarter-mile or so from the caravan, ahead and a bit to the north as they curved back east to reach Bandfast.

The animals weren't a threat, but Tala had made her desire for a couple of the bovines known.

Tala glanced to Mistress Odera. "What do you think about me going hunting? I'll top off the cargo slots before I go, just in case?"

Mistress Odera huffed a small laugh. "Fine. Try to keep properly oriented so you don't get lost." She glanced to the terror bird. "Are you going with her, Master Terry?"

Terry lifted his head and glanced at Tala.

Tala smiled and shrugged. "I want to do the killing myself, but if the mini herd is bigger than expected, you can have the extras."

He flickered to her shoulder and trilled happily, perching in such a way as to have a clear view forward.

Mistress Odera smiled. "Bring her back safe, Terry."

He trilled again.

Tala swung over the side and climbed down the ladder, jumping free of the wagon and smoothing down her tunic. "Mind if I ride, Terry?"

Terry flickered to beside her, already sized and crouched low for easy mounting.

"Thank you."

He let out an indifferent but playful squawk.

Tala tucked her feet under his wings and grabbed his collar, clipping her anchor to it and leaning forward to reduce her drag.

Terry was off like an arrow, quickly coming up to speed and angling toward the reported grazing place of the small group.

Less than a minute later, they were atop a rise, looking down on ten thunder cattle.

"Huh... that's more than were reported."

Terry looked back at her, tilting his head in question.

She grinned. "Yes, you can help kill them, but not all of them."

He let out a quiet trill, warning her before he flickered away, appearing next to her, a bit smaller than he had been.

Tala landed lightly, thanks to the warning. "Thanks." She nodded to Terry.

Now... Tala groaned. *How am I going to kill them?*

She sighed. *I did it again. I was so focused on finding one and going after it that I didn't decide how to kill it in advance.*

She had one, partial answer. She pulled out three tungsten balls, none of which contained her bloodstar, and none of which were currently gravitationally altered. With those in hand, she began amplifying their gravitation toward the three biggest animals.

If she had to guess, the herd down below was an alpha bull and two betas, each with a mate, and four calves. It was a bit of an odd grouping as she didn't *think* thunder cattle were monogamous. *Maybe they're all the alpha's mates, and the other two bulls are just hangers-on?*

Millennial Mage, 5 - Fusing

It didn't really matter. She was targeting the massive bulls' heads.

Even though it wasn't a quick process, she got ready, bracing against the pull that would begin, soon. *Now, the others.*

"I assume you want the little ones?"

Terry crouched a bit lower and bobbed a nod.

"That's acceptable. Quick, clean kills, please."

He glanced her way, then seemed to roll his eyes before bobbing again.

"Thank you." That would leave her with three cows to deal with, assuming her spheres were as lethal as she had reason to suspect. She was still a couple hundred feet away, and while she wasn't invisible to the animals, they weren't paying her too much attention. *That'll change in a few minutes.*

She would have loved to target more than three with metal meteors, but three was her current limit.

She imagined running in, Flow swinging, carving them up, but eventually, she sighed, shaking her head. *I'll take the boring way.* There was too much chance that they'd be able to kill her with lightning. *Or at least cut deeply into my endingberry power and inscription integrity.*

Large animals did not handle weight increases well, as a general rule, and while these cattle had magic that gave them benefits well beyond any mundane creature, it wasn't their primary magic, and it wasn't immutable. *The cows shouldn't be as robust as the bulls, either.*

The balls were beginning to pull, if not quite at her limit, but she didn't want one to slip free early. *Better on my timing than unexpectedly.* So she signaled Terry and let them go.

As soon as she released the balls to start their bloody journey, Tala had locked onto the three cows. *Increase.*

The three spheres began rolling downhill, quickly picking up speed until they lifted free of the ground altogether, practically streaking through the air to crack into the three bulls.

The first had been facing a bit away, so the ball hit it in the upper back, between the shoulder blades. A loud crack and a panicked bellow were precursors to the beast collapsing in what seemed to be a paralyzed heap.

Oops. I'll try to finish him off quickly. No need to be overly cruel.

The second was almost exactly broadside to Tala, so the tungsten ball slammed into the side of its head, decapitating it completely and anything but cleanly. The pulped remains of the head painted the nearby bushes a grayish red, even while the beast's heart continued to pump, spraying the grass in front of the slowly tipping, headless corpse.

Tala's eye twitched. *This… this is a lot messier than I'd anticipated.*

The third bull had been facing her, more or less. The sphere breached the top of its skull, driving downward and embedding in the neck before slowly pulling back up, causing the bovine to disgorge some of the eviscerated flesh that had followed the ball for the end of its devastating path.

That was, unsurprisingly, the cleanest of the three kills. *Well, two kills; the first still needs to be properly dispatched.*

She walked down the slope following her weapons' path, if much more slowly.

As the bulls were dying, the cows were already beginning to struggle.

Tala didn't see the calves die, and when she looked to see how Terry was doing, she saw him crouching on a nearby hill, just waiting and watching. There was no evidence of where the young thunder cattle had gone. Not one drop of blood in evidence.

Though, it would be hard to spot anyway, given the ocean I've unleashed.

She began to jog, even as the cows were looking around, stumbling in a way that seemed a bit drunken.

Tala reached the first bull and used Flow to end his suffering with a blow from behind.

The cows hadn't really paid attention to the small human before that, given the chaos surrounding them and her iron salve making her less visible to their magic sight, but all three oriented on her instantly as the alpha bull died.

And they were livid.

A raking series of lightning strikes shattered the ground starting halfway between Tala and the largest cow, moving toward her with unnerving steadiness.

The smallest cow let out a bellow of fear and rage and tried to charge Tala, only to immediately trip. The loud crack and chaotic tumble that followed was a clear signal of that animal's demise.

The middle cow was suddenly wreathed in power; with a flash of light, the bovine was towering over her, front hooves raised and already descending to trample her.

They can teleport?! Thankfully, her instinctive reactions were faster than her conscious thought, and Flow was transformed into a glaive and cutting upward before her incredulity fully manifested.

In her haste, she dumped more power than necessary into the weapon, and it blazed with power as it struck the bovine's chest and power tore through the animal, bisecting it and cauterizing the two halves in a single blow.

The largest cow stumbled to the side, its attacks faltering before they reached where Tala stood, already panting under the influence of an adrenaline dump, between two smoking sides of beef.

It was dead before it hit the ground.

Tala slowly calmed herself before clearing her throat. "Well. That worked." She swallowed. "I'm really, *really* glad I didn't just charge in here like last time." As she looked around at the carnage, she sighed. "Well, it could have been better, but progress, not perfection, right?" She looked to Terry as he flickered into being beside her.

He looked around at the red-painted grass and melting snow. He tilted his head in an obvious question.

"Yeah... I know I said clean."

He squawked.

Tala grimaced. "I'm working on it, okay?"

He trilled happily, giving an almost-shrug before plunging his head into the nearest carcass, skillfully extracting the guts and viscera without contaminating the meat.

"Eat up, buddy. You earned it."

Chapter: 20
Back in Bandfast

Tala took a long couple of minutes to completely come down from the adrenaline released by the butchery she'd just enacted.

Terry took that opportunity to devour the traditionally discarded parts of the corpses. He even went so far as to carefully splay open those that she hadn't already bisected and remove the innards cleanly. To do this, he used a talon almost like a gut hook, the rounded top facing inward to glide across the underlayers as the sharper point and interior laid the creature open. He cracked the sternums with casual ease.

After severing the esophagus, he grabbed that and pulled, dragging all the guts free before devouring them in their entirety.

The whole sequence was carried out with disturbing familiarity, once again demonstrating his monstrous strength and incredible dexterity.

Wait... "Terry, if you can do that, why did you devour so many of the slain in the forest? When we went out to hunt."

He regarded her for a long moment, then trilled, gave an avian shrug, and went on to the next fallen beast.

Tala felt her eye twitch. "You didn't know I wanted the bodies…"

He didn't look toward her but squawked in a way that conveyed that he'd thought that obvious.

Millennial Mage, 5 - Fusing

Don't think about it, Tala. That money's gone and won't be coming back. She again watched him devour an animal's guts.

That doesn't seem healthy... Tala would have guessed that at least the stomachs and intestines would be bad to eat. *At least what was in them.*

But what did she know? Terry seemed to regularly ingest animals whole. *He probably just processes the entirety into power... somehow.*

When he was done, and she was centered once more, Terry returned to stand before her, looking around at the six, massive carcasses laid out around them

He trilled questioningly.

"What am I going to do with them?"

He bobbed a nod.

She gave him a confused look. "Terry... don't you know?"

He shook himself.

A grin stole over her face. "Jerky, Terry. I want to increase our dwindling supply of jerky."

Terry froze in place, then looked around once more, taking time to stare at each downed thunder cow or bull. Finally, he trilled in happy triumph, almost seeming to dance in a circle.

Tala found herself laughing. "Come on, we need to find a way of transporting these." She hesitated, then groaned. "I'm an idiot, again..."

Terry seemed quite pleased and continued to flit about, trilling and chirping.

"Any ideas?"

He stopped, looking between her and the carcasses. Finally, he flickered to her side and nuzzled Kit.

"I could probably make that work, but I'd have to cut them into basically long strips." She looked between the bodies and finally sighed. "I can probably get them in fourths." *Kit can open wide enough for that.*

With no time to waste, Tala used Flow to carve the already bisected cow down until it was roughly as big around as Kit's opening, and much, much longer.

She wouldn't have been able to do so with a mundane tool, but Flow sliced through with little effort.

It took *quite* a bit of finagling to get the long quarters in, but she did it in the end.

Tala looked at the five other bodies in despair. All but one were larger than the cow she'd just dealt with.

Terry let out a musical squawk, looking up the hill from which they'd looked down on the thunder cattle.

Tala turned to see a couple of mounted guards looking down on them. She waved up and shouted a greeting. "Hello!"

One waved back and shouted in return. "Greetings, Mistress. Good hunting, I see." They rode the couple hundred feet down to her.

She glanced around herself at her acquisitions. "Good hunting, indeed." She tilted her head in consideration. "Is the caravan close?"

"Just a bit south, on the other side of this rise, Mistress."

Good, they kept to the anticipated path. "Could you send for Master Rane? I need him, just briefly, to help transport these."

The sergeant with whom she'd been speaking nodded and sent the other man to do just that.

"You were sent to check up on me, yes?"

"Nothing so brash, Mistress. We were meant to see if you needed assistance."

"Uh-huh." She cocked an eyebrow at the man.

"And it seems that you did."

Millennial Mage, 5 - Fusing

She let her eyebrow fall and forced a smile, stifling a grimace. "Fair enough, sergeant. Thank you."

He gave a seated bow. "Our pleasure to assist, Mistress."

*   *   *

They arrived at the outskirts of Bandfast just as the sun touched the far horizon behind them. The light seemed to paint the walls a stunning reddish orange.

The sight brought a smile to Tala's lips, and she felt a bit of her tension slip away. *We made it.*

The trip through the farmlands was largely unremarkable. There was some work being done in the winter fields but not much. Most of what was being done was contained to the occasional greenhouse.

If Tala remembered correctly, there were a series of growing chambers under the city that operated year-round. *I wonder if the entrances are out here to keep the agriculture all linked or in the city.*

She could look into it or ask, but she decided she didn't actually care that much.

Their arrival seemed to fall near the end of the workday as many workers were coming from their tasks and walking the road back to the city proper.

The familiar *crack* of defensive magics took an arcanous bird from the sky on the far side of the city, and Tala felt her smile widen.

Terry, for his part, was contentedly curled on her shoulder, showing no concern for the death of so similar a creature. Not that Tala expected him to care. *If he gave any thought, I bet it was just a desire to eat it.*

His collar was topped off and clearly still fully functional.

They rolled through the western city gate and turned into the nearest work yard.

Tala faced Mistress Odera, who was sitting in the center of the wagon top, and gave a bow. "Thank you, Mistress."

Mistress Odera gave her an inquiring look. "Whatever for?"

"For not lording your authority over me, for allowing me to learn." Tala shrugged.

The older woman smiled and nodded. "It was a pleasure. We should probably discuss our next venture soon."

"Breakfast?"

She laughed. "I'll see what I can do. Where would you like to meet?"

"I know of a place that has *excellent* breakfast sandwiches. They don't really have a place to sit to eat, but we can find someplace nearby?"

Mistress Odera frowned. "I think I'd prefer to eat inside somewhere, this time of year."

Tala looked at her again, more closely, and saw the heavy blankets wrapped around her, against the cool, winter-evening air. "Ahh, that's fair. I'm sorry for not thinking of that."

Mistress Odera waved her off. "That's more than fine. How about we meet at the Caravan Guild office and decide from there? My great-granddaughter should be in town. It might be nice to introduce the two of you. She's just a few years older than you, I believe."

I'm the same age as her great-granddaughter? Tala knew about how old Mistress Odera was, but she'd never really put it in that light. "Oh, sure." She shrugged. "That would work."

Millennial Mage, 5 - Fusing

Mistress Odera smiled. "Alright, then. I'll send a message if I'm unable to meet up tomorrow. Otherwise, I'll see you just after sunrise?"

"I look forward to it." Tala turned and crouched next to the ladder of the now-stopped wagon. "Thank you, Tion, for getting us back."

He glanced her way with a smile. "A pleasure to serve, Mistress."

Tala patted his shoulder, stood, turned, and stepped off the top, Terry reflexively sinking his claws into her shoulder to stay in place as she dropped.

She absorbed her landing fairly well, only feeling a minuscule drop in endingberry power. *You know, I should keep that in my system, even in the city. It really feels like it reinforces my pathways enough to warrant the use of resources.*

After a moment's thought, she shrugged. *After I visit Holly.* She rubbed the right side of her chest in remembered pain. *I wonder why it didn't protect against that injury. Maybe Holly will know.*

She'd also need to find more ending trees to harvest. *And a more efficient means of harvesting...*

She was about to head to the pay clerk but realized that it would take a bit for her cut to be calculated. Instead, she turned and walked to the chuckwagon.

Amnin greeted her. "You know, Mistress, we cannot possibly be done already."

Tala grinned. "Of course not, Amnin. I just wanted to say thank you for the wonderful meals on this trip. I know you all had to work odd hours more than a time or two to keep us fed and awake."

Amnin gave her a searching look, then smiled. "It was my pleasure, Mistress." After a brief hesitation, she added, "Are you sure you would like *all* the meat jerked?"

Terry perked up at that, and Tala glanced his way with a grin. "Absolutely. Are you sure that the bones, alone, are sufficient payment?"

"Definitely. They are almost too much." Amnin smiled. After a brief pause, she asked, "Was there something that I can do for you, Mistress?"

"No, I just came by to express my gratitude."

"Well, you are welcome."

Tala gave a bow of her head. "Thank you once again. I hope that we see each other again soon."

Amnin waved farewell as Tala departed.

Tala then made a slow circuit of the work yard, stretching her legs before walking over to the pay clerk and waiting in the short line. Ostensibly, Mistress Odera and the lead caravan guard had submitted their reports with Archive tablets. Even so, it still took a bit for all the calculations to iterate through the system and tally. When they were complete, Tala walked away with an additional forty-five gold and fifty-three silver.

Her pay this time was a bit less than the last leg but not by much. They hadn't lost anyone, so there were no death benefits to be paid, and the healing costs were lower, stars be praised, but they'd also, ironically, defended the caravan from fewer creatures in total.

And we have more guards to split the payout with, given they all survived.

She frowned. *Which would be more cost-effective?*

She shook her head. *Nope!*

She decided that she wasn't a fan of that line of thought.

Moving on!

Rane came through the payment line a little while after her, but Tala didn't mind waiting.

He smiled as he walked up to her. "What's the plan?"

Millennial Mage, 5 - Fusing

Huh, he immediately assumes I have something in mind. She almost prodded him about that, but then, she realized that she did, in fact, have some things in mind, so she shrugged. "I'll talk my potential next route through with Mistress Odera tomorrow, but I want to take a bit to round out some of my training." She hesitated. "You interested in joining me on the next trip? This one wasn't exactly the safest."

Rane barked a laugh. "That's true enough." Still, he smiled. "If you're not sick of me yet, I think I'd like that."

"Any preferences on where to?"

"Nothing specific." He gave her a searching look. "You know, most routes from here will go through Marliweather."

Tala grimaced. "Yeah."

He glanced away, his voice dropping as if to not be overheard. "You don't have to see them, even if you're in the same city."

A small, sad smile pulled at her features. "I know."

"But you don't want to risk it."

"Yeah." She sighed. "But before we leave for anything, I need to visit Mistress Holly for all sorts of reasons. After that, I think a couple of quick runs are in order." She sighed. "I wish that the Alefast route wasn't so coveted. But I think a circumnavigation of the mountains to Arconaven would be nice. After that? North, maybe? I've never seen a city being built. That might be pretty interesting."

"Any plans for tonight?" He seemed a bit uncertain.

"Find Lyn. See what's been happening. I haven't seen her in a long time, and I think it would be good for the two of us to catch up."

Rane nodded, glancing away. "Ahh, well, I should leave you to that. Care to meet up for training tomorrow?"

"Yeah!" Tala grinned. "We should definitely drop through and see Adam. We were gone longer than expected, but they might still be open for sparring and working together. I could use a different sparring partner."

Rane's face fell, but Tala smiled a bit brighter and patted him on the shoulder, having to reach up to do so.

"Don't worry, we'll still fight, but we know each other's fighting styles so well these days that I feel like I'm more playing a guessing game than fighting. Does that make any sense?"

He shrugged, smiling a bit at that. "It makes some sense, but we've still a lot we can learn from each other."

"Undoubtedly, but if we're going on the next route together, we'll have plenty of time for that on the road."

"True."

"Besides, they'll train with you, too, don't forget. Mages who are willing to train with the guard aren't *that* common."

He nodded. "True enough."

"Well, then. See you tomorrow?"

"Yeah. Midmorning? At the guard's compound we went to last time?"

"That sounds great." Tala gave him a quick hug goodbye, which he returned on reflex, and set off into the city.

Behind her, Rane stared after her, seeming mildly confused.

Huh, why did I do that? She shrugged. *Whatever. To Lyn!*

* * *

Tala stood in the darkened street, illuminated by well-spaced streetlights, staring at the large building which stood less than a block from Lyn's house on the opposite side of the street.

Wasn't this whole block a park? She felt an odd pressure from the building, but that might have just been the mass of humanity crowded within and the light and noise spilling out onto the otherwise quiet, evening street. *I suppose a tavern isn't that odd to see here, but I would have sworn that it wasn't…*

She shook her head, continuing on. *I'll ask Lyn.*

A couple of minutes later, she was standing outside the familiar door. It was locked, but that was no barrier. Tala pulled out her key and opened the door, stepping inside. "Lyn?"

The lights were on, subtle magic flowing through the air along with the light. *That's a bit odd.*

"Lyn, are you here?" She looked closer at the magical lights and noticed that the light they emitted had a hint of magic lingering within. *Like how magical fire carries a signature.* She'd never really noticed it, before. *Holly did say that my senses would continue to improve. I'll have to ask her, I suppose.*

A thump, reminiscent of a heavy book being set down on a side table, preceded that of bare feet, running through the house. "Tala?" Lyn pulled to a halt just out of arms' reach.

Tala frowned. "Are you okay?"

Lyn straightened a bit, cocking an eyebrow. "Am I okay?" She shook her head. "You don't write. You don't send word. I had to find out about your delay in Makinaven *third hand*, Tala." She met Tala's gaze, directly. Lyn's eyes were filled with barely contained irritation. "I'm your guild contact, your landlord, and your friend."

Tala opened her mouth but found herself speechless. She was completely on the back foot. *She's right.* "I…

I'm sorry, Lyn. You're right. I should have let you know, somehow."

The older woman looked marginally shocked but didn't respond right away, so Tala continued.

"I'm planning on looking into Archive tablets, and that should let me communicate more effectively, going forwards. I truly am sorry. I didn't even consider letting you know, and I should have."

Lyn sighed and nodded, clearly still a bit frustrated but not willing to press the issue.

Tala scratched the back of her head self-consciously. Then an idea struck. "Oh! Let me make you some tea. I got some in Makinaven, and I think you'll like it."

The mention of tea seemed to lift Lyn's mood. "Ha! Tala, that's brilliant, and a cup sounds wonderful. Thank you." She stepped forward and gave Tala a hug.

Tala returned it, hesitantly. *What is with the hugs this evening?*

"I really did miss you, Tala." Lyn still sounded a bit frustrated, but Tala didn't doubt the sincerity of the sentiment.

"And I you."

Lyn linked arms with Tala, drawing her into the sitting room.

Tala took a deep breath, reveling in the scent of the place. There wasn't anything specific that stood out, but it just smelled *right.*

"So, will you need help selling the tea you brought back?"

Tala gave her an odd look. "What?"

"The tea. Do you already have a buyer, or will you need help?"

"I just bought tea for myself. Why would I have brought extra?"

Millennial Mage, 5 - Fusing

Lyn turned to regard her. "Oh... Tea is one of Makinaven's primary exports. This season? It's easy to make a thirty to fifty percent profit if you have the right buyers here. More if you sell it to end users yourself, but that takes time that I think you don't want to spend. You can make more with specific types or producers, less if it's growing season here."

Tala groaned. "I even bought more for myself as I was leaving. And I even have some money..."

"I'm sorry, Tala. We never really discussed possible trade goods on your routes." Lyn patted her arm. "Come, now. It wasn't something we were thinking of because you were... less financially well off. It sounds like that's changed?"

Tala shrugged. "You could say that." She remembered recording her most recent payout.

Seventy gold, one-hundred-forty-eight silver, and fifty copper.

She shook her head in realization. "One moment."

Tala pulled a small notebook from Kit and flipped to the furthest page with writing on it. *I didn't carry over the conversion. Seventy-one gold, forty-eight silver, and fifty copper.*

"There. Sorry about that, I just realized that I neglected to do something." She sighed. "I do have another payment due on my debts tomorrow, too."

Lyn gave a small smile and cocked an eyebrow.

Tala grinned. "And I owe you twenty silver for this month's rent." She grimaced then. "Do I owe any late fee or anything?"

Lyn laughed, taking a seat in one of the chairs. "Let's have some tea and call it even." She hesitated. "I mean, if that's alright. I don't mean that you're obligated to—"

Tala held up a hand, smiling. "That sounds wonderful. I want to hear what's been going on with you."

Lyn smiled, in return, clearly relaxing a bit. "Only if you tell me of your adventure after."

"That sounds wonderful."

The night wore on as the two friends spoke and spun tales. They laughed as the chamomile tea flowed, keeping throats wet and words flowing. After all, it took a long time to fully discuss their nearly two months apart.

In the end, they didn't get to their respective beds until after midnight.

It is good to be home.

Chapter: 21
Aproa

Tala woke early and moved through her standard routine despite her late bedtime. *If I let myself sleep in, I'll just rotate my whole schedule around and muck up all my habits.* And that was the best result she could expect.

When she finally exited Kit, she felt relaxed, refreshed, and awake. Ready to face the day.

As she climbed out into her room in Lyn's house, she found herself frowning. *I should just rent a closet or something. I don't need the whole room when I'm staying inside Kit.* Probably worth discussing with Lyn.

That would only become more true as time went on and Kit grew bigger on the inside. *Speaking of which, that's not a bad use of funds if I have any to spare.* She hesitated at that. *No. I'll need to buy some goods to trade on my next route.*

She sighed. *I should set aside some amount of gold for trades and use the profits from that to expand Kit.*

She tilted her head to the side. *That is an excellent idea. It would allow me to expand Kit at a regular rate without taking from my other funds.*

Terry flickered to her shoulder, giving her a soft headbutt and pulling her mind back to the present.

"Morning Terry."

He trilled back, happily.

The sky was still dark outside, but Tala knew that dawn was near at hand.

Millennial Mage, 5 - Fusing

"To breakfast!"

Lyn was awake but seemed much less chipper than Tala.

"Good morning, Lyn."

"Morning."

"What are you doing up?"

Lyn gave her a quizzical look. "I have work."

"Ahh, right. When do you head in?"

She shrugged. "Any time now. You're meeting your mentor at the Guildhall, right?"

"That's right, but I need to drop through the work yard to charge the cargo slots first."

Lyn stood, heading toward the door. "Let's go then; I don't want to be late."

They locked the door behind them and headed through the still-dark streets.

As they passed the tavern, Tala was a bit confused, given that it seemed to still be busy.

"When did they build that place?" Tala gestured. "It seems quite popular."

Lyn gave her an odd look. "Tala, that's been there…" She shook her head. "Rust, I don't remember a time it wasn't there."

Tala looked at her questioningly. "There is no way that was there before I left. We'd have eaten there, at least once."

"Didn't we?"

"No. We most certainly did not."

They both stopped, looking at the tavern. After a long moment, Lyn turned and started walking.

"Where are you going, Lyn?"

Lyn glanced back her way. "To the work yard. You coming?" She glanced at the tavern behind Tala. "If you want, we can grab lunch there or maybe dinner."

"Aren't you the least bit curious?"

"Of course. That's why I suggested eating there later today." Lyn frowned, then shook her head. "Tomorrow might be better, and we definitely don't have time, now. Come on. I don't want to be late."

Tala rolled her eyes. *Whatever. I'll figure it out later.*

They walked on through the cold streets. There wasn't much snow on the ground, and the melded paving stones felt fantastic to Tala's bare feet. *I love the winter.*

They talked about small things as they went, but eventually, Tala brought the conversation around to a topic from the night before. "Like I mentioned last night, I do have the thunder bull horns and skins."

"So you said."

"They aren't tea, but I would like to sell them."

"I can deal with the horns for ten percent. The skins, I think you should take to the Constructionists to meld with your elk leathers."

Tala was hung up on the first part. "Ten percent?"

Lyn shrugged. "I can get six gold apiece. You got five before, right? In a waning city?" She smiled mischievously. "You'll end up with more in the end. Trust me."

Tala huffed a laugh. "I do, I do. Fine." After a moment, Tala frowned. "You really think I should use the thunder leather for myself?" *Ooo, I like the sound of that… I wonder if that's really what it's called.*

"Yes, and you should soul-bond those clothes before you run out of luck and lose them."

That was a very good point. She did intend to bond them eventually. *And I can't bond Kit yet.* She tsked. *Not for a long time, yet.* "Yeah… You've got a solid point, there."

If she did, she could finally get some use out of Merilin's other clothes. *All I've ever really done is try them on. I want to wear them, but it isn't worth the risk, either of damaging them or ending up naked.*

"Yeah. I think you're right."

"Oh, of course I am. I'm glad that you're beginning to see it." Tala laughed, and their conversation turned to more frivolous topics once again.

They reached the work yard, and Tala did her duty, quickly refilling the dimensional storage items' reserves of power.

From there, they quick-walked to the Guildhall, arriving about the time that Lyn needed to check in for work. They said a hasty goodbye, and Tala began looking around for Mistress Odera.

The older woman wasn't hard to find; she was waiting to one side, just inside the doors.

Lyn gave a slight bow to the woman as she passed but otherwise headed straight for the back.

Tala walked over to Mistress Odera and her companion, ostensibly her great-granddaughter. With a bow, Tala greeted the older Mage. "Mistress Odera. It is a pleasure to see you."

"Mistress Tala, thank you for joining us for breakfast." She turned to the side, indicating the woman beside her. "This is my great-granddaughter, Aproa."

Tala gave a second bow to Aproa. "Mistress Aproa, a pleasure to meet you."

Aproa bowed in return. "As it is to meet you, Mistress Tala. My great-grandmother has had many wonderful things to say about you."

Tala gave a half-smile. "Funny, I never took Mistress Odera to be a liar."

The woman laughed even as Mistress Odera rolled her eyes, and Tala took that moment to assess the Mage, combining what she'd already seen with what she could detect in the brief lull in the conversation.

The Archon, not Mage, she corrected. *Almost Fused.* Aproa was well ahead of Tala and Rane on the progression to Fused, though that was to be expected. By her looks, she was late twenties, but as Tala had well and truly learned, perceptions were only vaguely useful when trying to determine the age of a Mage.

She was traditionally beautiful, but more in the way a winemaker or craftsman was beautiful than the delicate beauty of a fairytale princess. Aproa's beauty was strong and vibrant, her face nicely framed by her almost perfectly black hair.

She wore very traditional Mage's robes, but they were made from sturdy leather rather than cloth. The clasps, at a quick glance, seemed wholly insufficient to hold the garment on despite the perfect fit. *There must be something else that adds to the security of the closure.*

There was a sense about the Archon that made Tala feel like she didn't have enough air, even though she knew that wasn't the case; she could breathe just fine. *What is her specialization?*

Aproa was obviously a Material Guide, specializing in air, and she wore two heavily inscribed bar maces hanging from her belt, one on each side. The weapons were inscribed identically. From what Tala could see, each was meant simply to drive air away from themselves.

Tala frowned. *No, it's more nuanced than that.* She'd have to study the inscriptions in more detail if she really wanted to understand them, but that wasn't something she could do right then.

The moment passed, and Tala was pulled back to the needs of the social situation.

Mistress Odera was shaking her head. "Self-deprecation doesn't become you, Mistress Tala. Come.

Millennial Mage, 5 - Fusing

Let us grab breakfast. There is much that we should discuss."

What? She almost frowned before she remembered. *Right. I joked that anything good said about me would have to be a lie.* Tala just smiled as they began to walk.

The three of them moved toward the guild lounge. In the silence, Tala decided to go for nostalgia. "Mistress Aproa, what is your foundation?"

The other woman smiled genuinely, responding without hesitation. "Having the wind knocked out of you should be more literal."

Tala gave her a quizzical look, then glanced down to the maces. She found herself chuckling. "Really?"

Aproa shrugged. "Yeah. Seems to fit, and it's very satisfying to drop a magical creature by driving the air from their lungs."

"I'll bet."

"There are obviously other things that I can do, but that is the foundation of what I pursued."

"I'd be curious to learn about those other things."

As they entered through the large, double doors, a vaguely familiar form stood up from a nearby table. "Well, as I live and breathe. Mistress Tala?"

Tala frowned for a moment before it clicked. "Master Cran, good to see you."

The man bowed. "Life seems to be treating you well." He grinned. "You don't have the same timidity about you as you did when Mistress Lyn brought you in." His eyes flicked to the two women beside her.

"Oh!" Tala cleared her throat. "My apologies. This is Master Cran. Master Cran, this is Mistress Odera and Mistress Aproa."

He bowed to each in turn. "It is a pleasure to see each of you once again."

Of course, he's met them before. Tala kept herself from rolling her eyes.

They gave bows of their heads in return, and the group exchanged mild pleasantries for another moment before Mistress Odera excused them politely, stating that they had quite a bit to discuss between the three of them.

Cran took the dismissal with grace, smiling and wishing them a wonderful day before he returned to his table and his book.

The three women took a table in a back corner, and Mistress Odera ordered a spread of food fit for a dozen people.

Aproa cocked an eyebrow, evaluating Tala again. "So, Gran wasn't pulling my leg? You really can eat that much?"

Tala shrugged. "Yeah. I almost have to, actually."

"Fascinating. Your defense is in the 'take the hit' category, then? Rather than avoiding or mitigating?"

Tala glanced to Mistress Odera. "She doesn't know?"

The older woman shrugged. "Your magics are yours. The curiosity of your eating isn't a secret, but the specifics of your defenses?" She shook her head. "That is not for me to share."

Tala actually felt a bit touched by that. Though she wasn't sure she'd have offered the same courtesy in Mistress Odera's position. *What does that say about me?* "Well, thank you." She smiled, turning back to Aproa. "I have heightened regeneration, as well as a good measure of increased resilience."

Aproa clucked her tongue. "Your regeneration pulls from your stores, hence the need to eat more."

"Precisely."

"Fascinating indeed." Aproa bit her lip, seeming to be contemplating how to ask something.

"What is it?"

The woman looked to her great-grandmother, who smiled but didn't say anything.

"Well..." Aproa swallowed, glancing away. "I'm in need of martial practice, but opponents are in short supply, unless I want to spend half a decade in the wilderness."

Tala immediately thought of Rane for a number of reasons and suppressed a smile. "Oh?"

Aproa nodded. "So, I was wondering if you would be interested in sparring on occasion."

"Sure."

The Archon blinked back at Tala. "Just like that?"

"Sure. I could use a greater variety of opponents. I'm going to the training yard after breakfast. You can come if you want."

She brightened visibly. "That would be fantastic! Thank you."

The food arrived shortly after that and put a damper on conversation. The words that were exchanged were simple small talk.

As the meal was wrapping up, Mistress Odera turned the conversation to their next venture. "I think that we should go to Marliweather next."

Tala stiffened. "Let's go to Arconaven."

Mistress Odera gave her an odd look. "Why?"

"I've never been that way?"

A single raised eyebrow was the Mage's only response.

Aproa suppressed a laugh.

Tala frowned toward the woman.

"Excuse me, sorry. I just am used to being on the receiving end of that look."

That made Tala smile and relieved some of the tension. "I'd rather not go to Marliweather, not just yet."

"Why." The inflection made it more of a statement than a question, almost a command to explain. Mistress Odera would obviously know that Tala had grown up in Marliweather, but she was likely unaware of Tala's feelings about her family. They had danced around the topic on occasion, but Tala really hadn't been interested in discussing it with the woman before, nor was she about to do so now.

"My reasons are my own, for now. As the forest cities are not reasonable options, I think Arconaven is a perfect choice."

Mistress Odera frowned but didn't press. "Most routes to Arconaven go through Marliweather, but there are a couple a month that go direct. I'll look into it. Will Master Rane be joining us?"

"That is my understanding."

"Good. I'll see what is available."

The three chatted a little while longer to let their food settle, but it wasn't too long before Tala sighed contentedly and pushed back from the table. "We should get going, Mistress Aproa. Master Rane is going to meet me for training, and now is as good a time as any to start sparring with you as well."

"That sounds wonderful."

The three stood in unison, the younger women bidding Mistress Odera goodbye and thanking her for the meal before departing.

Mistress Odera, for her part, sat back down and pulled out a book, content to sip her tea and enjoy the peace and quiet of solitude.

* * *

When they arrived at the guardsmen's training ground, Aproa pulled up short. "Here?" She looked to Tala. "I'd thought you would have rented a training ground for Mages."

Tala shrugged. "We're primarily melee fighters, so guards make good opponents."

"Huh." Aproa was frowning.

"What?"

"I mean... it seems unfair?"

Tala grinned. "Wait 'til you meet Adam."

Aproa still seemed skeptical but didn't object further.

Tala returned her attention to the training yard, filled as ever with men and women going through various forms, exercising, or sparring. As usual, there was a scattering of healing-focused Mages throughout, ready to attend to any injury.

Tala stepped across the almost invisible line between street and training yard, and immediately, the closest person stopped what she was doing and came their way.

She bowed low. "Mistresses. How can the guard serve today?"

Tala cocked an eyebrow. *A bit more subservient than before.* She glanced to Aproa. *Maybe, because there are two of us?* "What is your name, please?"

"Joa, Mistress."

"Well, Guardsman Joa, I am Tala. We are looking for Master Rane or Guardsman Adam. Are either here?"

"I'll go check. Do you mind waiting here?"

"Not at all. Thank you."

Joa turned and jogged through her fellows, toward the nearest building.

Tala glanced toward Aproa with a smile. "She shouldn't take long."

Indeed, Joa had barely disappeared inside before a familiar figure stepped out, waving their way.

Joa appeared again shortly thereafter, returning the way she'd come. "Mistresses, you are expected." She gestured to the main building. "Would you like a guide?"

"No. Thank you, Joa."

Joa bowed to the Mages once more before returning to her exercise.

Tala and Aproa crossed the yard, careful to not disrupt anyone that they passed.

Adam, the man who had waved to them, was waiting for them when they reached the building. "Mistress Tala, a pleasure to see you."

"Adam. How have you been? How's the family?"

"Good, good. Thank you for asking. I stick close to home through winter. So, we're all happier this time of year. I hear your adventure was more... adventurous than ideal."

Tala snorted a laugh. "I'll say." She turned toward her companion. "Adam, this is Mistress Aproa. Mistress Aproa, this is Guardsman Adam."

Adam bowed to the new Mage. "Good to meet you, Mistress Aproa."

"Likewise, I'm sure." Aproa gave a small bow.

"Master Rane is already here." Adam turned, gesturing into the building.

They walked in near silence for the short way to a familiar courtyard.

Tala found herself grinning. "Hey! You got us the same one."

"Indeed we did."

"Thank you, Adam."

He cracked a smile. "It was a small thing."

They came out onto the surrounding, open-air walkway, a few steps above the sand of the training yard.

Down in the sand, Rane was sparring against some eight guards, all on the younger side. Force was still at his

Millennial Mage, 5 - Fusing

waist, only evident by the handle sticking out of his dimensional storage. In the greatsword's place, Rane wielded a longsword and shield.

The fight was near its end, so the three new arrivals simply watched as Rane was finally overwhelmed by the sheer number of opponents.

Even so, he eliminated four before they took him down.

Aproa was frowning when Tala glanced her way. "What is it?"

The other woman clicked her tongue, behind her teeth. "It just seems… odd to have guards take down a Mage."

Adam smiled. "To be fair, he isn't using his main weapon. We don't wish for deaths here. And Master Rane can deliver death blows that are just that, more quickly than the healer in attendance can see to the injured."

Aproa nodded but still seemed… uncertain.

Rane kicked up from the ground, landing on his feet before he laughed and thanked those who'd been sparring with him. He noticed the new arrivals, then. "Mistress Tala!"

Tala waved. "Good morning, Master Rane."

He walked over, smiling. "I am Rane." He bowed toward Aproa.

"I am Aproa." She glanced to Tala. "Mistress Tala was kind enough to allow me to join you in your training, today."

"Oh?" He looked to Tala, who nodded. "How did you two meet?"

Tala smiled back at the big man. "She's Mistress Odera's great-granddaughter."

Rane blinked at Tala for a moment, then regarded Aproa once again before clearing his throat. "Well, then." His eyes took in her maces, then he looked back to Tala. "How did you want to start this?"

Tala shrugged. "I figured Adam could fight her. Give her a good picture of why we're here."

Adam cleared his throat, looking mildly embarrassed but not surprised. "It actually would be good for me to get a gauge on her abilities if we are to incorporate her into the rotations."

Aproa looked skeptical but didn't object, so Tala nodded. "That sounds wonderful. Mistress Aproa?"

"Yes?"

"We'll have you use training weapons, if that's acceptable. You can probably use your actual maces when fighting myself or Master Rane, but not against the guardsmen."

She shrugged, setting the maces aside.

One of the students came over, offering her a practice pair.

Aproa's eyes widened slightly as she took them. "Thank you. These are a near match."

The young man smiled. "I'm glad. They seemed the best of what we had on hand."

She gave a slight bow. "Thank you."

Adam walked out onto the sand. "Are you ready?" A student tossed him a short sword, which he caught with ease.

With a resigned expression on her face, Aproa joined him on the sand. "I suppose so."

Chapter: 22
Five Percent

Tala grinned as she watched the first, quick bout. Even Terry lifted his head from her shoulder before flickering to his favorite spot on the roof to sun-bask and watch.

Adam neatly sidestepped or bent out of the way of Aproa's attacks before moving in to place the tip of his practice weapon to her throat.

The Archon froze, simply staring at the man before she glanced at Tala.

Adam stepped back a few paces.

Aproa laughed. "Fair enough." Her grin was almost hungry as she looked back to Adam. "Again, please."

He nodded acceptance, lifting his blade back to a more formal, ready position.

"With magic defenses to incapacitation or surrender."

Adam hesitated. "If you wish, Mistress. That highly favors you, though."

She shrugged. "It seems that I need a reasonable set of advantages."

He still seemed hesitant, but he agreed. "As you wish." And Tala would have sworn he was trying to keep a small smile from blossoming across his features.

The second fight was considerably longer. Aproa, it seemed, could thicken the air in a weaker imitation of Mistress Odera's shields. What she gave up in strength, however, she gained in speed of manifestation.

Millennial Mage, 5 - Fusing

The thickened air could be almost instantly enacted, easily fouling the intercepted attempts to strike her down.

For his part, Adam quickly adapted, seeming to notice that Aproa had to see an attack coming to enact her defense. Additionally, there was a slight visual distortion caused by Aproa's defensive magic, which Tala guessed was how Adam saw the workings. His movements became quicker, and he added feints and redirects that Tala had trouble following.

A simple turn of Adam's wrist would radically change the point of attack, often bypassing the defenses Aproa raised.

Still, though Adam scored hit after hit, most likely leaving damaged flesh and possibly even bruised bones, Aproa persisted, her own weapons sweeping through the air in dizzying patterns, their momentum mostly maintained through the striking sequences.

Tala noted that Adam was at yet another disadvantage, given that his 'sword' wouldn't cut like a real one would, but Aproa's clubs would hit very nearly as hard as their non-practice lookalikes.

Even so, Adam didn't seem concerned. He rarely deigned to block her attacks directly, and when he did, it was almost always a deflection.

The final strike came suddenly, with nothing to set it apart from the flurry of exchanged blows that preceded it.

Aproa was swinging for Adam's head with her left mace, a look of growing frustration across her features.

Adam stepped in, cutting at the wrist of the striking hand. This counterstrike was stopped by thickened air, which also spoiled Aproa's own attack.

As he was cutting toward the attacking wrist, Adam stomped down on the Mage's leading foot, causing her to bend forward reflexively from the shock and pain. Taking full advantage of that exact reaction, Adam struck Aproa across the center of her face with his offhand, breaking her nasal bone and folding the entire nose over to one side.

Aproa cried out in pain, dropping her maces and clutching her face, even as blood spurted from her nostrils.

The healer was there in an instant, power washing through Aproa and reversing the injury.

Adam, for his part, had quick-stepped backwards, somehow wholly avoiding getting even a drop of blood on himself.

When the healer returned to the side, Aproa grimaced, then spat onto the sand, clearing her mouth of some blood. "That was... instructive."

Adam gave a slight bow. "Indeed. Are you alright, Mistress?"

The Archon shook her head, smiling. "The only lasting injury is to my pride." She glanced down with a small frown. "Well, and these bloodstains will be mildly irritating to get out." She shrugged and smiled again. "What did you learn, master Guardsman?"

Tala felt herself smile at the honorific given to Adam. *Well earned, indeed.*

Adam nodded. "You don't block what you can't see, for one."

Aproa frowned at that. "I *don't*? Don't you mean *can't*?"

"Not at all." He swept his sword in a tight circle around his head. "There, I have just blocked behind my head. I did not have to see behind me to defend my skull. You are capable of thickening the air out of your line of sight, yes? I believe you did so a few times when I made my next place of attack more obvious."

She nodded in return, considering.

Millennial Mage, 5 - Fusing

"Right, so here is my recommendation. You clearly have some training in striking and defensive patterns. We can map out standard defenses that cover for the openings in each of your patterns, and you can practice forming those defenses instinctively, whether you think an attack is coming there or not. Additionally, you need more practice against multiple opponents to increase your instincts for where attacks could be coming from based on the flow of the fight."

"That sounds wonderful." She bowed to the man. "Thank you."

The rest of the morning went largely as Tala had expected. Since the Mages were restricted to mostly mundane fighting to help them improve those skills to better complement their magics, they were usually beaten, whether by groups of newer guards or individual, more experienced fighters.

Throughout, the instructors gave tips and corrections to all combatants, and all in all, it was a refreshing way to spend the time.

Tala, for her part, cycled between three of Flow's forms, as well as empty-hand combat. She participated in matches with each of those four weapon sets in one-on-one, one-on-a-group, and group-vs-group.

The only style of traditional fighting she didn't practice that morning was fighting with Flow able to change shape mid-fight. *Not precisely traditional, but it will be good to add in tomorrow.*

She also deeply wanted more practice with her bloodstars, but that would also have to wait for now.

When lunch rolled around, the guards wished the Mages farewell and let them know that this training ground would be open to any or all of them for the time being.

Rane, Aproa, and Tala then briefly discussed the plan going forward.

Aproa smiled. "Thank you for letting me come today. I think it was a really good change of pace. I can see it adding a lot to my capabilities, going forward."

Rane cocked his head to the side. "What do you normally do for training?"

"A few of us meet up in one of the Mage training yards to practice defense and offense, target protection or acquisition, and a host of other things. You are both welcome if you'd like. We meet after lunch daily. Though not everyone makes it every day. We could go grab some food and head over?"

Rane glanced to Tala inquiringly, clearly interested.

Tala shrugged. "I definitely need to eat, but afterwards, I really should drop by my inscriber. There are a *lot* of things that I need checked into, including refreshing my scripts." *Memory modification not the least.* Truthfully, a large part of her had wanted to go straight to Holly when she arrived back in Bandfast so that she could learn what she could about what had happened to her, but another part was afraid to find out the truth. She pushed that aside. "Tomorrow? We can do more martial work here in the morning, then the magical training after noon?"

"That sounds good." Rane turned back to Aproa. "I'm free after lunch if the offer is good for just me."

She smiled in return. "Of course!" She looked back to Tala. "And that sounds like a great plan for tomorrow. So… lunch?"

Rane and Tala heartily agreed.

* * *

Lunch was fantastic, but Tala continually found herself distracted by her upcoming visit to Holly's workshop.

Millennial Mage, 5 - Fusing

Am I just an automaton, making my choices based on what some creature put in my head? Intellectually, she knew that was silly. Xeel had assured her that the influence had been slight, a nudge more than a push, and certainly not an in-depth hijacking of her will.

Even so, she found herself almost as afraid of learning as she was of not knowing. *That's just ridiculous.*

She bid goodbye to Rane and Aproa and set off to Holly's.

As she stepped inside the moderately warm building, a buzz of power rippled across her neck. *Connecting to Holly's systems.*

"Finally."

Tala almost shrieked in surprise as Holly stood from a chair right beside the door. Terry lifted his head to glance at her, then curled back down, unimpressed.

"I thought I'd have to track you down. Come on." Holly walked toward the back, beckoning for Tala to follow.

Tala rested her hand on the center of her own chest, feeling the need to calm her heart. *Was she just waiting there? How did I not sense her through the wall?*

Still, the older woman didn't slow, and so Tala followed her back to the familiar workroom.

When the door swung shut, a series of inscriptions activated across Holly's skin, which Tala had never seen active before.

Power hummed through the air, and a second series of inscriptions activated, this time in the shape of a cube around the entire workroom.

"Now, Mistress Tala. Have a seat."

Tala was looking around, trying to study the working embedded in the walls, floor, and ceiling. "What did you do?"

"I cut us off from any outside intervention or eavesdropping. Be sparing with your magic; you only have what is in your body at the moment."

Tala looked inside, frowning, but she found her gate... not gone, but closed off, somehow.

She began to hyperventilate. *How is this possible? You can close someone else's gate?*

Of course, it made sense in theory, but she'd never... *Breathe, Tala.*

Holly sat on her own stool, calmly waiting for Tala to move.

One step at a time. She walked over and sat in the chair left available to her.

"Good." She smiled. "First things first. You are not corrupted. Your mind is still under the control of the real you, mainly your spirit and soul." She frowned lightly. "Though, you haven't been treating your body very well, but that is a later conversation."

"So... I'm not being controlled?"

"No, not at all. There is a bit of a lingering influence, pushing you a bit more toward dangerous actions, but that is less pronounced than you might think. I'd give it a five percent stake in your decision-making, assuming you aren't in a high-stress environment."

"You mean like on the road? Pursued by armies of Leshkin?"

"Fair point."

"So... what happened?"

"The short version? You had your short-term memory erased, twice it seems, but I only have a record of one."

"Can you recover it?"

Holly gave a puzzled look. "No, dear. I don't have a brain scan to even begin restructuring your lost memories. All the inscriptions recorded were magics in and around you and physical stresses you endured."

"Would that help?"

"Maybe? If we expanded the capacity of your consciousness monitor, it could delve into your mind and pull out memory fragments." She shrugged. "We might be able to piece something together, but that would be a substantial upgrade to the functionality—and something I wouldn't recommend to anyone with a lower power density than you." She smiled. "So, the inscriptions in question would normally be reserved for those who are at least Fused, preferably Refined."

"But I could sustain them?"

"You could." She hesitated. "You would need a link to the Archive, though. No human mind below Reforged could handle the stress." She tapped her side. "I keep myself well-inscribed toward that end, but you don't like staying in cities, and losing a connection required for a working within your mind would be… bad."

Tala nodded. "What do you suggest, then?"

"Soul-bond an Archive tablet. An artifact style, of course."

"What would that even do?"

"Well, once you'd done that, I would be able to modify your consciousness monitor to use that link to copy out your mental structure and parse through it, among other things."

Tala's eyes widened. "You want my mind to be copied to the Archive?"

Holly sighed. "No, dear. I effectively want to take pictures of your brain's structure and cognitive pathways so that your scripts can analyze a static version. That is *much* less intensive than trying to analyze your mind as it is actively working."

"What then?" Tala was still quite apprehensive.

"It could then present you with recompiled memories as it reconstructs them. In time, it could do a lot of other things as well. It would expand your cognitive abilities further and utilize your increased mental capacities better than we've managed already, perform calculations, and in theory, it could even offer advice."

"Offer advice." She gave Holly a deadpan look.

Holly shrugged. "Any sort of sentience requires a soul or spirit, and since yours is the only one in there, it would be coming from you. But yes, 'advice' is the right word. It could process more information than you, alone, and then offer up the decision that you would have made if you had time to process it all yourself."

"That could work…" There were all sorts of odd implications, but it bore consideration. Tala had a thought, then. "What if my mind was altered again?"

"You'd have, available to your magic, ongoing versions of your mind. From those, your inscriptions could fill in the gaps and rebuild what you lost, presenting to you the memories that something tried to destroy."

Tala considered that. "All it would take is letting my mind map be available in the Archive."

Holly shook her head. "Not at all. Firstly, you should know by now that the Archive is inviolable. The information pulled from you would be stored in a way locked to you and your scripts. No one else would ever have access unless you granted them such." She held up her hand. "And before you ask, with your mental monitoring inscription, it would be virtually impossible for someone to force you to grant that access. The scripts would detect coercion and prevent the approval from going through. Secondly, the inscription will be *far* more than simply the capturing and transferring of mind maps."

The more she considered it, the more Tala sort of liked the idea. *Plus, I've been wanting an Archive tablet anyway.* "So, then could I pull other information from the Archive directly into my mind?"

"Technically, yes, but the conscious mind really can't handle true info dumps. You could call up specific books that you were authorized to access and read phantom copies. But you couldn't simply *wish* to know what a book said and imbibe it."

Tala considered. "What about subconsciously?"

"Subconsciously?" Holly tapped her lips. "I suppose we could train your subconscious to utilize the bond, but that would take time that I don't really have."

"I could use an inside-out Archon Star."

Holly frowned. "An inside-out Arch—" Her eyes lost focus like she was reading something that lay between Holly and Tala. "Huh. That's interesting." Her eyes began flicking back and forth, adding to the sense that Holly was reading. "Yeah, that could work. You'd have to learn how to make one, though…" Her eyes refocused, then she sighed. "Let me guess, you already did so, by accident, and found someone to tell you what you had done?"

That was almost hurtfully accurate. "Something like that."

Holly sighed again. "Alright, then. From what I understand, that would allow for some interesting things, but you would lose conscious control of the connection, at least until you trained that, specifically. I'd have quite a bit of research to do, in order to integrate it, but I like learning new things."

"Could the conscious control be mimicked by the inscription? That would eliminate the need for training."

"You mean you ask the inscription for a book, and it presents it to you?" Holly cocked her head to the side. "Interesting. It could work, but it would be at least a bit less efficient for that. More complex, too." She nodded. "It would be far better for the memory archive and analysis of your mind maps, though."

"So?"

"So, yes. I think that would actually be a fantastic use for you." She shrugged. "I'll have to finish designing the script with this in mind. As I consider it, I'd likely have come to the need for a subconscious bond in the end, and I'd have suggested it then."

Would you now? Tala grinned.

"What else do you wish to discuss?"

Tala frowned. "You mean, aside from the fact that an arcane seems to have altered my mind within this very city?"

Holly waved her off. "The Archon Council is looking into it. It isn't a concern for a Bound."

Tala narrowed her eyes. "It is my mind."

"And we are addressing that, yes?"

"Can I know what's been found?"

"When appropriate, I will let you know."

Tala felt some things click into place. "You want to wait until I'm inscribed with the mental monitoring." *She was leading me this way the whole time.*

"That is a consideration."

"So, you aren't really sure I'm not still under their influence."

"'Sure' is such a definitive word."

Tala growled. "What's going on, Mistress Holly?"

"You are you; you are human; and a Concept Arcane has taken a particular interest in you. Until we can get you fully protected, we are on a need-to-know basis, and that is really all I can tell you. Even that is more than I was advised to share."

Tala ground her teeth but then had a thought. "You know, Archive tablets are *expensive*. Given this is a fairly critical matter…?"

Holly sighed. "One will be provided for you to bond. *But!*" She held up a finger. "I am no longer going to be giving you my pity discount."

Tala rocked back as if slapped. "Wow, pity discount?"

"Yes. You were poor but interesting, so I didn't want you to go off and die for lack of funds."

"That... that is really heartless. You only helped me because I was interesting?"

"That's what you have a problem with?" Holly gave a small smile. "I wanted to work on you, due to your magical density, and I wanted to work on your desired schemas. You are fascinating, and I wasn't willing to let your poverty stop me from experimenting."

Tala grimaced. "So, why not give me the inscriptions for free?"

"Because that which you do not pay for isn't appreciated and is often abused. I calculated what I thought you could afford and charged you that." She patted Tala's wrist. "But you aren't poor anymore." She hesitated. "Well, not *as* poor."

"Fine." Tala was not happy, but she realized that she wasn't going to get anywhere by pursuing the topic further. "I'll inform the Constructionists to bill you for the tablet."

Holly rolled her eyes. "Very well. I'll deal with the Archon Council about getting reimbursed. Now, what else?"

Tala nodded once. "So, I recently encountered a hallucinogenic effect. Can we protect against that?"

Holly crinkled her nose. "We can't, really, because that's how the body functions. If we block hormones and the like from influencing your thinking, you would lose the ability to do... anything?" She shrugged. "I don't even know, really. Messing with hormones is almost never a good idea, at least not without good reason, and blanketly blocking 'mind-altering' compounds would be incredibly unwise."

"What about the mental inscriptions I already have?"

"Those don't block anything, they just streamline the processes already taking place. If anything, they might make stimulants and hallucinogens more effective, though I don't think they'd have that effect." She scratched her cheek. "You know, though... Once we add the expanded mental inscriptions, monitoring all of it could help you identify such manipulations more easily." Holly began nodding. "Yeah. That is well within the capabilities of what we'll be working with."

"What would that even do?"

Holly shrugged. "Depends on how you imagine it. I'd think of it as making hormonal and such influence be more... secondary? Like you would have a better understanding of why you're feeling and acting as you do. For hallucinogens, you'd likely see them more as figments, translucent and less real."

"That sounds pretty ideal."

"We'll have to be careful, but I think it should be a natural feature of what we're discussing."

That sounds reasonable. "Alright. There are a few other things I wanted to discuss."

Holly smiled. "Well, with the Concept magic discussion behind us for the moment, we don't need this anymore." The inscriptions deactivated around the room, and Tala's gate, once again, gushed power, refilling her reserves rapidly.

Terry didn't react, simply staying where he was, content to rest.

Holly stood. "Let's get some tea and dig into your other questions and ideas."

"That sounds wonderful, thank you." It was going to be an interesting afternoon.

Chapter: 23
The Right Call

Tala and Holly sat in the workroom, a table set up between them with tea. Holly had provided the beverage, and Tala was quite enjoying hers.

Terry had declined a cup when offered.

After only a couple of sips, Holly set her cup to one side. "Now, I don't have all day, and you have much to do as well, I assume."

"I do." Tala smiled around another sip of tea.

"So?"

She set hers down as well. "First, let's get some easy things out of the way. Is my magesight becoming more sensitive?"

"Of course. The longer you have your inscriptions, the more potent they will become. That includes your magesight."

That makes sense and is what I expected, but it's good to confirm. "Should I be able to see magic in the light coming off empowered fixtures?"

Holly hesitated. "That is a bit more sensitive than I'd expected until you finished fusing, but yes. That is within expectations." She smiled. "If you pay enough attention, you will be able to see fluctuations in the magic levels given off by various lights. The greater the fluctuations in inscribed lights, the closer they are to the end of their life—and the sooner they need to be reinscribed. Greater fluctuations in artifact-style lights are simply the result of

Millennial Mage, 5 - Fusing

the quality of construction and empowerment." She looked up, considering. "When you reach a deeper level of perception, you will be able to interpret a city's power status, simply by glancing at any artifact-style item hooked to the grid." She laughed. "Or, I suppose, the enchantments in the air within the city."

Fascinating. I'll have to start paying more attention to the subtleties I can now see. What should she ask next?

She glanced to Terry, feigning sleep on her shoulder. "Terry seems to store many of his vitals in extra-dimensional spaces. Is something like that possible for me? It would let me have much greater reserves and be less vulnerable."

Terry perked up, clearly curious as to the answer.

Holly frowned, then shook her head. "I see. That would explain how he is able to get smaller so easily and with seemingly no ill effects. Even so, no. It works for Terry, there, because he does it to change size. If he were subjected to anything interfering with his magic, he would simply grow in size to whatever his natural state is. His organs would have places to be, and there would be no issue. If that were to happen to you, with what you propose? Your 'extra stores' would splay out everywhere, and depending on how it was done, you'd burst—and not in a fun, 'that was a bad idea that I can learn and grow from,' sort of way."

"Ahh… I hadn't really considered that. What about just hiding away critical organs?"

"I see you weren't listening closely. My bet is that Terry shrinks and places the excess into what amounts to dimensional storage, yes?"

"That's what I understood."

"Good. That means, when he grows, he pulls out as much of the organ as is needed to fill the space."

"Right."

"So, you aren't changing size. You'd just be creating a vacuum within your body. In the best case, your body would fill it without injury, but that would leave you with no room for your critical organs to return to at need. At worst, you'd implode. It wouldn't be extreme, but it would be unpleasant."

Tala grimaced. "Fine. That idea's out, then."

"Quite."

What next, what next...? Ah, yes. "I need an area of effect option."

Holly shrugged. "Delve back into alchemy."

"Alchemy?" Tala frowned. "What?"

"That, or you can change your understanding of gravity. That would give you area of effect options."

Tala sighed. "I'm not going to fundamentally reshape my understanding of my own magic."

"Then I suggest Alchemy." She hesitated. "Or do you have a good grasp and concept over another branch of magic?"

Tala shook her head at both ideas. "I don't have time to practice another skill, mundane or magical."

Holly looked at her with genuine confusion. Then, she seemed to realize something. "Oh, I see. No. Don't do Alchemy. Go to an alchemist and get a solution. Bottled fire, compressed lightning, that sort of thing. Or, you get a magic tool that does what you want."

It was Tala's turn to consider. "Huh. Alright. I'll think on it." She frowned. "I'd have thought you would propose an inscription-based solution."

"I already did. Your active gravity manipulation *should have* allowed for area effects, but you don't seem to be able to make it work that way. That says your fundamental understanding is not compatible with such at this time."

"Alright then."

Millennial Mage, 5 - Fusing

Holly started nodding. "Speaking of your current inscriptions." She pulled out a stone tablet. "What the rust did you do to your *Crush* and *Restrain* inscriptions? Not only are you out of rings, but the base spellforms are utterly fried."

"Oh… I crosslinked them to stop one Leshkin juggernaut and crush another when I was out of standard uses."

Holly wrinkled her nose, sighed, then gave a small smile. "That is a disappointingly reasonable explanation."

"Disappointing?"

"I was a bit excited to lecture you on foolishness, but those things are… not worth messing around with. If you had two to face at once, and you were out of rings, I can understand some desperate action."

"Huh." Tala found a bit of warmth stirring in her chest. *Was that a compliment?*

"In that vein, though, you have been abusing your inscriptions *extensively*."

"What do you mean?"

"Well, you are so full of stimulants that only the inscription on your neck, which enforces your ability to sleep and remain conscious otherwise, is allowing you to function. Every detoxifying organ in your body has burned through six months of inscriptions in barely more than two. How much coffee have you been drinking?"

"Detoxifying organs?"

"Mistress Tala, I am no healer. Don't dodge the question."

"A…" Tala took a deep breath then let it out slowly. "A lot."

"So it would seem. And you've been sparring, I can tell by how often your body has had to heal from minor impacts and bruising. You've been working out almost as much as you've been drinking coffee. The scripts have almost completely rebuilt your musculature. You somehow lost your right arm entirely. That ironically allowed for a much more complete, robust reconstruction of everything there." She hesitated, then looked up at Tala. "Don't take off other parts just to get the same minor boost. You're nearly there anyway, with these scripts."

"With these scripts?"

"Hmm? Oh, yes. The physiological enhancement scripts are a series of inscriptions all focused on increasing the body's capacities over time. Each approach it slightly differently but close enough to prevent resonance issues. They are intended to build on each other. These, the ones you currently have, are almost done with their work, and their magic is almost set, which means that when I reinscribe you, we can do the next series." She hesitated. "I'm not describing it well." Holly bit her lip briefly. "Oh! That's it. Normally, the human body counts to three. We wanted more from your body, hence the inscriptions. So far, we've been having your inscriptions count to five over and over, reinforcing that sequence. Now, with your body acclimatized to its new pattern, we make the inscriptions count to eight."

"I understand the metaphor but not how it applies."

"I'll get you the technical breakdown to study on your own time."

"Alright."

"Now, your gravity manipulation, I don't think you need the hand positioning for regular targeting. You should have a pretty good mental model for that, now."

Tala thought about it for a moment, then shrugged. "Yeah. That's true enough."

"So, the question remains. What do we do with your right breast?"

Tala snorted a laugh. "That's quite the question."

Holly shrugged. "What do you want?"

"Well, when I use my *Crush* mental model with my new scripts, I get the same effect, but it really stresses the inscriptions."

She nodded. "I was wondering what had caused that. Go on."

"Is there any way we can incorporate the ring-style stress-sink from *Crush* and *Restrain* into my active gravity manipulation?"

"You mean as a fallback?" Holly looked up and away, considering. "To bear the extra strain if you do those heavy-requirement workings." She started nodding. "I should be able to make that work."

"Great! And can you cover my whole body with those rings? I never want to run out again."

Holly laughed. "That, I can't do."

Tala frowned. "Why not?"

"Because the strain can only be mostly redirected. I will already have to beef up the entirety of that inscription set to handle pulses of higher throughput. Best I can do is…" Holly paused, seeming to do mental calculations. "We should split them up so you don't lose all your castings with a hand, again. And we should give you a backup."

"Why put it on my hand at all?"

"So, you can easily tell how many you have left? I'd hate for you to think you had more than you actually did, mid-fight."

"That… that is a fair point."

"So, fifteen per hand, and a backup of five on your left breast?"

"Just five more than before?"

"But better distributed."

Tala sighed. "If that's the best we can do."

"It is until you integrate the spell-workings more fully. Your iron defense is helping with that, by the way. Your natural magics seem to be acclimatizing about twice as fast as usual, even taking your high magical density into account."

"So, what should we do with the space now available in my right breast?"

Holly began moving things around on her tablet. "You know, with the expanded functionality, I'd prefer to not try to cram the entirety of your mental-monitoring and consciousness-maintaining scripts at the back of your neck. The dimensionality now available would allow me to make it much more efficient, gold-wise, as well as increase performance."

Tala thought for a long moment, then sighed and nodded. "Alright, but we need a better name for it."

"Your imaginary friend?"

"Rust, I hope it doesn't manifest in that way."

Holly chuckled. "True enough. The name is important and will likely influence the functionality, over time."

"How about Nima? Neurological imaginary magical assistant."

Holly shook her head. "No, no. This needs more thought than we can give now. I don't need to incorporate the name into the schema. Take your time. Maybe use the spell-working for a bit to figure out what you think would work best."

"I will. Thank you."

Holly pushed back and stood up. "Now, I do have a lot to do—and not just in working through the minutia of how we're going to alter your inscriptions." She thought for a long moment. "You're a Mage Protector now, right? You get half your inscriptions paid for?"

"Yes. Why?" Tala didn't like where this was going.

"Earmark forty gold for the inscribing."

Millennial Mage, 5 - Fusing

"*Forty*! That's insane?"

"Is it? I need to reinforce and improve virtually every spellform in your body and add entirely new workings. Plus the redesign isn't free."

Tala grimaced. *There's not really any better option… is there?* "Fine."

Holly smiled. "Good. Now, shoo." She playfully flicked her hands toward Tala. "I've work to do."

Tala growled but nodded. "Fine… Thank you, Mistress Holly."

Holly gave her a long look. "We'll get you sorted. Say hi to Master Boma for me if you see him again at the Constructionists'. He said you are loads of fun to work with." Her eyes were glinting mischievously.

Tala, a bit hesitant, agreed as she departed. "Will do."

*   *   *

Tala paused as soon as she walked in through the wide-open doorway and into the well-appointed entry hall.

While the magics of the scan that identified her as a human Archon were nearly identical to what she'd come to expect, the *ding* of this branch of Bandfast's Constructionists' Guild was a bit different in tone than the one Tala had gotten used to in Makinaven. *Huh. Didn't notice that before.*

Boma himself came out, stopping as he saw her. "Mistress Tala. You're back."

"I am, Master Boma." She gave a shallow bow. "Mistress Holly sends her greetings."

He grunted, then gave her a wary look. "You aren't here to harass my people about a coffee incorporator again, are you?"

She chuckled, waving his concern aside. "No, no." She hesitated. "Wait. Harass? Again? I never harassed anyone."

He cocked an eyebrow at her. "What do you call showing up randomly, at all hours, and questioning, in detail, as many of our assistants as you could pin down?"

Tala grimaced. "Well, fine, if you put it that way." She took a deep breath and sighed. "I apologize for acting in that way. Even though it wasn't my intention, I can see how it might have been perceived."

Boma rocked back slightly, blinking. "I... Uh... Apology accepted."

"Thank you."

There was a moment of silence before Boma cleared his throat and smiled. "So, what brings you here today, if not the quest for a coffee incorporator?"

"Dealing with a simple soul-bonding, then incorporating a large number of things into the soul-bound item."

Boma sighed, his countenance falling. "Alright. What broke?"

She frowned. "What... broke?"

"Yes, broke. What happened that you didn't expect? What inconvenient magics manifested with the soul-bond?"

"Nothing broke. I want to soul-bond these." She patted the elk leathers. "And then incorporate a variety of magical and mundane items into them."

He cocked his head. "And you're coming to us before the bond has taken place?"

"Of course, I thought that the wisest course. Was I wrong?"

A smile broke across his features. "No! No, that's amazing. Most Archons bond whatever they feel like, then come to us for help patching the cracks and smoothing out the unwanted aspects." He wrinkled his nose slightly at the thought before his grin returned in full force. "This is way better. So, a clothing item. You found some armor to combine with it, I'd guess?"

Tala nodded. "Leshkin juggernaut."

Boma whistled. "Not bad. That's a fantastic base for building up the defensive abilities of soul-bound clothing."

"Really? Why? I'd hoped to get some utility out of them, but it sounds like you're suggesting that they're especially good?"

"Well, yeah. So long as they were harvested less than a week ago."

"They were."

"Perfect. So, Leshkin arms and armor aren't made in the mundane sense, nor are they grown in the animal sense. Their magic enters into matter, in this case plant matter, and changes it to match the form and function desired. The lower tiers of Leshkin often use all their power simply to create the shape required, but knights and juggernauts? They have magic to spare that reinforces and expands the capabilities of what they mold to their will. That magic should still be within the armor. Thus, we can draw it out and make almost any article of clothing function as a base for the armor magic."

"Wow." She hadn't considered that. "So, are Leshkin unique in this?"

"Hmm? Oh, no. Greater elementals, elder fae, and quite a few other creatures do similar things. A good rule, which mostly holds true, is if the creature possesses material to create its body, it has this effect on the results."

"Good to know." She made a mental note to keep an eye out for such creatures. *Not that they are that common in the human wilds.* As usual, none of the creatures mentioned were new to her, but most were simply stories, things of myth and legend.

Boma broke through her meandering thoughts with a question. "I assume you have a few sets? I've heard some stories about your latest venture."

"I've a few, yeah." Rane had given her all the Leshkin juggernaut harvests, save those he needed for his own weapon's improvement. She would repay him for what she used of his half of the spoils, if necessary.

"Wonderful. Let's go to a merging room and lay it all out."

"Don't I need to bond these first?" She patted her side.

"No, not at all. If we can get the merging set up, then when you perform the bond, it will incorporate everything set up at a much more efficient and deeper level." He hesitated. "You won't have as much conscious control over the outcome, but that's the point of the spellform. This one will be *complicated.* I'd not do it at all without our merging rooms." He grinned. "Oh, it is so wonderful to build a bound set from components instead of just patching them up."

Tala smiled in return. "Glad to have made the right call."

"Come on. Let's get to it."

*   *   *

Tala stood near the entrance, focusing within her finger, building up a bloodstar for the binding. *Easier than cracking open a piece of tungsten.*

Boma was happily humming to himself as he checked, triple-checked, and rechecked all the lines both on the surface and weaving through the floor.

Terry was tucked in a nearby corner, guarding Kit, and Tala was wearing a borrowed arming robe.

Millennial Mage, 5 - Fusing

"Alright, Mistress Tala. To verify, these are all the items you wish to incorporate, and you use a version of directional flow to empower your external workings capable of supporting up to eight paths?"

Tala nodded absently, pulling out a mundane knife. *The star is strong enough.*

After a flex of will temporarily disabled the defensive inscriptions in her finger, she used a quick motion to open her skin. A *pull* removed the bloodstar and brought it to rest in front of her chest.

"Archon Star is ready. It's not a fully powered one, but that should work, correct?"

Boma examined her from where he stood. "Yeah, I assume this is what you'd used on your knife before the merging when we first met?"

"This is actually a bit stronger than that."

"Then it should be perfect."

Tala smiled, looking in at their work from the last hour.

The room before her was fascinating. The elk leathers lay at the center, her simple, elegant, sturdy black belt atop them and her shoes beside. Her other outfits from the seamstress, Merilin, were arranged around the three articles of clothing. Around that were six sets of Leshkin juggernaut armor, spaced with thunder bull leather.

The Leshkin armor was of wide-ranging styles. On one extreme was wood closely mimicking a suit of full plate, but instead of padding or chainmail to protect the joints, there were only smaller, more articulated plates. The other extreme was simply heavy wooden rings woven into ring mail, with progressively smaller rings in tighter patterns behind. The others were mixes or types that landed somewhere between those two.

They had selected these specific sets for their resonance with each other, the elk leathers, thunder leather, and Tala, herself.

Most of the armor sets had had a strong counter-resonance with Tala, and her magics. That was likely because of the Leshkin hatred of those using endingberry power. The others had been a bit tricky to harmonize with. Even so, Boma was very pleased and had no doubts that they'd get a good result. Apparently, the spellforms acted to counter any imbalances, and he'd needed very little of that functionality in this merging and bonding.

Copper spellforms, as delicate as spiderwebs, covered the floor, obviously dipping below the surface as well. Around each item or set was a clear circle for it to rest within.

Additionally, around the elk leathers, Boma had left eight circles for Tala to dump power into, via her void-channels.

Boma had asked her innumerable questions as he worked. How did she want the items to integrate, what features did she want in each form, and so on.

They had grabbed onto the same ability that Flow had manifested from her bloodstar, the ability to change shape.

While shape-changing bound items weren't terribly uncommon, it was almost always a feature that had to be merged in from an outside source and was therefore never as core to the item as Tala's could be.

They were ready.

Chapter: 24
One More Thing to Practice

Tala surveyed the merging room one last time as Boma went to sit on the side in another open space.

With quiet solemnity, only mildly spoiled by his happy smile, he placed his hands down on the circles waiting for him there. "As discussed, I will be guiding the process and providing the shell of power, containing the merging. You will be fueling the actual process, however. Ready for that, Bound?" He was grinning.

They'd discussed price already, and Tala had paid before they'd begun. *Six gold is way better than I could expect if I tried to merge these in sequence, rather than all at once.*

Tala walked out into the room, careful to not disrupt or scuff Boma's work.

Finally, she stood over her trusty leathers. *You've seen me through a lot. Let's make this official.*

She grinned stupidly. *You are me.*

She let her aura expand and connected eight void-channels through her aura to the spellform's inputs, making the channels as large as she was able to with that many active.

Power roared through her as the spellforms began to light with power.

"Bind it now." Boma spoke calmly from the side, his own power flowing out of him.

Millennial Mage, 5 - Fusing

Tala looked down, still straddling her outfit, and willed the bloodstar down and into the subtle, embossed-like residue of the spirit binding she'd performed months previously.

Join with me. Take of my power and lend me yours.
She felt a pull somewhere deep within herself. It was as if she'd been doing soul-work exercises all afternoon. She almost staggered but managed to maintain her balance.

Power exploded through the room, consuming the inscriptions in the floor, the materials, and Tala's robe. *Ah, rust…*

After an instant of nakedness, the belt wrapped around her waist and cloth blossomed outward. In less than a blink, Tala stood in a cleared stone room.

She looked down at herself and laughed.

A simply stunning linen top covered her torso, cinched at the waist and her throat but otherwise flowing loose. The back was open most of the way down her spine, and her shoulders were bare. The base of the top continued below her belt to midthigh.

The pants were snug without being constricting, and while under the upper garment, they were perfectly modest. Shoes had even manifested to cover her feet.

"Perfect. Thank you, Master Boma."

He smiled in return. "Happy to assist."

Tala gave a little twirl in her outfit, enjoying the feel of something against her skin besides leather. *Though, the leather is still amazing.*

With a thought, she dove into the garments with her magesight and power, filling its reserves as she investigated.

There were dozens of paths of power within the clothing, but they didn't give off the same sense as those within Flow. These were all much closer together, and she had the sense that the only changes were cosmetic.

The one that felt most familiar accepted the power she offered.

Leather grew out from the belt and the choker. *Huh, the choker, too? I wonder why that manifested.*

The material flowed into the form of the elk leathers as she'd worn them previously.

There were still ties up each side, starting at her waist and going up to her armpit, but they were now purely decorative as she would never need to undo them again. The ties were of leather as well, of course, though she felt like she could change their appearance if she wished. *This might be a bit too much customization for me...*

The sleeves were loose without being billowy, and there were several minimal, stiff ridges that ran down the arms to hold them in place. Somehow, the stays didn't inhibit movement at all. The ridges were evenly spaced around each sleeve, creating a subtly beautiful pattern. They were mirrored by similarly flexible, yet ridged features on the torso's boning that held the shape, without inhibiting movement.

It was a masterpiece, or rather the perfect replica of a masterpiece. *I'm so glad that it so wonderfully preserved what Merilin was able to create.*

Both the first linen-seeming outfit and this one breathed almost as if she were still naked, though she could also feel the clothing upon her skin.

The leather of the tunic was a light gray, nearly white, while the ties were marginally darker, offering a nice hint of contrast. Below the ties, the tunic continued down to just above her knees, providing some modesty and adding to the look.

The pants fit exactly as well as they always had before. They were a dark enough gray to evoke thoughts of thunder, storms, and torrents of driving rain. They moved with her, and the flare toward her feet was as subtle as it was functional.

Boma offhandedly tossed a knife at her midsection. "Don't block."

And she didn't.

The knife struck her in the abdomen. *Wow. Is that all an enemy would have to do to stab me?*

Where the knife hit, she felt the leather stiffen, taking on a rigidity akin to an armored plate. To her magesight, there almost seemed to be the ghost of exactly that: an armored plate, protecting the garment from the attacking blade.

Instead of sticking into her tunic or her stomach, the knife deflected to the side, landing on the ground to skitter to a stop on the floor behind her.

The defense had taken power, though Tala judged that it was less power than it would have taken to repair a slit cut by such a strike. That also didn't account for the magic and resources it would have taken to heal the wound that would have been inflicted as well.

That's a nice improvement.

Moreover, the outfit now had a direct connection to her soul, her gate, and it topped itself off as soon as the power had been used.

That issue is solved, at least.

Boma went to retrieve his knife, and Tala walked over to pick up Kit, Terry simply flickering to her shoulder.

Tala pressed Kit to her belt and willed it to be hanging there.

Her belt, strand by strand, broke and reconnected through Kit's belt loop. Thus, in less than a count of three, Kit was back where it should be.

Tala pushed power down another path within her outfit and felt magic and her garments ripple across her, leaving her standing in the looser-fitting linen outfit from before.

"Oh, I'm going to like this so, so much." She looked to the Archon. "Thank you, once again, Master Boma."

Boma gave a happy bow. "Once again, I am happy to have been able to assist, Mistress Tala." As he straightened, he smiled. "Is there anything else we can do for you today?"

"In fact, there is. What sort of Archive tablets do you have on hand?"

He frowned. "Archive tablet?"

And his good mood is gone. She kept a smile off her face. "Yes, Mistress Holly would like me to bond with one. She's paying for the device."

"I hope you know I'll have to check on that."

Even though Tala knew that she was correct and Holly would pay for it, she suddenly felt nervous under Boma's scrutiny. "Of course."

He regarded her for another moment before grunting. "As for bonding, we should at least wait until tomorrow. Your soul needs to restabilize."

Tala nodded. "Sure. Mistress Holly needed the tablet today, though, so she could work on some integrations."

Boma gave her a long look, then sighed, shaking his head. "I don't want to know. Come on." He waved for her to follow him as he led the way out of the merging room and back toward an entrance.

When they were almost all the way back, he turned to the side, into a small sitting room. It was comfortable without being spacious. There were seats for up to four people, spaced for easy, quiet conversation, without being within reach of physical contact.

"Grab a seat." He sat down in one of the chairs and pulled out a tablet, beginning to search through the empowered device.

Millennial Mage, 5 - Fusing

Tala sat down and flicked out some jerky for Terry. She took the moment's pause to dive back into her garment, mentally flicking through the pathways.

Unlike Flow, she didn't have to maintain power through a pathway in order to maintain that form. She only needed to feed magic into the change, then the outfit would stabilize once more.

In searching, she began to get a sense of what each path would do. *I think that this one will...*

She pushed power down it, and her shoes almost seemed to liquefy. The material stretched out to connect to her pant legs and was seemingly absorbed.

Hah! I got it right. She hadn't cut off the power, and she felt all of her clothing start to break down to be reabsorbed. *Nope!* She cut off the flow of magic and looked down. The clothing had become a bit more malleable in texture but instantly snapped back into shape.

She let out a long breath. *Oh, good. I didn't just magically strip naked in front of a Fused.* She felt her cheeks heating, nonetheless.

Boma didn't react.

Alright. So, be careful trying things out in public.

"Here it is. Mistress Holly put in a requisition for you for a clip-based, full Archive connection."

Tala frowned. "What?"

"It's a little, circular metal clamp that you put around a writing implement, and any inquiry you make of the Archive is responded to by being written out."

"How does it know what I'm asking about?"

"You write it out."

Tala blinked back at him. "So, I have to have a written dialogue with the Archive?"

"In a sense, yes."

Her eye twitched. "Why can't I get a tablet?"

Boma glanced back at his device. "Well. Mistress Holly did add a note, here, in case you asked that question or something similar. I assume you'll know what it means. 'We only need the connection, dear, not the fancy means of display.'"

Tala thought for a moment. "Oh. That actually makes a lot of sense."

He gave her an odd look. "You know, even if you bind this to you, you won't be able to process the information directly."

"I know. Mistress Holly is modifying some of my inscriptions to make use of the link."

"That's... irregular." His eyes unfocused slightly as his magesight came to life. "Yeah, you are still a Bound." Power faded from his inscriptions. "You shouldn't have the power density or..." He stopped, then shook his head. "You know what? It's not my business. Mistress Holly won't kill you or fry your brain."

That made Tala vaguely uncomfortable, so she moved on quickly. "How much?"

"For the artifact version?" He hesitated. "Wait. You said she was paying for it. And this note says the same."

Tala shrugged. "I'm curious."

Boma cocked an eyebrow. "It's a bit rude to find out the cost of gifts someone gets you."

She snorted a laugh. "It is hardly a gift."

He opened his mouth to ask, then closed it, shaking his head. "Right, not going to ask. Fine. It will cost five gold, and I'll have to make it. There isn't much demand for this style of Archive node."

"I can't imagine why."

"Hey, they were quite popular some thirty years ago. Then, the tablets were invented and that type became mostly obsolete. They still work perfectly, though. In fact, they are the chief way of replicating physical books from the Archive's informational stores. The design is *incredibly* efficient. Even unbound, any Mage can empower it."

"Alright, alright." She held up her hands. "I didn't mean any insult to the invention." She frowned. "Wait. If she could send you a note on what she wants, and I imagine you can deliver it to her when it's finished, why did I need to tell you?"

He shrugged. "Doesn't say the delivery fee is covered."

She glowered at him. "When will it be ready?"

He smiled. "I can set up the process right now, but you'll need to come back in a couple of hours to pick up the product."

She sighed. "Alright. Thank you."

"Happy to assist."

* * *

Tala took the time until her Archive connection was complete to walk to Brand's restaurant and get a meal, catching up with him and Lissa. It was a pleasantly large meal, and the company was nice, even if they were interrupted fairly regularly by a sporadic stream of customers.

Though the main meal was a hearty chicken and barley soup, with buttered wheat bread on the side, they also served her what amounted to a garlic broth that was shockingly good.

With her dinner taken care of, and acquaintances renewed, Tala went back to the Constructionists and got the Archive link before taking it to Holly's workshop.

The inscriber didn't deign to meet with her. Instead, her assistant received the empowered item, asked Tala to fill it with her own magic, and then thanked her for bringing it by.

Apparently, Holly would like to have Tala back the next day, around sunset.

Fine. That will give my soul enough time to level out, too.

That done, she actually felt a little lost. *What should I do now?*

After a bit of meandering, she headed back to the Guardsman's training ground to get in another workout and to run through her martial forms.

* * *

The sun was setting when Tala finally finished her martial forms. *I'm getting quite a few of these to practice.*

Adam had offered the guard students' services in creating forms based around Flow's ability to change shape. She had to admit it was an appealing idea, and she'd tentatively agreed. *Right now, it feels like I'm constantly switching fighting styles. I need a coherent approach to what I'm doing.*

In the private bath room, off the training yard, Tala opened Kit on the floor, tossed a bit of jerky to Terry, and dropped in.

As expected, Kit's configuration was set up for her to bathe. These days, since she'd expanded Kit's capacity, that meant that most of her stuff was in another part of the space, partitioned almost completely away from her and the inevitable steam.

The tub-like depression in the floor was perfectly contoured for her, and her water incorporators were ready and waiting beside her comb and some soap.

"Now, I just have to undress." She delved into the pathways of her garments and found the one she'd used earlier. *Now, how does this work?* Before, she'd thought of removing her shoes, and that was what came off first, though the rest had tried to follow.

I need to bathe. She pushed power down the channel, and her clothing retracted up, into the choker around her throat. *Huh, not the belt?*

As she thought about it, however, she realized that the belt would be irritating to wash around. *That probably affected the manifestation.* There was so much to learn.

"Bath time!"

Clean and ready to go, Tala climbed back out of Kit sometime later.

She tossed another bit of jerky to Terry, which vanished without him seeming to stir.

She was in the linen, flowing halter-top and leather pants. She'd kept her shoes off. *I'm getting the hang of this garment thing.* Working with Flow for so long already had likely helped in her understanding and use of the clothing's various forms.

One pathway had intrigued her since she'd first noticed it, but she hadn't taken the time to try it out yet. *All things in time.*

She glanced around at the empty, locked room. *Now's as good as any, though.*

She pushed power down that path and felt material begin to grow up her neck.

It took a lot more power than the other changes had, but it was still well within her ability.

Once her head was fully covered, she had a moment of panic. What if it stopped there? What if it got stuck?

An instant later, the material pushed outward, forming a great helm-style helmet. She had a moment of irritation, given how hard it was to see.

She also had the realization that she likely looked ridiculous. *Who wears a full helmet over a halter-top?*

Then, as she contemplated her reduced vision, she had another thought. *I can aspect mirror!*

With an act of will that strained her current abilities, she mirrored her ability to sense through her various sensory organs upon her now soul-bound garment, granting her enhanced capacities to that empowered item.

Suddenly, she could perceive all around herself. The flood of information was overwhelming and disorienting.

She lifted her hand to her head in reflex. That motion caused her perspective to shift in radically unexpected ways.

In that moment, the anti-vomit inscriptions finished burning through their metal.

Tala had a moment of calm as the last vestiges of their Magic rushed through her, then she fell to her knees and filled her helmet with her head still inside.

* * *

Having her head in a bucket of her own vomit was decidedly unpleasant.

Tala was able to gain enough control of herself to magically reach into her garments and dismiss the helmet. That caused her bile to slosh down onto the floor around her hands as she knelt on the ground, still heaving. Every motion increased her disorientation and nausea. She could smell the sick from all around, not just her nose, and she could *taste* it where it had splashed on her clothing.

Release the aspect mirroring, idiot!

She did so, and her vision narrowed to what felt like an alarmingly small field of view.

She panicked. *Am I going blind?*

A moment later, she realized that this was her normal vision; it only *felt* small because of how extreme the previous sight had been.

Millennial Mage, 5 - Fusing

Not only had she been looking in every direction at once, but she'd also been looking out from every part of her soul-bound clothing at once, creating an overwhelming number of overlapping fields of view.

She groaned, heaving one last time.

As Tala looked up, she saw Terry perched on a shelf, regarding her with a bit of concern evident on his avian face.

"I'm okay." Her voice came out a bit thickly. She pulled out her cool water incorporator and took a long drink before continuing. "Mistress Holly did tell me that the anti-vomit inscriptions weren't especially robust. I'll have her correct that error in judgment."

Terry trilled softly.

"I'll be okay." She smiled weakly at the bird. "I think I discovered something pretty cool, though." She chuckled wryly. "Though, it does mean I'll have one more thing to practice."

Chapter: 25
Mage Hunters

After her second—*no… third?*—bath of the day, Tala combed through her hair one last time in a desperate attempt to feel clean after having her face and hair soaked in… ick.

She felt like she had expelled more than she'd eaten recently and suspected that her body had taken advantage of the exodus to get rid of some things it didn't precisely want.

Waste management… hurrah! She let the sarcasm ring loud and clear through her thoughts as she continued to move the empowered tool through her hair.

There was no need to comb through it more than once. Her brush effortlessly left her hair clean and dry with a single stroke, but she felt the *need* to continue combing at least for a short time.

She skillfully, deftly rewove her braid and attached Kit to her belt with a quick motion, once again willing her belt to move through the belt loop on the pouch.

"Alright, Terry. Let's go." She glanced down at the vomit still on the floor and sighed. "In a minute." *I can't leave this for some random person to have to deal with.*

She used the supplies already in this private bath room to clean up the mess and then headed out, Terry flickering to her shoulder as the door swung shut behind her.

Millennial Mage, 5 - Fusing

Night had truly fallen, then, and only the facility's magical lights provided illumination under the cloudy, winter sky.

Even so, there were guards moving through the compound. Those that saw her gave nods of deference but didn't stop to chat or otherwise acknowledge her beyond that.

She had to smile. *Don't talk to the Mage, and she won't give you extra work.* She could respect that. *Everyone wants to get home.*

She walked across the strangely desolate training yard, out front of the interconnected buildings. It felt strange, eerie even, without the presence of dozens, if not hundreds, of guards training and working to improve themselves. Instead, it was lifeless, barren.

Tala shivered. *Walk faster.*

With that, she loosened her steps and ate up the ground before her at a brisk walk.

As she neared home, she again saw the tavern, glowing cheerily in the evening stillness, raucous laughter and the murmur of uncounted voices drifting to her enhanced ears.

Is that place always busy?

Her stomach gurgled at her, and she glanced down. "I did just empty you without cause, didn't I?"

Her stomach growled as if in response.

"Fine. I'll see what all the fuss is about."

As she drew closer, she began to feel a pressure building across her skin, an emphasis on the warmth before her and the cold behind, a heightening of her hunger, and an enhancement of the scents of food wafting out of the establishment before her.

Something about it made her feel like something was off. *What is it? What's wrong here?*

Her steps slowed despite her growing hunger, and she stopped in the street, some fifty feet from the building.

Huh, you know, I don't see anyone entering... or leaving.

She forced herself to wait and watch.

One minute became five, five minutes became ten, and no one entered or left.

That's really odd. She could see people within the building or at least vague movements that seemed to indicate people were within.

What is going on here? Then the door swung open, and a group of three people stumbled out, joyously calling back goodbyes to those inside.

Tala relaxed and laughed to herself, turning toward home. *I'm being ridiculous.*

She was exhausted and needed to sleep in her own room, in her own bed. *Well, within Kit, but still.*

Terry didn't stir, instead content to ride on her shoulder in silence.

When she reached Lyn's house, she unlocked the door, entered, and locked it behind herself.

Her stomach gurgled again. *Right. I'm really hungry.*

With a grunt, she went to the kitchen and used the facilities there to prepare some of the 'venture food' that she had in Kit.

I really should have grabbed food on the way home. She sighed.

It didn't take long for the food to be ready, and Tala devoured it with abandon. Even so, she took notes on the preparation process and how the final results tasted in the small notebook provided to her for that purpose.

Her stomach satiated, she moved through her nightly routine and climbed down into Kit, now arranged for her sleep.

Millennial Mage, 5 - Fusing

* * *

The next morning, after her start-of-day routine, Tala walked to the work yard alone.

After charging the cargo slots for the last time until her next venture, she chatted with the foreman of the newly arrived day shift, then walked back toward the guildhall.

It was a beautiful, crisp morning in the city, and she enjoyed people-watching as she made her way toward breakfast.

Most people were wrapped in several layers against the cold, but it didn't seem like the weather was actively keeping too many indoors. The streets were full without being packed, and everyone seemed to be going about their days as normal.

Nor should the weather be an issue. It's gorgeous! Even before she could largely ignore the cold, she'd loved the winter.

Mistress Odera had requested that they meet at the guildhall once again, and Tala had no issues with that in the slightest.

The meal was uneventful, and they weren't joined by anyone else. Thus, it felt much like their meals in Makinaven; a discussion of Tala's training, any issues she was running into, and a dialogue on what might help her surmount them.

They agreed that she shouldn't try mirroring her senses again until the anti-vomit inscriptions were refreshed. When she did try it again, she would try to limit the mirroring to a smaller portion of her outfit to help prevent sensory overload.

They discussed a host of other things but nothing else of true note.

Well, except that Mistress Odera decided to let Tala know that she was trying something insane and fully expected to fail.

"Iron."

"That's right."

"You're going to try to create an Archon Star in iron."

Mistress Odera grinned. "Your medium contains a lot of iron. I thought it would be an interesting test."

Tala shook her head. "Now I know how most people feel when talking to me." *That's a ridiculous idea.*

Mistress Odera let out an almost cackling laugh. "Wait 'til you see it." She pulled out a caltrop the size of the last knuckle on her thumb. In this case, it was four short spikes, oriented so one would always point up when resting on a flat surface. It was technically small enough to swallow.

"That is truly insane."

The older woman nodded sagely. "I would have to be mad to swallow it, that's for sure."

That notable exception aside, the breakfast was fairly standard, from start to finish.

When their plates were clean, and the conversation had run its course, Tala bid the woman goodbye and headed to the training yard to meet Rane and Aproa for training with the guards.

That training also went quite to expectation until Adam went to land the first hit on Tala's side.

Power flickered to life and blocked his practice sword as effectively as a wall.

Adam stepped back, blinking in confusion.

Right, no magesight. To him, it would look like his sword had simply glanced off my side.

"Did you somehow upgrade your skin's density? That seems a bit foolish."

Millennial Mage, 5 - Fusing

Aproa, who'd been taking a drink after her own bouts, almost choked. Though if it was at the informality or the idea itself, Tala didn't know.

"Neither. I am simply properly armored now."

Adam sighed. "Do you know why we don't train in armor, much of the time?"

Tala frowned. She actually didn't. To be honest, she hadn't thought of it. "Too heavy?"

He snorted. "Hardly. If that were the only consideration, we'd be in it more, not less. No, we don't train in armor for two reasons. First, we never know when an enemy will be able to breach our armor, so we must treat every enemy as if we are unarmored. Second, we cannot accurately replicate armor breaching attacks in a safe manner, so we cannot properly train injury and the like in armor."

She nodded. That made a lot of sense. "I'm not sure I can turn it off?" If she really couldn't turn it off, she'd be ticked. *I'm not buying new clothes just to wear for sparring.*

"Well, yours is magical, correct? I mean rather obviously."

"It is."

"Then what about we get a sense of the magic expenditure, and you can regulate your losses by how much it takes to block the hit."

Tala grunted in surprise. "That would actually work really well." As she thought about it, she found herself smiling. "It would also help so that I could determine what I should block, dodge, or take."

He grimaced at the thought but didn't contradict her.

Tala smiled. "Well, I should delve into this and see if I can suppress the defensive functionality. I'll take next?"

Adam gave a half-bow before turning to face Rane.

Instead of watching the odd dance, Tala dove into examining the pathways within her garments.

To spare Rane's inscriptions from a war of attrition, Rane and Adam had decided that Adam's win condition was forcing Rane to flip three times in the same direction in quick succession.

Tala was a bit peeved that they'd never thought of something like that for her bouts with Rane, but it made sense.

Adam was vastly better than Rane, somehow, but the Mage was still virtually untouchable by the guard.

But that wasn't what she was supposed to be focused on.

It didn't take long for her to find what she was looking for. It helped that she'd begun with an intuitive sense of what the soul-bound item could do and how to make it happen. That understanding was growing deeper, or it seemed to be doing so over the last half-day or so.

Thus, she was able to find out how to deactivate the reactive armor. Interestingly enough, as she interfaced with that path, she was able to discover what it did.

It's not altering the material of the garment alone or even primarily. No, the defensive magics were grabbing onto whatever was close at hand to forge the armor at need. In this case, that meant the air.

I hope that doesn't mean that Leshkin could take forms other than tree people. That was a disturbing thought.

If one could create a form for itself out of the air... She shook off that idea.

No, we modified the magics through the merging and soul-bond. That was the more reasonable explanation.

The remainder of the morning passed uneventfully, though they all did agree to take a bit of time for Tala to take blows with the reactive defenses active and inactive so she could begin building an understanding of what sort of damage was mitigated and at what cost.

Even Rane and Aproa got in on the damage dealing, using practice weapons for now, of course.

With morning passed, the guards left for their various duties, and Rane, Tala, and Aproa went to lunch.

An enormous mound of meatballs in white sauce overtook Tala's attention for a long while. In the end, she licked her plate clean. *I need this sauce. I need it on everything.*

The other two Mages drew her away, but she promised herself that she'd be back.

Together, they headed toward a Mage's training area to meet Aproa's acquaintances.

The facilities were much the same as those Tala and Rane had used in Makinaven, though they were constructed mainly of stone rather than of wood—as would be expected, given the construction of the respective cities.

Tala found herself a bit nervous as they approached the reserved space, Rane and Aproa chatting about the events of the previous day animatedly.

Tala didn't really listen to the specifics, instead trying to calm her nerves. Behind those doors ahead was a group of Mages, roughly her age.

I specifically avoided people like this... She almost laughed. *I may have specifically avoided these specific people if they are close enough in age to me.*

That would be embarrassing if it were true and came out.

Maybe I shouldn't go...

But the choice was already made. She was here.

Strength, Tala. You're going to be fine.

Rane pushed the doors open, revealing a large space with an arching dome of thick iron wire far overhead.

It appeared as if there was a mesh of copper woven throughout the iron. *Huh, iron to prevent direct magical effects, and copper to activate when indirect magics approached. Clever. Expensive but clever.*

She almost laughed. *I suppose this is what's required when you don't have a god-king to ensure the city stays safe and intact.*

There were ten Archons engaged in various activities around the large open space. Two stood out immediately because of their bored, almost laidback expressions.

The first was quite obviously a healer, likely on hand in case of emergency. Given the glimpse Tala had gotten at the powersets in the room, that was probably wise.

The second, though, he held her attention, her mouth opening in wonder.

Her voice came out in a whisper. "Magnetism?" She strode across the sandy floor without acknowledging anything else, stopping in front of the man. "You manipulate magnetic fields?"

But the only reason he would do that is to interact with ferrous materials. She nodded, her magesight showing her what amounted to almost a cloud of iron moving in subtle currents around him. To that perception, it glittered like stars, moving in ever-changing constellations.

The slim, toned man, some five to six years older than her by appearance, looked up with one eyebrow cocked. "Ummm… Hi?"

She held out her hand. "I'm Tala." *Manners, Tala, keep it together.*

He hesitated. "Mistress Tala, good to meet you, but most don't want to get too close. I've a lot of iron dust around me."

"I know. I can see it."

He straightened, surprise replacing cautious puzzlement. "Really?"

Millennial Mage, 5 - Fusing

Her hand was still out.

He clasped it, shook it, and smiled. By the lines on his face, it didn't seem like he did that often. "I'm Cazor. It's a pleasure to meet you." He released her hand, and the small amount of iron that had clung to her skin pulled away.

I'm glad that I scrubbed off my iron salve, as I usually do in cities, or this could have been awkward. Tala nodded emphatically. "You overcame the difficulty of enacting magic through iron, too?" She laughed. "I mean, you must have, obviously. What methods did you use to train?" She grinned. "Did you have the spheres?" Her eyes widened, and she gasped. "Did you bond a magnet?"

Cazor stood, brushing off his pants, a frown returning as he took his time processing her flood of words. "Mistress Tala… are you a hunter? I wasn't aware a new one had been added to our ranks." His eyes flicked to something behind Tala, to her right, but then returned to her an instant later.

It was her turn to frown, then, some of her enthusiasm bleeding away. "I mean, I hunt on occasion, but—"

He shook his head. "No, I mean, are you a Mage Hunter? Most Mages avoid iron…" He stopped, shaking his head and rubbing his face. He muttered under his breath. "Why am I saying this? She obviously knows…"

She decided to ignore his mutterings and focus on the fact that he used iron! *So, a hunter. That's why he uses iron.* "Not a Mage Hunter." She chuckled halfheartedly. "I mean, it's not something I've ever considered."

"I see." He seemed at a loss as to what to say, after that.

Tala saw that Cazor had a number of open-top pouches on his belt, each seemingly containing iron filings.

He cleared his throat, forging ahead. "Most Mages don't even start to work on overcoming the iron impediment until Refined. Most never succeed, but then most don't even reach that stage." He cracked a smile once again. "But I suppose most also don't run straight up to a Mage Hunter and begin asking questions."

Tala suddenly felt incredibly self-conscious and looked around. A few of the others were staring at her in obvious confusion. *Oh... Great first impression, Tala.*

"But I have been rude. You asked a question." He nodded almost to himself. "I did, indeed, study with the spheres. I had to conquer the third set before I could enact my inscriptions to my own satisfaction."

"Third?" She groaned. "I just got the second."

A bit of mirth came back into his eyes. "Even that is impressive for Bound."

Tala cocked her eyebrow at him. "But... you're Bound."

He blinked at her in shock. "How...?"

How what? How could I tell? She took a moment to examine her own perception, realizing that most magesight wouldn't be able to pick out the color of his aura through the tightly controlled, swirling iron cloud.

Oh well. She opened her mouth to respond, but Aproa cleared her throat from back near the center of the space behind Tala.

"Well, I'm glad you met one of the hunters. He's only here to make sure none of us get carried away and go out of control." She was smiling as she spoke, though.

Cazor rolled his eyes, even as Tala turned away to regard Aproa.

He responded, a hint of a smirk evident in his tone. "You know why I'm here, Mistress Aproa. You all wanted to test yourself against someone capable of actually resisting you, and I wanted practice disabling different types of Mages."

Millennial Mage, 5 - Fusing

Aproa snorted a chuckle. "Fine, fine. Mistress Tala, let's introduce you around."

Tala immediately forgot all the names that were given to her, though she did note, again, the wide range of abilities arranged before her.

One seemed to be straddling the line between Creator and Guide. She was a water creator and a heat guide. *Ice Mage?*

An air guide, who seemed to specialize in the manipulation of oxygen and several other gases that Tala couldn't place, wore what looked like flint and steel strategically intermeshed with his gloves. *He snaps to make a spark? That seems like a fire Mage but with extra steps.*

The third simply seemed to be a Material Guide focusing on photons, but Tala didn't understand well enough to figure out exactly what she could do.

The fourth was another fire, but this one was the more standard, conjuring fire into existence as a Material Creator. *That seems so... wrong to me... Fire isn't actually a thing...*

The fifth seemed to have taken inspiration from the fourth. *Or maybe the other way around?* In either case, she was somehow a Material Creator, focused on lightning.

The sixth was an earth manipulator who reminded Tala of Atrexia, though this guy seemed to be more freeform with his spellforms. *Huh, I wonder if all Mages transition from more specific manifestations toward more general ones like I did?*

She could ask, and maybe she would, later.

The seventh and eighth were actually fraternal twins, apparently. Both were Material Mages, one Guide and one Creator, and they seemed to have focused on water.

And then she noticed a ninth, who had been sitting in the shadowed corner on the wall with the door, so she'd missed her.

Tala frowned. The woman was an Immaterial Guide, but all of her scripts seemed focused on magic itself. *Is that like how Master Jevin focused on aura manipulation?* Probably worth asking.

Aproa gestured and the Archon stood, moving their way. "This is Mistress Jean. She's the other hunter that we put up with."

Jean rolled her eyes, flipping her red hair behind her back. "You know you'd be lost without me, Mistress. I got you through the academy."

Tala's eyes were drawn to the woman's hip, where an iron device hung from the woman's white belt. *It looks like a crossbow without the arms, and a tube instead of a stock.*

Her belt held a dozen small items that gave the sense of being paired with the iron item, but each gave off a radically different magical signature. All the inscriptions she could see on the small things were gold. *What in Zeme?*

Aside from the starkly white belt, gloves, and boots, Jean's outfit was a simple, comfortably snug black shirt and pants.

Aproa then motioned to Tala. "Everyone, this is Mistress Tala. She's another addition to our practice."

Tala gave a little wave. "Hey. Good to meet you all."

The chorus of generic greetings came back her way.

Well, this should certainly be interesting.

Chapter: 26
Challenges

Tala stood across the training ground from the woman that she'd challenged.

Aproa had explained that they always began their time by allowing individual challenges, if any were desired, and Tala had immediately issued one.

Tala had challenged the Mage Hunter, Jean. Terry had used the momentary distraction to immediately flicker over to one side to watch.

Jean had seemed surprised for only an instant before a small smile tugged at her lips. "As you wish, Archon."

She drew the device from her belt and opened the back end.

Tala watched as Jean pulled out a smaller cylinder, heavily inscribed with gold, and replaced it with one covered and interwoven with copper.

"What is that?"

Jean chuckled. "I'm switching to a training round. I've no desire to kill a law-abiding Mage."

Tala was going to object, then realized that she was *far* outside her knowledge base. *Let the woman act as she deems appropriate.* "As you wish."

That was how they'd ended up here, facing off with nearly twenty yards of distance between them, Cazor ready to call a start to the fight.

I have to close the distance. I can alter her gravity as I do, but I'll have at most five seconds before I'm in melee range. So, she could add to her opponent's gravity to increase it by almost fifty percent or lower it down to around seventy percent. *Up it is.*

Jean didn't have her weapon drawn, and Tala had decided to mirror that. She briefly considered beginning the fight by tossing her anchor across the space. That would close the distance faster than anything else, but with her anti-vomit inscriptions gone, she shouldn't risk it.

Run, target, ramp up gravity, draw Flow, attack.
"Fight!"

Tala took a lunging step forward, her left middle-finger and thumb already together as she targeted Jean.

The lock wouldn't stick, and Tala snarled in irritation.

Jean was drawing her weapon, lifting it free of its sheath with casual speed. *Huh, she probably practices drawing it quickly.*

Interesting.

At the next step, Tala tried, again, to establish the target lock, throwing all her magical weight behind it. There was a moment of purchase before her targeting was thrown off.

Jean's weapon was rising, and there were still a dozen yards between them, at least. Tala drew Flow, pushing it into the form of a sword, even as she called her bloodstars out of Kit, pulling them to move protectively in front of her.

Mirroring. Can I solve my targeting issue with mirroring? This time, she mirrored her magical weight into all her bound items, bloodstars included. She then mirrored them back onto her enactment of the targeting.

She felt her left eye begin to twitch as something within her mind, her will, strained to its limit. The combination of so many aspects to mirror and those aspects being ones she wasn't familiar with was enough to jack up the difficulty.

The lock blossomed into being on Jean, the combined power of Tala herself and her bonds winning through.

Increase!

Jean's eyes widened, even as the tube of her weapon fully leveled toward Tala. The Mage Hunter pulled the trigger, not letting her surprise cause hesitation.

Tala saw in horror that all the magic in the area stilled before streaming toward the device in Jean's hand as quick as lightning strikes, even as the weapon settled, aiming steadily at Tala.

In retrospect, challenging the Mage Hunter for the first duel of the day might have been… ill-advised.

Tala's heightened perception made the eyeblink of time stretch into a seeming eternity.

It was hard to see inside the iron tube, even though it was pointed directly at her, but it looked almost like strands of heat and light were being woven within, each thread seemingly precisely modulated.

As Jean had pulled the trigger, Tala's bloodstars had come into alignment between Tala and the unknown threat.

The air seemed to scream out in agony to Tala's magesight as every drop of power was pulled from it. Even the edges of Tala's own aura seemed to be fraying.

Runic symbols lit up down the length of the weapon, not looking like any scripting Tala recognized as they glowed through a solid layer of iron.

As the spells within the device finished coming together, Tala saw her chance and enforced an aspect mirror across her three bloodstars and her elk leathers, giving each of them Flow's ability to deflect incoming attacks.

Millennial Mage, 5 - Fusing

As she had to release the other aspects she'd been mirroring, that caused her targeting lock to weaken, and Jean threw off the magic without any outward evidence of difficulty.

Tala had managed less than two seconds of gravity increase.

The world went white.

Heat, which balanced nearly precisely at Tala's upper limit, slammed into her.

Her attempt at defense had utterly failed from what she could tell. Her defensive stance broke under the wash of power, Flow slamming back into her chest, along with the tungsten sphere and rod.

Tala was thrown backwards and crashed into the far wall of the training ground.

Her breath exploded out of her, and she slid to the ground in a stunned heap.

Rust me. I'm glad she changed out for a training round.

As light and sound returned to normal, the healer rushed over to Tala but slowed as she approached. Tala felt the touch of diagnostic magics and didn't resist them. "She's fine, just stunned."

Tala groaned. The magic of the area returned to a smooth, even level as if it had never been disturbed.

As the healer went back to her seat, Aproa jogged over to Tala and offered a hand up. "That's why you don't fight Mage Hunters."

Tala snorted a halfhearted laugh and accepted the help up.

She looked around, expecting to see the sand melted and the wall behind her scorched, but there was no evidence of the heat and light. Even the air of the training space was still pleasantly cool.

Was it all in my head? No, she'd been thrown, and she knew what she'd felt. She patted her clothing and found the outside unpleasantly warm to the touch. The attack had just been *that* precisely calibrated. Tala looked to her opponent across the space and tilted her head to one side. "Did the attack modulate to my tolerances?"

Jean nodded, grinning. "Yeah." She seemed hesitant about something. Finally, she shrugged. "I can usually get a couple of shots out of a training round, but you required the entire capacity of this one." She smiled. "Nice."

Jean then shifted, clearly a bit uncomfortable.

"Um… would you mind releasing… whatever it was you did?" Jean did a couple of hops and came down more quickly, and harder, than was normal.

The watching Archons began muttering to each other, but Tala ignored them. "Oh! Right. One moment." She re-established the lock, Jean not opposing it this time. *Reduce.*

Two seconds later, Tala released the working and the lock.

"There you go."

Jean hopped again, smiling as she landed. "Thank you."

Tala cracked her neck and twisted back and forth.

Rane, standing off to the side, shook his head. "Oh, no."

The others, at least the non-Hunters, looked his way. One ventured to ask, "What?"

He simply gestured to Tala, and taking the cue, she smiled. "Again."

Jean hesitated, then shook her head, ejecting the spent round from the back of her weapon and replacing it. The used one was placed in a pouch on the back of the Mage Hunter's belt. "Like punishment, do you?"

Millennial Mage, 5 - Fusing

Tala shook her head. "Not at all. I like improving." Then, she looked within herself and paled. "But you're right, not another today." Her scripts were getting truly, dangerously low. Tala cursed.

Aproa frowned. "What is it?"

Tala sighed. "My inscriptions are almost dry. They've not been refreshed yet since our caravan just returned yesterday. I'll be getting reinscribed this afternoon. I'm sorry about that. What would you all normally do?"

Aproa patted Tala's shoulder. "We do begin with challenges if anyone is inclined, just like we said. After that, we do team bouts, contests, or direct oppositions of will. If your inscriptions are low, we can focus on contests of will today."

The lightning and two fire Mages grinned widely, while the others whom Tala didn't know by name groaned.

Tala shrugged. "Sounds good. What do we do?"

*   *   *

The remainder of the afternoon was much less exciting but no less enlightening.

Tala held Terry in her lap, scratching his head and neck as she sat a mere ten feet from the twins, engaging in a very one-sided conflict.

The contest in question was a simple one: who could touch the other with their aura first. No attacks, items, or magical workings were allowed.

It was a delicate balance of offense and defense. An Archon had to press their aura forward against the resistance of their opponent, while not allowing them to take advantage of the longer route to reach from the sides or over the top.

Or, that was the theory.

Tala simply punched straight through any individual among the Archons there.

The Mage Hunters had declined for the moment, but Tala thought she was beginning to intrigue them.

In the end, the others had paired up against her, using their combined magical weight to hold her back and their two minds to try to outthink her.

Again, that was the theory.

"Victory, Mistress Tala," Cazor called from the side.

"*What?*" The male twin stood. "Her aura is completely held at bay. How did she win?"

Cazor shrugged. "You all appointed us as judges. Her aura touched you."

Tala gave a half-smile. Her great breakthrough had come when she realized that she could extend a tendril of her aura underground and no other Archon had magesight of sufficient precision and sensitivity to notice.

She suspected that even Cazor couldn't see the part of her aura that was underground.

It wasn't fast, so she still had to hold off the incursions of her opponents while she slowly poured power into the sapping maneuver, but it worked every time in the end.

Tala stretched back, pulsing her aura outward to clear the remainder of the twins' probing tendrils from the space around her. "Well fought. You had some good tricks there."

She rocked back before kicking up to a standing position. Terry had flickered away as she moved and flickered back to her shoulder when she was upright. Tala tossed him a bit of jerky and walked to her opponents, hands held out.

They sighed, taking the offered help up.

They'd all long since realized that Tala, small though she was, had the mass to act as a good anchor for such things.

Millennial Mage, 5 - Fusing

The sister leaned in close. "How are you doing it? Did you pay off the Mage Hunter?"

Tala laughed. "No cheating or bribery, I promise."

The twin sighed. "I kinda wish you were. It would make our repeated defeats easier to bear."

Her brother shrugged. "It's good exercise. I haven't felt this worked, on a will level, in…" He blew air through his lips, making a sound that was a bit like a horse. "Well, ever really. With these contests, it's usually pretty even, so we don't push our hardest. With you?" He grinned. "I push as hard as I can, and it feels like you barely slow down."

Tala smiled happily at the compliment. "Well, thank you. I've put a lot of effort into aura manipulation, and I had a good teacher to get me started." *I really do need to be practicing my bloodstar orbits and increasing the number I can use.*

"Oh?" They both looked quite interested.

The quiet of the courtyard was interrupted by a loud voice as Jean called out, "Victory, Mistress Aproa."

Rane groaned and flopped backwards, holding his head. "Well done, Mistress. I need a moment."

Tala watched as Aproa stood and went over to help him. "Don't strain yourself, Master Rane. It is good to improve but not to damage yourself along the way."

"Yeah… I know." Rane turned his head Tala's way, peeking between his fingers, and Tala grinned at him. "Rust you, Tala."

Tala snorted a laugh. "Come on. I know it's a bit early, but I need food before I meet with Mistress Holly." Tala glanced around.

There were, once again, wide eyes and disbelieving stares. Finally, Cazor glanced around and shook his head. "Come on, it's not that unusual that she has Mistress Holly inscribing her."

The lightning Mage snorted. "I'd give an arm to have that Inscriber work on me."

The oxygen manipulator laughed. "It'd cost that much, from what I hear."

Tala felt a bit awkward. "Well, ummm... For dinner, you are all welcome, of course."

Rane took Aproa's offered hand and stood. "That sounds wonderful. You can celebrate, and we can commiserate." He glanced to Aproa. "Thank you for the hand, Mistress."

In the end, they all agreed to come as it was early yet, but most wouldn't eat as they tried to have dinner with their families whenever possible.

Huh, I guess I didn't really think about some of them being married. Turns out all but Aproa and the hunters have spouses and kids. She didn't really know how to process that. *They are quite a bit older than me.* She decided to think more on it later.

* * *

Dinner was surprisingly fun. The whole group was there except for the healer, who had departed after the last duel and before the contests of will.

Tala had been surprised at the inclusion of the Mage Hunters as they'd seemed pretty set apart up to that point. Even so, they seemed to join in the conversations with abandon. Apparently, this group had been close enough in age that they'd all been at the academy at the same time, at least for a few years. They'd worked to push each other and improve.

That was likely a core reason for their age and relatively high rank.

Millennial Mage, 5 - Fusing

This also wasn't their whole group, as they were scattered on various jobs or tasks, and they'd added some since like Rane and Tala.

As for their group, apparently Jean and Cazor had stood out enough from the others that they'd been approached to become Mage Hunters.

At least, that was what Aproa said.

Cazor said that it was just because of their foundational principles, desired magics, and personalities.

Tala did get to learn a bit more about Mage Hunters. Each city had around a hundred of them, though rarely that exact number. They were tasked with handling the Mages and inscribed who thought themselves above common law. As a result, they also investigated crimes that seemed to have a magical component.

Tala ended up sitting between Aproa and Cazor during dinner, across from Rane and Jean. Terry opted to stay on Tala's shoulder, snacking on the occasional bit of jerky that Tala tossed for him.

Rane and Aproa had a bit of fun with the hunters, each extorting a small wager out of the one nearest to them on whether or not Tala could out-eat them.

Tala briefly considered ruining their fun or throwing the contest, but in the end, she let them have their amusement and a few silver changed hands, along with awed, almost horrified glances.

Tala didn't let it bother her and ate her fill.

The group parted ways just before sunset, having eaten a fairly early dinner. It seemed that no few of them had tasks to complete that evening.

Thus, Tala found herself alone, darkening Holly's warehouse doorway, just after sunset. *Really, it's still late afternoon…*

"You're late."

Tala turned to find Holly, once again, in the chair beside the door. "Gah! Why are you waiting here?"

"Because you're late." Holly stood and walked toward the back.

Following behind, Tala continued the conversation. "You never waited for me before my return from this last trip. What's the issue?"

Holly glanced back her way, sighed, and looked forward once more. "There's a syphon in the city that we haven't been able to find. You have a history of being influenced by mental magics, and I don't want you to vanish for a day to who knows where, having your magic drained like some grape for juice."

She's worried about me? Tala stopped walking. "Wait... what do you mean?"

Terry lifted his head in interest.

"Come on, dear. I'll explain."

Terry and Tala glanced at each other and shrugged. *This should be interesting.* She hurried to catch up, doing so just as they reached Holly's workroom.

"So, a syphon is a term for a class of magical creature that pulls power from humans harmlessly. In general, the worst that happens is that they feel a bit drunk after. It's often accompanied by lost time. In some cases, however, the people just vanish."

"And there's one in the city?" *Why does this seem familiar?* Maybe she'd read about this creature type in the past.

"Yes. The city overseers have noticed lower-than-average ambient magic, given our population, but it's spread out. No obvious hunting ground or target group."

"So... how can it be within the city?"

They'd taken their usual seats; Mistress Holly on her stool, Tala in the client's chair, and Terry watching them

Millennial Mage, 5 - Fusing

both from the corner. "Come on, Mistress Tala. Think before you ask."

Tala did think, then, and had to sigh. "If they are subsisting on human magic, then the only magic that could be detected is human."

Holly gave her a strange look. "No. Not at all." She shook her head. "That's like saying if you only eat potatoes, it's reasonable to expect that you might poop mash." She muttered something under her breath too low for Tala to hear. "No, child. If humans are their primary prey, and most of us are in cities, then the only way such a thing still exists is if it can adapt itself to go unnoticed by city defenses and high-level Archon perusal. It would, of course, be obvious at close inspection, but we can't investigate every alley, park bench, or new door to a dimensionally expanded space."

"It can be any of those?"

"Yes. They can also be humanoid in appearance, but that's rarer. There's a subtype that is more often lethal, which seems to enjoy hiding in ruins and pretending to be treasure chests." Holly shook her head again. "No one really knows why. They also seem to be much more physically aggressive, rather than wielding conceptual magic, so…" She shrugged.

Alright then, something else to be concerned over. "Well, that happy topic aside, let's talk inscriptions."

"Ahh, yes. Your inscriptions. I dug through your records more thoroughly, and I want you to explain exactly what caused you to cook your own muscles via overexertion."

Oh… right. Tala glanced to Terry. "Yeah, so… About that." Without further delay, she began a more detailed retelling of her time away.

Chapter: 27
Alternate Interface

Tala had finished her tale, and Holly was simply sitting, contemplating.

"Is everything alright?"

Holly grunted, standing. "Quite, yes." She hesitated, then pulled a seemingly raw steak out of thin air and tossed it toward Terry.

It vanished before reaching the halfway point between them, just a hint of dimensional power giving knowledge of where it had gone.

"What was that for?"

The older woman paused for another moment, then smiled. "Courtesy never hurt anyone." Without another word, she went and grabbed a small box from the side of the room. "This is the Archive connection we will be utilizing. I need it bound to you before we inscribe you."

Tala nodded. "About that. Is it really worth such a bond? I only get eight, if I remember correctly. I have my weapon, my clothing, and I will have my storage. Is this really worthy of the fourth slot?"

"Unequivocally. Yes. Every Archon that reaches a high enough level that their mind and magic density can make it work gets something like this. Speaking of which"—she pulled a book out of thin air, handing it over to Tala—"read the marked section and ask any questions now. I won't give you an inscription you don't fully

Millennial Mage, 5 - Fusing

understand. Everything else is based on what you know, and so you can expand your understanding afterwards."

Tala shrugged. "Sure." She took the book, flipped it open to the marked page, and read. Tala really did take her increased reading and comprehension speed for granted. She read through the ten pages in half as many minutes, closed the book, and looked up to Holly, questions prepared. "So, I understand what this will do, and how. What I don't understand is why you trust the Archive so completely. How can we know it's secure?"

"Because its security is keyed to a combination of your soul and your will. The access and input functions for each bit of information are literally impenetrable. Trust me. There are a *host* of locked notes and information that Archivists have spent centuries trying to get access to, to no avail. In a few instances, the fount of the owner of those files was tracked down. They tried to manipulate it to help grant access, but it didn't work."

Tala still felt skeptical, and her look must have conveyed the same.

Holly sighed. "The information doesn't exist in any physical place, so that cannot be breached. It exists in a dimension of magic. Within the magical matrix, there is a random distribution of information segments and redundancy. The right, authorized soul-combination will gain access easily. Nothing else can. Even if someone were able to find the exact right magical coordinates for a given bit of information, any unauthorized mind in the information space immediately corrupts and eliminates the data." Holly shook her head. "Even this is an oversimplification. It cannot be breached."

Tala grimaced. She was about to comment when Holly's eyes lit up.

"Oh! This is perfect. About a thousand years ago, an Archivist earned the favor of one of the arcane sovereigns. She was granted one boon. Being an Archivist, she asked for access to the 'lost' information within the Archive."

Tala leaned forward, curious as to the result of the request, though she suspected that she knew, given the context in which she was being told the story.

"The sovereign tried. He tried for a hundred years. Finally, he stated that the Archive was unbreachable and granted the Archivist two boons in recompense for his failure."

Tala huffed. "He probably got access and just lied."

Holly let out a long-suffering breath. "No, Mistress Tala. A boon is a magical contract that will rip apart the soul of someone who fails the obligation. The fact that the boon was requested, not fulfilled, and the sovereign lives is the true testament to the impossibility of the task."

"What do you mean?"

"A claim on a boon cannot be impossible, else a sovereign could be slain by a cleverly impossible request."

Tala grunted. "How reliable is this story?"

"The Archivist is my aunt."

Oh. "Well, you heard it firsthand, then. That's pretty reliable."

Holly sniffed. "You can go ask her, yourself, if you wish."

Tala shrugged. "I might. But I think I am satisfied, for now."

"I'd hope so."

"Shall we, then?" Tala glanced at the item in Holly's hands. "Bonding first, right?"

"That's right." Holly opened the little box and held out an oddly adjustable ring. It looked like a perforated band with a small screw gear, which could be used to shrink or expand the size.

Millennial Mage, 5 - Fusing

"So, this is usually put on a pencil, pen, or some such thing?"

"That's right. I've sized it close to one of your fingers. I think you should put it on before you bond it."

Tala shrugged. "Sure." She slipped it over her right ring finger and manually used the mechanism to tighten it until it was a comfortable size. Next, she opened Kit and *pulled* out her inside-out Archon bloodstar.

"Alright. The bonding process should be the same as with a standard Archon Star."

Tala shrugged, focusing her magesight on the odd, magically-empowered, circular clamp on her finger. When she found the tell-tale gap in the spellform, she moved the drop of blood into that space, pushing it more in a magical direction than a physical one.

There was a resonant *click* within the ring and within herself.

Tala felt the bond take hold and gasped at the outrush of power and strength. Her soul felt stretched—as made sense. It had been forcibly expanded to include something else.

She took a few deep, almost panting breaths. When she recovered her focus, she looked down at the ring.

More accurately, she looked at her finger and the ring of red, magical symbols that were now set into her flesh.

As she looked, they pulsed once with a bloody light and faded.

"Um… Mistress Holly?"

Holly was looking as well. "Fascinating. It appears to have simply incorporated with your flesh."

Tala glared. "Why? What does this even mean?"

"It means that you'll never have to worry about it breaking or being stolen or corrupted. One moment." Holly put her hands on either side of Tala's, not touching her skin but with her palms oriented inward. Scriptings blossomed with power across the woman's flesh, and suddenly, Tala could see spellforms in the air around her own hand and arm.

They weren't the same shape as her metal inscriptions, but she could see that they had the same purpose. "Are those my ingrained magics?"

"Very good." Holly smiled. "Yes, this working displays the ingrained magics of the target, though it isn't perfectly accurate, by the nature of representing a thing that is magically dimensional in physical dimensions."

"I don't really understand the difference."

"Not surprising. The human mind doesn't really assimilate extra dimensions very well."

Tala grunted, looking closer. Sure enough, around her right ring finger, she could see spell-lines for the connection to the Archive.

Holly was looking as well. "Truly fascinating. Your subconscious took over during the bond—as expected for a subconscious soul-bond. It—well, you—felt that you only needed the connection to the Archive, and so it shed everything else, even the natural physical form of the item. I imagine that your medium being fluid, as well as a part of you to begin with, allowed that. You can likely force a physical form in the future when you get conscious control, but for now, this will be incredibly efficient." She was practically glowing with glee. "I wish I could have accomplished something like this for myself."

Tala smiled hesitantly. "I'm glad?"

"You should be, dear. I'd had a small concern that having an active, constant connection to the Archive would be a power drain that would add difficulty for you until you elevated yourself to Refined, but my concerns were unfounded."

Millennial Mage, 5 - Fusing

Tala's eye twitched, but she held her tongue. *Those concerns would have been nice to know about beforehand.*

Holly grinned, going to a cabinet off to one side and bringing out the auto-inscriber. It was much bigger than Tala remembered it. Apparently, Holly had been pleased with the results to the point of making a full-body version. "Alright. Remember, you must be conscious to prevent power from flowing into the scripts, since your gate doesn't close with unconsciousness."

Tala shook her head. "Rust that. Enact that privacy spell you used before. It closed off my gate well enough."

Holly opened her mouth, thought for a moment, then closed it in thought before nodding. "You know, that would probably work. Good idea, Mistress."

Tala's eye twitched again. *She didn't put any thought into a solution, at all.* "Thank you."

She was about to lift up her arms to have the device slipped over her head when Holly sighed. "You will need to deactivate the armor, dear. I don't want to break these needles on it."

"Oh! Right." Tala dove into the garment with her magesight, found the proper path, and sent power down it to deactivate the defensive magics.

"Thank you."

Tala worked with Holly to wriggle into what now seemed like a one-piece, oversized outfit that included an inverted hood.

"Here you go, dear. Sleep well."

She felt the cool, hard stone press against the base of her neck. As her consciousness fled, Tala sensed the auto-inscriber tightening to fit her perfectly, completely encapsulating her within its needle-armed embrace.

*　　*　　*

-Ding-
-Consciousness disabled for reinscribing.-
-Reinscribing complete. Consciousness restored.-
Tala groaned, stirring and blinking her eyes open.

Below her was a surprisingly comfortable chair. Over her head was a simple, well-built ceiling.

Where am I? She blinked a few more times, and it came back to her. *Right!*

She heard some movement from the far side of the room.

"Mistress Holly?"

"Yes, dear?" The woman came over to her.

"Are we done?"

"Yes. I just put away the auto-inscriber. Do you notice anything different?"

Tala stretched, looking around. "Not immediately." Then she frowned. "No. You know what? I feel like I heard something right after I woke up… or maybe as I was waking up?"

Holly was nodding. "That is in line with what I expected. How do you think you should interact with it?"

Tala thought for a long moment. "Hey, please… detect lost or repressed memories."

-Ding-

-Instruction received. All other functions will be unavailable until deep neural scan is complete. Thank you for your patience.-

Just as with the consciousness restoration inscription, the voice Tala heard in her mind was her own but somehow not her. It was more distinct this time, almost… emotionless? *What happened to the snark?*

"Mistress Tala?"

"Hmm?"

"Am I to intuit that you found something?"

Millennial Mage, 5 - Fusing

"Oh! Yes. It accepted the command, but it seems... lifeless?"

Holly shrugged. "I overlayed and interconnected it with a deeply complex set of inscriptions. The consciousness-maintaining script is a minuscule subset of this new spellform. It will develop as it is used. It might start showing some 'life' next time you interact or in five years, but I'd wager that the first is vastly more likely than the second." She paused for a moment of thought, then nodded. "That was a very good first command, by the way. It will give it the impetus to map your mind for later comparisons."

"So, everything else is refreshed?"

"It is." Holly held out a slate with the total bill.

Tala sighed but confirmed the transaction, placing her caravan token on the slate afterwards to allow Holly to bill them for the inscriptions of a Mage Protector.

Forty gold, just like she said. It didn't help that Tala felt like she was still being given a discount, even if not as great as before. *The cost is going to scale with my earnings for years... I just know it.*

Everything felt as it should, except around her stomach. She looked within with her magesight and found the inscriptions at issue.

She sighed. "Anti-vomit scripts are settling back in."

Holly nodded. "You really shouldn't use any of your inscriptions completely."

"Yeah, I know." Her stomach gurgled. "Oh... wow... I am hungry." Now that she'd noticed it, she couldn't really ignore it. She felt positively ravenous.

"That'll be the next step of your physiology inscriptions." Her look and tone turned stern. "Don't drink so much coffee. It's not good for you physically or financially."

Tala grimaced. "Fine."

"Good. Now, how do you like the rings?"

She hadn't actually looked. Lifting her hands, Tala examined the new design of golden rings that now decorated the back of each hand. "Lovely. Thank you. It's as much art as inscription."

Holly smiled brightly, clearly pleased with the compliment.

"Well, anything else we need to do?"

"No, I think we're all good here." She held out the book that Tala had read a portion of for her new mental scriptings. "These are the updates to your inscriptions. The only one we haven't discussed is the improved heat dissipation. I put that one at the beginning, so you could brush up quickly."

Tala stood, took the book, and gave Holly a bow. "Thank you, Mistress Holly."

Holly gave her an odd look but bowed in return. "I am happy to assist."

Terry flickered to Tala's shoulder and squawked.

Holly hesitated, shook her head, and snorted a laugh. With a smooth motion, she tossed out another seemingly fresh, bloody chuck of meat, pulling it from thin air.

It vanished in a similar fashion.

"Now, go. I have other work to be about."

Without another word, Tala left.

*   *   *

Tala had an almost insatiable hunger, so she went and got herself two cheesy little caravans.

Oh, rust. I've missed these. She sat in a nearby park, utterly demolishing the food, which could have fed a grown man after an entire day of hard work.

As she ate, she read through the book provided by Holly. *Ahh, that makes sense. An increase both to heat*

Millennial Mage, 5 - Fusing

capacity and conductivity. Her body could now hold more heat safely and dissipate it more rapidly, though a good portion of the first was an artifact of her increasing mass.

She could feel her magics working within her, adding density and structure to her bones, enhancing her musculature and reaction rates, and consuming her reserves, both magical and mundane, to do so.

So… hungry… Tala had a thought. *Is this natural, or am I being magically influenced to be hungry?* It was a silly question, but she thought it was worth asking.

Please, is my hunger mundane or magical in nature?

-Ding-

-*All functions are offline during deep neural scan.*-

Tala sighed. She had expected as much, but she still found herself mildly disappointed as she took the next massive bite.

-*Tala*-

-*Obviously, you are simply hungry, but you are hungry because of your new inscriptions, which are magical. Thus, your question was asinine. Please consider your questions before you query. Time is valuable, and you've wasted it for both of us.*-

Tala startled at the second response, then snorted a laugh, taking another bite.

Fair enough. That was a pretty poorly worded question.

No further responses came as Tala continued to eat, not that she expected any.

It was odd, having even that short exchange with something inside her head. *But it's still me, just with a different interface. I interact with the physical world and she with the Archive.* Tala perked up at that. *Ohhh, I like that; Alternate Interface. She's my AI.* After a short thought, Tala shrugged. *I'll ask her at some point if that works. No need to force a name on this new aspect of myself. I can decide.*

She hesitated, there. *Wait. I don't want to force a name on myself... I want to let myself decide.* She groaned. *This is ridiculous.*

Again, the contemplations were becoming odd and convoluted. She sighed and tore into the second feast-in-a-package.

This. Is. Perfect. No need to contemplate the upcoming existential crisis of her soul operating what was, effectively, two consciousnesses. *No reason to consider it at all.*

She took another glorious bite and continued to study her new book.

*   *   *

Tala finished her meal too soon, and while she was still hungry, she suspected that she would be hungry a lot in the coming days. She'd delay at least a little while before getting more, else she'd be eating constantly, and that wouldn't do.

I should drop through the Archive and kick that hornets' nest in regards to the Culinary Guild. As she considered, she realized that she'd been avoiding doing just that. *I just want to train... This is going to get political.*

If it got political, Lyn might be able to help... *Yeah. I should go get Lyn and see if she wants to come.*

With that decided, Tala set off toward her home.

The city, as always, was stunning. The sky overhead was clear, and the stars were bright to Tala's enhanced vision. *I so prefer exterior cities...* It was an odd thought, really. She'd never really contemplated what it would

Millennial Mage, 5 - Fusing

mean to live in a city that was entirely contained in a single structure.

While she could see the faint spell-lines of the city's defenses tracing their way through the sky, they were dim to the point that she could easily tune them out, unlike in Alefast.

Now she knew what it was like to be in a fully contained city, and she preferred a more traditional approach.

As she neared home, she noticed the tavern again. *Right. I wanted to try the food there. It seems popular enough to warrant investigation.*

-Ding-

Tala stopped. What was this? Had she found something already?

-Please refrain from exposing us to mental manipulation while I am mapping our brain. It greatly increases the difficulty of my task.-

Tala's eyes widened. *Exposing myself to mental manipulation?* She stared at the tavern. *Is that—*

-Tala-

-Yes, that is obviously the source. Please leave or stop the influence in some way. Our mind is convoluted enough as it is, without adding external factors.-

Tala took another moment to simply stare at the building before her. *Well... I guess I found Holly's syphon.*

Chapter: 28
Syphon

Tala frowned, forcing her thoughts in order against the subtle push from outside.

I need a plan. How should I handle this? The part of her that wasn't being influenced to go eat in the tavern wanted to burn the thing down, but that seemed unwise.

First, find a way to remove the influence. Then, go tell Lyn. Then, go tell the Archons.

That was a solid plan. *But how do I do the first?*

The other her had noticed the influence, and she only had access to the same senses as Tala.

What am I missing?

She delved through herself with her magesight, and as she concentrated on her mind, she was able to see ripples of magic slowly moving through it.

A weaker, but more precise one acting internally seemed to be coming from the inscriptions at the base of her neck and in her right breast. But then, there were other ones coming from outside. They were broad, undirected, and strong.

There you are. But how could she counteract them?

I'm resisting somehow, at least a bit. Probably my magical weight? That made sense. *That also explains why I wasn't really affected during my first time passing by. I still had my iron salve at that point.* She sighed. *I wish I'd known to keep it on.* But no, that wasn't right. She hadn't been affected as strongly, but she'd still been affected.

Millennial Mage, 5 - Fusing

So, magical weight. She bit her lip in thought, moving to the side of the street and pulling back from the tavern a bit.

Can I shift my magical weight? It made some sense. It would likely leave the rest of her vulnerable to direct magical manipulation, but she should be able to protect her mind more fully.

With a great effort of will, she forcefully guided her power up into her head. She didn't form it into any shape, she just packed it in there.

There. As an Immaterial Guide, it wasn't a difficult process. And it seemed to have the desired effect.

The external influence now felt more like a small hammer tapping on a rock than a finger poking a waterskin.

Alright, now to go to Lyn and...

Tala's eyes widened in horror as the rhythm of magical taps changed, speeding up and becoming more focused on her.

Still, she held her concentration and resisted with little difficulty.

Hah, you can't overcome me that easily.

It was then that two great eyes opened, high up on the walls of the tavern. They looked around, searching, and stopped to stare directly at her.

Oh... That wasn't part of the plan.

She quickly dove into her garments and sent power through the path that would reactivate the defensive magics. *I really should have done that before leaving Holly's—or at the very least, made that step one of my plan.*

Flow was in her hand in the form of a glaive. *All the better to stab you with, my dear.* She let out a little giggle, more from nervousness than humor.

Terry's head jerked up, and he looked around in the closest thing to a panic that she'd ever seen him express. With a flicker of power, he was gone.

She could sense him staying close by, within safe range for his collar, but he was hidden. *Probably for the best.*

What on Zeme should she do next?

Crush it? No, there were people inside. Crushing the building would kill them all.

Do I just... start hacking at the façade? What would that even do?

Only one way to find out, I suppose. She hesitated. *Wait. It hasn't attacked. It's just staring at me.*

She had a realization. *If it attacks, it will likely become detectable to the city's defenses or at least the Archons.*

She smiled, slowly moving down the street toward her home, keeping her eyes and weapon oriented on the syphon.

Is it going to let me go? That didn't seem like its best option... *Was it? What is it thinking? What is it doing?*

She tore her gaze away from the monstrous eyes still staring straight at her. She looked through the windows and saw the forms inside beginning to slump. As she thought about it, she realized that the noise coming from inside had died down.

Oh, rust me. It's draining them dry in a last grab for power. She no longer had a choice. People could be dying. She couldn't go for help and leave them to their fate.

Tala growled and charged.

As she came close, the front porch tore itself free with the audible snap, crackle, and pop of wood breaking and fasteners pulling free. The newly ambulatory limb whipped out, slamming into her faster than she could dodge.

Millennial Mage, 5 - Fusing

Even though she got Flow in the way in time, mirroring her mass into the weapon, she was still lifted free of the ground and thrown to arc through the air before slamming into the cobbled street.

She landed in a tumbling roll farther down the way, on the opposite side of the tavern from her home.

Nothing was broken, but she could feel her scripts pulling more than their base rate of power. *Strained but not overcome.* She could work with that.

She hopped to her feet and threw Flow with all her might, letting the weapon reshape into a sword so that it would be a spinning wheel of death as it approached.

A gutter detached to slap at the incoming weapon.

Flow sheared through the adornment-turned-limb but was still knocked aside. It would have missed the main body of the house, so Tala pulled her weapon back to her hand.

They were making a *lot* of noise, and people were coming out of their homes to stare in bemusement at what was happening.

Good, someone will go for help.

Incredibly, most simply looked at her with confusion, shook their heads, and went back inside. Tala could feel the power radiating through the air, knocking at her mind, trying to overcome her cobbled-together mental defense.

In the doorway of the house closest to Tala, an older lady turned to her and yelled, "What's wrong with you? People are trying to sleep. Those who drink too much should just go home." She then huffed and slammed the door.

Tala stared after her for an instant of bewilderment. *Don't let it distract you, Tala. It's still influencing their minds, but it's thrown subtlety out the window.*

Farther down the street, Tala saw Lyn staring at her in obvious confusion.

"*Lyn*! The tavern is attacking people."

Lyn cocked her head. "What are you talking about?"

"Please! Go for the guard, even if just to arrest me. Attack the tavern if you can."

Lyn gave her a long look, then shook her head. "If I go to jail for this, you're paying bail, and *you* are paying to get me reinscribed."

She lifted her hand, and Tala saw Lyn use battle magic for the first time.

Brilliant golden inscriptions blazed to life across the woman's body, burning away in an instant of glory as she spoke a single word. "Crumble."

A spell with greater weight than two of Tala's *Crush* enactments tore down the street, and Tala witnessed the conceptual magic in the air splinter and crumble.

Lyn's eyes widened now that she could seemingly suddenly see the tavern as it truly was.

Her spell-working tore into the gigantic creature, and its material began to shred, revealing the twisted, disguised flesh that really composed the seemingly mundane establishment.

Unfortunately, Lyn lacked the power to dispatch such a monster.

Even so, its pained roar shook the surrounding city, causing both Lyn and Tala to stumble, and the being's aura was unleashed, fully visible to Tala for the first time.

Blue filled Tala's vision.

Oh, rust. Oh, rust! Why had she been able to resist it? *Its power was diffuse, and it was trying to remain undetected.* That was gone now.

She felt something strike out at her mind and frantically jerked her magical weight to the side. Somehow, that let the attack glance off, if only for a moment. In the distance, Lyn crumpled.

Her mind was spinning. Too much was going on. *I've got to get to Lyn. I have to—*

-Tala-

-*That is really distract*... What the rust is that!?-

Tala began to laugh. *At least we're in agreement.*

-Kill it! Kill it with fire!-

I don't have fire.

-...*We should reconsider that. Alchemist's fire is a good option to have at hand. Please don't die. I have work to do.*-

A staggering blow hammered against her mind, and Tala's vision fuzzed. She barely held her magic in place, focused around her mind.

She thought she could hear a small whimpering from the back of her mind. *Other me probably has the right idea...*

Her vision returned as lances of fire and spikes of lightning began to rain from the sky. The city defenses had detected the threat and began the purge. As the first attacks landed, several cloaked figures seemed to materialize out of nowhere on the street in front of the monster building.

With waves of power in the form of various spell-workings, human bodies were pulled from the increasingly unrecognizable tavern, and once they were clear, the fight truly began.

Some of the new arrivals were establishing a perimeter, erecting defensive and dampening shields to protect the surroundings.

An Archon whose aura was utterly undetectable to Tala pointed at the syphon. A beam of pure light extended from the finger, and as the Archon moved their finger in a random zig-zag, the beam sliced through the creature effortlessly.

Tala saw another Archon on the other side absorbing the beam of light in a cloud of darkness so it wouldn't continue into the city beyond.

The syphon didn't go down so easily, however, its body pulling together in new, mind-bending shapes as it healed from every wound it received.

It lashed out with body and mind.

Tala staggered under another mental attack, but it was wide-area this time, and so it didn't cripple her even for a moment.

Several of the other Archons, who were much closer, stumbled, one even going to a knee before recovering.

After that initial largely ineffective attack, the syphon mostly used fleshy tentacles to slap and slam anything it could reach.

The Archons who were closest engaged the flailing limbs as best as they could, but it was obvious that some were more skilled than others.

A few in the group appeared to be healers, and they were tending to the humans who had been pulled out of the false tavern.

Tala ran over to them as they seemed like the least likely to be hurt if she distracted them. "Is there anything I can do?"

A woman glanced at Tala. "You helped draw it out of hiding?"

"Yes, Mistress."

"Then you've done enough. Draw back so you don't get crushed in the crossfire. We know what we're about." After a moment, she continued, "Don't go too far. We'll want to talk with you once the creature is dispatched."

Tala nodded and moved past on the far side of the thoroughfare, skirting behind a shield Mage who was simply protecting the houses across the street from the raging beast.

Millennial Mage, 5 - Fusing

Once she was in the clear, Tala ran toward Lyn, who was sitting up on the street holding her head, clearly in pain and just as clearly exhausted.

Tala sat down next to her friend. "Are you okay?"

The beast screeched, but it was dampened, the sound barely reaching them just a few dozen yards away.

Lyn nodded tiredly. "I've not used that working very often."

Tala snorted a laugh. "What was that, anyway?"

"My defense of last resort. My foundational understanding made manifest."

"Oh?"

"'Words are power.'"

"Rust. That's pretty cool." Tala chuckled.

Lyn grinned. "Yeah. Too bad it's single cast." She sighed, leaning back to enjoy the show. "I should be able to support a multi-cast variant when I reach a higher tier of advancement, but we'll have to see."

"When? Not if?" Tala smiled mischievously at her friend.

Lyn rolled her eyes. "Yes, when. I'm over the biggest hurdle. Basically, everything else just takes time, and I'll have that in gold. I'm not going to stop now."

Tala bumped her friend's shoulder with her own. "Good."

Together they settled in to watch the show, and a show it was. The city's defenses were relentless, but they weren't designed for this level of threat. Thus, they were only an aid to the true heroes of the moment. The Archons displayed a wide variety of abilities from earth rising up to crush parts of the enemy to the light beam that Tala had seen earlier.

One Archon apparently favored fire and used it liberally.

There was a mix of other workings as well, but from where they sat, it all distilled down to a beautiful light show, punctuated by increasingly desperate, rage-filled roars and screeches.

It took nearly an hour, and a truly staggering amount of power, but the Archons wore down the beast, cutting it apart until it could no longer heal.

Tala had watched as its aura slowly moved down the spectrum. When the aura had faded from red entirely, she knew that the fight was done.

Less than a minute later, a final, mournful cry escaped the mound of flesh, and it shifted for the last time, settling into a dead, bloody lump of used-to-be-creature.

Lyn shook her head in wonder. "Imagine, a Revered getting into the city. That shouldn't be possible." She barked a short laugh. "And no one died! It was contained and destroyed."

"Yeah…" Tala frowned. "It shouldn't have gotten in at all, but I doubt it was that powerful when it arrived. It's probably been gorging itself on power for weeks."

"True enough." Lyn shuddered, some of her good mood fading away. "I've gone to that tavern, Tala. I *liked* the food and ale. I drank so much I missed work the next day…" She shivered again, all mirth gone. "I fed it…"

Tala wrapped an arm around her friend. "You're okay now. It's gone."

Lyn leaned into Tala's embrace. "I feel disgusting, violated."

"Anything I can do?"

"Food. I want food, prepared by a human while I watch. No crazy magical creature drawing me in with inhuman delights."

Tala smiled at the attempted humor. "I can do that. Let's find somewhere that's open. But we should check in

Millennial Mage, 5 - Fusing

with them first. The healer I talked to said they'd likely like to speak to us, now that it's over."

As they stood together, they garnered attention, and one of the Archons came their way. "You two. You fought the beast?"

They hesitated, then nodded.

"Tell me what happened, please."

Tala shrugged and recounted what had led up to the fight, though she left out any mention of voices in her head.

"Clever use of your magical weight. It's a good skill to practice if you're able, and you've a leg up as an Immaterial Guide."

Next, Lyn filled in her side, short though it was, and the man nodded his acknowledgment.

"Thank you, both, for your assistance." He handed a token to Lyn. "That will allow an Inscriptionist to charge us and cover the cost for reinscribing." He grinned. "That was some spell. It lit up our detection grid like the breath of a god. I can't wait to see what you're capable of in a few centuries."

Tala laughed, patting Lyn on the back, the other woman coloring at the compliment. "Thank you, Master."

He then turned to Tala. "Mage Protector, right? Blood Archon Tala?"

She blinked at him, processing the fact that he knew her name. She was instantly suspicious. "Ummm… Yes? How do you know who I am?"

He gave a half smile. "We were briefed on your encounters and discovery. We were also asked to watch out for you, when possible. I'm glad you survived even such a small engagement with that thing."

She laughed nervously. "Yeah…" *Well, it does make sense that the Mages watching over the city would have been told about mind-altering creatures within their walls.* It also made sense that they'd be told who the source of the information was.

"You helped slay it, so you're entitled to part of the rewards. Your friend's pay is the reinscription, and I imagine that's worth more than you'll get, but here." He handed her a different token. "Come to the Archon's compound any time after tomorrow morning and turn that in for your portion of the calculated pay." He bowed and was about to turn away when he paused, sighed, and looked back to Tala. "I was also instructed to inform you, if our paths ever crossed, that the city lord would still happily accept you into our ranks." He gestured at the group who had responded to this internal threat. "I can promise it's not a boring job."

This time, he got a half-dozen feet away before he paused and turned back. "In case it wasn't obvious, we'd prefer you not spread information about this incident. If you choose to, or if you must, talk all you want, but it would be a kindness if you didn't." He bowed again. "Good night, Mistresses."

Without another word, he departed.

Lyn and Tala shared a look, each holding back a smile and some stress-induced laughter.

The older woman sighed, still clearly fighting down a smile. "Food?"

"Food!"

Terry flickered into being on Tala's shoulder.

"There you are. I was worried about you. You vanished right as that thing showed its true form."

Terry squawked at her irritably and headbutted her cheek.

"I'm fine." She tried to wave the terror bird off.

He squawked again, this time clacking his beak near her nose.

Millennial Mage, 5 - Fusing

"Alright. I'm sorry. I didn't mean to worry you." She tossed him a bit of jerky and then scratched the back of his head and down his neck.

He harrumphed but seemed to accept her apology as he curled up on her shoulder and tucked his head in to rest.

Lyn shook her head, clearly barely holding back laughter. "Come on. Let's find something to eat."

Tala nodded emphatically. "Yes. Yes, please."

Chapter: 29
By Design

Tala and Lyn sat in the park nearest to the cheesy little caravan restaurant. Blessedly, that place seemed to keep odd hours.

Lyn had been a bit cold, but Tala had produced a couple of blankets to put down on the bench and then pulled out the massive bearskin to enshroud them as they ate.

Terry curled up between them, on the blanketed bench, content simply to sleep.

Even so, the night was getting chilly, so Tala had used her hot air incorporator to complete the bastion in the snow.

Lyn had laughed at the lengths Tala had gone to but seemed genuinely grateful for the gesture.

Tala, in a fit of appreciation of her own and generosity, had bought Lyn's dinner for her, much to the other woman's thankful surprise.

On the funny side of things, apparently Lyn had left the house without her coin pouch.

They'd been eating for a bit, slowly and contemplatively, when Lyn took a drink to clear her mouth and shifted to look to Tala. "So…" Lyn cleared her throat. "That happened."

Tala huffed a laugh around her own most recent bite, even as she swallowed. "Yeah, it did, didn't it?"

Millennial Mage, 5 - Fusing

Lyn shook her head. "Now that it happened, I'm glad to say I hope to never think of the creature again. Does that work for you?"

Tala thought for a moment, then shrugged. "Yeah, I can work with that." She rearranged the bear skin a bit. "What do you want to talk about then?"

"Anything else would be fine. I'd just like to turn my thinking toward something else, please."

Tala's eyes widened, and she smacked herself on the forehead, once again disturbing their improvised fortification against winter itself. "Right! I was going to go to the Archon Library, and I wanted to know if you'd like to come."

"This late?"

"I was coming to get you, originally, almost two hours ago…"

"Fair enough, I suppose!" Lyn spoke quickly, likely to keep the topic from returning to the earlier unpleasantness. Even so, the clerk frowned, taking another large bite. She spoke around the food as she considered. "Probably not tonight?"

Tala sighed. "Yeah. I think I could use the sleep, too. What about tomorrow?"

"Yeah, that could work. Morning or evening?"

She fought down a yawn. "Seems like evening would be wiser than waking up even earlier than usual."

Lyn nodded vigorously. "I second that." After licking some of the juices from her fingers, Lyn made a noise of surprise. "Oh! Right, I sold the six horns you passed into my keeping. I have thirty-two gold and forty silver for you, back in our house."

Tala gave a happy laugh. "Thank you! That's after your cut, right?"

"Naturally."

She laughed again. "Thank you, truly."

Lyn only smiled in return.

The conversation fell into a lull, then, the two working at finishing their food more quickly than they'd been doing before. When they'd swallowed the last bites, they stood, and Tala stored the blankets and bearskin back in Kit, topped the pouch off, magically, and smiled. "Let's head home."

The walk was pleasantly brief and made in companionable silence.

As they passed the park, which once again took up the entire block across the street from their house, there was no evidence of the fight that had taken place there such a short time ago.

"This is impressive clean-up work."

Lyn nodded her agreement, clearly not wanting the conversation to veer back toward the cause of the earlier chaos. "I'll say. I suppose it makes sense, though. No need to cause a panic."

Tala shrugged. "Yeah, that makes sense." She frowned. "Won't people be curious where the tavern went, though?"

Lyn's eye twitched, then she sighed. "Honestly?"

Tala nodded.

"Probably not. I, for one, never thought of it unless I could actively see it. Probably an effect of its magics. Most people will never even remember it was there."

She shook her head. "That is terrifying."

"Just a bit, yeah." She cleared her throat. "Now, as I said, I'd prefer to never speak of it again?" She made the last a question.

"Right! I'm sorry, Lyn."

Lyn half-heartedly waved her off. "I understand it's unreasonable for it to *never* come up, especially so close in the aftermath, but I'd appreciate some space from it."

Tala nodded, and silence covered them again as they arrived home, locked the door behind themselves, and parted for the night.

As Tala and Terry were closed into their room, Tala couldn't help but shudder. "I am so, so glad that thing is gone."

Terry let out a tired trill before flickering to her bed, already sprawled out in seeming slumber.

"Night, Terry."

He vaguely waggled one taloned foot in her direction and cooed softly.

"Sleep well."

* * *

Tala didn't dream at all that night.

It felt as if she closed her eyes and immediately opened them again.

Huh, that's odd. She somehow knew that the night had passed and that it was time to get up. Even so, she felt well-rested—incredibly so, in fact.

That's odd, indeed. She shrugged, stretched, and dove into her morning routine.

That morning, however, she ended the time by mirroring her perspective onto Flow as it sat off to one side. *One more thing to practice.*

At first, she cheated, closing her eyes and only perceiving through the weapon, but by the end of that morning's session, she could have her eyes open, so long as she didn't move.

Even without vomiting being an option, the disorientation of differently moving perspectives was too much. *For now.*

That accomplished, she bathed, gathered up Terry, and headed out.

Breakfast time!

Mistress Odera had requested that they meet for lunch instead of breakfast, so Tala was on her own.

She dropped through her old favorite breakfast place to get a breakfast deal.

The breakfast deal came with six tasty sandwiches and a whole gallon of coffee, all for just a single silver.

Oh...

One gallon of coffee.

Holly asked me to cut back on the coffee...

That wasn't precisely true.

No, she implied that I should stop entirely.

Tala groaned.

The poor attendant working behind the counter waited patiently for her to place her order.

"Could I get the breakfast deal, but can I replace the coffee with more sandwiches?"

The attendant brightened. "Oh! Certainly. That will be one silver for eight sandwiches, please."

Tala grinned. "That sounds perfect." She felt an ache of longing for the no-longer-coming coffee, but she pushed it aside. *Food will help fill the void.*

She paid, found a nearby park bench, swept it free of snow, and sat down to enjoy her steaming sandwiches.

She found water lacking as a breakfast beverage. Her head started to hurt in sympathy with her bereft palate, and food only helped a little.

Tala grimaced. *I don't want to spoil these glorious creations.* A thought came to her, and she smiled. "I do need to be reinforcing my magics, after all." She pulled out her flask of endingberry juice and took a long drink. It paired perfectly with her meal.

Unfortunately, she was beginning to run low on the magic juice, and that just wouldn't do. *I need to find a closer grove than Alefast... Oh! The library should have that knowledge. I'll ask when Lyn and I go this evening.*

That decided, she dug into her repast with a vengeance. As she ate, she had a thought, glancing to Terry, tucked in on her shoulder. "You have to try this."

She broke off a bite of the current creation and tossed it for the terror bird. Terry flickered to snatch it from the air. He barely swallowed before letting out a happy trill and shimmying contentedly on her shoulder.

Tala grinned. Thus, she gave Terry a good-sized bite of each of her sandwiches, telling him the name, in case he liked one more than the others.

Overall, it was a very pleasant way to spend the meal.

I should ask Mistress Odera to meet me for lunch every day, instead of breakfast. This is sooooo good.

* * *

Since Tala didn't have to go to the work yard or the Caravan Guild's headquarters, she found her morning freer than her previous two had been.

With that extra time, she decided to see if her jerky was ready yet. *If I'm calculating it correctly, between Terry and me, we're going through just about five pounds of jerky per day.* That sounded about right. After all, she'd gotten around twelve hundred pounds from Rane's hunting trip and Brand's jerking, and she'd guess that she was coming up on having used a third of her stock.

Given the strength-enhancing properties of the meat, I think that Terry and I should both up our intake. If she did that, she should really take the time to sit and meditate to ensure the power went to the right places. She tsked. *Another task.* Still, the power would likely just build up in her system until directed—either subconsciously due to exertion, or consciously by her abilities as an Immaterial Guide.

So, she'd be eating thunder cattle jerky and drinking endingberry juice and taking time each day to ensure that the accumulated power was channeled to the right locations. *I suppose I could make gelatin out of their bones to strengthen mine further.* She grimaced at that. *Yeah, no. I'm okay without that.* She hesitated. *Wait… are the bones what's used to make gelatin?* In the end, it didn't really matter; she wasn't interested.

She was going to up her intake and try to get Terry more as well.

I'm so glad I went hunting. She was going to have to do more hunting, too. *I'm glad that thunder cattle are so prolific around here…*

As she thought about it, she realized that with Lyn selling the horns, she could make a *killing* by killing the cattle and bringing back their bodies.

She chuckled to herself at her own joke as she walked toward Brand's restaurant. She didn't know where the Culinary Guild offices were in Bandfast, and he would likely be best able to direct her to where Amnin could be found.

There were only two problems with her theoretical gold vein. First, there were only so many buyers for thunder bull horns in the city, and most wouldn't be willing to pay full price. *If I'm willing to flood the market, I'll probably end up having to take as little as one or two gold per horn, and at some point, people won't be interested at any price.*

The second issue was that thunder cattle really did prefer to travel in big herds. True, there were more little herds than big—by the very nature of numbers, that had to be the case—but the vast majority of the area's thunder cattle would be in one of the three or four massive groups.

Millennial Mage, 5 - Fusing

There is no way I'm up for taking on anywhere close to that many. She paused, considering. *Well, if I perfectly aligned some tungsten spheres and targeted the far side of the herd...*

In the best-case scenario, that would cut lines of death through the animals but leave most of them intact and vengeful.

How do they respond to predators? Her understanding was that most mundane herd animals would flee before even a single predator, leaving the weakest among them to fall prey to the attacker. *Are magical herbivores different?* She'd have to ask Ingrit, the Archivist.

Tala already knew, though, that thunder cattle fought viciously to avenge their fallen herd-mates. *At least against humans. I suppose they'd treat a pack of wolves differently?* She didn't know. She'd definitely need to ask.

Brand's business was open—but not open for business. From what Tala understood, they would be working to prepare the food for lunch and dinner customers and had their doors open so that large orders could be placed, but no food was ready for immediate sale at that moment.

She pushed open the door and smiled at the entirely mundane *ding* that resounded through the space as the door pushed passed the little bell hanging behind it for just such a purpose.

"Mistress Tala! What a pleasant surprise, seeing you here this time of day."

"Lissa, always a pleasure to see you." The women exchanged a brief hug. *My goodness. I'm very huggy of late.*

"What can we do for you?"

"Well, I was hoping that Brand would know where I could find Amnin."

Brand's voice came from the back. "Is that Mistress Tala who I hear?"

"It is! Come out, dear. She's got a quick question."

He came out, wiping his hands on his apron. "Mistress, good to see you. What can I answer?"

Tala gave a nod of acknowledgment. "I'm looking to find Amnin."

Brand grinned. "The jerky, right?"

She blinked at him. "How do you know about that?"

He laughed. "She checked with me on the recipe I had used. Here, let me show you where she's most likely to be found." He walked over to a decorative map of the city, hanging on one wall. "We're here." He pointed to the location of his restaurant before dragging his finger down various streets. "If you follow this way, you'll find the guildhall you want here." He tapped the map twice to emphasize the final location.

"Perfect. Thank you!"

Tala had no issue finding the Culinary Guildhall, and to her surprise, she found that there were nine massive bundles of jerky, each wrapped in treated canvas and bound tightly to last, theoretically, forever. *Assuming they don't get wet, invaded by pests, or exposed to temperature extremes.*

So, within Kit? Indefinitely.

Tala grinned, pulling Kit from her belt, opening it wide, and dropping each of the bundles inside.

Someday, I'll have to ask how they lock the magic into the meat like this. Maybe I can use the same technique to improve the shelf-life of endingberry juice.

Now that the jerky was all stored within, she could sense that Kit was getting on the full side once more.

I really need to expand Kit again... There was a lot that she 'needed' to do.

Amnin wasn't actually working that day, so Tala just interacted with the receptionist who seemed *incredibly* uncomfortable talking with a Mage.

Millennial Mage, 5 - Fusing

Tala spared the poor man, taking the jerky and departing as quickly as she was able while remaining polite.

She did pause to leave a grateful message for Amnin. *No need to be rude, after all.*

With all that complete, the morning was still young, and thus she arrived at the training yard only a little later than she had the day before.

* * *

Tala spat out sand and groaned, rolling over onto her back.

Two. I held my own against two! It had even been Adam and one of his peers. True, it had only been for a short bout, less than two minutes if her sense of time was accurate, but she'd done it!

She'd incorporated the first of the multi-shape weapon forms incredibly quickly, and it had done *something* to pull her fighting style together and give her movements a unity of purpose.

She was no longer jumping between unique weapon types.

No.

Now she was using one, highly versatile weapon to best effect.

Adam offered her a hand up. "Well done, Mistress Tala." He was breathing heavily but had enough control to speak almost normally despite his clear fatigue. "I could not have taken you alone."

Tala's eyes widened at his words.

Of course, they both knew that if they were really fighting, Tala would win handily, but under the current restrictions, Tala felt immense pride at the compliment.

"If I may ask, you seemed very surefooted, more so even than you were before your trip to Makinaven."

She grinned. "That's not a question, but I think I understand what you're getting at." She nodded. "I kept the pressure distribution scripts on my feet. I've gotten used to the sure-footedness they grant, not to mention it makes it easier to move quietly and without damaging what I walk on." She gestured at the sand. "And they give much better purchase on uncertain terrain."

Adam nodded, clearly a bit lost in thought. "That should serve you quite well, I'd think."

"Yeah, Mistress Holly and I discussed it a bit, and it seemed worth keeping for the time being."

The sun was almost directly overhead, the training time with the guards at an end.

Rane and Aproa were finishing up their matches as well, and Tala could already see that each would end with the Mage's defeat.

That was by design.

The Mages were here to hone their martial skills, not lord their magic over mundanes.

Because of that, the bouts were always stacked against them, even if never to the extent of a quick loss. The point was to push them, not frustrate their attempts to improve.

When the inevitable ends came, the two thanked their respective sparring partners and walked over, panting.

Aproa was all smiles. "This really is fantastic training. Thank you for allowing me to join you all."

Tala grinned and Adam bowed, responding with grace, "It is a pleasure to have you here, Mistress."

Aproa glanced to Rane expectantly, and the young man flushed. "Oh, uh… Mistress Tala?"

"Hmm?"

Aproa asked Adam a question and led him off to the side to discuss the answer.

Millennial Mage, 5 - Fusing

Rane scratched the back of his head. "Would you like to grab lunch with me? I mean, just me and—"

Tala cut him off with a wave of her hand. "I've got to meet with Mistress Odera for lunch. Maybe later?"

He hesitated, the words dying on his lips. "Oh. Sure. Yeah. That makes sense."

Tala smiled. "I'm sure Mistress Aproa is free. And we'll meet back up in the Mage's sparring arena?"

He nodded, then shrugged. "Sure. Yeah. I'll see you there, I guess."

He turned and walked over to where Aproa and Adam were still talking.

Aproa gave him a questioning glance, and he shrugged again. The woman gave Tala a confused frown, then shook her head, and the two Archons left together.

-*Tala*-

-*You are going to have to deal with that boy's feelings for you, and yours for him, eventually.*-

Tala sighed. *I know. I'm not an idiot. I just don't want to think about that type of thing, and—* She straightened. *Wait! You're talking with me? Why? I thought all functions were offline?*

-*Ding*-

-*Earliest lost or repressed memory, not lost due to the natural processes of time, partially recovered.*-

Tala's eyes widened. *One moment.*

She bid goodbye to the departing guards and went to one of the private bath rooms, Terry following her in before she locked the door.

Alright. I'm ready. Let me see it.

She sank to the floor in a cross-legged position, eyes closing of their own accord as she was pulled into a memory.

Chapter: 30
Finally Time

Tala sat in the lap of a giant—the comfiest chair in the world.

Before her, a book lay open, a massive finger pointing at funny black lines.

A steady cadence of sound washed over her, and though she couldn't understand it, yet, she knew it had meaning.

More than anything, she knew that she was happy to be here, held by the giant, safe and loved.

*   *   *

Tala came out of her memory, cheeks damp and eyes swimming.

Rust you. Why did you show me that?

-Ding-

-That is your earliest repressed memory.-

Why would that be repressed? As soon as she asked, she knew the answer and didn't want it stated, but it was too late, the question had been asked.

-Tala-

-You dislike how it makes you feel about your father.-

Tala grimaced. *Great...* The other her was being snarky. She should change the subject before things got too personal.

What should we call you?

Millennial Mage, 5 - Fusing

-I need to continue following my last command.-
Let's settle on a name first.

There was silence for a long moment, to the point that Tala thought that she'd have to wait. But, finally, *-That is acceptable.-*

What do you think about AI?

-For Alternate Interface?- Other her could clearly pull from Tala's own mind for the reasoning behind the initialism.

Yeah.

-I think it will be confusing.-

How so?

-I'm not sure. It just seems too obscure. I don't really like it, either.-

Tala grunted. *Fair enough, I suppose. You should like the name we use for you, after all.*

-I appreciate that.-

So? Should we call you Sue? That's a pretty good name.

-I'm not a boy.-

...I know?

-What other suggestions do you have?-

You know you're basically me, but you can think much faster.

-That's true. So, I'm Tala, what should we call you?-

Tala rolled her eyes. *You know that's not what I meant.*

-True, but it's harder to do humor based on misunderstanding when we share a mental space.-

I should call you Dorris.

-That's hurtful.- Dorris had been Tala's imaginary friend from her childhood.

When other kids had made fun of her for bringing her fake friend out to play, Tala had asserted that Dorris was real, simply invisible.

When they couldn't touch Dorris, Tala had stated that Dorris was intangible, too.

Thus, the neighbor kids had asked Dorris to speak to prove that she existed.

Of course, Tala had informed them, Dorris was mute and so couldn't speak.

We could say we got a Mage to cure your vocal cords.

Other Tala snorted a laugh within Tala's head, which begged the question of *how,* but that would have to be explored later. *-We did promise to do that, didn't we.-*

So?

-No.-

Fine. What do you want to be called?

-Well, I'm you, just as you are me.-

We already established that.

There was a momentary pause. *-Do you just want me to tell you, or should I walk you through it?-*

Tala considered for a moment.

-You know, I can hear your considerings, too.-

She sighed. *Just tell me the end result.*

-Alat.-

Alright. That sounds great. You are a lot.-

-...I see what you did there, and I don't appreciate it.-

How? They sound the same.

-I'm literally in your head, Tala. I can read your thoughts. In this case, that is relevant because homonyms are incredibly obvious.-

That makes sense. But you had to know I'd make that joke.

-I thought you might be better than your baser humor.-

Alat?

-Yes?-

For someone who lives inside my mind, is built from me, and is basically just another aspect-manifestation of my soul, you don't seem to know me very well. Tala felt herself relax a little. She didn't really know why, but having the voice in her head not pre-guess her actions was relieving.

-You enjoyed that little rant, didn't you?-
I did.
-Did it help you feel more comfortable with me?-
…Yes…
-Good.- Tala got the feeling of smug contentment, radiating from something *else* within her head.

Rust.

-Ding-

-Continuing the implementation of the prior command. All other functions will be unavailable during this process.-

Tala sighed. *Of course.*

Oddly, the implication that she'd been set up and influenced to feel less iffy about Alat didn't undo the relief. *This feels like it should be a bad sign, but I don't think it is.* If Alat was basically her, why would she want to hurt herself?

She let out a dismissive, groaning sigh. *I'm starting to get a headache over this. I can think more on the implications later.*

Tala stood and pulled Kit from her belt. *Stretch and bath time, then lunch with Mistress Odera.*

She mentally dove into her garments and sent power down the path to retract them into the band around her throat, even as she climbed down into her dimensional storage.

* * *

Lunch was uneventful, and Tala enjoyed her conversation with Mistress Odera as much as usual, though her headache didn't fade as she'd hoped.

The older woman took them to a sandwich place for a quick bite to accompany the shorter-than-usual time together.

Apparently, Mistress Odera helped teach at a local primary school when she was in town, specifically helping to identify students who might have the ability for either inscriptions or training as a Mage.

Ahh, pre-magic. It was a mixed bag as far as classes went. Tala actually hadn't enjoyed it very much, but she had done reasonably well. That was why she'd been given the entrance exam for the academy.

And why my family was able to unload their debt on me.

At the thought of her family, she again was reminded of her father reading to her even before she understood his words.

She pushed that aside, and the conversation moved to other topics.

When she arrived at the Mage's training ground, she found everyone else already there, a challenge in full swing.

Fire tore through the area in precise lines, crisscrossing through the air and moving to encircle the fire Mage's opponent.

Tala's magesight allowed her to see the paths of altered gas as they were carved through the air before being ignited.

Lightning struck through the leading edges of the paths of fire. Unlike Tala would have expected, the counterattacks seemed to sever something in the flows of magic and disrupt the air manipulator's hold over and control of the concentration of that flammable gas, allowing the lightning to effectively disrupt the attacks, even if imperfectly.

Millennial Mage, 5 - Fusing

The two Archons seemed on almost equal footing, exchanging strikes without being able to directly affect the other, but Tala saw what almost anyone with their magesight active would have.

To be fair, in the strobing arena, under the clashing influence of two Mages, it was marginally painful to see that aspect of reality, but it did give her insight into what was going on.

The lightning was fascinating, as it wasn't coming from anywhere. The Mage was creating it, already en route to her targets.

The air manipulator was protected by layered, segregated zones of hyper-modified air.

As the lightning breached one of those pockets, it would ignite the space, causing a blowback that would prevent the attack from breaking through.

A similar, constantly forking network of electric lines flickered around the lightning Mage, disrupting any trails of encroaching flammable air that tried to close in.

To the mundane eye, it seemed like a standoff, but Tala saw the end coming.

The lightning Mage had no real defense against oxygen deficiency, and the air around her was being bled of oxygen. The woman was clearly beginning to become light-headed.

It seemed that she was aware of the tactic as her aura was spread wide, locking down the area directly around her. Even so, by pulling oxygen away from all the air nearby, not within her aura control, as well as preventing any other oxygen from entering in, her opponent was all but assured that the conclusion to the match was only a matter of time. The explosions stirring up the air had likely greatly increased the pace of the oxygen depletion as well.

As such, Tala arrived less than a minute before the end of the bout.

The lightning Mage began panting in deep, useless breaths, clearly feeling a bit lightheaded.

When she dropped to a knee, she mumbled out, "Rust you, Stan. I surrender." She collapsed to the sand of the arena, and the healer rushed over to her.

Tala watched as the air manipulator—Stan, apparently—pushed the life-giving substance back into the air around the downed woman now that her aura was no longer blocking his control, and her breathing leveled out.

So, he has methods of winning, both fast and slow. Tala immediately wanted to fight him. She honestly didn't know how she'd do, but she had a few ideas to tip any conflict her way.

Cazor unnecessarily called the match. "Victory to Stan."

Stan bowed toward his opponent, then toward Cazor. "Thank you for officiating."

Aproa cleared her throat, walking in from the side. "Any other challenges?"

Tala grinning. "I'd love to fight Stan."

Stan cocked his head to the side, examining her, then grinned.

Aproa sighed. "Anyone who has already fought may deny a challenge."

Stan waved that away. "No, it's fine. I'd love to see what the Blood Archon is really capable of."

Rane walked over to Tala. "Talk after the bout?"

She looked him up and down, noting his nervous posture. *He's going to ask again...*

She really had had enough time to figure out how she felt. Too bad she'd never taken any of it to think through her feelings.

Millennial Mage, 5 - Fusing

"Yeah. Okay." She smiled in what she hoped was a reassuring way.

Rane hesitated, then straightened a bit, smiling in return. "Alright, then. Good luck!"

Tala strode out into the designated area, her opponent stretching just a bit, limbering up for another fight.

Cazor lifted a hand, and his magic swept through the space, bringing with it a dispersed cloud of iron.

Stan shivered as the iron moved past him, even though none stayed in his vicinity.

Terry flickered away before the wave of magic-nullification swept over them.

Tala extended her aura to protect her iron salve. She'd determined that it was worth the difficulty of reapplications to take advantage of the benefits of having her magics reflected and contained within herself more completely. Even so, she was not eager to reapply it so soon.

Cazor gave her an odd look but didn't comment. He was sweeping the space to prevent any lingering magical influence of Stan's from affecting the upcoming battle.

"Ready?"

Stan and Tala each nodded.

"Fight!"

Tala crouched and launched herself forward, locking onto her opponent as she did so. *Increase.*

Stan's will opposed hers, causing the inefficiency of her working to spike.

Tala growled. He couldn't shake her lock, but he wasn't trying to. Instead, he was disrupting it enough to render it moot in the short term, unless she wanted to burn rings for a bout. *Yeah, I'm not rich enough for that. Not yet.*

It was actually a bit of a revelation. Jean, in fighting Tala off until she was overcome, let Tala end the battle of wills with a full lock and fully effective magics. Stan, by not opposing the lock itself, and only fighting the working, ended up being better protected than Jean, even though Jean had a *much* stronger will.

So, oppose outright those who I can block fully and hamper those I can't. That alone was a valuable insight.

The revelation was so foundational that Tala almost completely missed the sudden working of power, which pulled a line of highly flammable air into existence, with a larger pocket created just in front of her.

Stan snapped, his hand passing through his end of the trail with expert precision just as his glove created the needed spark.

Fire ripped through the air, but Tala dropped and slid to get under the blast.

Stan anticipated her and a line of fire tore down a secondary path to an ancillary gas-bomb pocket, which appeared just ahead of her aura, in the path of her slide.

The two zones detonated simultaneously, one almost directly over her, the other just ahead.

Tala was driven back and down, but not nearly as much as Stan likely expected.

Increased mass for the win! Her physiological inscriptions were still increasing her density, even though she was already at least twice as heavy as she really should be.

Focus, Tala.

Her momentum had been utterly countered, so she was just lying there on the sand.

She kicked up to a defensive stance just as more explosions rocked the area around her.

Tala felt the activations of power as the defensive magics in her clothing activated to counter the blows.

She was satisfied to see Stan's eyes widen as he evidently noticed the armor.

Millennial Mage, 5 - Fusing

Alright, play this smart, Tala. She took out two tungsten balls and began gravitating one toward her opponent, even as she simply threw the other.

Her opponent gave her an odd look as he easily stepped aside to avoid the thrown metal sphere.

He glanced back at it a few times, clearly scanning it with his own magesight, but he seemed to determine that there was no working on the ball that would stab him in the back.

In that time, Tala was bouncing around the battlefield.

Some of her movements were volitional as she dodged and wove around the ever-moving fields of fire.

Some were involuntary as the explosions changed her trajectories and moved her in ways she didn't expect.

Well, this is good anticipation and reactionary training at least.

She drew Flow and threw it in sword form.

Stan's eyes widened as the magical weapon spun through the intervening space, but when the superheated blade hit one of his protective zones of manipulated air, the pocket detonated, throwing Flow back and away.

It seemed that the Material Guide's defenses were as effective against Flow as against lightning.

Tala called Flow back to her and continued throwing it at regular intervals in both the form of a sword and a glaive. It always encountered those pockets of hyper-flammable air and was deflected, but that provided a good distraction and allowed her to slowly work her way closer.

She threw Flow one last time as a sword, and Stan ignored it, confident in his defense against the weapon.

It was finally time.

At the last moment—before Flow's blade would have entered and triggered the explosion of one of Stan's defensive zones—Tala reshaped her weapon into a knife. The knife form did not have a superhot blade.

At the same time, Tala extended her aura a bit to one side so that the Mage was directly between that part of her aura and the tungsten ball she'd thrown earlier, the tungsten ball containing one of her bloodstars.

Tala *pulled* even as she changed her direction of movement and let the ball still in her hand pull her forward just slightly, adding to her speed. The fight wouldn't last long enough for it to be a useful weapon, but it could help with this.

Her opponent didn't have time to notice that his defense had failed, let alone to even attempt to stop Flow before the blade sunk into his shoulder.

Such a wound would hardly have been the end of the fight, even though it would obviously be painful, but that was just a distraction.

Normally, Tala's pull would have been incredibly obvious, and Stan could have been expected to defend himself with ease.

Now, with Flow in his shoulder, he had an instant of less-acute focus.

In that instant, Tala mirrored her mass into the proper bloodstar, and the tungsten ball slammed into his back, near his upper spine, cracking ribs. Additionally, it pulled the mage forward and even more mentally off balance.

The sphere behind him continued to pull him toward Tala, even as she closed the last few feet.

His eyes were unfocused as he'd clearly been taken off guard in quite a few ways.

She slammed her right fist into his gut, driving the wind from him.

As he bent nearly double, the tungsten sphere helped push him over, and Tala changed the direction of her pull, drawing the bloodstar toward her right knee, even as she drove it upward into his falling chest.

There was another sickening crunch as the colossal strength of the hit lifted the Mage off the ground, compressing his chest dramatically in the process.

"Victory, Tala!" Cazor called, the healer already halfway to them.

The sphere in Tala's hand lost the little attraction it had had toward the Mage because he was no longer her opponent.

Huh… I wonder if I can use that somehow.

Stan dropped to his knees, gasping and wheezing.

Tala quickly knelt next to him, bracing him up and holding him steady even as she tucked Flow back in its sheath and the spheres back into Kit.

The healer slid into place next to the two of them, her magic rushing through Stan, identifying the issues. Without a word, the other Mage placed her hand on the damaged Mage's shoulder, and healing magics rushed through him, restoring him to perfect health almost instantly.

Stan let out a gasping whimper, then grimaced and spat out a mouthful of blood.

He turned his head to the healer, nodding his thanks, then looked to Tala. "What are you made of, Mistress? You kick like a bull." His voice sounded a bit thick, and he coughed again, cleared his throat, and spat out more blood. "You take fire like you're made out of mud."

Tala grinned back. "I'm just a poor woman, made out of muscle and blood." She hesitated. "Well, muscle and blood and skin and bone."

Stan snorted a laugh, then made a gagging sound, coughed, and spat up yet another mass of blood. "Yeah. No more challenges for me today."

Tala chuckled. "You did great, keeping me at a distance."

"I did, didn't I?" He gave a half-smile.

She offered him a hand up, and he took it. "Thank you for the match, Master." She bowed over their linked hands.

"Well fought, Mistress." He bowed in return, and they released their grips.

Rane had walked over, and he clapped them each on a shoulder. "Well fought, both of you."

They nodded in thanks. Then, Tala glanced away.

I did promise... She sighed internally and looked back toward Rane. "Ready to have that chat?"

Chapter: 31
Brutal

Tala and Rane walked over to one side of the Mages' training area and through a door before walking up a flight of stairs to a small room that overlooked the private arena.

There were a few seats set up so that people could watch the goings on, but neither of them sat.

They stood and watched as another set of Archons fought, but Tala didn't really register what was happening. Instead, she was waiting for Rane to say something. He obviously would, at some point.

I've been doing that this whole time, haven't I...?
So, what did she want?

I don't want a relationship. I don't want to have a family. The pain caused by her own family still loomed too large, though she knew, more and more, that she had and was likely overreacting to hard choices made in a difficult situation.

But she didn't want to face that either.

Is it fair to expect Rane to wait for me to be ready? She hesitated. *Do I want him to?*

Rane still hadn't said anything.

Tala gave him a grimacing glance.

He saw her move and smiled her way before turning back to gaze out at the fight below.

She looked back as well, once more folding into her mind and her own thoughts.

Why isn't he saying anything?
She kept herself from growling.
Why am I not saying anything?
She did growl at herself, then, but internally. *Gah… this is giving me a headache…*

Rane finally took a deep breath and let it out slowly. "I'm glad that we're in a place where we can just be here, watching a fight together in silence, and it isn't weird."

Tala felt her eye twitch. The one on the far side from Rane, of course.

"I did want to talk to you, though."

She gave a tight-lipped smile but didn't turn. "Mmhmm?"

"I'd like to go to dinner with you, just the two of us."

She shrugged. "Sure. I have to eat, after all."

Rane huffed a laugh. "True enough." After a moment, he nodded as if to himself. "I want to be clear. I want us to get dinner, not as friends."

Tala turned to him and sighed. "I knew what you meant, Rane."

He hesitated, caught with his mouth open. No further sound came out.

Now or never, Tala. "I need you to understand a few things: I don't want anything more. Not right now, maybe not ever. Casual can't exist in light of eternity." She shook her head. "We could both live for thousands of years, if not longer. That feels like an eternity at the moment." She sighed. "So, I don't want casual, and I'm not in a healthy place for anything serious."

He shrugged. "I can understand that. What do you need?"

She shook her head again. "Rane, I can't give you a list of things I need before I go on a date with you. There isn't one, and even if there was, it wouldn't be fair to give you a 'to-do' list."

"So, you need time, more than anything." It wasn't a question.

"It really isn't fair to ask you to wait for something that may never come."

He shrugged again. "You aren't asking me to. Your answer is simply, 'Not now.' I hear you. Beyond that, if I wait, it's on me. Fair?"

"Yeah... that is fair." She gave him a searching look. "You are having far, far too well-crafted responses to all of this."

Rane blushed, looked away, and scratched the back of his head. "Well... Mistress Aproa pretended to be you, and I practiced..."

Tala blinked at him a few times, then snorted a laugh. "That sounds like something Mistress Odera would do."

He grinned in return. "Yeah. Turns out, like grandmother like granddaughter."

"So it would seem."

They went back to looking at, but not really watching, the fight below.

Only a short time later, Rane cleared his throat. "So... do you have any interest in me?"

Tala sighed loudly, but Rane held up his hands defensively.

"I don't mean now, of course. We just settled that I understand that now is 'no.' I mean, is this something that could *ever* work out, or am I just not of interest to you, no matter the circumstances?" He pointed between them to indicate what he meant by 'this.'

Tala reddened, not looking at him. "There is nothing objectionable, no."

Rane snorted a laugh. "That's probably as good as I can hope for."

She reflexively punched him in the shoulder, not hard enough to be considered an attack.

Even so, he staggered to the side a bit, the blow having pushed him off his footing.

Huh, that might be a weakness, though he probably doesn't regard me as an opponent at the moment. She shook her head. Now was not the time to be thinking of how to overcome him in a fight.

Rane rubbed his shoulder, not trying to hide the motion. "Ow."

She glanced his way, suddenly feeling guilty. "Sorry… I didn't really think before I did that."

He shrugged. "It's fine. Doubt it will bruise."

She smiled self-consciously. "Even so. I apologize. I shouldn't have done that."

He smiled in return and dipped his head but didn't say anything else.

They lapsed back into silence for an extended time, watching the match finish up.

Finally, as the winner was announced, Rane broke the silence. "So, dinner?"

She gave him another searching look.

"As friends. I know that's all it can be."

He didn't add 'for now,' but Tala heard it anyway.

Should I keep my distance? Pull back? She didn't want to lose one of the better friends she'd made since leaving the academy. She huffed a laugh internally. *Not that I had any good friends before that.* "Sure. Invite others?"

He hesitated, then shrugged. "Sure."

"Looks like the challenges are done. Ready to get some practice in?"

"Yeah, Mistress Aproa said we'd be doing focused skirmishes today."

"What's that?"

*   *   *

As it turned out, 'focused skirmishes' were team fights centered around conflicting goals rather than elimination.

In some cases, the outright elimination of the opponent was a negative.

At the moment, Tala was cradling a blown egg. Her team was tasked with defending it for five minutes without 'killing' any of their attackers.

They had been forbidden from simply placing the egg in a storage space, and the other team had no restriction on the elimination of the defenders, though that wouldn't win them the round.

Their unrestricted goals were made obvious by the *storm* of ice and other magics that absolutely shredded the designated arena.

Jets, walls, and columns of freezing water flowed around the other attacks, making the battlefield a slurry of danger.

Tala would have been unable to fully protect the target from even those magics—despite her speed and resilience—if it weren't for Stan and the other fire Mage.

Aproa had thought it entertaining to pit fire against ice and water.

Lightning also wove among the ice and through the water, filling in the gaps in the all-encompassing assault.

The fire Archons continually met incoming spears, spikes, and blocks of ice with detonations of flame, pushing the attacks aside more than melting them. Their explosions also disrupted the workings of water but had the negative effect of creating a constant smattering of sleet that quickly soaked them all.

Water is stupidly heat-resistant…

Aproa was surprisingly the best counter to the lightning attacks, as her ability to create voids in the air made it impossible for the electricity to pass through those spaces, foiling the lightning strikes.

Millennial Mage, 5 - Fusing

If that was the full set of Mages, Tala would have been tempted to simply stand in place, allowing her teammates to defend her as she lightly clutched the egg. Sadly for her team, there were others.

The earth and light Mages were dueling titans, working across the battlefield at cross purposes. The earth Mage was using every spare moment to alter the terrain to the attackers' advantage as well as send crushing attacks at the defenders. The light Archon, however, was keeping those spare moments to an absolute minimum, using her opponents' ice and water to refract and redirect her quick, harrying light attacks.

It was only her efforts that kept the attackers on their toes and prevented them from solidifying a victory.

The earth Mage raised the sand and other bits of earth to deflect or intercept the light attacks, but the light Mage was an artist, often forcing the earth Archon to choose between letting his comrades be hit or knocking them aside himself.

She was the star of the show by a long stretch, but even their interwoven back and forth wasn't the end of the chaos.

Rane pressed Aproa and Tala relentlessly.

Every attack from either side seemed to allow his defenses to move him exactly as he wanted, and it took both of the women to counter him, while Tala was hampered by the need to protect the egg.

It was brutal.

The air was so full of magic that Tala felt her eyes beginning to ache under the strain of her magesight. That, in turn, was an accompaniment to her head throbbing with pain.

She didn't disable it, however, as she needed the split-second's advantage it gave against the few attacks that did reach her.

After what felt like days, Cazor called a halt. "Time!"

Spell-workings faded from the air, leaving a sopping slurry of sand behind.

The Mage Hunter walked over to Tala and held out his hand.

Tala blinked and rubbed at her eyes, trying to clear the lingering fatigue from magesight use in such an inundated area and the ache in her head from processing all the information.

When Cazor cleared his throat, Tala jumped a little. *Right!*

She proudly presented him with the perfectly intact egg... Well, not perfectly.

The shell had cracked but not deformed.

The Archons all groaned; the attackers because they'd hoped to press her enough to shatter the target, the defenders because it wasn't perfectly intact.

Aproa laughed. "Does that mean it was a tie?"

Cazor shook his head. "I guess? We've never really had this happen before." He gave Tala a searching look. "How did it happen?"

She glanced to one side for a moment, shrugging. She felt incredibly irritated and grouchy at her own mistake. "Well, I backhanded a block of ice with the hand holding the egg, and I guess the impact transferred through, just a bit." She looked to her teammates and forced the appropriate reaction. "Sorry, everyone. It was instinct."

Everyone waved it off as fine. The point wasn't really the egg, or winning or losing, it was to train them in varying situations.

In truth, she did feel somewhat bad, but mostly, she just felt irritable, and her head *hurt*. She didn't remember taking even a glancing blow to the head, and her scripts should have taken care of it if she had. Still, there was no

Millennial Mage, 5 - Fusing

reason to whine about it or take out her discomfort on others.

Cazor seemed to have a thought. "You know, I rule this as a win for the defenders. The target is banged up but alive. They could get him healed in no time."

Half the Archons let out whoops of victory, the others, groans of defeat.

True, winning wasn't the point, but it was still gratifying.

* * *

They went through several more situational matches.

Some were more physical like infection tag, where the Archon who was 'it' just had to hit any of the others in any way, physically, and the contacted Mage would switch to the 'it' team.

Those trying to escape were restricted to the use of non-lethal methods to keep them back.

Unsurprisingly, Rane dominated that one, easily remaining as the last survivor and staying such for long enough that the Mage Hunters called it a win. He did have a rather unfair advantage.

Some were more magical like aura domination.

In that, each Archon sat three feet behind a post, equally spaced from the others in a ring.

Each post would light up with the color of the dominant aura in contact with it.

It was, in essence, an eleven-way contest of wills.

To her surprise, Tala struggled in that one. She was utterly unused to battling so many other wills in so many directions at once.

With regard to contests of aura and will, if she was used to tug-of-war, this was tackle-tag.

Still, she learned, and the game-like setting helped her enjoy it more than she might have if she had attempted to train the same skills on her own—if she even could.

The final thing they did that day was rotate through having each one of the Archons take a turn as the 'rogue Mage.' The others had to work together to subdue the rogue without harming them. As made sense, the rogue had no such restrictions.

To no one's surprise, Rane won as the rogue. What was a surprise, however, was that the rogue won every round. With the restriction of non-harm, they were each able to hold their own well enough to force the containment group to hurt them in order to end the fight.

All in all, it was an amazingly fun afternoon of training.

I could have been doing this the whole time?

True, not every skill Tala wished to work on was practiced that afternoon, but every one that she did work on was *much* advanced by the exercises.

I'll have to think of ways for the group to compete on the other skills I need to improve. The addition of new contests was encouraged. Each game they played had been added by one member or another of the group over the last years of on-and-off group training.

Everyone but Tala required the healer at some point during the day, and Tala actually received *much* more healing than the rest, even if hers was self-administered.

She did ask the healer to take a brief look at her when a building headache wouldn't go away, but nothing was found to be amiss. So, Tala just bore through and guzzled water.

As the day wrapped up, Tala and Rane invited the others to join them for dinner, but each had other plans for the nightly meal. So, they all went their separate ways, agreeing to meet up again the next day.

Millennial Mage, 5 - Fusing

Tala and Rane went and got cleaned up in private bath rooms, meeting up half an hour later.

She stood out of a stretch from against the wall as he came out, having finished a bit before him. "Let's go see if Lyn wants to join us."

He paused, then shrugged. "Sure."

With that decided, they turned to go, only to be stopped by Terry.

He flickered to Tala's shoulder and bumped her cheek. "What's up, Terry?"

He flickered to the corner, curled up, and let out a dramatic sigh, then returned to her shoulder and trilled.

Oh! "Getting bored, bud?"

He trilled again.

"Well, maybe we can have you join in?" Tala looked to Rane.

Rane hesitated once more, then grinned. "Let's do it. I think he could add a lot to both the morning and evening training sessions if the others are okay with his participation."

Tala smiled back at Terry. "How does that sound?"

Terry squawked contentedly and curled back up.

That decided, Terry seemed much happier, and the three headed for Lyn and Tala's home, Rane and Tala chatting about small things along the way.

When they got close, Tala once again marveled at the lack of evidence for the massive syphon's foiled hunting ground as they walked beside the perfectly maintained park. Terry went so far as to flicker over to the spot that the syphon had stood and poke around with his beak.

Rane didn't comment on Terry's actions, and as Tala thought about it, she realized that it really wasn't out of character for Terry to flicker off to a random location for a moment.

Instances of passing curiosity? Or does he often sense things that I completely miss?

"Oh!" Rane's exclamation pulled her out of her thoughts. "Someone went to investigate the ruin you opened up and we reported."

"Really? What did it turn out to be? Did they say?"

He nodded. "Just an old storeroom from a cycle or two back. Still, there was a small finder's fee." He gave a soft chuckle. "Though in this case, it's mainly a 'thank you for not investigating yourselves' fee." He pulled out a gold coin and handed it to her.

"Really? That much just for finding a random old cache?"

Rane shrugged. "They want such things reported when found, rather than having random Mages delving into places like that and trying to scrape together enough remnants to make it worth the time. The professionals are safer, faster, and more efficient."

Tala grunted. "Makes sense, I suppose."

Terry flickered back to her shoulder, and she scratched his head before tossing some jerky.

"Well, thank you." After a moment, she asked, "You got a part, too, right?"

"Hmm? Oh, yeah. We found it together, and that's what we discussed."

"Good."

With that, their time was up; they had arrived; their walk was done.

Tala let them in, and they found Lyn reading.

"Do you just sit there, reading, when I'm not around?"

Lyn looked up. "Well, good evening to you, too."

Tala grinned. "Evening, Lyn."

Rane gave a shallow bow. "Good evening, Mistress Lyn."

Millennial Mage, 5 - Fusing

Lyn shook her head, placed a bookmark on her page, and set the book on a side table. "So, what's up?"

"Dinner?" Tala put a playful hint to the word and was rewarded with an amused smile.

"Why not. Let's go eat."

It was a pleasant late afternoon. The three of them ate slowly, though Tala much more quickly than her companions, and they talked of small things: life in the city, new plays, new magelings, and so much else.

There were apparently a smattering of new mageling arrivals, those who had graduated in the weeks after Tala's departure from the academy and who had chosen Bandfast as a destination.

One had even joined the Caravan Guild as an apprentice clerk. So, there was a reasonable chance of them seeing the new arrival, given Lyn's job and Tala's breakfasts with Odera.

Oh, breakfast deal, how I will miss thee. Unless... She could always get the food, then have it for lunch? She groaned internally. Her head was still aching, and it was making it hard to focus on such things.

Lyn mentioned offhandedly that the teleportation rooms were still in a stir from one or two arrivals coming in naked in the last few months. Though, apparently, it had been intentional on the part of the mageling.

Tala quickly changed the subject.

Rane suggested that they see the occasional play here in Bandfast, and Tala heartily agreed. They had been incredibly pleasant, effective diversions in Makinaven, and she saw no reason to forgo the mental breaks now that she was back in Bandfast.

Even so, it was still not quite evening when their meal drew to a close, and they stood to go.

Lyn stretched contentedly. "Didn't you need to go to the Arcanum, Tala?"

"Yes, yes I did. Do you two want to come?"

The other two Archons exchanged a glance before grinning. "Of course!"

Chapter: 32
It All Started with Some Chicken Soup

Tala, Rane, Lyn, and Terry entered the Archon compound, and Tala immediately felt a difference.

It was subtle, likely something that she only noticed because of her heightened magesight.

The power within the building was held on a much shorter leash, as it were. Even the little magic in the air was all claimed by various spellforms, in one way or another.

Honestly, it felt like Makinaven, but where that city had had a single, unified overlord, this felt like a patchwork of authorities overlapping one another.

Huh, there is no free-floating power at all. The city usually had at least a little. There must be incredibly efficient collectors within this complex.

She rubbed her temples briefly, vainly attempting to dispel her headache. At this point, she'd suspect mental shenanigans, but Alat had remained silent. *No use worrying about it, I suppose.*

The overall sensation was like having her clothing pulled tight across her skin, but it was external power tightening around her own, internal power.

She bolstered her aura, just at the boundary of her own skin, and felt a lessening of the pressure within herself, though it meant that it was concentrated on the edges of her power. *It's even trying to strip power from my aura.*

Millennial Mage, 5 - Fusing

These scripts must have been laid and activated by truly powerful Archons.

She rubbed her forehead against the still-present headache and took a deep drink of water.

When they entered the entry atrium, Tala suddenly remembered the round disk given to her by an Archon, after the fight with the syphon. "Oh! Right, my token."

She pulled out the token that she'd been given, ostensibly for her contributions toward finding and removing the creature. She'd not actually looked closely at it, and now that she did, she had a moment's hesitation.

It was a thing of beauty.

A stylized golden skull was inset into wood. The skull wasn't actually gold, as the image was slightly translucent, somehow, but it represented the color well enough.

Around the outside were twisting, interweaving lines that looked like inscriptions but weren't. *Just decoration, or is it some sort of script?* She could look into it later if she had time.

For now, though, she was standing in the Archon Complex atrium, staring at a small wooden coin.

She cleared her throat and continued forward, ignoring the inquiring looks from her companions. *Well, not Terry. Terry's content to sleep, for now.*

Feeling a bit hesitant, as she wasn't quite sure this was exactly where she was supposed to take it, she walked up to the central desk and cleared her throat. "I believe that I was told to bring this here?" She held up the circular item.

The young man behind the counter looked up. "Oh, certainly, Mistress." He held out his hand, and Tala placed the token into it.

Lyn patted Tala on her shoulder. "Yeah, I cashed mine in at my inscriptionist after lunch. Took most of the afternoon, but I'm all refreshed now." She gave a half-smile. "Best part about that token was it got me out of the afternoon of work to have the inscription done."

Tala smiled at her friend briefly before returning her attention to the Mage behind the counter

He placed the token on a small, empowered circle that was clearly intended for the purpose. He read something on his slate and nodded. "Oh, I see. You assisted with one of the last syphons."

Tala managed to keep her astonishment off of her face and out of her tone. *One of the last? How often does this happen?* She supposed that if they didn't kill anyone, they could be pretty prevalent and be little more than a nuisance. "Yeah." She tried to act casually, but the assistant's small smile said that she'd given away something of her surprise. "Has the reward been set?"

"Yes. It says here that you are to be given the choice between three gold and the syphon's alteration fascia."

Tala blinked, all pretense at understanding utterly forgotten. "Excuse me, but its what?"

"Its alteration fascia."

When Tala simply returned a blank look, the assistant sighed, manipulated his slate, and read from what seemed to be a prepared information packet.

"Syphons use a mix of dimensional, material, and illusion magics to create their perceived form, both interior and exterior. Its alteration fascia are the tendrils, nodes, and interconnected networks which contain and transport that power throughout its form."

"How would such a thing even be harvested?" Tala imagined trying to remove a creature's circulatory system, intact. *That sounds tedious to the extreme, not to mention finicky beyond belief.*

"With great precision, care, and precisely modulated spellforms. There are several specialists within the city who are masters of dressing arcanous kills and extracting the useful bits whole and in working order."

"Hunter's Guild?"

"Most of them are, yes."

"Huh. So, why is it being offered to me? Not that I'm not grateful, of course." Tala held up her hands placatingly.

"Of course, of course. All the Archons that participated in the slaying of this creature in an official capacity have already merged their dimensional storages with one or more syphon alteration fascia, so they have a lesser claim. Syphons are true magical creatures, not the result of founts, so they are both prolific and seemingly unending. The law requires that such harvests be offered to participating Mages before they are sold off by the city, though that basically never actually happens. If you do not claim this as a reward, it will be offered to the Mage with the next fewest such, merged with their bound items." The young man looked up from where he'd clearly been reading from a script. "Do you have a preference?"

Tala was still dumbfounded. "What is something like that worth?"

He got a hesitant look on his face. "Well, that should not factor in as you would be barred from selling the harvest if you accept it as your payout. It is intended as an incentive to find and fight such creatures, not as a source of income."

Tala waved that away dismissively. "Yes, of course, I've no plans to sell it if I accept. What about for curiosity's sake?"

He frowned, looking back down. He took another minute to search through information on his slate before grunting in seeming success. "Here it is. The last time one was offered on the open market was some two hundred thirteen years ago. It sold for two hundred and thirteen gold, seven silver, and six copper." He laughed. "That's a funny coincidence. Some two hundred and thirteen years ago, it sold for some two hundred and thirteen gold, plus change."

"Huh, yeah. Funny." *Two hundred gold?* She hesitated. *Maybe I should sell it...* No. This was clearly a valuable resource, and they wouldn't let her sell it anyway. "Yes, I'd like the fascia, and how can I be authorized to hunt more of these?"

"If you mean as a private citizen, there is no authorization required. We encourage such, in fact."

"What if I wanted to be called in to assist in taking down ones found by others?"

The young Mage put on a pained smile. "Unfortunately, slots for exterminating such creatures in an official capacity are highly coveted and only available to the city lord's personal guard." He glanced down, then added, "Oh! My apologies, the item I found, which was for the sale, was the fascia of an elder syphon. This one was two stages higher when it was engaged."

Tala's eye twitched. *Worth more than two hundred gold... The city lord's guards get to hunt these and claim the harvests... I could always still take that position...* She had *drastically* underestimated that offer of employment. *No, stay strong, Tala. You don't want to be trapped here...* It was obviously tempting, nonetheless.

"As I said, you are still encouraged to engage any syphon you find within the city as a private citizen." He straightened a bit, seeming to return to the script. "As you have selected the fascia for your reward, you will receive no further compensation for your participation in the removal of a clear and present detriment to the citizenry of Bandfast. Is that understood and acceptable?" He slid a slate across the counter to Tala, and she read it, reading through its contents.

"That is acceptable." She placed her thumb on the stone and pulsed her aura through the identifying magics, confirming the agreement.

"Thank you, Mistress. I will go get that for you now." He stood up and walked to the center of the round reception desk. In the floor in the center of the space that was surrounded by the circular desk, Material Guide scripts activated, moving the stone aside with a touch of magic, coming from inscriptions set around the Mage's ankles. Below the new, opening door was a spiral staircase leading down, presumably into a storeroom.

It only took a few minutes for him to return carrying a large, iron-clad box with obvious effort.

Tala could see further inscriptions running throughout his muscular-skeletal system, strengthening and stabilizing him, and he was having difficulty even so.

One of the other attendants stepped forward and helped hoist it up onto the counter, where they set it with a *boom* that echoed through the large room.

"There you are. Per the agreement, please do not open this except in the presence of a Constructionist Archon, in order for them to assist you in the merging of it with your dimensional storage."

"Understood. Thank you." Tala grabbed the box and hefted it free of the counter.

The young man's eyes widened at the apparent ease with which she lifted it.

It *was* heavy. Likely close to four hundred pounds all told, but Tala was *much* stronger than the average human.

"Thank you." Her voice was slightly strained, and that seemed to allow the Mage to recover some of his pride.

"You are most welcome, Mistress. Is there anything else we can do to assist?"

Tala briefly considered asking them to keep the box for her until after she was done in the library, but she couldn't bring herself to make the poor man carry it back downstairs. "Not at the moment. Thank you." Terry shifted on her shoulder but was otherwise not disrupted.

She turned around to see Rane and Lyn giving her bemused looks.

"What?"

Rane shook his head, and Lyn grinned before responding, "It's just very you."

Tala shrugged, causing the iron chest to bob up and down. "Well, I can't fit this in Kit, so I've got to carry it. I'll drop by the Constructionists after." *Ignore the headache, Tala; it's not that bad.*

"Fair enough."

"To the library?" Rane asked.

"To the library!"

The hallway of monsters passed in a flash, and Tala didn't allow herself to focus on the arcanous depictions.

The iron chest was irritatingly bulky, but otherwise, Tala didn't really mind carrying it.

When they entered the library proper, Ingrit was waiting for them, along with the other two assistants who had previously helped Rane and Tala.

They bowed in greeting, and Ingrit spoke to Tala, who was in front. "Do you each require an assistant, or will one be sufficient?"

Tala glanced to her companions. "I think they're just here because I am, so just one?"

Her companions shrugged, and Rane responded, "That sounds fine."

The other two assistants briefly addressed their respective Archon before departing, back to their other duties.

Tala turned to Ingrit. "How do you do that?"

Ingrit cocked an eyebrow. "You are scanned at multiple points as you head this way, giving us ample time to meet you here."

"Ahh, that makes sense." *I guess...*

Ingrit glanced at the iron box. "Do you wish a secure place to leave that until you depart?"

"That would be kind of you."

Ingrit walked over to one wall and pushed lightly with her fingers and more strongly with her magic. There was a soft *click,* and the panel opened, revealing an empty space just larger than the iron box. "Here you are."

Is that always there, or is it a dimensional storage? Did she size it precisely, or did she simply choose one that was the right size already? She could ask, but that wasn't really why she was here. Tala shrugged and placed the iron box within. "Thank you."

After Ingrit pushed the compartment closed, once again, she smiled. "Shall we find a private place to chat?"

"Yes, thank you."

Five minutes later, the four humans, plus Terry, were sitting around a table in a small alcove. Though, in truth, Terry was simply sprawled on his seat, content in his seeming sleep. A copper inscription had been activated to grant them privacy, and Tala was able to sense the weight of a deeply powerful will behind the working. *Ingrit is even more powerful than I'd have guessed.*

"Now, Mistress Tala, what can I do for you?"

"Well, I have one serious inquiry, one mild curiosity, and one somewhat involved discussion."

"Let's start with the passing curiosity, then hit the inquiry, and finish on the discussion, shall we? That way we ensure everything gets covered."

Tala nodded. "That sounds great. Thank you." *And it gives me time to think on how exactly to bring up the Culinary Guild, its research, and its fear of Mages...* She really should have been thinking about it before, but she'd never taken the time. "So, do arcanous herd animals behave like mundane ones? Meaning do they generally leave the weakest to be taken down by predators?"

Ingrit shrugged, clearly oblivious to Tala's frantic, mental scrambling. "Our studies have shown no differences in that regard, save when the predator is human. Arcanous animals, almost universally, treat humanity differently, usually with violent intent."

Tala grunted. "That's what I would have guessed. Thank you." *Rust, that was too quick. Think, Tala! Should I test the waters? Should I just dump it all in her lap? No, I promised to obfuscate...*

"Absolutely. And the inquiry?"

Inquiry? Oh! "Are there any endingberry groves nearby?"

"Of course. There's a rather large one some twenty miles from the city's southeastern outer defenses."

"Can I get a map?" *So, I have to be circumspect... Can she access anything I have access to, by default? Does she already have access to the Culinary Guild's records but doesn't know it?*

Ingrit shrugged. "Certainly, if you explain why you want it."

Explain what? Rane and Lyn were looking at her curiously as well. *Oh! Endingberry use, right. Have I never explained my use of endingberries to them?* "Well, I drink endingberry juice, and I'm almost out."

Lyn closed her eyes and leaned back. Her lips moved but no sound came out as she clearly was speaking to herself.

Rane looked thoughtful for a moment, then seemed almost to shrug. Clearly, the information didn't faze him.

Ingrit was taking a long breath. "Mistress Tala, I assume you know how dangerous those trees are."

Millennial Mage, 5 - Fusing

"I do." *If I didn't, I'd be dead.* She hesitated at that. If she were dead, she'd have first-hand knowledge of how dangerous they were. So, all told, that was a fairly stupid question. *Ingrit's not stupid, though...* It was possible she assumed that Tala had purchased the juice from someone else. *That's as likely as anything, I suppose.*

"And you know that the berries, and the juice, would effectively be a mildly crippling agent for virtually any other Mage, any Inscribed, or anything naturally magical?"

"I do." *Well, I didn't 'know,' but that is close enough to a pithier wording of what Grediv told me, so same difference.*

"Will you make a statement of intent to never give, sell, or in any way voluntarily pass on the berries, juice, or any other harvest from the trees?"

Tala grimaced. She could make good money selling parts. "Is that absolutely necessary?"

"If the trees weren't such a pivotal part of humanity's history, we'd have wiped them out centuries ago. They are dangerous in the extreme, every part of them. Yes, it is absolutely necessary to have such a commitment if I am going to provide locations to you."

"I could just hunt them down on my own."

"You could, but you would receive no assistance from the Archive in that endeavor."

She sighed. "Fine. I want the things for my own use, anyway."

"Alright. I'll ensure that you have clearance to access endingberry grove locations in the future. That is generally restricted information for the reasons just explained, but you'd qualify for a dispensation."

"Thank you."

"You can sign the statement of intent and pick up the map at the front desk on your way out." She smiled.

"Now, what was the last item that you wished for us to discuss?"

Last item? She blinked, pulling herself out of musings about ending trees and their harvest. *Oh! Right...*

"Mistress Tala? Is everything alright?" Ingrit looked genuinely concerned.

"Oh, yes. I am just ordering my thoughts." *Start simple. Yeah. That's the way to go.* "Do you automatically have access to all the parts of the Archive that I do?"

Ingrit gave her a curious look. "In a sense. If you make an inquiry, I can query the Archive as if I were you, and then I am granted access to anything that you would be able to see."

"Why is that better than me querying it myself?"

She grinned. "That is an excellent question. You could run all these queries yourself, Mistress."

When Tala reddened, Ingrit let out a small chuckle.

"But I offer insight and the quick compilation of the results into coherent answers. I can also alter your access, as with the ending tree locations. That query would have simply returned that you were unauthorized to access the information."

"Alright." Tala nodded. *Here it goes.* She smiled broadly. "Alright! The non-Mage, human consumption of arcanous harvests. What can you tell me about it?"

Ingrit sighed. "Mistress Tala, you know the answer to this question. You've even asked it of me before." Then, she hesitated. "Something's changed though, hasn't it." It wasn't a question.

Tala nodded. "Please, humor me."

Ingrit shook her head, then glanced up and to the left. Her eyes widened ever so slightly. If Tala hadn't had her enhanced senses, she'd have missed it entirely, and even so, it was a subtle thing.

Tala grinned, and she looked over to her friends only to see confusion on their faces.

Rane cocked his head to one side. "What's this about?"

Tala gestured to Ingrit. "Wait and see."

The Archivist Archon's eyes were flicking back and forth as she was clearly processing a lot of information. "I can tell you a lot, it seems. In general, any non-elementally aligned harvest can be used to enhance the same biological processes in a mundane. The enhancement is temporary but seems to last longer with each successive use. There is a long list of specific harvests I could direct you to, to enhance various things from healing to reaction time. Do you want a list?" Her voice had an almost unbelieving quality to it.

"That isn't necessary. Thank you. If I were to inform you I was going to research further, would that be an issue?"

"Not at all."

"What if I told you that someone with my new access, a mundane, was going to do this research?"

Ingrit hesitated, clearly inquiring. "No issue whatsoever."

Tala let out a happy little laugh. "I knew it."

"Mistress Tala, what is this about?"

She hesitated, then shook her head. "No. I need to check with… someone first."

Ingrit frowned, and Tala hurried to continue.

"I'll do my best to come back tomorrow, though!"

"This is going to create a headache for me… isn't it." Again, it wasn't a question.

"I deeply hope not. My intention is to mend fences and soothe headaches."

Ingrit huffed a little laugh and couldn't keep a small smile off her face. "Do you have anything else for me or that you needed from me? Or was this the only puzzle you needed to put upon me?"

Tala smiled apologetically. "I will try to be back tomorrow."

"Very well, Mistress." She then turned to regard the other two. "Did you both really just come to sit there and listen?"

Rane scratched his temple, grimacing. "Seems I had a lot to learn, so yeah." He glanced to Tala. "Can we get the full story?"

Lyn nodded her agreement. "Yes, please. I would greatly like to know what is going on."

Ingrit frowned just a bit but nodded. "Very well, then. I will leave you to it. This booth is yours for the next hour."

"Thank you for your assistance."

Ingrit smiled brightly. "You are most welcome, Mistress Tala."

Without another word, the woman departed.

Tala turned back to find her friends regarding her with undisguised intensity. She felt herself start to shrink back from their gazes but steeled herself. "Alright, alright. So, it all started with some chicken soup."

Chapter: 33
Siphon Fascia

Tala told the tale of her interactions with the Culinary Guild in about fifteen minutes, during which Rane and Lyn were consummate listeners, never interrupting and paying rapt attention.

In truth, Tala felt there really wasn't much to tell, but she humored them, nonetheless.

Lyn and Rane then peppered her with questions for the remainder of their time. They dug deeper into the situation than Tala thought was warranted as it seemed pretty cut and dried, in her opinion. Rane, in particular, seemed skeptical that a simple misunderstanding could have iterated so far and for so long.

Lyn didn't seem to take issue with that part, but no matter what Tala said, she couldn't seem to understand how Tala had been the one to discover the disconnect.

In truth, that hurt a bit, but Tala understood. *It's not like I'm one of the great investigators of the world.*

Tala drank lots of water both because she was talking a lot and because it seemed to help her head, if just a bit.

Terry, for his part, ignored them all, by and large, only stirring when Tala tossed jerky for him, which she did quite often. *No shortage of jerky, now, and I'm only planning on getting more.*

Once the hour was up and the privacy scripts deactivated, they stood and departed. Lyn and Rane were

Millennial Mage, 5 - Fusing

still full of questions, but by that point, they were mostly derivations of ones already asked.

They had internalized that this was a secret, and not theirs to share, so they didn't continue the discussion as they left, but Tala could sense that they wanted to.

When they reached the entrance to the library, Tala had a moment of panic as she didn't know how to open the storage cubbies, but it turned out to be a non-issue.

As they stepped into that last part of the library, an incredibly subtle scan slipped through her iron salve. Tala only noticed because a very slight warming of her skin caused her to look closer. *How in Zeme did they get this subtle of a scan through a script?*

However they'd done it, it worked, and her identity was confirmed. The wall panel that Ingrit had previously activated popped open, revealing her prize.

Well, Ingrit did say that I'd been scanned several times… Did they compensate for my iron salve? If the Constructionist Guild seemed to take her iron salve into account, she'd ask.

Tala grabbed her heavy iron chest without having outwardly paused to consider and lugged it back to the front desk once again to sign the statement of intent and pick up her map.

The same attendant assisted her once again, giving her the slate to confirm and then a large, rolled-up piece of vellum.

The map was a thing of beauty, really, which was why the fee of four silver didn't come as a surprise. In truth, it seemed quite the bargain, all things considered.

It showed the city and surrounding countryside, with three groves of ending trees clearly marked. Each was tucked away in some fashion, hidden from casual discovery, even by the frequent caravans passing through the area.

One was in a grotto of sorts, set down below the standard level of the plains. *That's a bit terrifying. An enclosed space, filled with the magic of dissolution.* She had a passing thought, as she considered. *I wonder if you jumped off one of the surrounding cliffs if you'd ever reach the ground?* It was a dark line of thinking, so she moved on.

One was in a mountain valley a few dozen miles to the north. *Not along any major thoroughfares, and it looks like there is a twist in the valley, so even if I stood at the mouth, I couldn't see the grove.*

The last seemed to be hidden somewhere on a lone mountain that rose up to the southeast. *That's a lonely mountain there. I wonder how it came to be formed like that.* After a moment's thought, she shrugged. *Probably a dwarf mountain and not as big as I'm thinking.*

All together, this painted a picture of trees tucked away from easy view, very different from the grove near the waning Alefast. *Each city may handle the ending trees near them differently? Maybe it's at the discretion of the head of the city?* Yet another benefit to working for the city lord. *Not now, Tala. Maybe in a few years.*

"Thank you." She nodded goodbye to the attendant, put the map into Kit, and picked up her iron chest once again.

Once they were outside, Tala shifted the weighty thing. It was late, but she didn't want to hang onto the massive burden of the iron chest for longer than she needed to. "I'm going to the Constructionists to bug Master Boma and get this merged."

Rane nodded. "That makes sense. See you tomorrow?"

Tala hesitated. "I actually have a few things that I *really* need to do. Meet back up for training the day after?"

"Sure."

Millennial Mage, 5 - Fusing

Well, that was easy. "Can you let Adam and Mistress Aproa know for me?"

"Absolutely. I'll still train with the guards, and I imagine Mistress Aproa will, too."

"Thank you, Rane."

Lyn looked between the two of them, a small smile on her face, but all she said was, "I need to go home, too."

Tala grinned. "Don't stop through any taverns on the way home, alright?"

Lyn grimaced. "Don't even joke." She shuddered. "I hope you do go hunting for those things. I'd feel better knowing they were gone."

Tala was touched at the implications of that. "I'll try not to let you down."

Rane grunted. "They're like spiders, Mistress Lyn. Most won't hurt you, even when you pass them by, and if you only knew how many were close to you at all times, you'd realize that most of the danger is in your own head."

Lyn gave Rane a withering glare. "First of all, how was that supposed to *help*? I'm more worried about the number of syphons in the city than before, and now, I'm anxious about spiders, too; thank you very much. Second, city Archons don't go around wiping out spiders when they're found, so syphons seem a good deal more concerning, thank you very much."

He ignored the blatantly obvious social cues and shrugged. "Well, they don't go after mundane spiders, but there are quite a few magical varieties that pervade human cities. Spiders, by their nature, are infiltrators, so those that achieve natural magic can almost always get inside magical defenses rather easily."

Lyn was twitching slightly. "Not. Helping. Master. Rane. Please, shut up."

He glanced at her and noticed her rubbing her own arms and looking around her feet with slightly too wide eyes. "Oh… Uh… I apologize, Mistress Lyn." He seemed genuinely apologetic, apparently not having intended to play on her fears.

She glared again, then turned to Tala. "Goodnight, Tala."

"Good night, Lyn." Tala did not laugh at her friend's discomfort, but it was a near thing. She had a brief urge to find a fake spider, or a hundred, to play a joke on Lyn; another glance at the woman and her better sense prevailed. *That would be in very poor taste and not very friendly at all.*

Lyn and Rane awkwardly said their goodbyes and went their separate ways as Tala toddled down the street with her heavy load.

The familiar scan and *ding* greeted her as she entered the building. *So it did compensate for my iron? I wonder why Makinaven didn't. Is it because they didn't need as detailed of scans in the tree city with Master Jevin overseeing the defenses?* That actually made good sense, now that she considered it.

An attendant came out to bow to her. "Greetings, Mistress. How can we serve this night?"

Tala regarded the Mage for a moment. *Huh, he's chipper.* "Is Master Boma available?"

The attendant hesitated but only briefly. "Yes and no. He is in, but is currently working on a personal project. And while he is doing that, he does not like being disturbed. He should be available tomorrow if you'd like. I can even schedule you a timeslot to ensure such."

She nodded. She could understand where the assistant was coming from. Even so, based on what she knew of the man, Boma should be the one to decide if he wanted her to return later. "Can you let him know that Mistress

Tala is here with some syphon fascia? I'm happy to come back tomorrow if that is his preference, but I'd hate to drop through and not at least let him know I was here."

The attendant looked hesitant, then he sighed and reluctantly complied. "As you wish Mistress. One moment, please."

True to the attendant's word, Boma arrived a couple of moments later. He paused when he saw the box. "What grade is that?"

Tala glanced down. "The box?"

Boma sighed. "The alteration fascia, girl."

"Oh, Revered, I believe."

His eyes sparkled, something akin to hunger seeming to kindle within them. "Perfect. I'll give you two thousand gold for it."

Tala dropped the box from suddenly numb fingers. It slammed into the ground, barely missing her toes and sending a resounding ***boom*** through the space. She also thought that she heard the stone crack under the impact.

The poor attendant poked his head out before confirming Boma's presence and wisely withdrawing back into whatever room he waited in for clients to arrive.

Two… thousand gold? I could take the money and run. But what would she use the money for if she ran? She closed her eyes and grimaced. "No… thank you."

"Ten thousand."

Her eyes snapped open, and she glared at the man. "You know I can't sell it, don't you." It wasn't a question. *He's messing with me.*

His expression didn't change. "And I'll get you out of the consequences of breaking the contract."

Tala frowned. *Can he even do that?*

There was an almost malicious glint to the man's gaze.

Is all this just to get back at me for interrupting his personal project time? It seemed… excessive.

"Well?"

She sighed. *A deal this good has to be broken in some way.* She didn't think about the man who had been fond of that turn of phrase. "No. Thank you for the offer, though."

Boma grunted, closing his eyes and sighing with resignation. "Fine. Now, you did interrupt my project time." He glanced down to the box, then tilted his head seemingly examining the floor around it. "I'll cover the cost of repairs to the floor. That's not on you." He scratched his chin and frowned. "Is that really a Revered, syphon, alteration fascia in there?"

"That's what I was told."

He rubbed his hands together, the gleam returning to his eyes. "Then let's get to it. This won't take too long, and it isn't free." Boma seemed to really enjoy his work at times.

Why am I not surprised? "Of course it isn't. How much?" *Ten million? My life as a slave?*

"Eight gold." It was an almost disappointingly reasonable amount.

Tala frowned with suspicion. "That's very specific. And you didn't have to look it up."

"First, I was forewarned of your coming, though I'd thought you'd have the decency to wait until tomorrow." He gave her a meaningful look, heavy with recrimination. "Second, we do these fairly often. One a week or so, on average, though quite few of this grade." The excitement was leaking back into his expression as he continued. "This one must have been exceptionally good at hiding, it seems. It wasn't greedy and bided its time well." He shrugged. "I suppose it didn't really help it in the end."

"Yeah, I suppose not." *I hadn't really thought about it in those terms, but he's probably right.* If humanity kills all the easy-to-spot spiders, are they not helping breed

Millennial Mage, 5 - Fusing

spiders to be sneakier and harder to spot? *Don't think about that, Tala. Do syphons even breed?* She immediately decided that she didn't want to know.

Their banter stalled at that point, but Boma only waited a couple of breaths before clicking his tongue and turning on his heels to walk from the room. "Right this way."

As they walked, Tala decided to ask. "Master Boma?"

He glanced back at her. "Yes?"

"How is the scan on the doorway able to penetrate to scan me? I have a defense made of iron on my skin."

He looked back again, contemplating. "While that is a wonderful baseline defense, it is hardly impenetrable."

"I'm aware of that, but my understanding is that it had to be powered through or the touch had to be so subtle it could slip through."

"That's accurate enough. It sounds like you already understand then."

She shook her head. "No. In Makinaven, my defense caused a misunderstanding at the local Constructionist Guild."

Boma snorted. "Unlikely. If anything, their workings are both more powerful and more delicately executed."

Tala frowned. *What does that mean?*

The only reason that she could think of was that Master Jevin had wanted the misunderstanding to occur.

But why?

It had allowed them to meet and given the Archon a reason to assist her himself.

Was he just curious about me?

She supposed that if she'd tripped his senses, and he'd been interested in getting a closer look without violating her privacy, he'd have to arrange for something.

And a message out of nowhere would have been highly suspicious…

It was still a bit odd that Master Jevin might have orchestrated such a show…

Boma grunted. "Though, now that I think about it, the basic scanning scripts might be set up more simply, due to the more powerful workings on the city as a whole." He shrugged. "I'm not an expert in the differences between the cities."

Tala sighed. *Thus, I'm back to ignorance.* She supposed that was better than building the shadows of nefarious plots on false assumptions.

Boma finally led her to a large merging room, but this one had some differences from those that Tala had seen before. First, all the surfaces were lined in overlapping iron plates, not just the walls, and a set of thin, gold inscriptions was already in place, laid into the iron. Second, the walls, floor, and ceiling held a large smattering of hooks welded into place.

"Set the box in the center." Boma pulled the door closed. "Your… bird should wait in that corner."

Terry looked to where Boma pointed, glanced to Tala, seemed to shrug, and flickered to the indicated position. There was a three-foot-high partition of iron that blocked direct line of effect from the center, where Tala rested the box.

"Now, you haven't become an idiot and bound your dimensional storage since we talked last, have you?"

"No."

"Good. Then this will simply be the clash of two empowered items, and we don't have to take your soul into account."

Wait… Kit is at most Bound, given the power I've been feeding it, and the fascia is Revered. Tala hesitated. "Won't mine lose?"

Boma shrugged. "It shouldn't. This"—he kicked the iron chest—"is an organ without a mind behind it. It will have to be mastered, but it's no different than placing electrodes on a muscle sample, just more complicated and longer lasting."

Tala frowned. *What?*

He clearly saw her confusion and sighed. "Your storage item will be an apprentice, given access to her master's tools, instead of those usually given to apprentices."

"Oh, that makes sense." That brought to mind another oddity. "Master Boma?"

He hesitated, seemingly sensing something in her voice. "Yes?"

"How is it Revered? I watched the creature stripped of power, down through the ranks until it was less than red, to my magesight."

"Ahh, you are conflating power level with level of advancement."

Tala frowned. "I'm not sure I understand."

"That's what I just said, actually." He shook his head. "In humans, our power level and level of advancement are virtually always on equal footing, but for magical creatures, that is not the case. Advancing in power alters the body, mind, spirit, and soul." He clucked his tongue. "An imperfect example is a container that once filled is replaced with a larger one. Then, later, even if there is less water within than before, the new container doesn't shrink or transform back."

She grunted. "I think I understand."

"You don't, not by copper or gold, but you at least have less ignorance."

Tala glared at the older Archon. "How do you know I don't understand?"

He gave her a quizzical look. "Your question was one of ignorance, and there's nothing wrong with that. In that ignorance, I showed you the silhouette of the first, most basic premise. Thus, as I am the source of your knowledge on this subject, and I haven't told you enough to grant understanding, I can state that you don't understand."

She grimaced. *That's a fair point… if a bit heavy-handed.* "Fine. Care to enlighten me further?"

"No." He was already looking over the room once more, clearly refocusing on the coming working

"Oh… alright then."

Boma tilted his head, continuing his contemplations, and grumbled unintelligibly to himself. Then, he glanced back her way. "When I tell you to, toss the pouch into the box and step back. On my second command, come forwards and dump power into the item. Do you follow?"

Tala nodded.

"Good. Now, step back and let me do my work."

She did as he asked, and Boma bent, opening the iron box. The lid came entirely free, and he set it just beside the container.

Power rippled through the air, bouncing off the iron and resonating oddly within the space.

With speed bordering on superhuman, Boma shot his hand into the open box and yanked out a tendril, almost like a tendon, and pulled it to the wall, using one of the hooks there to hold it extended.

It was clean, with no blood or viscera on the length, but it was still obviously flesh, and as such was a bit creepy, stretching across the room.

Boma returned to the box and repeated the process, over and over again, creating an ever-growing, irregular network of flesh. Each extended tendril changed the pulsing resonance of power in the air of the room.

The zeme. Tala chided herself for not using the correct word. *The zeme is the currents of power in the environment—like weather but magic.* She shook her head. *Why am I thinking about that now?* It didn't really matter, but she thought this was probably the highest concentration of power she'd ever been in, and it called to mind her lessons.

As she was examining the room's zeme, Tala noticed a hollow space in the power, a place where none of the magic moved or shifted. The shape of the iron wall protecting Terry kept any of the magic from reaching her friend.

Good. It was interesting as she doubted it would work with any other spellform. This room had been designed, specifically, to work with the syphon's alteration magics.

Even so, the resonance didn't seem harmful. She, herself, was standing in it, after all, but safe was better.

Some of the strings of flesh were interconnected, smaller strands pulling taut as Boma expertly positioned each piece.

It took the experienced Archon almost half an hour to finish the task, and even with that experience, he had to shift a few of those that he'd placed early on, changing the feel of the power in the room ever so slightly.

Finally, he seemed satisfied. "Now. Place the dimensional storage in the box."

Tala had long since pulled Kit free to be ready, and she strode forward through the literally humming air.

Her magesight wasn't required to see the symphony of spellforms twisting through the air, harmonizing with what Tala had finally identified as flesh-medium spellforms, which made up the fascia.

A clear path forward had been left for her, and she took it. A moment later, she dropped Kit into the box and stepped back.

The gold inscription on the floor flared with power, and the magic in the room pulsed, the flesh seeming to be *pushed* out of phase with physical reality, though Tala's magesight could still see it.

Kit's spellforms uncoiled, once more taking on an almost feline shape, though this time it seemed to be resting in the center of an insane spider's erratic web.

The cat settled into the position of command and seemed to *pull*.

Boma's voice was calm, firm, and insistent. "Now. Give your power."

Tala stepped forward so that she could touch Kit's physical form, that of a small leather pouch. She immediately connected four of the largest void-channels that she was capable of forming to the item.

Magic roared through her, and Tala gloried in the feel even as Kit seemed to imbibe the incredibly complicated spellforms of the syphon's fascia.

If Kit's lines of power had been a simple, if beautiful, tool, they now looked like the last work of a great artist, almost more lovely than any tool should be. At the same time, they gave a feeling of resilience that was stone compared to the cloth of Kit's previous makeup.

The resonating power in the room gained a new depth, and the music of it seemed to fade, pulling back into the pouch.

The inscription faded from the floor, the gold utterly spent.

The merging was complete, and Kit still seemed to drink quickly and deeply from the power that Tala offered, seeming as unquenchable as a forest fire before buckets of water.

Tala sagged to her knees, maintaining the flow with her full concentration, and finally, a tipping point seemed to be reached, and Kit almost relaxed, solidifying and filling to the brim with Tala's power almost instantly.

Millennial Mage, 5 - Fusing

She cut off the flow and gasped, falling back to sit, staring at the pouch before her, which was now sitting on the floor outside the iron box.

I thought I tossed it in. But the fascia was gone, so a slight positional change was hardly the most striking physical change in the room.

"Good." Boma walked up beside her. "Now, throw it against that wall and wish for a door into your storage space."

Tala was too tired to argue, and her headache was returning in force, so she silently apologized to Kit and tossed it against the wall, wishing for a door so that she could go in and sleep.

A door blossomed into existence in the wall.

It was a simple thing, looking almost exactly like the single door that already existed to exit the room. In fact, it suited the room so well that if Tala hadn't known better, she'd have thought that door had always been there.

Even knowing what to look for, and being sure she should find it, she only barely caught hints of Kit's magic, threading through the doorway.

Boma wore a smug, satisfied smile. "As ordered, Mistress. One fully integrated syphon fascia."

Chapter: 34
The Normal Rate

Tala looked at the new door out of the room. *Huh, that's Kit.* The dimensional storage had formed a doorway, hard up against the iron wall, seeming like it belonged there.

She then looked back to Boma as he held out a slate to her for confirmation of the work done, and her payment therein.

She fuzzily confirmed the transaction, still awed by the nearly entirely ordinary-seeming door. "So, this is what it allows?"

Boma froze, tablet halfway withdrawn after she'd touched it. "Excuse me?"

Tala sighed and waved at the door. "This is what the fascia allows, then?"

He slowly finished pulling back the empowered device before tucking it into his own storage space. "Am I to understand, Mistress Tala, that you just paid me to merge an unknown item with your magic-bound dimensional storage?"

"Of course not, both you and the attendant at the Archon's compound said that it was a wonderful addition to a dimensional storage."

Boma rubbed his forehead between his eyebrows furiously. "I *meant*, did you really not understand what it would allow for your item?"

Millennial Mage, 5 - Fusing

Tala shrugged. Now that her headache was coming back to the forefront of her thoughts, it *hurt*, and it was making it difficult for her to think clearly. "It was good, it was valuable, and now it's done. What does it do?"

He made an oddly inhuman sound, somewhere between a grunt of astonishment, a squeal of surprise, and a whine of indignation. Boma took a deep breath and let it out slowly, eyes closed. When that was complete, he repeated the process. Then again.

Tala looked longingly at the door that ostensibly led into Kit and her bed. *It would be so, so nice to sleep.*

Finally, Boma opened his eyes. "Mistress Tala, I will not waste both of our time by explaining how much what you have just conveyed smacks of idiocy. I will simply state that my opinion of you has dropped. Markedly."

Tala felt like she'd been slapped in the face, but before she could respond, Boma raised a hand.

"That said, I will still correct your ignorance as much as my already limited time allows." He took another deep breath and let it out. "At its most basic level, your storage item now has a greater ability to alter itself, both inside and outside, to meet your needs. This will have come with a percentage increase in the overall dimensional capacity that will remain as it expands, meaning that any increase to its capacity will be likewise increased by this percentage. For a Revered fascia, I expect this to be effectively a doubling of storage size."

Tala's eyes widened. *A doubling of the current size and a continued doubling of any expansion I do?* That was beyond incredible.

"The greater control will allow a fine-tuning of your dimensional space beyond what you've experienced, thus far. I would have to know exactly what you've experienced to tell you how it would change." He gave her a critical look. "But I can see you are fading. Sleep, experiment with the capacities of the item, and if you have any questions, come back." After a moment, he added, "At a reasonable hour, please."

She nodded. "Come on, Terry."

Terry flickered to her shoulder as she opened the door to Kit and walked inside.

The last thing she heard as she stepped through, letting the door swing shut, was Boma's startled exclamation. "No! Not in here, girl!"

But she was too tired to really process what he was trying to say.

* * *

Tala woke bright and early, feeling that she'd gotten exactly as much sleep as she needed.

Her eyes snapped open, and she was fully awake.
Bright? I thought I was in Kit.

The light level within the space was, indeed, slowly increasing. Moreover, she was sure she was in Kit based on the underlying feel and magical sense of her surroundings.

The illumination was especially of note because Kit had never really seemed bright or dark inside. It was always exactly light enough to see clearly and not a lumen more. Though, she'd always kind of wished the lighting was more varied.

Wish granted, I suppose.

The new ambient light in the space seemed to be increasing from near total darkness—likely so that she could sleep more easily—to the golden light of morning.

It was glorious. *Exactly what I want for waking up.*

There was no real source for the light, per se, even though it was coming through a 'window,' and Tala had

Millennial Mage, 5 - Fusing

an intuitive feeling that plants couldn't use this light to grow by. *Illusion, then? Not real light?*

That had some interesting implications. *If the light is an illusion, does it light the space as it is, or does the illusion have to include everything within the space?* It was an interesting philosophical question but hardly relevant at the moment.

She looked around and found that she was curled up in her bear fur, which was situated in a bed-sized nook in one wall of a small room, and folded over her to be both top and bottom for her sleeping arrangement.

Across from her bed, the giant window looked out across rolling wooded countryside. If she focused even a little, her magesight revealed the view to be purely an illusion, but it was utterly convincing to her mundane sight.

The illusion was a mix of magically generated light, texturing, and coloration added to the space beyond the window, and a subtle push on her mind to see it as intended. Her defenses didn't automatically reject the mental nudges as it was her own power, wielded through Kit, which was doing the work.

She decided to simply appreciate the end result.

Beautiful. The detail was stunning. She could see a little creek winding its way among the hills, variation in the type and age of the trees, and even the occasional bird flitting between the branches. Her mundane vision was enhanced well beyond what any normal human would have, let alone process effectively, and yet she couldn't see anything that stood out as out of place.

Is that because the illusion is perfect, or is the illusion altered to perfectly match what I expect to be there to believe what I'm seeing? The second sounded the most likely, especially given the source of this new ability for her storage.

She turned her attention away from the stunning vista and examined the rest of the room.

The walls seemed to be made of well-fit stone, like a shepherd's cottage in some rocky highland. *Not that there are too many of those around.* Still, it evoked the idea from some of the old stories.

She looked out at the wide, open space through the window, and even though she knew it wasn't real, it still seemed to help her relax, loosening tension she hadn't noticed. It evoked a sense of peace, a sense of *freedom.*

She stood and stretched, finding the space between the bed and the window perfectly sized for her morning stretches.

Those complete, she looked back toward her sleeping area and noticed her comb beside the bearskin. *That is a good idea.*

She took a moment and ran the comb through the fur, detangling and debriding it after her night of sleep. The small magics involved were lovely in their simplicity, and now with her increased magesight sensitivity, Tala could see it easily.

The comb basically decreased the coefficient of friction to any natural fibers running through the tines and for a short distance ahead of their movement. That allowed any debris, any water, and any tangles to come out with a single pass.

So simple, yet so useful. It used so little power that, even in a city, it didn't need a Mage to refuel it. *You know, I've never seen one of these for sale before… I wonder if the Constructionists could replicate it?*

If so, the market for such a product would be immense. *I'll ask someone.*

Afterwards, she replaced the comb on its little shelf and folded the bearskin back into a pleasingly neat state.

There was no sign of Terry, yet.

Millennial Mage, 5 - Fusing

To the right of the window, perpendicular to that wall, was a plain wall with an inset shelf containing her notebooks and a pencil. On the other side was the door out. It matched the simple, clean, craftsman aesthetic of the rest of the space, the handle seeming of wrought iron and the wood well-shaped.

The iron surprised her, but she supposed that it was unlikely to actually be iron, just like the view wasn't actually a true vista.

All told, this room was a bit smaller than Kit had been when Tala first got it.

Time to see what else is here, I suppose.

She opened the beautiful door and stepped through into a large main room constructed in the same aesthetic.

There were four doors out of this larger space, besides the one she was standing in.

One was clearly the main door to the house, and Tala intuitively knew that it was the exit of the dimensional space as well. That was directly opposite her, across the well-sized room, which was roughly thrice the size of the bedroom.

Terry slept in the far-right corner, on her folded bedroll.

To her left, there was a small counter in a kitchen-like area, and her incorporators were arranged on a rack, along with her other cooking-adjacent items. On either side of the counter, near those two corners of the room, were two more doors.

Even somehow intuitively knowing what she'd find, Tala poked her head through each door. The farther door from the entrance held all her food stuffs and food-related items that didn't fit neatly in the kitchenette. The other door held everything else, except her books, otherwise unaccounted for.

The books were inset into a wall in the main room—the same wall as the bedroom door.

I need a comfy reading chair...

There was one final room, and she verified its contents quickly.

It was the bath room with a glorious tub, ready and waiting.

When she looked, her two water incorporators were there beside the tub, ready to be used, along with the comb that she'd just used to clean the bear hide's fur. She glanced behind her and saw the two incorporators still on the rack.

She suspected that if she checked the bedroom, the comb would be there as well.

Turning back to the bath room, she verified that the items were there. *Dimensional manipulation, indeed. I bet if I had another Mage in here, we couldn't both use them at the same time, but I'm not absolutely sure.*

"Well done, Kit." She placed her hand on the wall on a perfectly sized, decorative handprint in the stone and dumped power into the pouch. While it did take almost a minute to refill Kit to full, it was still proportional to the total, increased capacity. So, Tala wasn't really concerned about the power usage. *Though, I need to grow my throughput before Kit gets too much stronger, or I'll have to spend an unacceptable amount of time recharging it every day.*

That complete, she moved through her morning exercises in the larger space of the main room.

As she did so, she found that room was big enough for the task, though she would have sworn it wasn't before. *So, it expands at my need, even while I'm in it.*

As she considered, she realized something else, too. *I suppose the other rooms don't need to exist, to take up space, when I'm not in them.*

Millennial Mage, 5 - Fusing

She'd need more capacity for Kit before she had guests. *Well, one would probably be fine. This room shouldn't be using all the space, and the others aren't so large as to take more than the balance.*

Exercises done, she gloried in a nice, relaxing bath.

Finally, ready for the day, she decided she was ready to face the city once more.

Almost immediately upon deciding that, she heard a knock on her front door.

It wasn't a quick, solid knock like someone trying to get in, nor was it a tentative knock like someone hoping not to disturb her.

It was firm but somehow lazy. Like someone who felt obligated to knock but didn't care one way or another if there was an answer.

"Terry?"

Terry lifted his head and let out a single, short note of acknowledgment.

"Ready?"

The terror bird flickered to her shoulder.

Tala strode forward and opened the door. There was no one directly outside.

The first thing she noticed was that she was looking out into the iron-clad room from the merging.

Oh, right. Oops.

Second, she saw a Mage, laying on his back, fingers interlaced on his chest, twiddling his thumbs. He seemed to be making random noises with his lips, but when she opened the door, his eyes widened in shock, and he stood quickly.

"Mistress Tala." He bowed, flushing brightly.

"Random Mage boy. What can I do for you?"

His flush deepened. "I was set to watch for your exit."

"Oh?"

"Yes, Mistress. Master Boma was... displeased that you placed the entrance to your dimensional storage within our facilities." He looked incredibly uncomfortable as he held out a slate. "I was instructed to give you this upon your return."

She glanced back to Kit's closed door, and on instinct, she reached out and grabbed the frame, pulling on it.

The door fuzzed and vanished, leaving Kit, the pouch, in her hand. *Huh, neat.* She pressed it to her belt, and the pouch, obligingly, stuck in place. *Nice.*

She then took the slate and glanced at it. "What is this?"

He cleared his throat. "An hourly rental fee for the room, and a charge of an attendant's hourly rate to await your return."

"I'm to be charged two gold per hour for this room."

"That's right, Mistress."

"And you get paid a silver per hour?"

"I am a mid-level attendant. The initiates are not trusted to be in this room."

"Of course not, they might lie on the inscriptions in the floor." She looked pointedly at where the Mage had been lying, which was, indeed, directly across the gold inscriptions. *Rusting foolish, that.*

He reddened again. "So it seems."

"Hey! I was only in there for five hours? That's wonderful. So, a total of ten gold and five silver."

"That's right."

She clucked her tongue, looking over the transaction. "Yeah, I'm not paying this."

She handed the device back to him with a smile.

"Have a great day!" Without a backward glance, she strode from the room.

She left the gap-mouthed Mage behind as she swept through the halls. *Where is that man?*

Millennial Mage, 5 - Fusing

After taking a couple of turns, she sighed and stopped, allowing the quick-walking Mage to catch up to her. "What time is it, again?" Even as she asked, she somehow knew. *It's 2:07 in the morning.*

"Just a couple of hours after midnight, Mistress."

Tala frowned, then sighed. The information must have come from the subconscious bond to the Archive link. *Not the time for such contemplations, Tala.* "This would be a rusting rude time of night to bug him…" She glanced back at the Mage. "Incidentally, why did you knock when you did?"

"What do you mean?"

"You knocked. Why did you choose then to knock?"

"I'm so sorry, Mistress, I don't understand. I've been knocking every ten minutes since Master Boma set me to the task. Is that what you're asking?"

Huh, Kit didn't allow the sound to transmit through the door until I was ready to interact with the outside world. That's fascinating.

The young man held out the slate once again. "I really must insist that you pay your balance, Mistress." He looked quite uncomfortable.

Tala cocked an eyebrow at him. When he didn't budge, she sighed and rubbed the sides of her head. Her headache was coming back to the forefront of her mind. It had been there since she woke up, but she hadn't paid it any mind, hoping that it would simply go away. It hadn't. *I suppose I have been a little bit rude.* "What is your name, good Master?"

He seemed taken aback at that. "Well." He swallowed. "I am called Simon, Mistress."

"Good to meet you, Master Simon." *Material Guide, specializing in the alteration and study of empowered materials?* That was interesting, to say the least. What could he even do with that? *Maybe…*

Simon seemed a bit confused, the slate dropping slightly as he lost his focus on that matter. "Oh, umm. Thank you?"

Tala stepped forwards and took the slate back. Next to the fee of two gold per hour was listed 'Rate for active, Magical use.' Tala frowned. *Does using it as an entry point for my dimensional storage really count?* "This seems excessive. Are these the true rates?"

He glanced to the side, then shook his head. "Master Boma was less than pleased with you, so he instructed me to use this rate for the room."

"What about for you?"

He squirmed a bit, clearly uncomfortable. "He wanted me to charge you a gold an hour for my time as well, but that seemed excessive. That portion is the Guild rate for my time."

Tala found herself touched, and then she felt irritated at herself for how she'd treated the Mage previously. "My apologies, Master Simon. My actions put you in quite the awkward position." *I should apologize to Boma, too, but not now. I'll do so next time I see him.*

He glanced down and shrugged.

"What would the proper rate be? If you are allowed to say."

"Two silver per hour to reserve the room, more to use it for mundane purposes, more still for magical use. What you did would qualify most closely as reserving the room."

Tala contemplated for a long moment. "Will you get in trouble for charging me the normal rate?"

Simon looked up at her, frowning in confusion. "Most likely not? Master Boma probably wouldn't check the exact amount of the receipt, and even if he did, once he's less... displeased, he likely wouldn't mind, in truth."

Tala nodded. "If it's alright with you, let's do that."

Millennial Mage, 5 - Fusing

He hesitated a moment longer, then shrugged and nodded, taking the slate back and manipulating it to make the changes.

Tala verified the new total of fifteen silver and confirmed the transaction.

"Thank you, Mistress Tala."

"And thank you, Master Simon. I'm sure you had better things to do than wait for me to re-emerge, even if it was just sleeping."

"True enough."

"Now, where can I find Master Boma to wake him up?"

Simon paled, his hand trembling, slightly.

Tala held up her hands in a warding gesture. "I'm kidding!" She chuckled awkwardly. "I'm only kidding. I'll come back once the sun is up."

He visibly relaxed, clearly relieved that she hadn't been serious. "Oh. Oh, good."

Tala was about to turn away from Simon when her thoughts coalesced despite the headache.

"Master Simon?"

The Mage seemed a bit nervous. "Yes?"

"Would you, or the Archon you work under, have any interest in examining a simple, useful artifact for potential reproduction?"

Simon frowned. "But we cannot make Artifacts, Mistress."

Oh... right... rust... "Of course, I was meaning to pull the idea and learn from the spellforms."

He gave her a searching look, then shrugged. "Probably. Master Queue would probably love to discuss it with you. He was my master before I attained Magehood, and he continues to oversee my projects."

Disaster averted, good. She smiled. "That sounds excellent. I'll ask for him after I speak to Master Boma, once the sun is up." *I do have an apology to make.*

Chapter: 35
Black, Please

Tala had a lot of time on her hands, unexpectedly. She was used to sleeping later, at least until morning was near at hand.

Why did I wake up so soon? If her reckoning was correct, she'd gotten what felt like a full night's sleep in around four hours.

I've been needing less sleep, but this is a marked difference. The inscriptions throughout her body felt more settled, improving her physiological functions more than ever. She had her iron salve in place as well, amplifying and condensing all the magic within her. *It makes sense that would translate to more efficient sleep, I suppose.*

As she stood outside the Constructionist Guild, on dimly, but sufficiently, lit streets, the question was, what now?

She could find a place to train or a place to anchor Kit and train in there.

She could...

Her head twinged with ignored pain, and her stomach rumbled.

Food. I need food. Specifically, she was craving dessert. *A nice chocolate cake or caramel pudding.* She licked her lips in anticipation.

She was walking through the virtually deserted city streets, aimlessly searching for an open restaurant. She would be meeting with Mistress Odera in a few hours, but she was hungry now.

The cold stone of the streets and the occasional piles of snow felt good on her feet, and the cool air seemed to be helping her head, even if only as a side effect. She really did love the cold.

Food, food. Where would there be food…? Somewhere that caters to late-night workers… or Archons?

That's an obvious answer. She smiled. *Seems like I'll be at the guildhall early today.*

Tala turned her path and went to the Caravan Guildhall. As she'd hoped, the lounge and food area were open, even though the main space, in which clerks like Lyn worked, was closed.

By the time she arrived, her headache was more manageable once again, but she was feeling incredibly dizzy. *How can I be this hungry? I know my stores aren't low.*

She could feel her own weight with each step, not that she jiggled. She could simply tell that she was still markedly heavier than a normal person would be.

Maybe, I'm missing a specific nutrient? That was a thought—probably a good one. *Well, I'm craving sweets, so maybe I'm low on sugar, somehow.*

The place was hardly empty, but she was able to grab a table with ease in the mostly empty space. The few other people there seemed to be deeply focused on their own business, so they and Tala did little more than acknowledge each other in passing.

When a server came by to check on her, Tala knew what she wanted.

"I'll have the double-fried donuts, stuffed with sweet, cream cheese filling, and to drink, I'd like some fruit juice—whatever is least expensive."

"Of course, Mistress. Our apple juice is fresh pressed and in season with the winter harvest coming from the grow complex daily. How much of the juice?"

"A gallon should do it."

The server seemed to hesitate, but then something in her stance changed, and she smiled. "Certainly, as you wish. How many donuts would you like? And what toppings?"

Tala glanced down at the menu again, looking at the price. The late-night menu was much more limited than the standard but also quite a bit more reasonably priced. *A dozen donuts for a silver.* "Let's start with a dozen… and powdered sugar over the cream cheese icing, please."

"Very good. The total for those and the juice will be two silver. Would you like any donuts left out to eat before you go?"

Tala blinked up at the older woman. *What?* "Oh! I apologize for the confusion. I'll be eating them all, here. The sooner the better, if you please."

The server hesitated again before she nodded. "Shall I get you a larger table, or move one of the others over? How many are you expecting to join you?"

Tala sighed. "No, no. I'm not being clear." She smiled up at the woman, trying to remain calm despite her growing irritation and headache. "I will be eating them all, myself, right here, as soon as possible."

The server swallowed and nodded, clearly realizing that she wasn't going to fully understand her customer. "As you wish, Mistress. Do you want any coffee with that? Help you kickstart the day?"

"*Coffee!*" Tala exclaimed, lifting her hands in a gesture indicating realization of the obvious. "I'm having caffeine withdrawals." *No wonder the headache is so awful…* There were probably other reasons, too, but coffee was an easy enough core cause to explain it.

Millennial Mage, 5 - Fusing

The older woman had taken a step back at the exclamation. Then she gave a little chuckle. "I'll take that as a yes, then."

"No." Tala shook her head, sadly. "I drink too much of it and need to stop."

Yet again, the server seemed utterly baffled. "So you're going cold turkey? That seems unpleasant."

She just wants to sell some coffee... Tala grimaced. *That's uncharitable. She's just trying to help.* "I'll survive. Better a lot of pain for a short time, than a moderate amount for weeks."

"Whatever you say, Mistress. It's your head." The server nodded once. "Alright, a dozen double-fried donuts and a gallon of apple juice as quick as I can get it."

"That's right."

"I'll be right back, then."

Tala placed her head into her hands. *Of course it's the coffee. They weren't kidding when they said I was addicted...* She wasn't exactly sure who she meant by 'they,' but she was sure they had been right.

Would that explain the dizziness, though? *Why am I so, so hungry?*

Her mind felt pretty fuzzy, so it was no wonder she was startled when the server placed her food down beside her.

Tala jumped, causing the poor woman to step back quickly in alarm, leaving the food and jug of apple juice behind.

"Oh! Thank you." Tala tried to smile to calm the woman once more. *My manners are all over the place.*

The server bowed and departed, though Tala hardly paid attention; her eyes were now locked on the treats before her.

She took a long swig from the jug of apple juice, and something deep within her projected happiness. *This is what I need. I'm not sure why, but I definitely do.*

She'd have to drop by Holly's workshop to ask. *One more thing to do.*

She pulled out one of her books and continued reading through. *There is so much to learn.* True, she could wait until Alat finished going through her mind and then just have her find any info at need, but Tala didn't want to rely on Alat too much. *Certainly not a lot.*

She laughed, shook her head, then sighed while licking her fingers clean of frosting.

She glanced down. *What?*

The donuts were gone.

"Terry, did you eat my donuts?"

Terry trilled a negative, and Tala thought she detected an eye roll in the sound. *Either I'm understanding him better or starting to project.*

"Huh." She waved down the server and ordered another dozen, along with a chicken-fried steak for Terry. They didn't normally sell just the steak, but when Tala explained it was for her companion, they relented.

Half a silver. *Not too overpriced for nicely fried meat.*

Terry did take a small bite of donut when Tala offered, but he didn't seem to like it.

In the end, Tala ate four dozen donuts, drank two gallons of apple juice, and gave Terry two chicken-fried steaks.

All told? Seven silver.

Not too bad for satisfying a late-night craving. It was a blatant breach of her daily food budget, but since it wasn't day yet, she justified it to herself.

It was four in the morning. *I know, I know. A budget isn't a budget if you don't stick to it.* She'd do better next time.

Millennial Mage, 5 - Fusing

Three hours until breakfast with Mistress Odera. Tala paid, thanked the server, and left for home. *I'm going to talk to Lyn.*

She was halfway home when a pleasant sound resounded in her mind.

-Ding-

-Further lost or repressed memories, not lost due to the natural processes of time, recovered. Please indicate when you are free to relive them.-

Well, that's something to do until Lyn wakes up.

*   *   *

Tala sat, weeping, with her face in her hands and tears running down her forearms in one of Lyn's chairs when the woman herself placed a hand on her shoulder.

"Tala? Are you alright? What's happening?" Lyn sounded at a complete loss, her tone uncertain and careful like she was talking to a wounded beast.

Tala looked up through watery eyes. "My family."

Lyn knelt down next to her. "Did someone die? Did you get a message?"

Tala shook her head, drawing in a ragged breath. "I just miss them so much."

The memories drudged up by Alat were almost entirely related to her family and all that she had experienced growing up with them. There were good and bad memories mixed in, but the common thread running through them all was how much they were *family* and how much she had loved them, and they her.

There had been a few embarrassing memories that she'd repressed, too, and which Alat had dredged up for her to relive, but they didn't seem quite so bad now that she'd reexamined them. It was quite amazing how little they actually embarrassed her now.

She even felt more embarrassment from how she'd reacted to the embarrassment of the moment than from the initial action. But that was twisting her in mental knots, and those had been presented to her early in this set of memories, so that was not what dominated her thoughts.

"Why don't they want me anymore?"

"Oh, Tala." Lyn pulled her into a careful hug as she wept.

Tala just stayed there for a long time, unable to stop the tears from flowing as Lyn stroked her hair and back, shushing and speaking soft, calming nothings to her.

An unknown amount of time later, Tala leaned back, pulling free of the comforting embrace. She knew it was almost time to meet Mistress Odera, but she hadn't thought to check the time when Lyn had joined her in the living room.

"I have to go." Tala pulled a rag from Kit and wiped her eyes before blowing her nose. *Holly blocks vomit but not snot. They're there for good reasons, of course, but still.* She sighed. Then, she looked closer at the rag and felt herself smile slightly. It had been a part of her shirt that the plant creature had torn to ribbons when she'd slept on it, so long ago. *Well, torn to rags, I suppose.*

Lyn's voice brought Tala back to the moment. "You're going to need to work through this, Tala."

"I know." And she did, too. She'd hidden from this for long enough. *At the very least, Alat probably won't let me repress it again.*

Lyn gave her a deeply skeptical look.

"I do, I promise. I just had Alat dump on me, and I wasn't really ready for it."

"Oh? Like what? What besides your family?"

Millennial Mage, 5 - Fusing

What? Oh. "No, not a lot." Tala left an obvious gap between the two words. "Alat." She spoke the name quickly, to ensure that it sounded like a single word.

Lyn cocked her head and frowned in confusion. "You'll have to explain that one to me."

-Tala-

-You are going to be late unless you leave soon or are willing to run.-

I thought you went back into 'deep-diving' my memories.

-Firstly, you are distressed, and mental functions are impeded during times of heightened emotion. I determined it was wiser to wait for you to calm down. Secondly, I'd have told you if that were the case.-

Tala grimaced, then processed that Lyn was waiting for her. "I'm sorry, I can't explain now. I have to go. Talk later?"

Lyn nodded, smiling reassuringly. "I'm here when you're ready."

Tala placed a hand on her friend's shoulder. "I know, and thank you."

Lyn gave her a quick hug, then pulled away, heading back to get herself ready for the day. "Don't wait for me. I know you have a breakfast meeting."

"Thank you, again," Tala called at her friend's retreating back.

Lyn waved over her shoulder as she walked back toward her own room. "What are friends for?"

The meal with Mistress Odera was uneventful, though Tala yet again was drawn to the sweetest available breakfast options.

As she bid her overseer Mage goodbye, she had a choice to make.

Constructionist Guild, Culinary Guild, Holly, blacksmith, or alchemist. She clucked her tongue. *I've a lot to do, today.*

-Tala-

-You seem better.-

What? Oh... She grimaced.

A sigh resounded within her skull. -*And you're worse again. I'm not waiting anymore. We're so close to being done. All other functions going offline, now.*-

Alat?

There was no response.

Fine. She hesitated. *Oh, right, I need to talk to Lyn.*

She should do easy to hard. *Well, I can't talk with Lyn 'til she's home. So, that's got to be last.*

So, alchemist first. Tala stopped, hesitating then. *I'm an idiot.* She'd forgotten something incredibly important. She glanced to Terry. "You were going to start training with us, today, weren't you?"

He met her gaze and gave an affirmative, soft squawk.

"I'm sorry, Terry. I went and changed our plans without thinking about that or how it would affect you."

He gave the avian equivalent of a shrug.

"Will tomorrow be fine to start that? I can probably still make it to the training yard today if you want."

Terry considered for a long moment, then shook himself.

"Today?"

He shook himself again.

"Tomorrow?"

He bobbed his head in agreement.

"Thank you, Terry. I'm sorry for not remembering sooner."

He trilled happily and flickered away to catch a bit of thrown jerky before curling up on her shoulder once again.

Millennial Mage, 5 - Fusing

That decided, Tala set off, back to the alchemist who'd made her original iron salve after she arrived here from the academy. She was on her last bar of the stuff, which was one reason for the visit.

When she entered the well-appointed alchemist's shop, the smell of the herbs, tinctures, and reagents hit her with a tide of memories.

Many of the remembrances that Alat had brought to the forefront of her mind were filled with similar smells. She took a moment, eyes closed, to compose herself.

When she was ready, she opened her eyes once again and turned to the man working behind the counter. "Good day."

"Hello, Mistress." He turned to greet her. "How can I help you?"

"I don't know if you remember me, but I came through here a few months back to get some iron dust combined with a salve for application onto my skin."

His eyes brightened with recognition. "I do! I do remember you. You gave me a lot to think on, Mistress, and through that, have allowed me to earn quite a bit of coin."

"Oh?" Tala walked farther into the shop. She was curious. *I know no other Mages are using the iron salve.* Well, she didn't *know*, but she doubted that they did.

"Yes. If your goal is to get as full coverage of yourself with iron as possible, I think I might have a better solution." He was grinning.

"Do tell."

He pulled out a small jar. "This is a cosmetic paint, often used for festivals—face painting and the like. It is also the base that most of us use for beauty products if we wish for them to last a long time."

Tala frowned for a moment, then shrugged. *I have seen some ridiculously long-lasting artificial colorations. They might actually be a good basis for this.* "Tell me more."

"Well, I was able to make an even finer iron powder for combination with this, and it worked! The medium drinks in the iron to a ridiculous extent and binds with it and whatever it's painted onto." He grinned at her.

"You can't have done this just because I put gold in your mine."

"Oh, you started it, that's for sure, but I realized that this works to make anything able to take a magnet, too. I took that to the Constructionists, and they were thrilled, though they tell me it has other applications as well. So, I doubt they're using it for the magnetic applications. That is of no consequence to me, however. All that matters is that they buy it from me by the gallon."

Tala's eyes widened. "That's amazing." *If the Constructionists are using it, it must have close to the anti-magic properties of a solid plate of iron as that's their go-to method of containment.* "Can I test it out?"

"Of course!" He hesitated, seeming to consider. "But first, I overrode you when I realized who you were. What brings you in today?"

She grinned. "Well, this new idea will cover one need, assuming it works."

"And there are other needs?"

She nodded. "I'm looking for a way to deal with many monsters at a time. Alchemist's fire, or something like that."

He shook his head. "Oh no, Mistress. I'm neither cleared for such a dangerous concoction nor skilled enough to create it. You might want to check with some of the alchemists attached to the Guardsman's Guild, as they tend to have more use for and experience with such things."

Millennial Mage, 5 - Fusing

Tala sighed. *That makes sense, I suppose.* "Alright, then." She didn't let her disappointment drag her down, however. "Let's test this stuff."

The alchemist grinned. "Certainly! I've been able to produce it in black, yellow, and red. Do you have a preference?"

"Is that a true yellow or closer to a gold?"

"Definitely not a gold. And truth to tell, the black is closer to gray, and the red isn't a true red, more of a rust color." He grinned at that. "As one might expect."

"Ahhh, I see. Then, not yellow." She imagined herself with rust-colored skin and shuddered. *Red eyes are quite enough, thank you.* "Black, please."

"I'll get a sample for you to try."

Tala had a thought as he ducked down behind the counter. "How much does it cost? Assuming it works as I need it to, I might need a lot of it."

Chapter: 36
Not Pregnant

Tala was excited to test out the iron salve improvement, which was why she'd asked how much it cost. *I can't pay rivers of gold, but if this works as well as I hope, it could be worth a lot to me.*

"Half a gold per gallon." He handed over the test vial, complete with a little brush mounted to the lid, just like the glue she'd used to protect her palms for the application of her iron salve.

Half a gold per gallon? Tala's eye twitched. "That's not cheap."

"It is a bit more expensive than the salve I made for you last time, yes."

A bit, yeah. That was only a few silver; this is fifty.

Though, as she thought about it, all the bars she'd purchased together would likely have been less than a gallon.

Maybe the costs are closer than I think. "Well, I'll give it a try and see."

The paint was thick as Tala used the little brush to paint her left hand using her right. "I recommend you do three coats to ensure complete coverage. With those, it should last until you scrub it off, and believe me, you will have to *scrub*."

She gave him a skeptical look.

He simply grinned back. "It is surprisingly robust—intentionally so."

She grunted in acknowledgment and shrugged. "I'll definitely put it to the test."

Even as she applied the first coat, she could feel a noticeable difference. Her magics were being better contained and reflected back than they had been with iron salve. *Maybe I should be sleeping in an iron box if this is the result.*

Unfortunately, an iron box wouldn't actually work for that. True, an iron box would keep her from losing magical power, just like it did for harvests and items, but the iron would not be evenly distant from her skin in a box, and the random angles at which it would be in relation to the spellforms would mean wonky angles of reflection that would not well complement her existing magics. All told, an iron box was useful for containment, not training.

She also realized these results helped her to understand why most Mages did not like iron. *Their spellforms are not as safe as mine to have amplified and applied internally.*

The paint was surprisingly quick drying, and so in less than ten minutes, her left hand was thoroughly coated with three layers of the flexible, somewhat stretchy material. She had used the entire test bottle to accomplish the three layers on that part of her.

The result had a bit of a metallic sheen to it, without being shiny, and it was a beautifully deep, dark gray.

An odd side effect of the nearly perfect containment was that her spell-lines, usually much too fine for mundane eyes to see, were shining through the layer.

No, that's not right.

Only the most prominent through lines were visible, those that carried the most power naturally, and even those were only just visible. The sheer amount of power flowing and resonating within the scripts seemed to be causing a resonance in the air that manifested as light.

Tala could only tell all of this because of her enhanced vision and magesight. The mundane alchemist had no idea.

"I apologize, Mistress. It seems it is not as impermeable as I'd thought." He was frowning. "That seems even worse than the iron salve, somehow. But that doesn't make sense. Didn't you put it on over the iron salve?"

Oops. She had, in fact. *And the paint is still staying this well?*

It was amazing stuff, it seemed.

"Oh, no, it's nearly perfect. This is a resonance in the air, right against the outer layer of the material." It was stunningly captivating, even just on her hand.

Tala flexed her hand, stretching her fingers and wrist with her other hand, but the layer didn't breach, crack, or in any way show signs of failing, seeming to move flawlessly with her skin.

Oh. Oh yes. She hadn't left her palm bare as she would have in the past, because her magics no longer needed an avenue out of her physical body. *No, now they reach through the dimensions of magic itself to enact my will upon the target.*

It took a bit more power to do it that way, but was massively more effective. It also took a will. In her research, she'd found that independent scripts, operating automatically, couldn't work within the dimensions of magic. The analogy that she'd liked best was a ball on top of a river.

The ball would go where the water flowed, but it took a will, an action, to push it under or lift it up. The only other way to get the ball underwater or above it was for the water to be churned up to an incredible degree. The

Millennial Mage, 5 - Fusing

analogy actually held in this case. The analog was that magic could actually bypass iron with sufficient power, turbulence, or with the right type of currents.

In either case, it was something that she could do fairly easily at this point. She continued examining her hand as she grinned. *And it allows me to do this.*

She ran a couple of tests, trying to extend her magics through her hand, and found the first issue.

The iron salve she'd been using was apparently permeable enough to let her aura draw power through it. Now, she could extend her aura but couldn't move power through it without the same effort required to utterly bypass the iron layer.

The result was that her aura didn't extend as far on its own and seemed weaker, somehow, like it was missing a layer of support that was usually there.

Thankfully, she didn't need magical power to pull on her soul-bound items. Unfortunately, it would mean that she wouldn't be able to easily do what she'd seen some higher-level Archons do; mainly, create spellforms around themselves, with their aura as the medium and magic, itself, as the spell-lines.

Magic concentration first, then when I'm a bit more advanced and have a bit more time, I can work on spellforms in my aura. She still had the ability to work with them in her lungs, but she'd decided long ago that that was too dangerous a place to do her tests. *I can learn how to breathe fire after I can create fire in a safer location.*

"I like it."

"I'm so glad." The man was studying her hand with obvious fascination, fixating on the glowing lines hard against, but outside, the dark, metallic gray layer atop her skin. "May I… touch it?"

Tala hesitated. "I don't actually know what that would do or if it's safe. It might be hot?"

"I will be careful and go slowly." He thought for a moment. "Let's be wise about this. Here." He pulled out a piece of paper and set it on the counter. "Place your hand on this, please."

Tala looked at her palm and the glowing lines there. *That's a pretty wise first test, actually.* She placed her hand down on the paper and waited for a count of fifteen. That done, she pulled her hand back.

The alchemist placed his own hand on the unmarred paper. "A bit warm to the touch. Not room temperature, but certainly not dangerous." He held his hands out, and Tala carefully placed her left hand into them.

He turned her hand over as he examined it from all sides, running his fingers carefully through the lines.

"Fascinating. I can feel… something, but it isn't quite heat. It seems to be resonating with something here." He placed his hand on his chest. "Somewhere behind my heart."

His gate. Tala looked closely at the man's hand, focusing on what her magesight was showing her, and she saw little eddies and echoes of her defensive magics in his natural magical pattern. As he moved his hand back, those artifacts faded, but they were definitely there.

"Imprinting? That magic is resonating powerfully enough that it is imprinting on the powers around it. I believe you feel it because the natural magic in your hand is taking on, very temporarily, my spellform." *Is this how they create artifact-style items?* It made sense, now that she thought about it. *Resonate a spellform strongly enough around an item and it could build up an echo or imprint.*

Her thoughts were disrupted as he pulled back his hands. "Ahh. Well, I don't want to blow anything up or—"

Millennial Mage, 5 - Fusing

Tala waved him off. "It's purely defensive and regenerative. No danger."

He looked skeptical and didn't touch her hand again, but he didn't argue.

She decided to change the subject. "How much will it take to cover me fully?"

He hesitated. "Fully?" He frowned. "Well, I believe a colleague of mine sells body paints for various artistic purposes, and she sells three quarts at a time. You are on the smaller side, so that should be about right. That is factoring in using the proper number of coats."

Then, three gallons would cover me four times, but that's probably a bit excessive. "I'll take two gallons."

*   *   *

Tala left with the iron body paint carefully stored inside Kit. She wasn't happy to part with a gold, but she understood the value of a non-toxic, long-lasting iron paint that she could cover herself with.

She didn't have time to apply it immediately as she had much too much to do that day, and she'd already spent more time than she should have with the alchemist.

She retraced her steps from so many weeks ago and found the blacksmith that Ashin had taken her to for a camp knife.

There, she had a lovely conversation with the master smith in residence and ordered four steel triangles into the corners of which she could put bloodstars before mounting them to shields.

She'd claimed two curving tower shields and two large round shields from the Leshkin loot, and that had pretty much exhausted her claim on the haul.

Rane had, apparently, sold most of the rest, only keeping the swords for merging with Force.

She did not look forward to taking a blow from the newly enhanced weapon, which, of course, meant that she needed to do it sooner rather than later.

She also had a bit of back and forth with the blacksmith about another idea and ended up leaving him with one of her tungsten spheres to properly size the contraption. She would have left him with one of her anchoring darts, too, but they, by their design, couldn't really be left behind.

Instead, he took good measurements of the empowered item and asked some pertinent questions.

All told, he expected that he and his underlings—*apprentices?*—could have her work done in a few hours.

They settled on a price of forty silver, and they both seemed happy.

Tala paid half in advance and went on her way.

At that point, she was ready to drop through and see Holly.

The inscriptionist was, as expected, quite busy, but the moment that Tala walked into the workshop, the Archon came from the back, practically at a sprint. "What have you been doing to yourself, Mistress Tala?"

Tala took a step to the side, trying to dodge without stepping back out of the building. "I was coming to ask you about my cravings. They started suddenly this morning."

Holly shook her head. "You're not pregnant, obviously."

Tala reddened. "What? Why would you—"

Holly waved her off. "Cravings, changes in health in the morning, better to dismiss it early so that we don't have to consider it any longer."

"But I haven't—"

"I don't want to know, dear. Now"—her eyes flicked to the side, seeming to be reading something—"a sugar craving? Yes, your increased mental activity is using much more of that macro-nutrient." She hesitated, then added, "I mean carbohydrates, obviously, not sugar specifically."

Tala immediately felt like an idiot. *Alat. She's using my brain more than is usual for a mundane human, so it needs more fuel than usual. Just like my increased exercise had me craving more fats and proteins.*

"So, you need to alter your diet. You are off caffeine; I can see that. Good for you, but that headache must be murder."

Tala glared. She'd been successfully ignoring it, but having it so blatantly pointed out made continuing that impossible. "Anything we can do about it?"

"Well, yes. Drinking a lot of water would help considerably."

"Can't my scripts prevent this?"

"Mistress Tala, I will not mess with your neurochemistry so directly. Natural decisions have natural consequences. You won't die or be permanently harmed by the headache or the irritability." She hesitated again. "Well, assuming that you don't direct the foul mood foolishly."

Tala sighed. "So, nothing nefarious is going on?"

"No, dear. You just need more sugar in your diet."

"Well, that solves that, then." Tala almost turned to go but noticed that Holly didn't seem to have heard her as she was staring at Tala's left hand.

Tala lifted it up, and Holly grabbed it, seemingly without thought. The spectacle created before Tala's magesight by her iron-painted hand in Holly's inscribed ones was fascinating.

Holly's aura seemed to harden at the borders of her skin, preventing any outside magic from influencing her natural magics or inscriptions.

"What have you done to your hand?" Holly's voice was distant, barely above a whisper.

Tala gave a brief explanation as to what she and the alchemist had done.

Holly nodded along, commenting at the end. "This would be a swift, incredibly painful death for anyone with different scripts than yours. Even your gravity alteration spellforms are equally weighted for increase and decrease in their normal, active state." She tsked, shaking her head in wonder. "But this is so beautiful."

Tala tried to pull her hand back, but Holly held fast.

"You are going to be pressure-cooking yourself in magic, and I cannot wait to see how you turn out."

That's a pleasant image. "Is that… bad?"

"Oh, no dear. It is getting your body adjusted to a *much* higher power content that will increase your power density proportionally as your body tries to adjust to containing such, on its own. I assume the plan is to paint your entire body with it?"

"That was my thought."

Holly cackled lightly, then caught and schooled herself. "That's amazing. You will progress your magical weight in months as much as most do in years, if not decades. How far are you on the road to becoming Fused?"

Tala hadn't thought about that in a while, but when she did, she felt the work continuing in the back of her soul and spirit. She looked inside, looking closer at the ongoing stitching. "Half done?" No, that wasn't right. She was close to halfway from the center to the outside, but each layer outward was bigger than the one before. "No, one quarter, if I'm remembering the area calculation formulas correctly."

Millennial Mage, 5 - Fusing

Holly grunted. "Not bad for a bit less than a month's dedicated work. Some may have done it faster, but most take years longer even to get this far."

"Why?"

"Why do they take longer?"

Tala waved that away. "No, no. Why do you ask?" She knew that most people didn't pursue advancement at the same, arguably insane, pace that she did.

"Oh, because every step of advancement deepens your connection to power, and all aspects and features of yourself that relate to it, depending on the stage of advancement, of course."

"Ahh. I think I understand."

"You don't, but that's fine. You will in time."

Tala sighed, Holly's words harshly reminding her of Boma's similar feelings about her understanding. Feeling a bit defensive, she turned to go. "Well, I've much to do. Thank you for answering my questions and for your assistance."

Holly gave Tala a level look. "*You're* busy?" She opened her mouth to say more, but then she just shook her head. "Not worth the time. I appreciate you dropping by to chat, though. Good day, Mistress Tala."

"Good day, Mistress Holly, and thank you again."

Tala left and went straight to the Constructionist Guild.

She again enjoyed the cool air and stone as she trekked across the winter cityscape.

She arrived at the guildhall and walked through the open entryway.

She'd never noticed before, but there was a marked increase in temperature as she walked down the short hall, and the subtle hints of magic in the air, only barely visible to her even now, gave her the reason as to why it was so.

Seems like it would be easier to just use a door.
Though, as she thought about it, one of the core purposes

of a city was to bleed off power and use it up, helping to keep the barrier between worlds intact for longer.

Huh, syphons might actually be helping in a certain way, then. That was an interesting, if marginally disturbing, thought. *So long as they don't kill people, they might actually be better to leave alone.*

She guessed that if they got too powerful, that would no longer be the case, however. *That's probably why they are hunted. We don't want a Sovereign Siphon rearing its head in a human city, after all.*

She was scanned, greeted by the pleasant ding, and waited the short moment for an attendant to come out. It wasn't one she'd met before.

"Mistress. How can we assist you today?"

"I'm looking to meet with Master Boma and Master Queue. Are either available at the moment?"

"Let me check. May I tell them who is requesting a meeting?"

"Tala."

"Thank you, Mistress Tala. I will be right back. If you'd like, we have a waiting area right over there."

Tala glanced that way and saw the coffee dispenser. She swallowed involuntarily, feeling her body groan in desire, her headache spiking, almost as if it were promising to go away if she would just have one little cup. *Yeah, I better not get any closer to that.* "I'm fine waiting here, thank you."

"As you wish."

Chapter: 37
Vestiges

Tala waited just within the Constructionist Guild for one of the two Archons she was seeking a meeting with.

She stood in the entry hall, specifically not looking toward the waiting room, from which she could easily detect the smell of fresh coffee, if only faintly.

Stay strong, Tala. Not drinking coffee is better for you. She grimaced and groaned internally. She'd gone most of her life without coffee, but now it felt like air or water. She *needed* it, even though she knew that she didn't.

Her eyes flicked to the side, glancing over and taking in the earthenware mugs set out for easy use.

Tala resolutely turned away. *Nope.*

A change of air currents, likely due to an open entryway behind her, brought a particularly strong waft of coffee goodness to her nose.

She spun to face the waiting room. *One cup won't hurt. One last cup.*

At that moment, she heard the sound of footsteps and turned back in time to see the assistant returning with a man who could only be Master Queue.

The Archon had a very tightly controlled, hardened aura that completely blocked Tala's ability to view what type of Mage he was, let alone what he could do, but it did put his aura on easy display. The power encasing him shone forth, a happy yellow-green.

Refined. Well on the way to Paragon.

Millennial Mage, 5 - Fusing

His eyes only flickered to Terry for a moment, showing interest but not overpowering curiosity, as he crossed the floor.

Terry seemingly took no notice of his surroundings.

Queue stopped a few paces from her and bowed, allowing his long white coat to billow around him. "Mistress Tala, I presume. How may I be of assistance?"

Tala bowed in turn. "Master Queue, your Mage assistant, Master Simon, directed me to you. He seems a competent fellow."

Queue's eyebrows went up in surprise. "Oh? Well, thank you. I quite like his work. I will pass on the compliment."

She nodded in acknowledgment, then pulled out her comb. "I wanted to discuss this with you. Somewhere private might be better?"

The Archon took the comb, turning it over in his fingers before shrugging. "Sure. I'm not sure what there is to discuss, but I can give you five minutes."

Tala nodded her thanks, then glanced to the assistant. "This in mind, I'll be looking to meet with Master Boma in the next half-hour if he's available." *If Queue only has five minutes for me, that should be enough time so that I don't keep Boma waiting.*

The assistant bowed. "I'll see what I can do."

"Please don't inconvenience yourself or him. I'm happy to schedule something when I come out if he isn't free."

The assistant nodded in acknowledgment as Tala departed after Queue.

Tala followed Queue into a side room, where the Archon activated some privacy inscriptions with a gesture. "Now, Mistress Tala, what do you have in mind?"

"Could this artifact be replicated?"

He gave her a long look, then examined the comb again. "Most likely, yes. I'm guessing that you don't want to know what it takes to do so, just that it can be done?"

"That's right, though I might be able to guess." She kept her left hand back, slightly behind her body for now. *No need to complicate things.*

Queue grunted. "So, why would we replicate this? It is a fairly standard artifact. Like most, it is probably unique in some way or other, but still, the uses aren't overarching enough to justify the expense."

"That doesn't need a Mage to power it, even in a city."

He glanced back down. "I did notice that it wasn't attuned to you. This is a wonderfully efficient device, then. Even so, such things aren't unheard of. Probably one in a hundred artifacts don't need to be magic-bound to survive, but what's... your... point..." He trailed off there at the end, seeming to consider. "This detangles hair at a stroke, yes? I'm interpreting the magics correctly?"

"Detangles, debrides, and dries, without damaging the hair."

His eyebrows rose once more. "That makes sense, but I'd not have thought of it."

"So, you see the utility?"

"I think I understand what you are getting at. It is quite useful."

Not willing to dance around it anymore, she grinned. "And could be used by mundanes."

He was nodding. "Yes. Artifacts for mundane use are rare. There would certainly be a market for such a comb. How could we disguise that we can create artifacts, though, if we flood the mundane market with nearly identical items?"

Tala shrugged. "Claim some new material coating with a natural magical resonance? A proprietary process to

Millennial Mage, 5 - Fusing

capture and lock such into place for use by any, even mundanes?"

He snorted. "That's mostly nonsense. No material's natural resonance is anything close to this convoluted." Then, he paused. "But it might just be believed. This certainly isn't the first artifact created for widescale, mundane use, but it might be the most... personal so far. Most are embedded in buildings or the like." He tapped the comb against his palm. "It would be an undertaking to build the impressor for a new artifact-style item, plus we'd need to have the combs made in one of the factories. They'd have to be identical in size and composition. We're talking a few thousand gold to do this right."

Tala balked. "That seems extreme. Couldn't we find a comb already on the market and use that?"

He shrugged. "There are a few mass-produced combs, true, but not many, and I don't think any are made in Bandfast." He clucked his tongue. "At best, we could get it up and running for a hundred gold, but then we'd be dependent on another city to supply the base item."

"Is that bad? Also, I don't have that much."

He waved her off. "The money's not really important." He seemed to be considering.

Tala checked the time and cleared her throat. "I'm sorry, Master Queue, but we've gone a bit over the five minutes you said you had. I can come back tomorrow?"

He gave her a sideways glance. "I can make the time for this. This shouldn't take too much longer."

Tala bit the side of her lip. A host of things flitted through her mind, including how poorly she'd treated Simon the night before and how much help Boma had been. With that, and much else, on her mind, she made a decision. "While you're considering, I have something to do quickly."

"Sure, sure. The bathroom's down the hall and to the right."

"That's not…" It really didn't matter what he thought she was doing. "Thank you."

She quickly walked back out to the entryway and found the assistant waiting in a side room.

"Excuse me."

The assistant's head snapped up, clearly engrossed in his book. "Oh! Mistress!" He scrambled to stand up.

"I'm sorry to bother you."

"No, I'm here to help. How can I assist?"

"It seems that Master Queue and I will take a bit longer than I'd expected. Can you convey that to Master Boma and ask if I can meet him in his office when I'm done?"

"Certainly. I'll let him know."

"If he isn't available, or that doesn't work, I understand. I'll check with you when I come out."

"As you wish."

Tala quickly returned to Queue and as she walked in, he started talking almost as if she hadn't left.

"Buying the combs in bulk shouldn't be an issue. I can put in the order now, after I find a sample in the city that will work, and the shipment could arrive by the time we need it. We'll have to advertise it to the masses, somehow, but that wouldn't be hard." He glanced at her. "I'll also need to verify it does what you say for myself, I hope you understand."

She shrugged. "Certainly." She'd honestly expected no less.

"They could sell for two silver?" He nodded, then clucked his tongue. "Most costs are in the start-up, so we'd recoup costs in five thousand units or so." He frowned. "That's too optimistic. Double that. Ten thousand units."

Millennial Mage, 5 - Fusing

"For two silver, you would eventually sell one to every woman in the city and many men." Tala grinned, thinking. "I imagine the guard might want them as standard for their supplies, given they can be a bit of an effective dry bath, at least for those with hair."

"True enough." He seemed to be doing some calculations in his head. "If you can leave this with me for a week, I can front the start-up costs and give you"—he seemed to consider for a moment—"five percent of any income after those costs are recouped?"

Tala's eyes widened. *Ten copper a comb… for nothing more than lending him mine for a week?*

He misinterpreted her reaction. "I can probably take what I need from the item in a few days, but a week would be better."

She narrowed her eyes. *Not his limit on that, so probably not his limit on the percentage.* "Five percent is too low. The item is mine, and therefore the spellform is mine." Tala's understanding of law when it came to spellform ownership was shaky, at best.

He waggled his hand. "In a sense, yes, but that wouldn't stop me from reproducing it."

"It would if I don't lend you the item."

He held it out to her. "That is true enough. Backwards engineering the spellform wouldn't be worth the effort, even if we sold a comb to every human in every city."

She took the comb. "What about a fifty percent split? True, you're doing the work, but I'm allowing that work to be profitable."

He gave her a flat look. "Fifty."

"Seems fair."

He shook his head. "Fifteen."

"Of gross. I don't want my portion being limited by costs at only fifteen percent."

Again, he shook his head. "It will be after expenses, but I can go as high as twenty percent and not a copper higher."

She thought about it for a moment. *I probably would have taken it at five percent, so twenty is amazing. I don't even have to do anything.* Another thought occurred to her, though. "Can I come and use the comb during the week you have it?"

After a moment, he shrugged. "I don't see why not."

"Then, agreed."

Queue pulled out a tablet from seemingly thin air and began working on it, clearly entering the details of their agreement.

Tala held in a sigh at yet another Archon with an untethered dimensional storage. *Though, it makes sense that if anyone were to have them, it would be those who are members of the Constructionists Guild.*

Less than five minutes later, Queue handed over the short, simple contract.

She read through it, verifying it matched what they'd agreed to, and confirmed it. "A pleasure doing business with you. When do you think we can start selling them?"

Queue shrugged. "Two or three weeks, I believe, unless the spell form is incredibly stubborn."

She considered for a moment. "Can I see the process?"

He shook his head. "Unfortunately, that is proprietary to the Constructionist Guild and its sub-guilds. Some others do know the method, but I cannot share it."

She nodded. "Very well." Without further discussion, she handed the slate and comb back to him, then offered her hand. "Thank you."

He took her hand and shook it. "I appreciate you coming to me with this. May it profit us both, immensely."

Millennial Mage, 5 - Fusing

Her magic tingled at the close press of his hardened aura, but she didn't feel any invasiveness, and he kept his aura perfectly aligned with his own skin, so it never even attempted to dip into her hand.

They left the little side room and parted ways, Queue going back into the depths of the facility and Tala heading back to the entry hall.

Tala checked with the assistant and was directed toward Boma's office. As she turned the corner, she saw the Archon stepping out into the hallway. When he saw her, he stopped and nodded her way.

Just more than half an hour. She hadn't left enough of a buffer, it seemed.

Tala walked up to just out of arms' reach. "I apologize, Master Boma." She bowed over clasped hands in a formal gesture that she hadn't used since graduating. "Both for the delay now, and for my rudeness last night. My exhaustion, while a factor, does not excuse the result."

He seemed genuinely taken aback by her apology, even pausing for a moment to collect himself before he responded.

Tala straightened and smiled.

"Well, I suppose that the apology is accepted, Mistress." His face had lost most of the edge of wariness that she'd noticed when she first saw him a moment earlier. "What can I do for you?"

"I've some questions about my dimensional storage. Is now a good time?"

He nodded and gestured for her to follow. "As good a time as any, and better than most."

They went into what she presumed was his office.

There was a workbench off to one side, but surprisingly, the space was mostly dominated by a large desk, the entire top of which seemed to be a device for integrating with and accessing the Archive.

There were light creation scripts in addition to the normal color-changing features standard on an Archive tablet, and Tala was able to see exactly what they allowed.

The image of a bracer revolved, floating above the desk with a veritable cloud of magical notations, which seemed to be scrawled around it.

"What is that?" She pointed to the bracer.

"I assume you aren't familiar with vestiges?"

She frowned and shook her head. "No."

"That's actually a relief." He gave a humorless smile. "To come at it from a direction you'll catch, this is an artifact found in the prison of a shattered foe from long ago."

Tala walked over and looked more closely. "This seems to indicate that it doesn't require bonding or power of any kind, but even what I can see would indicate a massive power usage. How is that possible? Or am I misunderstanding what I'm seeing?"

"Oh, no. You aren't misunderstanding, and your assessment is accurate. A vestige is an artifact-style item that has a gate within it."

Her head whipped to the side, eyes locking on him.

"Yes, I can see you grasp what that means. Someone bound a human soul into that item. If the soul bound itself in there, that would be something entirely different and unrelated. As it is a vestige, we've been trying to make contact with the soul inside. We can't free the soul without destroying it, so it's a question of an eternity bound to the bracer or non-existence. We'd like the soul's opinion before the choice is made." He sighed. "Or, conversely, all sapience and sentience have left the soul, and it is nothing more than a bound fount, in which case, the item can be put to use defending humanity and preventing at least a few more people from suffering from this or similar fates."

"That sounds like a horrible mess of a situation. Reasonable of you to make the attempt to contact it, but horrible all the same."

"Indeed." He moved around to sit in the chair behind the large desk and motioned for her to take one closer to the entrance. The image of the bracer drifted to the side, clearing line of sight between them. "Now, what can I do for you?"

"I am interested to know how I can achieve certain things for my dimensional storage, and I want to know if other things are possible."

"Go on."

Alright, first should be what I know is possible, else I might just irritate him again. "How can I get an artificial sun within the space so that I can grow plants if I want? I'm also interested in artificial weather so that I don't have to maintain the biome, specifically."

Boma nodded. "Well, first things first. Nothing about such things is artificial. Your dimensional space is effectively its own world, and you are simply hoping to give that world a sun and weather patterns."

"Okay." *Interesting way of thinking about it, but I can see the logic, I suppose.*

"Given the syphon fascia we just merged with your item, I imagine that you've already seen an artificial sun and that it didn't satisfy. Yes?"

She thought back to the illusory vision of a sunrise. "True enough."

"So, what is a star? What are weather patterns?"

She took the seemingly parallel line of questioning in stride and gave the best answer she could. "Well, a star, from the perspective of a planet, is a source of heat and light and an anchor within the cosmos as a whole."

"Surprisingly good answer. You don't need your storage's star to be an anchor, but the rest is required if I understand your request properly."

"So, I need an item that generates light and heat? I just need a fire artifact?"

"You will need the right kind of fire artifact and the proper integration spellforms, but essentially, yes. Your storage must be sufficiently large to warrant such, though, and it has to have at least some static features, else the day-night cycle won't function properly, and that will cause all sorts of issues. Moreover, the artifact must be able to be turned off unless your storage gets to the size of truly mimicking a small world and you wish to form a sphere, or at least a cylinder, within the space. Thus, the fire artifact can't be an ever-burning torch, for example. Even better than simply being able to be turned on and off would be if it had the ability for a variable output."

Tala quirked a smile. "And I suppose you have such an artifact on hand?"

He raised an eyebrow at her smirk. "We have several, yes."

"Conveniently ready to sell to me, I suppose."

"No."

She blinked at him. "What?"

He took a deep breath and shook his head. "You aren't listening. Your storage must be large enough and have static sections for such a merging to be useful. I could perform it now, but it would be worthless to you until you'd at least quadrupled the size of what you're working with." He frowned. "No, that's not right. Your storage is what, about fifteen hundred cubic feet? A little less?"

She thought about it, then shrugged. "Give or take? I've not measured." *Probably a bit more, actually.*

Millennial Mage, 5 - Fusing

"Yeah, then we need to increase the capacity by at least ten times that before a magical star would be truly useful to you."

Tala grimaced. That would cost a lot of gold. "What about weather?"

He waved that away. "Weather patterns just take standing water, a star, and a desire for such weather. Your storage will take care of the rest."

That made a lot of sense, actually. She was familiar enough with the water cycle in the world that it should translate fairly well into her desires as conveyed to her storage space. "How much for the item and integration?"

"Not a lot. Ten gold, give or take, depending on exactly which item you choose."

"And expanding my item's capacity by tenfold would take…?" She knew it would be a lot, but she wanted that confirmed. In truth, she hoped that something would factor in, somehow, to reduce the cost.

Boma turned to his desk, and the image of the bracer was replaced with a depiction of Kit, overlaid with descriptions of what the Constructionists' Guild knew of the item. "It looks like merging with your storage is quite efficient. The item has an incredibly stable base matrix and takes on additions with ease. So you probably have closer to two thousand cubic feet to work with, probably a little more. That said, even with the ongoing multiplier from the Revered syphon fascia, we'd need to merge in at least twenty of the generic expanded space boxes with your item. At thirty gold a piece, for the item and merging, that comes to six hundred gold. I'd recommend a couple more, but that's where it sits, at the moment. We do have larger versions of our storage boxes for merging, and they are a bit more cost-effective if you can afford them, but the cheapest I could get it done, all told, would be between four and five hundred gold."

Tala grimaced. "Yeah, I don't have that much."

"Understandable. Most don't have that much in ready cash." He grinned a bit ruefully. "Most immediately spend what they get upgrading their bound items, rather than saving up."

She grunted. "Well, thank you for the information." It made a sort of sense. Any upgrade to any item could be what saved a Mage's life. Was it worth saving up for an upgrade the Mage might not live to get, when spending a bit more, overall, could keep that Mage as equipped as possible at any given time?

"You had another question?"

She was drawn out of her contemplations. "Oh! Right. Can I create a permanent entrance and exit to my dimensional storage?"

"I assume you don't mean just leaving your item in the form of a door, attached to a wall permanently."

"No, I mean something like a door that always leads to and from my storage space, no matter where I am with the item itself."

He nodded. "I assume you'd like a few, ideally. One could lead to where you actually are in the wilds. One would lead to a sea-side city, and another to a more upscale place like Bandfast. And you simply must have four, so the fourth should lead to a plateau, high in the mountains, covered in flowers. Am I guessing correctly?"

Tala sighed. "You're making fun of me, again. There's no reason why it shouldn't be possible."

He grinned. "Yes and no. Many have tried to do exactly as you are suggesting. And if you'd like to pursue it, I'll gladly help as you're right; there is nothing that prevents it from working, in theory. We just have never figured out a way to do it. If we ever do succeed, then caravans would become a relic of the past, and we'd simply create dimensional storage tunnels between the cities."

"I knew it should be possible. As you said, it would be rusting useful." *It did seem too useful to not be used by everyone.*

Boma smiled sadly. "Indeed. Now, is there anything else you wish to ask?"

"I think that is it." She stood and gave a shallow bow. "Thank you."

"You are most welcome, Mistress. Good day."

"Good day."

Chapter: 38
Blessings Never Cease

Kit was in heaven. The influx of blessings never ceased.

The human who had dared claim her had gone above and beyond in offering recompense. She served Kit well enough to earn her continued existence a thousand times over. Though, Kit was beginning to suspect that the human had other motivations for its largess.

Kit held sway over more and wielded more power than she had ever thought possible, and the increases seemed unending.

Now, she was not just a devourer but also a creator. All within her expanded space was under her auspices; she could form it at will. The human had somehow granted her the ability to form illusions and reshape the properties of that which was under her control.

From her meager tests, the changes she made to physical matter did not endure outside of herself, but there was time, still. She could now alter her exterior, if not as much as the physical space she contained, and she could see outside herself if just a bit.

The latter was likely to facilitate her exterior changes, which Kit took special pride in. She could hide anywhere.

Kit did *not* consider how closely her new abilities mirrored those of her near kin, the syphons. It was probably just a coincidence. After all, a syphon of sufficient power to have physical remnant magics able to

Millennial Mage, 5 - Fusing

grant this level of power would have been *strong*. Its power would have been far beyond the ability of her human to overcome.

It was obviously just a coincidence.

The human continued to feed Kit a seemingly unending supply of power, which was beginning to make Kit a bit lazy, if she was being honest.

She hadn't been wantonly eating anything left within her for a while, now. Though, she did still sequester things that the human was unlikely to miss. Mostly, that included scraps of bio-matter and excess material, stubbornly grabbing onto the items that the human *would* miss.

It was a comfortable life.

Too comfortable.

Deep within Kit, she was still the Devourer of All. That was still her nature.

She was sure of it.

Because of that, the greatest shock in this new iteration of existence had come when the beacon of death had begun accompanying the human into Kit's domain. Thankfully, it was only on occasion, but ever since Kit's last upgrade, it had been increasing in frequency.

The beacon was a being of such deep power and hunger that Kit truly began to question if she had ever been worthy of the name 'Devourer of All.'

She had, only once, attempted to take a nibble from the seemingly infinite supply of power and food that was the beacon.

It had been like trying to bite a rock.

No, that wasn't right. Kit regularly devoured little rocks and bits of sand that came in with the human.

It had been like... Kit shuddered. It had been like trying to take a bite from the Consumer, back when she was but a little devourling, surrounded by her broodmates in the deep nothing, outside of existence.

Her progenitor had been so far above her that, had the Consumer not so named her, Devourer of All would never have dared presume the moniker.

As it was, Kit was glad to have another name now.

Identity crisis avoided.

Still, she occasionally saw the beacon watching her, somehow, its eyes seemingly looking beyond the extra-physical space, in which Kit was the absolute master, and into *her*.

Her human did not know what it was doing by giving such a being a cutesy name like 'Terry.'

Author's Note

Thank you for taking your time to read my quirky magical tale.

If you have the time, a review of the book can help share this world with others, and I would greatly appreciate it.

To listen to this or other books in this series, please find them on mountaindalepress.store or Audible. Release dates vary.

To continue reading for yourself, check out Kindle Unlimited for additional titles. If this is the last one released for the moment, you can find the story available on RoyalRoad.com for free. Simply search for Millennial Mage. You can also find a direct link from my Author's page on Amazon.
There are quite a few other fantastic works by great authors available on RoyalRoad as well, so take a look around while you're there!

Thank you, again, for sharing in this strange and beautiful magical world with Tala. I sincerely hope that you enjoyed it.

Regards,
J.L.Mullins

Printed in Great Britain
by Amazon